A few weeks later, Tobias' daytime tedium was dispelled by two horsemen entering the village. This in itself would not be unusual or worthy of note but for the fact that both riders were priests. To be more accurate, one was a full priest and the other, judging by his gown, an acolyte. As such, they came along the road in due order of precedence. At first the priest gave Tobias no more than a glance – villages seemed to have at least one idiot with nothing to do but lay about and gawp – but a few seconds and two steps on, his head jerked around to appraise the youth more closely.

'Good day to you, are you . . . Tobias Oakley?'

'Good day to you Father, brother,' he replied; the hitherto silent acolyte nodded at this greeting. 'Why do you want to know?'

A flash of strong ill-will and impatience visibly crossed the priest's face. Tobias' opinion of himself had been so bolstered up in the last few weeks that he had not appreciated the obvious impudence of his reply.

'Come, come,' the priest said, 'either you are or you are not he – which is it?'

'I'm Tobias Oakley, yes.'

The priest's calm, friendly mien returned. 'Good. I thought so – I sensed you have the talent. Years of acquaintance with it gives one a certain perceptive ability, you know. I am Father Guido Mori from the Holy Thaumaturgic College – in Rome,' he added as an afterthought.

A Roman, thought Tobias, but speaking *perfect English . . . A Magician? Could it really be?*

JOHN WHITBOURN

A DANGEROUS ENERGY

VGSF

First published in Great Britain 1992
by Victor Gollancz Ltd

First VGSF edition published 1993
by Victor Gollancz
A Cassell imprint
Villiers House 41/47 Strand, London WC2N 5JE

© John Whitbourn 1992

The right of John Whitbourn to be identified as author of
this work has been asserted by him in accordance with the
Copyright, Designs and Patents Act, 1988.

A catalogue record of this book is available
from the British Library.

ISBN 0 575 05576 6

Typeset at the Spartan Press Ltd,
Lymington, Hants
Printed in Great Britain by
Cox & Wyman Ltd, Reading

DEDICATION

To: LIZ (of course)

To: THE FAMILY

To: ROSEMARY PARDOE – and all those
who frequent her 'Haunted Library'

'Harden not your hearts.'
The Book of Common Prayer 1662:
Psalm 95.

CONTENTS

BOOK ONE

August 1967 – March 1979

BOOK TWO

May 1982 – November 1985

BOOK THREE

August 1990

BOOK FOUR

November 2003 – November 2026

BOOK ONE

AUGUST 1967 – MARCH 1979

LOYOLA COLLEGE, OXFORD
BACHELOR OF ARTS DEGREE
1993
HONOURS

PAPER FOUR:
HISTORY – EUROPEAN SECULAR 1500–1950

TIME ALLOWED – THREE HOURS
ANSWER *FOUR* QUESTIONS, TAKING AT LEAST *ONE* FROM
EACH SECTION

ALL QUESTIONS CARRY EQUAL MARKS

SECTION A – ENGLISH HISTORY

1 Account for England's survival as the sole 'Protestant' state in
Europe 1601–1649.

2 Outline the main events of the English Civil War 1642–1649.
Give THREE reasons for the 'Protestant' Parliament's defeat.

3 'Charles I's conversion to Catholicism in 1635 made a Civil
War inevitable.' Discuss.

4 To what extent did Charles III's policy in the late 19th century
prevent the formation of a United Kingdom in the British Isles?
Did the Anglo-Scottish wars of 1819–1821 and 1899–1901 destroy
all prospects for unification?

5 Write brief notes on TWO of the following:

OLIVER CROMWELL – either birth to 1649 OR 1650–1666 (exile
and conversion).
THE EARL OF ESSEX – with particular reference to the revolt of
1601.
CARDINAL ARCHBISHOP CRANMER.
The accession of MARY II and 'HENRY IX' in 1563.
The 'SPANISH ARMADA'.

11

6 Describe the main events of the Great European War of 1708–1820 and account for the Holy Roman Empire's eventual success.

7 What were the main reasons for the Polish-Imperial War of 1896–1901? In what sense was the outcome to neither side's advantage?

8 'France is no longer a major power; indeed the forces ranged against it bring into question its long term survival as a nation.' Discuss Professor Griffiths' comments with particular reference to Burgundy's expansionist policies.

9 Describe the major Polish/Imperial Crusades against the Tartars, Magyars and Ukrainians in the period 1900–1950. To what extent did HETMAN PILSUDSKI'S campaigns ensure European security during this period?

10 Describe and account for the rapid collapse of 'Protestantism' after the destruction of Hamburg in 1600. [Restrict your arguments to the purely historical field. Theological considerations are dealt with in a separate examination paper.]

11 Trace, by the citation of Church Council decisions and papal Bulls, the Church's developing attitude towards magic and magicians in the 9th – 15th centuries.

12 Describe the process of conversion of the IROQUOIS peoples and account for their present domination of the New World Provinces. To what extent did this vindicate the papal/imperial 'Nativisation' policy? Why is this policy considered to have failed in Australasia?

13 Examine the political relationship of the Arch-Magician RONCEVAT and the Emperor CHARLEMAGNE. To what extent is RONCEVAT responsible for the political structure of modern Europe?

14 Describe the three major historical schools of thought on the initial discovery of the magical arts. To which one (if any) do you subscribe and why?

15 Describe the major Crusades to the Holy Land from the 11th – 17th centuries. Why was the 'ENTERPRISE OF RICHLIEU' a lasting success when all previous attempts were not?

CHAPTER 1

In which our hero is introduced and receives an education.

The slender pale woman raised her eyebrows in surprise and peered closer at the shiny metal in her hand. Curse the gloom for deceiving an old, old soul so, she thought, but there was no mistake – the fine needle-like arrow emanating from the centre of the silver circle was swinging wildly to and fro. She hissed violently, and the young males crouching tiredly about her tensed their long limbs and gave ear.

'Prepare, the mistress calls – be watching and report the approaches to me.'

Two of them, hefting light spears, vanished into the surrounding dusk, and the old woman dropped the still-active silver circle to paw and search in the bag which hung about her neck. At length she brought out a tiny pack of cards, and in an intent manner laid three on the mossy ground before her. While she studied the portents thus revealed, the two spearmen returned and one bent low to whisper into her ear.

'There is a newcomer-breed, a brat, late for one such to be — '

She silenced him peremptorily with a wave of a white, gnarled hand, 'Take him, no blood; I will watch and later talk.' As an afterthought she added, 'The cards have promised much.'

The one to whom she spoke slid elegantly backwards and led the small band out of the shallow grassy depression in which they had been sitting.

The boy, enjoying the minor thrill of an unauthorised and post 'bed-time' walk, had no warning at all of their approach. All at once he found himself in the middle of a ring of wicked-looking spears which were held by dimly glimpsed figures, seemingly sprung out of the earth itself. The lad was no more than six or seven years old, slight for his age with black, bright eyes and long straight hair. Surrounded by his tall, slim assailants he felt as though he were standing at the bottom of a well. So far as he could see in the dim light, they wore long, dun-coloured cloaks and wide hats. But it was their faces that caught and held his attention, to the exclusion, even, of the spears they held. In his very limited experience the boy had never been looked at with such an utter lack of sympathy

13

before and an icy feeling took possession of his stomach. Then he noticed their almond-eyes which contained no pupils and which glowed faintly yellow.

With no avenue of escape, his hand flew to a skinning knife hung about his leather belt. This drawn, he tripped and stumbled through the 'warding words' the village priest had taught the children. And all the while he was gamely brandishing the knife (which suddenly seemed so small) before him.

'In the f-face of iron, by Christ, I tell you b-begone.'

The spearmen did not even stir in acknowledgement and tears began to spring into his eyes. But he did not give up the ghost; studying the knife before him, he considered it with reference to his own throat and then that of his nearest tormentor. He did not want to fight in such a hopeless mismatch, but knew, even in his growing panic, this was what he had to do.

The old woman had been watching this little scene throughout and concluded, with grim satisfaction, that her instincts and tools had yet again been vindicated. The newcomer-boy had seen his own death in the humourless eyes about him, but had not abandoned himself to despair. He had had the presence of mind to remember the laughable iron superstition, and then when all else had failed had considered suicide, but then decided on selling his life in preference to giving it away. All this was very good, doubly so in one so young; a precocious brat, even for the newcomers, she thought with a smile.

His first (and potentially last) test was over. The woman made herself visible to the boy, who immediately seized upon her appearance with relief and gratitude, because it postponed his fatal course.

The old lady, drawing herself up to her full six feet, made a dramatic sweep with her shawl and studied the boy with her ancient deep-set eyes, from the prominence on which she had chosen to make her entrance. Nevertheless it was he who first broke the silence. (Such promising impudence, she thought.)

'Are you elves?'

His voice was high but steady, and tears had ceased with the arrival of hope. She ignored the question and fixed him with a glare so penetrating that this time he flinched.

'Look boy,' she said, 'and observe closely; you are safe.' (It seemed unnecessary to add *now*.) 'But even so you must answer everything I ask as truthfully as you can, if you wish to return home, and,' – she spat ferociously – 'I will know if you lie to me. Now watch.'

She looked up to the sky and gazed all about, even though darkness had come. Having settled her eyes towards one direction, she spoke a word, barely audible and quite meaningless to the boy, but a strikingly profound one. For it brought a small bird, a robin, which flew straight as a die at the old woman and settled on her arm, singing wildly. She smiled amid wrinkles, and with grand-motherly charm asked him, 'Would you like to be able to do this, boy?'

As she spoke, the bird increased its noise to an almost frantic level and the boy forgot his recent fears. He considered it advisable to be truthful, and at length said, 'Yes, madam, I would.' (For it *was* a clever trick, and moreover this seemed to be the answer required of him – with a little bit of flattery masquerading as respect.)

'That is good,' she noted. 'Now, would you like to be able to do *this?*'

She spoke another outlandish word and the robin, still cheeping furiously, flew away at high speed, only to hurtle with a tiny thud straight into a nearby sapling, falling lifeless at its base.

The watching spear-bearers flashed a quick, mirthless grin with perfect white teeth, and the boy, horrified and once more fearful for his safety at this new manifestation of violence, shouted. 'No, NO!'

It was noticeable however, that his last negative, although louder and more vehement, contained obvious hesitation and doubt. Instead of the little bird (for which he felt genuine pity), he saw a hated schoolmaster, the village bully and a number of other nightmare figures hurtling impotently towards destruction, in response to one mere gesture. A sudden flame of ambition and a wish for power sprang up within him.

'Untruth, untruth, UNTRUTH!' the old woman screamed at him. 'Tell me the truth.'

This outburst, combined with a sense of guilt at his own unworthy thoughts, proved to be the final straw for the lad's over-tried nerves and he descended into a deep slurry of tears.

Patience, patience, Joan, the old woman thought, *the boy is yet unversed in the world; it is all different with the newcomers. Still he is entirely as foretold, and worthy of cultivation.*

'Where are you from?' she asked. It had some minor relevance and an easy question would serve to settle him.

He looked up, found his verbal feet and answered: 'Clarkenhurst.'

She knew it well – in an elfish way and from a distance – but well. Clarkenhurst: a hamlet become sizeable in a thousand years of incremental growth. One church, one inn, one school, one smithy, one street; all that was needed for an uneventful, isolated newcomer-life. The proximity of Reading had helped it no end, although few villagers would care to admit it: the city being 'Little Babylon' to the great 'Babylon' of London itself. Of late, mild prosperity had touched some of the village houses, turning wattle into brick and thatch into tile. Not too rich, not too poor; nothing of real note, for good or ill, had ever disturbed its happy history. *We'll change that* . . . thought Joan.

'Listen to me just one more time, little boy,' she went on, 'and then you can flee to your family. Should you wish to learn these tricks and many more besides, should you desire to know more of us and should you want to become greater than normal men, return here, to this very spot, on the evening of the new moon. Be unafraid little one, for we intend you only kindness.'

The boy raised his tearful head, but in the little time it took him to do so, they were gone, vanished silently, and only the grassy hummock, silhouetted in the moonlight, remained. Wary, and still with knife in hand, he took one more wide-eyed look at his surroundings, and then fled home.

Safely away from prying eyes, some distance away, Joan rested once more with her silent spearmen. He would return, she felt sure of that. His moment of hesitation had given him away and she was infallible when it came to detecting someone with qualities adaptable to her people's needs. Should the child be so unwise as to prattle to his family or village neighbours he would soon have such 'nonsense' and 'fairy tales' knocked out of him; what humans did not want to believe, they most assuredly would not. No, he would return, more was the pity for his poor little soul. Not that that was any of her concern, of course; she merely served another with higher purposes. She was therefore graciously allowed many powers and much knowledge. (She acknowledged the debt with a reverential nod.) It was not her part, or her nature to make judgements. In any case, she remembered long ago (so long ago) another wise woman saying that no one, not even the black eminence, can take a soul: it must be freely given. And that, if justification were really needed (which she did not think it was) was good enough for Joan.

From Tobias' point of view, his return to Joan was ensured, for all small boys dearly love to cause mischief, and so much the better if it can be done without a clipped ear at the end of it. This was the bait that she held before the lad to entice him on and further in. He was special she said, not like other mortals; and if he did but concentrate, he could play many games, both malicious and amusing, on the villagers. As a special 'pretty' when he returned at the new moon she gave him an ugly little arrow-shape of rowan wood: as instructed he had covertly directed the point at the retreating back of his chosen target and concentrated. In consequence Father Allingham, the parish priest, was confined to his bed (and its environs) for a fortnight with a looseness of the bowels which the village surgeon had termed 'quite remarkable'.

Accordingly, young Tobias Oakley had escaped the boredom of church attendance and Sunday Bible instruction for that glorious period, since no replacement for Allingham could be secured at such short notice. A less happy consequence of Tobias' actions was that old Grannie Hammond, aged ninety-one, a devout church-goer and much in fear of death, died in her bed without the solace and benefit of the Church's last rites.

He was not a naturally vicious boy, but with all the ruthlessness of childhood he was greatly disappointed when the arrow failed to work a second time. In this case his target was his father, who had anointed Tobias' ear with a large hand for liberating a meat patty from the family larder. It was only then that he realised these things did not come as easily as he had imagined, and that if he wished to learn (and he did) he had to persevere with the fearsome lady's teaching.

His sleep in the intervening ten days had been interrupted and uneasy, but it was not the agony of indecision that kept him awake, rather an elementary struggle of conscience with the decision he had already made. Seven years old was too young to appreciate the spiritual pitfalls along the path to salvation, despite Father Allingham's bellowed threats in the pulpit every Sunday (or nearly every Sunday). With all the sheer practicality of childhood, Tobias' main stumbling-blocks were fear of physical harm to himself and the invention of excuses plausible enough to explain his absences to his suspicious family. In the end, because he was both a courageous child and a convincing liar, conscience was driven mumbling to its bolt-hole in the inaudible distance.

He had presented himself at the new moon, a little way off from the original meeting place, and laid in wait. Just in case, he had sharpened his knife specially for the occasion and had appropriated his brother Jeremiah's prized boar-spear, even though the latter was far too heavy for him to use properly. Within the security engendered by these implements he felt both confident and grown up.

This fragile bubble was soon burst when, despite his efficient (he thought) concealment, he felt a sharp pain in his backside and turned to see Joan, and a grinning elf (one of the previous party? It was impossible to tell) who was lightly gripping the spear with which he had just been jabbed.

That night Tobias learnt a great deal that (if he did but know it) scholars and magicians of the Papal Thaumaturgic College itself would have given their first son or favourite maid to know. Joan told him all that her protégés needed to know of her people. That proved to be very little, but just sufficient to settle Tobias' spirit of curiosity. She did this so that his mind could be duly turned to more apposite matters. Reviewing his knowledge at a later date, Tobias was to find it added up to next to nothing. The elves, the heath people, call them what you like, were not human stock; 'newcomers' was what they called the larger folk with whom they shared the land and the term carried an implied sneer. He heard names that meant nothing to him: Bassion, Rhegged, Suth-Rege and Bins-Kom: once mighty kingdoms that were no more. These elves were the remnants, embittered custodians of displaced glory, nursing cold dreams of restitution. They were whimsical, strong and violent; they did not worship the crucified God and were, in sum, wise and cruel beyond the measure of men. They came and they went, and no one knew the manner of their passing. Everyone knew of their existence and nearly all (especially the Church) sought to forget this knowledge. This was quite easily done, for the elves normally had nothing to say to man and he, in turn, had no desire to converse with them. In this way the elves lived only in the dark corners of winter fireside-conversation or in mysterious window tappings at the dead of night.

Tobias learnt a trifle more than this, but not one hundredth part of the truth (if indeed that was known by anyone on earth) and, despite all the arcane knowledge he came to accumulate during the course of his long life, he did not ever significantly add to Joan's few disclosures that night of the new moon. Only later did he come to appreciate that the elvish people were spiritually dangerous and, from then on, he no longer despised the common sort for their unrationalised fear of them.

On the occasion of that second meeting he listened for some twenty minutes to what Joan had to say. All the while the crouching spearman continued a cold appraisal. At the end he was given the 'pretty' that was to so ravage Father Allingham's internal workings. After a characteristic dismissive wave from Joan's shawl, Tobias was obliged to drag a slow, meditative way home under the milky gleam of the slender moon. Already his childish thoughts were being inexorably drawn down trackways unknown to those of his school-room contemporaries, and his rowan-wood arrow gave him an acute sense of power. Compared to the arrow, the clumsy, mundane spear he carried seemed by far the inferior weapon. Now he would show them.

He was, however, quite wrong: there was no showing to be done. Joan alone held the real power and all she passed on to him in their subsequent meetings was information. Even the dramatic attack on the priest's health and dignity had been solely due to Joan's skills, not to those of Tobias. New moon after new moon he spoke to the old woman; all the time she patiently edged his blossoming mind along, forward and (most important of all) sideways, yet she truly taught him nothing at all. Eventually he rebelled and threatened to tell the priest of her existence, so that the Holy Office would be called in and then she'd be sorry, because she would be caught and tortured and burnt . . .

Joan shouted a word by way of reply and Tobias instantly felt such anguish that its very memory could raise cold sweat for years to come. It felt as if someone had gripped his heart and the thing (soul – call it what you will) that made him what he was – and then squeezed very hard. The elves were not careful or considerate with their charges, and the ever-present spearmen had laughed long at Tobias' writhings. Later on that night, at home in his bunk, he had tearfully sworn never to contact the sorceress again.

But at the next new moon he was at the appointed place, sullen and curt perhaps, but there all the same.

Farmer Todd Williams had buffeted young Tobias the week before for trespassing in his orchard. That night, rather than push her charge too far, Joan gave the boy a talisman which, placed strategically in a paddock, caused the farmer's precious ten-beast dairy herd to sicken and die. The following year was hard to the Williams family, for they had become reliant on the income from these useful animals. They were obliged to call upon the 'Church-dole' and two of their daughters had to go away into service to supplement the family's diminished earnings. One returned soon after, pregnant by (it was alleged) the master of the house.

Once again though, to Tobias' disgust, the talisman, stealthily retrieved, was ineffectual when produced for a second outing. Nevertheless he did find himself in trouble with the villagers in other ways arising from his secret education. Joan's attentions had so imbued him with the concept of his own superiority that he came in time to believe in it and to act the part. With no complementary power to back up his airs and graces, Tobias found that life became quite hard until he learnt to hold back his tongue and keep his ideas to himself. After a while he could effortlessly maintain a façade, behind which he lived out, unknown to anyone, his private and real life. This is just how the elves would have it, and as a result Tobias found village life less trying. His parents were pleased that his inexplicable delusions of grandeur had turned out to be a mere passing phase. Thus everyone was happy with his progress.

By the time of his ninth birthday. Tobias had all but irretrievably moved away from his peers – noisy, brawling brats for the most part – and people commented on what an unusually quiet and polite boy he was. Some went so far as to say that he was unhealthily reserved, and in this the bitter, old maiden aunt and melancholy neighbour in question were wiser than they knew. Tobias rarely expressed any opinion and was never seen to be boisterous. Yet behind his shield of reticence, he forgot or forgave nothing, and a mighty ledger of grievances grew in size day by day, awaiting full and correct payment. He became a bitter youth, but his act was so polished that no one noticed.

Tobias' father could both read and write, and so was of some standing in the village. Less happily he was also a small, pedantic and fussy man, but these minor cavils aside he was a good father to his children. Like his father and grandfather before him, Mr Oakley worked as the local clerk to the Papal tithe-commission based in London. The term 'tithe' was a misnomer; his Holiness' requirements were more lenient. This body levied a penny in each shilling from the earnings of all but the highest in the land and then transferred the revenue collected on to Rome. In due course much of the money found its way back to England to maintain the national Church's work and to alleviate poverty. Hallowed by age, the imposition was commonly known as 'Peter's Pence'. It was also bitterly (if secretly) resented. It was therefore a tribute to Tobias' father that his transparent fairness and moral rectitude prevented any of the tax's unpopularity transferring itself to its local record-bearer. In cases of serious hardship it was not entirely unknown for Mr Oakley to overlook certain small debts, or even pay them himself, and for this the villagers repaid him with respect.

Having nine other products of his loins to consider, Mr Oakley could devote little attention to Tobias save to ensure that the rudiments of education were driven into his head. The patriarch of the Oakleys entertained fond hopes of installing all of his male offspring into posts within the vast and complex machinery of Church government. Such employment would be their passport to an assured lifetime of moderate prosperity and respectability and so was much to be desired.

Tobias' father also considered it his duty to ensure his children lived according to the tenets of the catechism and the Bible. To this end, every Sunday saw Mr and Mrs Oakley with their progeny behind them like ducklings, off to be uplifted by Father Allingham's ministry. At some time during the evening of the Sabbath the family would also gather together to hear Mr Oakley read from the only book the household possessed, a large and battered Bible. The reading would be hesitant and stumbling for the text was in Latin and Mr Oakley's grasp of that language was far from complete.

When not about his various duties, Tobias' father's only visible pleasures were his pipe and an evening spent reading the *Albion Journal* (several weeks old and lent to him by the schoolmaster, Mr Pegrum). One of Tobias' earliest memories was of his father sitting in his crow-black frock-coat and high white collar, separated from his family by bluish coils of baccy smoke and 'tut-tutting' at the outrages he read in the out-of-date newsheet.

Mrs Oakley, by comparison, was small, worn out by childbirth and very quiet. She had never lost her sense of gratitude at marrying slightly above her station (for her family were churl-status and a literate husband was therefore a notable catch) and she showed this in a life of utter devotion and obedience to her spouse. Thanks to her good husbandry of their income, the family ate better than most on rye bread, soup, fat-bacon and eggs. On High and Holy days, they even ran to fish and poultry. Even so, to survive, all members of the family had to cooperate and so the children were kept industrious. There were certain periods of free time, however, and no one saw fit to question the fact that Tobias chose to spend his in early evening wanderings . . .

By the time he was twelve he had absorbed most of what Joan had to tell him of the elves' peculiar views, and with understanding came agreement. Intellectually he embraced the cold, ironic morality of Joan's people, although at no time was he pressed to do so. To him the elvish stance seemed enormously stern, hard and manly, and so he was glad to adopt it. At this early stage in his life the elf-influence did not run particularly deep and his humanity was not displaced very far. Often he weakened and was warm-hearted.

It is said that roving seamen, because of their contact with widely varying social mores, tend to become amoral or immoral, depending on one's point of view. By travelling a few hundred miles they can see that what might be counted right in one place is regarded as sinful in another. If, therefore, Right and Wrong are determined solely by longitude and latitude what application could either possibly have to a peripatetic life? So the reasoning went.

In the same way, Joan showed Tobias the parochial nature of his village's morality and, beyond that, the similar arbitrary constraints in his nation and the civilisation which gave it birth. This was all unfamiliar and heady stuff but, bit by bit, unhampered by ethical considerations his ideas and scope of thought widened.

Therefore at the age when his society first deemed him to be a man (at fourteen years old, for life was brief and childhood, of necessity, short), his personality was considerably more developed and mature than his years would suggest. Around this time Joan's teaching finally appeared as a consistent whole to Tobias, whereas before it had been largely unconnected fragments of disturbing, fascinating knowledge. It came to this: Joan had taught him no cure-all conjurings, no spectacular bolts of lightning such as he had fondly hoped for at first. Instead she had brought to life whole areas of his mind hitherto dormant; areas otherwise destined to remain forever passive. The comparison that occurred to him was a homely one: that of a heavy blanket being slowly lifted off a person in bed; the body once relieved of this unnoticed burden feels a new freedom of action and lightness of spirit. The simile perhaps showed his lack of experience outside the realms of village life but it was an apposite one nevertheless.

New ideas floated behind Tobias' savage self-control; he freely entertained concepts which, expressed publicly, would have drawn upon himself the baleful attention of the Holy Office. Yet the powers demonstrated by the fate of the robin and hinted at in most of the moonlit meetings remained steadfastly Joan's alone. He did not feel cheated because of this for he knew (on the basis of a somewhat uncritical assessment) that he had been given, if such a thing were possible, a powerful, energetic and tightly controlled intellect. The 'common masses', his parents, his schoolmates, troubled him not at all, for Tobias knew he was superior and whatever else Joan cared to teach would be based on this sound foundation, and would come in her own good time.

In actual fact the 'good time' in question came at the very next new moon after Tobias had reached the above conclusions, abstracted and brooding at the back of a wearisome Friday divinity-lesson. The old fool Pegrum had wittered on about the estate of man and how God's wishes were manifested in the arrangement of society. Tobias very quickly concluded that Joan had summarised that particular proposition far more accurately and with infinitely more sensitivity several years ago. Accordingly he blocked out the schoolmaster's bleating (a job made easy by years of constant practice) and moved on to more profitable, private trains of thought.

On the evening of the new moon, Tobias waited with weakening patience for the family meal to end. After this was over he was obliged to help his brothers repair the fencing around the compound which housed the family pig. By the time this was finished he had to hurry away if his usual meeting was to be completed before the light faded totally. Joan did not approve of his bringing a lantern and would only permit it on the very shortest days of winter. He often had to stumble and feel his way to the general area, and wait in the pitch darkness for Joan to arrive. The elves never seemed to have the slightest difficulty in finding him and usually appeared silently at his side directly after his arrival.

His father and brothers did not question his quiet slipping away that night or any other for that matter. He had become a taciturn boy, obedient enough but capable of iron resolution in rebellion. His father had once or twice entertained thoughts of making a point over parental authority with the lad, but no one incident had ever merited such a confrontation. According to the nature of these things the matter drifted and the patriarch of the family retained his position unchallenged but untried.

Sometimes Joan would be alone on the heath, at other times there would be up to a dozen of the silent males. Very occasionally another female would arrive alongside Joan, but no one save the old lady would ever speak to Tobias. With all this in mind the young lad chose at random a small hummock beside a line of scrub bushes and sat down upon it. Dusk prevailed now, and in the village, visible to Tobias between two stunted trees, lights were beginning to be lit. He had long since ceased to gaze at the new moon; it had been his constant companion since the dawn of his childhood memories and had become one of the accepted, invisible objects of familiarity to him. The heath itself was held in similar regard since he quite often came out for evening walks on it, if only to make his regular new-moon visits less conspicuous. People eventually assumed he had an obsession with the charmless place and ceased to regard his behaviour as necessary of remark.

At fourteen Tobias was a slightly undersized young man with unfashionably short hair. ('That is not necessary to ensure your head is free of livestock', his father had said to him, 'we are not churls after all.') Due to the fortunate circumstances of his birth, lack of proper nutrition had not acted to stunt his growth or twist his bones as it had with some of the ragged people who eked out their life on the 'Church-dole' in tumbledowns at the end of the village. That evening he wore the britches and woollen sweater typical of his lower-artisan class. As usual a knife hung from his belt, but by now it was a proper man's working blade. It was also large enough to be a ferocious weapon, although the villagers' tiffs were usually fought out with fists and working men's steel-tipped boots. Tobias did not live in a violent society; confused drunken brawls outside The Lamb and Flag on a Friday night were common and wife-beating was not entirely unknown, but these affrays rarely resulted in any serious injuries. Even so it was just such a knife, produced by the village smithy, that the infamous Glyn Benny had used in his fury to gut an Italian pardoner some forty or so years ago. Benny had been duly hanged for this deed soon after, but he lived on in village memory, partly because it was the last memorable thing to have happened there and partly because he had only put into prctice what a lot of people roundabouts had long dreamed of doing. As they would have put it, 'It was high time that some of those twisty, widow-swindling, pansy jack-priests had a knife put in their pockets and got sent back to Rome as they were.'

Few were stupid enough to say as much though. Tobias' father had once told him how, as a young man, he (and most of the village) had travelled all the way to Reading to see justice done to the irreligious scoundrel. As has been said, this probably represented a minority viewpoint.

So Tobias found the knife served as a practical comfort. For example, one never knew what one might meet on the heath.

A low cough told him that Joan was there and he raised his guarded unquiet eyes to see her and two elf-warriors. Instantly he perceived that this particular session was something special; the minutiae of detail he noticed (thanks to Joan's teaching) revealed it as plain as speech. In a somewhat melodramatic way the trio had appeared where the moon made a pool of weak milk-shine, and so they were coloured in nothing but sharply contrasted black and white. It had the nearly superfluous effect of making them look anciently evil.

'To work!' she said. 'Tonight we're going to perform a test, a little piece of revision shall we say – of everything you have been told . . . and a little more.' At this private whimsy she moved the wrinkles of her face into her own version of a smile. 'Are you prepared?'

'I am.'

'Good. Firstly: do you know and understand all that I have told you about personal force?'

'I do.'

'Do you know and understand my teaching concerning the links between mind, emotion and reality? How each can mould the other?'

'Likewise.'

'Do you remember what I have told you of the cosmic order and all that creeps, crawls and flies on, over or under the surface of this world?'

'I do, but do not believe it in its entirety.'

'As you wish.'

'Just so.'

'Finally: do you remember the words and sentences of power that I have taught you?'

'I do, but they remain meaningless to me.'

'Not for much longer. Now, beloved, come closer to me and listen.'

Tobias strode three steps forward; obedience to Joan was by now an unquestioning item of trust.

The two male elves moved forward as well, dragging with them a sizeable draw-string canvas bag. Tobias fancied that he saw it move; there was something living inside it. With effort, the warriors held the bag up between them and slightly loosened the string.

'Now,' said Joan, 'place your hand, nothing cautious, into the bag.'

Tobias stepped forward and did so. Immediately he felt a strong set of teeth fasten about two of his fingers. One he twisted free at once, but the other was bitten clean through to the bone. The pain was like intolerable rapiers – no – *pins* of white-hot steel thrusting up his arm. His finger was released and he pulled his hand from the bag. The bitten digit hung loose, half-severed, and blood splattered merrily around; precious little skin remained on the palm either. He set his teeth in a grimace due to pain and (controlled) anger.

'In that bag,' Joan told him, 'is a brutal animal; horrible beyond your conception. We will let it out now and you must kill it. Have your revenge.'

As she spoke, the two men undid the string further and then upended the bag. Something white and stringy landed on the grass, whining loudly. Too quick for recognition it hurtled across the hummock diagonally away from Tobias and his tutor. Tobias saw something that was pallid-white, that whined nastily, and he felt the starburst in his hand. His eyes lost their customary shield and flared; with his good hand he pointed at the limping, scampering creature. He shouted one of the gibberish phrases he had heard Joan use.

At once the thing slowed and for the first time permitted scrutiny. It too was an elf, save that it was naked and covered with scars; its long hair was not billowy and gossamer-like as was normal with elves, but dull and matted. He (for it was a male) stopped dead; blood erupted in a waterfall over his lower lip, then trickled from his ears, nose and eyes. One staggering pace on, the figure dropped with the finality and grace that lifelessness bestows.

Tobias, profoundly shocked, lowered his arm and a silence fell. At some point (how long after, Tobias could never say) Joan spoke into the cathedral-like peace.

'I have consulted the cards, beloved, though perhaps it is an impudence on so minor a matter. Should you bind the finger tightly straightaway, you will not lose it.'

Tobias addressed himself to this awkward task and in due course, although his kerchief was transformed to a magenta colour, the flow of blood was staunched. No one had offered to assist. Then he stared at the corpse again, slowly regaining control as he did so. He slapped down the initial, natural desire to blurt out something nonsensical.

'Well, Joan: why and what?'

'Tobias, my chick, my lovely,' she replied, 'you are a magician.'

He looked pained. 'But did it have to be a killing?'

She studied him for a brief while.

'Would it help if I said he was an abomination and a murderer of helpless infants?'

'It might.'

'Then he was an abomination and a murderer of helpless infants.'

The two spearmen grinned.

'You mock me, Joan.'

'Indeed not, child. I only seek to ease you in your troubles.'

'Which are of your making.'

'Not entirely; you had a hand in the matter too, if you'll excuse the term.'

Tobias abandoned the point; his thoughts had moved elsewhere. 'How did you know that I could become a magician – what if I had failed?'

'Our mistress told me,' Joan replied in a decisive tone, 'and she does not lie.'

Tobias turned his head sideways and smiled with an expression of patient cynicism.

'Ah, so wise and so old you are at fourteen summers,' she said. 'So clever and disbelieving.' There was a stern note in her voice.

Her charge refused to be drawn on this point either. 'What now, Joan?'

'Well lad, don't you have any ideas and notions about the world? It's there like a great game for you to play and thanks to me you know all the rules from the very start; and how to cheat at it too.'

'So?' he said weakly.

'So there it all is, the whole wide world, filled to sweating point with maids to be swived, men to fight or befriend, money and good things to accumulate; loves, hates, sorrows and joys to be ridden on their course. I should have to tell a young man all this?'

'You make it sound an exciting prospect, but at the moment the thought of being a magician excludes all others.'

'You should be glad always. But remember this clearly, for it is of the utmost importance: magic is a major part of power but not the entirety of it. The key to everything is power – *hear me.* Power is the only real thing in the universe. You have started to understand its nature: now make it your lifelong lover and devote yourself to its exploration. Find yourself a purpose or not, as you may wish, but live it whatever you decide and never give less than total attention to the love of your life.'

Tobias looked at her and frowned. 'What I don't understand is what you gain from this. You wouldn't do it unless for gain.'

'Your life is our life now,' she said with awful finality, 'ours, and our gain.'

Tobias, however, could no longer be so easily intimidated. 'You do not have and cannot have that.'

'In a sense, yes. In another, no,' she replied. 'The next time we meet, the question might be easier to answer.'

Tobias looked at the body again and then deeply into Joan's pupilless eyes. Both of them simultaneously saw, unbridled, wild power, and were abashed.

'Is there anything more tonight, Joan?'

'No, indeed, beloved. Goodnight.'

He turned and strode off clutching his injured hand, but abruptly about-faced a dozen or so paces away. To his surprise Joan and her two accomplices were still in position, dramatically outlined against the moonlight. He called back, a note of anguish in the upper ranges of his voice.

'It needn't have been a killing Joan – not a killing.'

He returned at the next new moon but as he had more than half expected, the elves did not come. He did not bother ever to go again, for he knew that his strange education was finished.

CHAPTER 2
In which our hero makes practical use of his knowledge and thereby makes himself known to a wider public.

Two years later Tobias was sixteen, and had given an enormous amount of thought to all that had transpired in the course of his unusual childhood. He concluded that the work Joan had performed on his mind and opinions was both unique and vital. In the field of magic, however, she had merely 'awoken' his talent and given him a head start. The seemingly meaningless 'words of power' she had taught him by rote now assumed new significance when he understood (he thought) the underlying principle. They served as the shorthand of magic, saving the trouble of constructing the spell anew each time. Indeed, so far had he progressed in the intervening two years, and so hard had he worked that he now had several new words of his own devising. It was, he found, a matter of comparative simplicity to adopt a word and imbue it with power. The trick lay in believing the thing, so utterly, so implicitly, that word produced belief and belief, through power, produced effect. This last stage was far, far, the most difficult part, and only Tobias' bitter determination made it at all possible. At the cost of enormous travail and stress he cajoled his mind into accepting a few new 'spells'. He was not yet fully aware of it but he was possessed of considerable skill and, considering that he was now unaided, was increasing his powers at an impressive rate. It was fortunate, therefore, that he had learnt at least one virtue at Joan's feet, namely modesty.

His sorcerous development remained a secret from the rest of the village. For although magicians were familiar-enough figures in the fields of politics, war and the higher echelons of the Church, the humble community of Clarkenhurst had never yet boasted such a son or daughter. Long before living memory the Church had set its face against the practice of magic, and although this had, almost a millennium ago, proved to be impractical, not to mention unwise, still a faint whiff of hell-fire attached itself to the magician's art. Tobias was therefore unsure of the reception any disclosure on his part might receive and, after due thought, this and other considerations led him to bide his time before committing himself.

He made no attempt to contact Joan or her people again, partly because their last meeting had been so unpleasant but mainly because it would be a pointless enterprise. He well knew that such searches were exclusively unsuccessful or fatal. In a moment of introspection he suddenly realised that the Church was right to try and suppress conscious memory of the elves. It might be done for half-forgotten, ill-understood, reasons but it was justified.

At fourteen his other, more conventional, education had ended as well and it was time to don the black fustian suit of the working man. His father, by use of what little influence he had, secured for him the post of under-clerk to the Parish Remembrancer, Mr Fitzsimmons. This worthy, by dint of his fancy name, claimed a connection, albeit distant, with one of the wealthiest families in Berkshire. This led him to put on a grandeur of manner which ill-fitted his unprepossessing character and uncertain place in the village hierarchy. His allotted duty was to record the busy life of the immediate area – the births, deaths and marriages, the harvests, the bastards, affrays and contracts. In short he noted down the very stuff of life and despatched it; written in dog-Latin and compiled in metal-tipped, leather-bound volumes, to the Bishop of Reading's administrative office, and thence eventually to his library. Since Clarkenhurst was a relatively peaceful and pleasant place in which to live, these volumes were seldom, if ever, consulted; although some were to survive to occupy the gentle scholars of an era far in the future and undreamed of in Tobias' time. Mr Fitzsimmons would not have been either gratified or made dejected by this foreknowledge of his work's reception; to him the compilation was the thing, the ensuing utility being very much a secondary consideration. In view of the somewhat thankless nature of the Remembrancer's post, this was perhaps a very healthy attitude for its holder to adopt. However it took certain types of people to think in this way and Tobias was not numbered among them.

The only reasons that he had been accepted for the post were because of his acknowledged ability at his letters and the less than incidental factor that Fitzsimmons, a bachelor, held romantic aspirations concerning Maria Oakley, Tobias' eldest sister. Under his breath Tobias cursed his employer for a filthy old lecher, but was little surprised when, a scant six months subsequent to his starting work, Maria Oakley became Maria Fitzsimmons. Even this short interval was perhaps too long, for Maria's voluminous wedding gown barely concealed the significant thickening about her waist; and but for Fitzsimmons' position in the village, Father Allingham would have had some stern words to say to the couple. As it was he merely glowered throughout the ceremony; a few of the coarser sort in the congregation were heard to chuckle.

· Tobias' new brother-in-law was not too hard a taskmaster, but long service at his chosen occupation had rendered him incurably pedantic and fussy. These qualities did not augur well, for the Oakleys were of a more straightforward and easy-going disposition. Before long, Fitzsimmons' very voice could irritate both wife and assistant clerk, but both (for different reasons) kept their thoughts to themselves.

To spend one's days endlessly compiling other people's petty pastimes was anathema to a youth who had been shown a glimpse of greater and wilder things. However this was balanced by the indolent streak in Tobias and so he carried quietly on, ever more discontented and constrained by the village context. Bit by bit the things that Joan had spoken of seemed less applicable, less and less anything to do with the dull, day-to-day, real world. The monotony began to affect him, disrupting the logical, 'streamlined' mind he had been so proud of, making him moody and fractious. As things turned out, this emotional state proved to be his friend and salvation, just as if part of a plan, and in the end the change Tobias dreamed of was imposed upon him.

To achieve their ends the fates. had seized humble Mr Fitzsimmons as their catalyst and *agent provocateur*.

On a hot July day Tobias was sitting drafting a long-since deceased cleric's spiderly writing into fair Church script. The part of his mind that was not yet in a slumber registered the fact that the letter was attempting to call the Bishop of Reading's attention to the ruinous state of St Matthews in Bradley, a nearby hamlet, and the dangerous condition of the church roof. The missive was over twenty-five years old and had recently come to light in a dusty search through a long neglected, indeed forgotten, strongbox. The writer, the resident priest of St Matthews, had been fully justified in his alarm, for an accompanying letter, dated a mere two months after the first, recounted the roof's final collapse. God had seen fit, the letter revealed, to allow this to happen while a service was in progress and a number of the faithful had been badly hurt. Thus vindicated, the priest was less temperate in his second letter than his first, and for his own good it had been intercepted by one of Mr Fitzsimmons' predecessors. It did not do, it was not wise, to address a prince of the Church, however minor, in angry ringing tones, however justified.

Tobias entirely failed to appreciate that compared to his usual work, this copying was quite animated. Lethargy and mounting frustration combined to make each pen-stroke a dull effort. As his assistant approached the apex of the monotony mountain, fortune directed Mr Fitzsimmons' feet away from his luncheon table and his once-again pregnant wife to see how his under-clerk was progressing. He had dined very pleasingly on Maria's home-made pie and porter, but whereas this would imbue in most people a more charitable and forbearing attitude to the world about them, in this particular gentleman it only served to reinforce his conviction that the world should be tidy, correct and without fault of any kind. Walking to his office he saw two dogs greet each other in their characteristic manner, and this brought home to him that all was not neat, clean and concise as it should be and his vague idea that he should do something about it rose more clearly than usual to the surface.

Discord, therefore, had a great richness of material to work on: the heat; an annoying, persistent bluebottle in the office window, two innocent, if unfastidious dogs, Tobias' boredom; a dead man's out-of-date correspondence and, best of all, Mr Fitzsimmons' pedantry.

The aforementioned gentleman entered his little kingdom and peered for a long while over his clerk's shoulder.

'Master Oakley, pray tell me how you have headed this letter you purport to be copying.'

Tobias looked at his work, could see nothing obviously wrong and so answered boldly. 'Your Grace, sir.'

'So I see Tobias, so I see.'

'But that's correct isn't it? That's what the letter says.'

'Sir.'

'*Sir.*'

'And, might I ask, who is this letter written to?'

'The Bishop of Reading.'

'Precisely, Tobias. And therefore you well know that the heading is incorrect. To address a Bishop in writing one uses the term "my Lord Bishop". Kindly change it.'

'But, Mr Fitzsimmons, I've only faithfully copied out the letter – the fault, which I acknowledge, isn't mine, it's with the priest who wrote it.'

'Then should he have started the letter to the "all-high Emperor of Atlantis", you would presumably have copied that out.'

'No, but — '

'But me no buts, Master Oakley – do it again.'

At this point Mr Fitzsimmons most unfortunately chose to emphasise his point by drawing the inkstick he carried in his breast pocket across Tobias' copied document. The youth looked coolly at his morning's labour, now ruined, and then at its destructor. Tidal waves of fury rose high enough to overwhelm the sea-walls of control that he had built up. He spat a word of command. That little part of his mind not consumed with anger or dulled by work doubted anything would happen, but doubt was instantly allayed. As if a giant's hand had pushed him up, the wailing Mr Fitzsimmons was lifted and propelled backwards on to and through the front windows of his writing house. The wooden frame splintered and the small glass panes either cracked or fell out entirely. Slightly bloodied, his frock coat torn to ribbons, the village Remembrancer lay panting outside, watched open-mouthed by two passing matrons. They were entirely unused to the respectable Mr Fitzsimmons making such spectacular appearances.

Very self-consciously, and stiff-legged, Tobias strode out into the street and dispassionately viewed his ex-employer. His ex-employer returned the gaze but with less equanimity.

'I wish you to remain quiet concerning this, Mr Fitzsimmons Sir,' he said, and spoke another word of command. Leaving the small pantomime behind him, Tobias then headed off down Clarkenhurst's main street while all about him his bridges burned merrily.

After this the village was split into two camps which might be roughly described as 'pro-Tobias' and 'anti-Tobias'. At first the strongest expressions of feeling were confined to debates in the village pub or gossip between neighbours, for the issue was very far from being clearly defined. No one could be sure about what had happened to Mr Fitzsimmons and he was saying nothing – literally. Every time he attempted to speak about Tobias or the much-discussed incident, his tongue clove to the roof of his mouth, so that he only produced an amusing 'glug-glugging' sound. Nor could his palpitating hands clutch a pen when he tried to set events down on paper. Everyone agreed that something supernatural had occurred, that was sure, for no undersized sixteen-year-old could hurl a portly man twelve foot or so through a window and bind him to silence afterwards. People began remembering all sorts of incidents from Tobias' past, both real and fancied, to confirm their own particular viewpoint.

Tobias found that the controversy which surrounded him brought various consequences, both good and bad. In the former case, he started to receive all sorts of goodwill presents from impressed or placatory villagers. Among these gifts was the ample and pleasing body of Betty Lockwood, a farmer's daughter two years older than himself. This was an entirely novel and exciting experience for Tobias and one in which he indulged to the full while it lasted. But she was an experienced girl, 'a much-loved person' as the village young men put it, and she soon threw him over when he refused to take her on a guided tour of fairyland.

On the contrary side he found that he lost those few acquaintances, never close, that he had managed to retain through the long, strange years of his training. His father, while perhaps furtively pleased to number a sorcerer in his clan, felt uneasy in the boy's presence; partly because of the evil reputation of magic unsanctified by the Church's authorisation, and partly because the natural hierarchy of the family was nullified at a stroke. What power did a man have in his own house if one of the younger children could put his father and his elder brothers through the window if it took his fancy? Mealtimes became tense and strained affairs in the Oakley household and Tobias took to staying out of the house in deference to the discomfort he was causing his family. Eventually reticence was cast aside and his bed was moved out into a lean-to adjoining the garden storeshed and there he made his home.

No other village employer cared to risk a rump-first voyage through a window and so young Oakley found himself devoid of an occupation. Solitary, and to all intents disowned, he spent his days sitting on a slight hillock on the approach to the village from Reading, like an old-time penitent, most profoundly bored. Joan had missed out one facet of power in her impassioned speech during their last meeting he thought – it was very lonely.

He also discovered a new, harsher side to the Church in the person of its representative in the village, Father Allingham, the ogre of his childhood. A neat handwritten message, summoning Tobias to the presbytery, had found him in his new, ramshackle 'home'. Over the heady novelty of a glass of sherry wine, the priest had been kindly but very determined. With the freedom and power concomitant ('Pardon?' said Tobias) to the status of magician, the priest had told him, went great responsibilities and restrictions on one's behaviour. Oakley was safe, if not welcome, in the village as long as he did nothing further for ill. Otherwise the Parish Council (under Allingham's browbeating control) would feel constrained to make a demonstration of public displeasure. Tobias was not entirely sure what form this would take, and it was left unspecified, but he knew his novice sorcery would not protect him from a mob of murder-intent villagers armed with knives and fowling guns. It was therefore no surprise that the tête-á-tête ended amicably with Tobias well aware of the general limitations set upon his life style.

Even from the most positive point of view it was a somewhat spartan life style, however far apart his limitations of action were set. Within village society no niche existed for an exalted figure (save for the Squire, an absentee landlord addicted to life in London) who furthermore compounded his jarring maladjustment by originating from local low-born stock. People mistrusted and were wary of Tobias Oakley's reputed powers, and this soon acted to inhibit social intercourse like a slow poison, so much that within a month his sole conversation was with captive audiences, namely himself, animals or infants. More and more often he would spend the day aimlessly studying the sky from his favourite hillock, only returning home for meals; meals that his father was starting to begrudge since Tobias' labour was now no longer added to the family's collective effort.

He had hoped that the recognition of his new status would have led to more contact with the 'higher' minds of the community, such as the surgeon, or even Allingham at a pinch, for he strongly suspected that much of use could be gleaned from educated folk. But because of his abnormality, he was effectively ostracised. Once they realised that he could not foretell the future, cure their sick cow or brew up an infallible love-philtre, the villagers steered clear of Tobias. On one occasion Maria Fitzsimmons née Oakley called to see him to petition for the return of her husband's former eloquence. In truth she only did this for form's sake and at her spouse's fervent prompting, and so when Tobias decisively shook his head she did not press the point. Upon reflection she even began to warm to the idea of her husband being just a little more contemplative and taciturn than hitherto.

The truth of the matter was that Tobias was in no position to effect a cure even if he had wanted to. He did not know how. It was all very well to harness a strong emotion to produce a tangible magical effect, but another thing altogether to reverse the process when no equally strong wish accompanied the requested act. Anyway, Tobias found himself totally indifferent to Fitzsimmons' future good health; he had passed from his mind. What was the point therefore of exerting oneself on his behalf?

If only Tobias had roused himself to slightly deeper thought, he would have known that Father Allingham, as overseer of Clarkenhurst's wellbeing, could not accept the present state of affairs as a *modus vivendi*. The thin brooding figure on the hillock disrupted the well-regulated pace of village life by his presence alone, and so could not be tolerated for long. Allingham had met several magicians in the course of his theological college days, but at heart he was as unsettled by them just as much as his less well-travelled flock who were, after all, of the same stock as he. Ever one for direct action in human affairs (with God holding a watching brief), he had sat at his writing desk immediately after Tobias' interview with him and made arrangements, in a letter, for Master Oakley's future career.

This explains why, a few weeks later, Tobias' daytime tedium was dispelled by two horsemen entering the village. This in itself would not be unusual or worthy of note but for the fact that both riders were priests. To be more accurate, one was a full priest and the other, judging by his gown, an acolyte. As such, they came along the road in due order of precedence. At first the priest gave

Tobias no more than a glance – villages always seemed to have at least one idiot with nothing to do but lay about and gawp – but a few seconds and two steps on, his head jerked around to appraise the youth more closely. While the acolyte drew up behind him, the priest stared for a short while, and then a smile spread slowly across his face. He was old, grizzled and florid, but his eyes were still full of life and seemed kindly. Tobias stood up and returned the smile without committing himself. As he did so the priest slowly, stiffly dismounted and turned once again to face him. Tobias' thoughts raced – *something special*? His hopes rose as he realised he was about to be addressed.

'Good day to you, are you . . . Tobias Oakley?'

'Good day Father, brother,' he replied; the hitherto silent acolyte nodded at this greeting. 'Why do you want to know?'

A flash of strong ill-will and impatience visibly crossed the priest's face. Tobias' opinion of himself had been so bolstered up in the last few weeks that he had not appreciated the obvious impudence of his reply.

'Come, come,' the priest said, 'either you are or you are not he – which is it?'

'I'm Tobias Oakley, yes.'

The priest's calm, friendly mien returned. 'Good. I thought so – I sensed you have the talent. Years of acquaintance with it gives one a certain perceptive ability, you know. I am Father Guido Mori from the Holy Thaumaturgic College – in Rome,' he added as an afterthought.

A Roman, thought Tobias, but speaking *perfect English* . . . *A magician? Could it really be?*

'And this is Pierre Bodu, my temporary assistant. We have come from London to make you a proposition, Tobias. Will you show us to your . . . to Father Allingham please, and we'll talk things over; how's that, eh?'

Tobias didn't have to think about it. Preoccupied with novel thoughts, he nodded eagerly and fell in beside the horsemen. For all his abstraction there was an unmistakable air of triumph about him.

Guido remounted and set his horse to follow the youth. He felt old and weary, and his buttocks ached with riding. He was so tired, and faced a task that did not appeal to him. Even so, at least this would not be a coercive job, there was that consolation; no need for force or bloodshed. *Mind you*, he thought, *I suspect we only just caught this one in time.*

In the Archbishop of London's expansive library, in the vast ibex-skin 1973 edition of the *Encyclopaedia Britannica* in particular, a servant of Church or State might open Volume Thirteen of this work and find:

1. *Thaumaturgic Colleges (including Holy)*
'... practice. Those who display above average ability or who lack proper guidance in the usage of magic are allowed to go to Rome. There they are trained by the very best exponents of each particular sorcerous art and in moral, magical and political philosophy. Less able candidates, or those urgently needed to fill vacant journeymen posts in the Church's Temporal Administration are trained at national colleges, several of which are maintained in the most advanced countries.
   Each graduate from the various colleges has priestly status, but is free of explicit pastoral duties, thereby making him free to serve the expedience of the moment as, when and how his Holiness sees fit.
   In this way magic is made a useful and respectable tool of Church affairs and statecraft, and the colleges serve as a guarantor of magical orthodoxy and propriety opposed to the ever-dubious operation of independent thaumaturges.
   SEE DRUIDS, JACK-MAGICIANS, WITCHES, WIZARDS, WARLOCKS.'

In common with most of the Encyclopaedia, this was substantially true, in fact entirely true; but it was not all of the truth. The Holy Thaumaturgic College itself was a grim, prison-like edifice that rose six storeys high, just outside Rome's walls. Talented young magicians went there when rounded up by servants of the Church, such as Father Mori, retained specifically for this purpose. Willing or not they went, the younger the better, and their potentially subversive talent was regulated and harnessed for the good of Christendom. Nowadays even young girls were taken in, whereas before their skills had been pointedly ignored or, if necessary, extinguished by fire. Although they could never become priests, as their male companions did, sorceresses had gradually become an accepted part of the Church apparatus, and the experiment (for such had it been) looked likely to become a permanent feature. Writers often cited this development as evidence for the growth of Christian charity and forbearance.

Whatever their sex, the usual product of such training was a dedicated and loyal top-notch magician of around twenty-five years of age, who could also be useful in the performance of various Church duties. Occasionally there were rejects, for the study of magic was inherently perilous, and a small but steady number of gibbering idiots and discreetly buried cadavers was also produced. The instructors refused to admit of any magical defences other than those appropriate to the mental configurations of a devout and orthodox Christian. An (intentional) consequence of this was that the pupils, lacking access to alternative defences (for they did exist) were forcibly obliged to conform or perish; accordingly the obstinate infidel or atheist succumbed and failed very quickly. Therefore as a reliable training mechanism, it can readily be seen that this system worked pleasingly well for the Church. Long before, the Church had been of a different attitude and had tried to extirpate magic by papal bull and auto-da-fé; then when this inevitably failed, it sought to make the practice its own exclusive tool. This policy was, of course, similarly doomed to failure; no visible sign marked out a magician from his fellow men, and many, for a great variety of reasons, kept the knowledge of their abilities hidden from general view. In consequence an unknowable but probably large number of sorcerers escaped the Church's net and 'Druids', 'Satanists' and unconventional practitioners abounded. On occasion they were better than anything the Church could produce, which was distinctly worrying to that body.

Tobias, however, had never seen an encyclopaedia and only had the most flimsy concept of the Roman college or any other for that matter. In his mind it conjured up pictures of subtle and dangerous wizards, power and prestige, all of which he found agreeable. Applied to himself, such images and ideas were positively stimulating. He knew little and cared less about service to his Holiness and the Universal Church; this was partly due to ordinary adolescent rebelliousness, and partly because he knew that a more mysterious, and possibly greater power and knowledge moved out in the wild places. Needless to say this attitude was concealed, quite invisibly, behind his cold control; indeed he began to regret his unusually open behaviour when talking to the priest. In all probability it was of no moment at all in this early stage of what promised to be a prolonged acquaintance, but Joan had said that first impressions were of vital import in dealings with all but the most intelligent of humans. At such a promising time it was more essential than ever that he did not forget his training. He acknowledged his fault and, being young, just as quickly forgave himself.

Father Guido, meanwhile, in the privacy of his thoughts reviewed a vast parade of transitory acquaintances. He had presided over the direction of a long stream of youth being fed as grist to the orthodox magical mill and, year by year, found himself more critical, more sad, less . . . convinced. The memory of his own training still had the power to generate icy chills and disturbed sleep. He had confessed his feelings, had the necessity of it all patiently explained, but still could not cast off the feeling that he was spending his one life pandering to something . . . wrong. How could he let others become scarred in the same way? Perhaps his gift, his 'talent', was a curse — a mere prop to the wickedness of the world? In the early, wakeful hours he sometimes felt . . . burnt out.

His spiritual struggle had not escaped the attention of the more subtle confessors. The more they considered the problem, the more obvious the solution became: the Church possessed many isolated monasteries and religious houses where men of great spiritual gifts (often a severe disability in terms of the world) could go to fight their inner battles away from material distractions. Just such an establishment was pencilled in on Father Guido's file in the office of the Archbishop of London; when and if his utility was quite exhausted the entry could be inked in, thereby settling the issue as neatly and painlessly as possible. Such a course of events was not in the least uncommon and no one, at least no one who mattered, thought the process sad or cruel; people served the Church in one way, and when they could do so no more they served it in another. Any theologian would affirm that the sufferings and struggles of a good soul were every bit as important to the Church as services to its tangible body. It seemed to be an eminently sensible arrangement and one that was beneficial to both parties.

Father Guido, however, did not possess the Church's millennia-long perspective and thought his travails to be solitary and unremarked upon. To him, Tobias was no different from the rest — a brief, bright splash of colour soon to be a blurred memory.

Acolyte Bodu was also engaged in mental conflict and turmoil, although on an altogether less exalted plane. In fact he was deeply concerned for the sanctity of his priestly skin, for Sister Theresa had missed her second period, and it seemed a branding was in prospect unless he could lie very hard and very convincingly . . .

In this way, engaged in disparate thoughts, the trio came to Father Allingham's door.

Father Allingham feigned surprise and was all deference and amiability. Tobias tasted sherry wine for the second time and went through the mockery of a discussion about his future. His final confession was heard and the provisional documents of indenture signed. The next time he came this way he would be a priest, and Allingham would, in all probability, be in the bosom of God's care. To Allingham himself this was an eminently attractive prospect compared to a rather stark and lonely existence as the shepherd of Clarkenhurst. The existence of a magician in the village was just another irritant and a problem he would be well rid of. He was a man who, rather late in life, had discovered a burning need for warmth and compassion, but it seemed clear to him that he would have to die before he would find them. Accordingly his faith was vastly increased.

Tobias was still young enough and human enough to feel a tear in his eye when he bade farewell to his family. His father had added his perfunctory signature to the relevant document, and his seventh child became, body and soul, Church property – which meant one less mouth to feed, hugely increased prestige in the neighbourhood and yet a gap in his fussy but essentially good heart.

Their farewell was the first genuine affection between father and son for years. Long after such emotion was no longer available or possible, Tobias remembered it warmly.

Mounted behind Bodu, young Oakley, apprentice magician, rode from Clarkenhurst, leaving behind both negative and positive achievements. On the one hand a dubious, even evil reputation and a near-dumb Parish Remembrancer. On the other an embryonic version of himself currently nestling, unguessed at, in Betty Lockwood's womb; and a relieved priest, left in peace to the thankless task of ushering the villagers to heaven.

All in all, quite a respectable legacy for a sixteen-year-old.

CHAPTER 3

In which our hero goes to London and is obliged to remain there.

Destiny was evidently a cautious, subtle creature mused Tobias as he sat beside a large fire in a Church lodging house in Whitehall. This was not a revelation to him at all; the same idea had presented itself after the very public announcement of his talents via the Fitzsimmons incident. No rapid advance in his interests had attended that particular drama, so he should not have expected overmuch from his meeting with Father Guido Mori. His disappointment was, however, only a natural youthful thing and not at all deep. His tuition had clearly taught him that progress rarely came in leaps and bounds; generally speaking it was concealed in the slow and tedious unfolding of time. This thought was a ready consolation and comfort for any present sorrow.

The journey to London occupied a day and a half of unhurried travel through small villages like Clarkenhurst and intervening woodland. Bizarre and inimical creatures were supposed to live in the forests, but none of them materialised for his entertainment. It was a pity, he thought: to see a real papal magician in combat with a slavering demi-demon would be both educational and diverting.

In only a short time Tobias had grown to like Father Guido; he seemed to have a genuine empathy for young people, and Tobias was not to know that this was mixed with no small amount of sympathy. Unlike most adults, gowned in prestige and position, he seemed prepared to discuss rather than issue proclamations from on high. Tobias felt his own special abilities granted him enhanced status over and above that of his contemporaries, and so was not afraid to attempt conversation with a man obviously his superior. Mori seemed inclined to indulge his charge in this minor presumption and so they talked, in question and answer form, for most of the journey, whenever circumstances permitted. Occasionally Mori would weary of it and wave Tobias to silence and they would ride on in peace for a few hours; then he would remember the charity enjoined upon him and permit conversation once more. Invariably Tobias would single-mindedly confine his questions to the realm of magical theory and this surprised Mori, in two respects. Firstly, he was impressed by the boy's precocious knowledge (although

laughably homespun and faulty in parts) and secondly, he noticed
an entire lack of the usual stock questions about life in Rome and
the Thaumaturgic College. Either the boy was dull and incurious
about his fate or (and this was the theory he accepted after
consideration) he was mature enough to make full profit from
association with a qualified sorcerer and leave Rome as a bridge to
be crossed in due and inevitable course. The coolness of thought
this betokened seemed to be in keeping with what else he knew of
young Master Oakley. But it had taken him a long while to perceive
this, Mori thought; nowadays his attention seemed only too ready
to slip. Generous by nature, Mori obliged Tobias by relating to him
several ideas and magical formulations that were the product of his
own personal research. From one magician to another it was a great
personal favour. For the entire final half-day before they entered
London, Mori and Tobias went over a currently controversial spell
that was yet to be included in the official basic grimoires – 'the rite
of cheerful subjugation' as Mori called it. The magician-priest
patiently expounded, and the apprentice-to-be probed on the
points he did not understand. Such was the latter's absorption, that
he was in full sight of London's massive walls before he noticed
where he was.

The first sight of London, 'Babylon the Mighty' and home to Kings
and Papal Legates, shocked him for all his later coolness. He even
allowed Mori's spell to fall from his mind for a little while.

Piled high within constraining walls and bastions were tenements, palaces, barracks and factories, termini and quays, the
heart and mind of a nation-state. Smoke lay heavy over all, thinning only slightly over the few spacious accommodations: the
papal citadel and royal dwellings at Westminster (conveniently
close for communication and beady observation), the park where
the Tower used to be, the Guildhall and a few other protected
sites.

Elsewhere, hemmed in by the Church-protected walls – modern
work upon Stuart, upon Plantagenet, upon Saxon, upon Roman
endeavours – steam-and-water-driven industry lived cheek by jowl
with housing and each made the other miserable with smoke or
noise or complaints. One day the pressure might cause the boil to
burst and ease itself and spread, but not while the papal word lay
against it. No man, it had long ago been decreed, should be more
than the merest walk from the works of God displayed in Nature.

Accordingly, green fields, albeit smoke-blackened and refuse-strewn ones, crept up to the very sides of the metropolis.

Tobias did not particularly mark these miraculous survivals: pasture was nothing noteworthy to him. Instead he marvelled at the spires and chimneys, the ships and trains and thought that nothing could ever prevail against the power manifested there. It was the forgivable mistake of the ignorant.

The enspiked heads over the great Western gate excited rather than repelled him. Magic of King or Pope kept them perpetually fresh and proclaiming their crimes.

'Levellers and Mohammedans' explained Father Mori, not wishing the boy to be distressed.

Later that night in his tiny bed (he shared a room with acolyte Bodu) Tobias utilised a mind-clearing technique taught to him by Joan, and began work again. He took that part of Mori's knowledge which he had managed to understand, and tried to attach it to a new power-word he was in the process of creating. After an hour of trying he temporarily gave up. Spells, especially new ones, did not spring into existence easily or quickly, that he already knew. He could afford to take his time in their creation, and it was an old adage that the more painstaking the construction was, the more efficacious the spell. As it was the spell did not attain life in his mind (and thus would not work), but the priest's information had definitely brought him closer and he felt a degree of gratitude. Not for the first time, he realised the inestimable value of experience.

Turning over to go to sleep, Tobias noticed in the gloom the bulk of the acolyte Bodu. He seemed to be having a bad dream. In the short time they had been together, Tobias had never really got to know the man, for he always seemed preoccupied; perhaps, Tobias thought, one of the religious-fanatic types. Then Tobias slept, unaware that, not a mile away, south of the clean and busy Thames, fate was preparing a change of destiny and, indeed, destination which was dramatic and clean-cut enough even for his tastes.

Sir Matthew Elias, Master of Magic to his Grace the Bishop of Southwark, was seated, brooding, in his large tatty office. The aftermath of untold experiments was strewn anarchically about, and such furnishings and decorations as were visible above the wreckage were remarkable for their complete lack of good taste. It was very late, his candle was low and a meal lay cold and forgotten beside him. Sir Matthew had delved very deeply into arcane matters on his various masters' behalf, often into subjects that magicians deemed perilous, and due to this he was very nearly mad. Putting the matter into simple terms and avoiding the use of such concepts as soul and horror, it could be said that he had seen far too much to remain humanly stable, and had come to a mental accommodation of a particular idiosyncratic nature. Not surprisingly, people tended to avoid him.

Nevertheless, he was an outstandingly able magician and when in conventional residence his mind was extraordinarily sharp and perceptive. It was entirely possible that magic had eroded his logical faculties, for vast jumps of intuition, invariably correct, were his widely acknowledged speciality. He habitually experimented with hallucinogenic herbs.

On this particular night, Sir Matthew was puzzling over a personal problem. Journeyman Hobbs had taken a strong fancy to a woman from over the river and instead of resorting to the usual arrangement, had chosen to renounce his vows and marry her. Sir Matthew, among others, was curious as to where this humble magician had found enough money to buy himself out of the Church and the Bishop's service; perhaps an unofficial, slightly dubious magical commission? No matter; he was to be replaced; that was the only important feature in the story and rather a pity since he had been a straight, no-nonsense chap and no bother at all.

Supposedly there were only a few, regulated, ways of recruiting magicians, all of which required prior approval of the Church Universal. However Sir Matthew no longer recognised convention; indeed he did not ever think of it, which made him a useful servant and a dangerous enemy, and this fact allowed a wider range of solutions to the problem. There was nothing but rules and convention to stop him venturing forth into the countryside, to search for a lad or lass with the required temperament and talent – nothing that is, bar Sir Matthew's *own* temperament. The difficulty was that the matter would require his own personal attention, for it needed very finely attuned magical perceptions to spot the right kind of embryonic talent. The thought caused Sir Matthew to shiver with distaste; after so many years in Southwark's vice and squalor his tastes had become very specialised. He needed tall tenements and narrow busy streets, and the thought of empty fields and smiling healthy bumpkins filled him with unresolved dread. No – definitely not the country, he thought.

This impelled him to find a town-based solution which meant, being so close to the ever-watchful eyes of the Archbishop of London, a reasonably orthodox solution as well. Searching for inspiration, Sir Matthew took from the drawer beside him a battered and bound set of papers. He flicked through and two-thirds of the way down, on a page entitled, 'PAPAL THAUMATURGIC COURIERS. SECONDED TO ARCHBISHOP'S STAFF – LONG-TERM TEMP', he noticed the name of Father Guido Mori. Sir Matthew knew this name from somewhere and with a shaky hand noted the man's contact address. He'd be worth a try – maybe he was en route already with someone suitable for Southwark's needs.

Relaxed now, the previous task immediately and completely forgotten, he leaned back in his wicker chair and stared out of the window at the brightly glowing Southwark night. He liked to sit and speculate on what was going on out in the township he had made his home; in an obscure but pleasing way such thoughts emphasised the wide and growing gap between him and the rest of humankind. This corrupting private communion was one of his favourite pastimes, but its joys were of a sad and limited nature. Eventually, therefore, he felt in need for something stronger and he called for a pot of tea to be brought to him. To this he would add some dried and powdered fly agaric mushroom and thereby escape.

In the due course of time and fate, Sir Matthew wrote a letter. Father Guido Mori's immediate superior during his secondment period in London, one Father O'Mally, received it, read it, and drafted another himself. Mori received this second missive whilst enjoying a large English breakfast, one of the few points of foreign culture he found superior to his own, but the reading of it rapidly deprived him of any pleasure to be found in his food. He looked around him with some agitation, an outward sign of inner turmoil, but no one seemed to notice his loss of appetite. Tobias was at the same table (possessing the talent immediately bestowed a degree of status, however base one's origins) and was fully absorbed in his first encounter with that most prestigious and exclusive beverage, coffee. Mori had told him how the beans were shipped at enormous expense from the vast but precariously held papal plantations in

the Southern Americas, and while Tobias had only the most
tenuous grasp of the geography involved, he fully appreciated the
value and mystique it conferred on the simple drink. It was the start
of a life-long love affair, one that would linger on when all his other
loves were dead. And just as no one noticed Father Mori's distress,
similarly this momentous occasion in Tobias' life went unremarked
upon.

Acolyte Bodu was toying with some food but, as usual, fully
occupied with his own problems, he impinged very little on the flow
of events.

Mori's mind was full of confusion but seemed, of its own accord,
to be making decisions that frightened him. His years in London had
given him some degree of familiarity with Southwark and an even
greater understanding of the specialist rôle its spiritual establishment played in the English Church. It was all coincidence, a
chance of time. If Father Allingham at Clarkenhurst had written
his letter a week earlier, if Tobias had defenestrated Fitzsimmons a
month sooner, Sir Matthew's disordered thought-processes might
not have settled on poaching Mori's young charge.

And it just so happened that something in Father Guido snapped
this time. *No, not this one*, he thought, pushing his meal aside. *Not
Southwark of all places*!

Pierre Bodu, attuned to his master's moves, hurried off to fetch
the good Father's outer cloak.

Father Guido had to wait forty minutes to see Father O'Malley and
therefore had time to muster and amend his arguments. In his
somewhat cooler mood, he realised how rash and unthinking he
had been in attempting to change, if not flout, direct orders.
Outrage and concern were good motives but poor explanations. He
had always been an obedient priest and magician, so why, he
thought in a nervous, cautious moment, rebel at this late stage? But
even after forty minutes for second and maybe third thoughts, he
still possessed ample resolve to carry him through O'Malley's study
door, and to fight the last tempestuous battle of conscience versus
duty.

O'Malley was a short, fat man with an air of urbanity achieved
only by the ruthless rooting out of all traces of his Irish-Welsh
origins. To rise as high as he had in spite of his serf-born status, he
had adopted the sophisticated, cosmopolitan manners of the higher

Church officials, and now, save by name, he was almost indistinguishable from them. It was a very notable achievement in a world that disapproved of undue social mobility and one he endeavoured to enjoy to the full. With the pleasure came the burden of concealing from scrutiny his early career.

His father had not only been a slave in all but name to the great Irish landowners in the Dyfed peninsula but, even worse, O'Malley was not a magician of the Roman school. His magical training had come in early youth from a local tribal wizard and general malcontent who had hoped to train sorcerers in order to raise rebellion and thereby lift his people from their centuries-old servitude. O'Malley had seen his tutor captured, and burnt by Royal troops put up to the job by a cartel of frightened landowners. The sight firmly taught him the worldly wisdom and realism he had previously lacked. Duly impressed and convinced by the lesson, he had soon after presented himself at the vestry door of Llandaff Cathedral as a lad of nineteen years, an accomplished magician and willing to carry out the commands of the Church. The Church in its turn could ill afford to ignore such a gifted person so predisposed to their rule, and accordingly a deliberate blind eye was turned to his dubious antecedents. This was not an enormously uncommon occurrence and could plausibly be justified by saying that it was far better that these individuals were gathered under the Church's wing (and surveillance) so that guidance might be given and service received where it would otherwise not be. Better this, in the Church's eye, than to let them wander 'free'.

Being a person of natural ability and diverse skills, O'Malley rose fast and learned even faster. As assistant Master of Magic to his Grace the Archbishop of London, he had done, seen and heard a very great deal, some of which, given a free choice, he would rather not have done, seen or heard. Even so, unlike some magicians, this did not graft a hard edge on to his sensitivities; rather he became more tolerant and compassionate to the strange people that were his charges.

Therefore Father Guido Mori was supremely fortunate in possessing a superior with the ability and inclination to consider his plea in a spirit of understanding, although not sympathy. Others might have felt less incined to humour him and had referral to their codes of discipline. Not so, Father O'Malley.

'Well, Father, I must confess I'm somewhat surprised at this.

48

What reasons can you offer me for countermanding the lad's transference to Southwark?'

'Only personal ones, Father O'Malley. I strongly suspect that the boy has been subject to malign moral influences, possibly for some considerable time and it seems to me that he cannot afford further exposure to wrongdoing, however good the cause.'

Mori felt this to be partially true and therefore justified; there *was* something suspiciously cold and abstracted about the boy, and Southwark would hardly help to remedy it. Yet his real concern was not specifically with Tobias, more with an abstract conception of all the children he had previously collected and handed over. But if he was to save this one from Southwark, he would be forced to recommend Rome as an alternative and the thought of doing so, reinforced by his vivid memories of his own Roman apprenticeship, made Mori feel nauseous and hypocritical.

O'Malley's curiosity had been roused. 'Do you have any idea of what these influences were?'

Mori knew a little of his superior's history and realised he was on the right track.

'It's only speculation Father, and the boy, of course, says nothing – but I fear that elements of paganistic thought were involved.'

This guarded comment was the nearest Mori could come to any actual mention of magical learning outside the jurisdiction, and perhaps even knowledge, of the Church. It was not a subject on which free discussion was safe or encouraged. He half suspected the truth about Tobias' education and this made him more determined than ever to save the boy from complete ruin. It would serve as a small act of reparation on his part on behalf of all the others, and as a grain of comfort for the years to come.

'Point taken, Father,' O'Malley said wisely. 'I won't press the subject further. Even so, I would have thought that the rigorous regime of Southwark would be the ideal solution for the lad. He'll be among his own, watched and guided on a constant basis, it's just as good a school as any other and if he acquits himself well his career will prosper, just as if he'd been to Rome. Why *do* you particularly wish him to go to Rome? If there is a good solid reason I could probably fob Sir Matthew off, even at this late date, but for the life of me I can't see it.'

Mori was an intelligent man, and could have devised a good solid reason with ease, but he was very conscious of his priestly status and would not tell a direct lie. 'It's not so much Rome I'm keen on, but . . . Southwark I'm against.' The last phrase he blurted out hurriedly to get the whole business over and done with as quickly as possible.

O'Malley's face hardened noticeably. 'Why, may I ask?'

Mori coloured slightly and went ahead to burn his last bridge. Slowly and coolly he announced, 'I feel . . . no – I *know* that Southwark is the very last place this boy should go to, for the good of his soul. As I've hinted, he's had no good influences up to now – are we to compound that by placing him in the worst establishment we can think of, and thereby set the pattern for his future career? No, it's the wrong school; the wrong . . . lessons.'

Father O'Malley leant back on his chair, his face still rather stern. 'I think you over-dramatise, Father Mori. It is true that Southwark has a training programme slanted to the more . . . practical, shall we say, elements of magic, but the use this training is put to is solely in the cause of good. It may be that in their later career the Church will occasionally pick out Southwark-trained people for specific tasks suited to their talents, but they otherwise remain perfectly normal magician-priests, just as if they had been at Rome or any other training school. Liverpool, for instance, devotes itself to the magical interactions between minds so that its pupils can assist in negotiations, interrogations and so on. Southwark, in turn, fits its charges to serve the Church in the vicissitudes of politics and affairs of state – hardly the "wrong lessons" you speak of. Surely you can't believe that?'

Mori knew he could have no answer to this simple statement of the facts. One school was probably as good or bad as another, what stuck in his craw was the system in its entirety – and against that there was no struggling. The securing of Oakley's passage to Rome would have been a minor victory for him; at least the training there was general and non-specific. It would also have been a salve to his troubled thoughts, but for Tobias himself the ultimate difference between the two courses proposed for him was probably minimal. Because his case and his strong feelings were based on sentiment, Father Guido had no real argument. He had lost.

O'Malley perhaps sensed the growing spirit of resignation in the man facing him across his desk, and since the matter was now beyond dispute he felt able to be conciliatory. 'Father Guido, I think I know what is worrying you. You've got a good heart, but on this occasion I suspect you are allowing purely personal, even selfish considerations to overrule your good sense. Even worse, you're masquerading them as concern for another.'

Father Guido coloured for the second time. 'Alas, you are correct in saying that, but . . . not wholly correct . . . I mean that other considerations intrude.'

'You refer to your anxiety for this youth's moral welfare I presume.'

'That and more. Father O'Malley, if we fling him into this system he will be lost. Entirely lost.'

The senior priest folded his arms and looked down at his desk to signify that the short exchange was at an end. *The old man has lost control on this one*, he was thinking. *He's on the edge. I must tread carefully if I'm not to break him – must keep this quiet from his superiors – how can I placate and save him?*

He lifted his head and caught Mori's gaze; something impelled him to charity. 'Between you and me, I know Southwark *is* a bit of a rough house, and perhaps there are a few scoundrels in the training school – perhaps even a few more than you might find elsewhere. Even so, rest assured that they are kept well under control. Their lawless exuberance is harnessed; put to good use. The setting tempers the talents into useful tools for the Church, does it not? That's the whole purpose and motive of placing the school there. Now if, as you say, this boy has had some bad teachers, surely the best thing that can happen to him is to be sent somewhere where such bad lessons are turned around and put to good use, eh? Perhaps we can even see God's hand in all this?'

Mori looked unconvinced, but O'Malley persevered.

'The crux of it all is that I see no good reason at all for countermanding this transfer. On the contrary: I think it will be the making of the boy . . . '

Mori slumped dejectedly.

'But don't despair, Father, don't despair.' O'Malley was a sensitive man; he could perceive deep emotions and so his last exhortation was not a cliché, but more of a command. 'What I will do for you is this; touched as I am by your Christian concern and diligence, I solemnly promise that I will make this . . . Oakley's welfare my special responsibility. Normally my brief would end when he arrives at his destination, but I will ensure that he comes to no subsequent harm, whether it be physical or moral. For you and for the respect I bear you, I will make him my charge, how's that eh? I can't say fairer than that now, can I?'

Mori heard this and took it in, but the proposition, given in all sincerity, left him untouched. He had come to the end of the road, his own and the Church's. Yet at least, he recognised, he had chanced upon a sympathetic ear, when he could just as easily have earned himself the perilous enmity of Southwark's Bishop.

'I must accept your kind offer, Father O'Malley, and I will pray for strength and clear-sightedness to be granted to you in this matter . . . please don't forget,' he added in an uneven postscript.

'Assuredly not, never fear,' smiled O'Malley. He was determined to be as good as his word for, unbidden, stray memories had returned to him of his own tough days as an apprentice and his clinging 'hedgerow wizard' reputation. No – with his power and influence (and perhaps even a little magic) he would endeavour to keep this particular child relatively unspoiled. It would be his offering to a good priest and to the young man that he himself might have been.

Father Guido left feeling more weary than ever, but thanking God for his leavening of good souls. He'd almost welcome the marsh or moorland monastery now.

Fate, the power that Tobias thought slothful, decided against him having a chaperon.

Two months to the day after his interview with Mori, O'Malley (after the prescribed fasting) withdrew to his quarters to summon a spirit. He did not inform his staff as to the object of his attentions but the name 'Astaroth, Prince of Hell' was whispered about his house.

No one ever knew what happened. Perhaps O'Malley fumbled over the dismissal or mayhap his guarding conjuration lacked sufficient conviction and therefore the required strength for a split second.

Whatever the cause, whether Astaroth or some other, Father O'Malley's head was neatly twisted off and placed, ready to be found, in the middle of his glowing pentagram.

Manifesting itself as an endless red-hot bronze plain, the force that human magicians named 'Pikestaff' idly tormented the residual life-essence of one such magician. Amusedly he, or it, looked down from a dizzy height and boomed in a metallic voice that filled the world. 'You thought you had bound me, did you not? You considered me so safe that I would do your every whim, did you not? But now it is *my* whims that count because, clever and confident as you were, you made a slip – only a tiny weeny slip mind you, but sufficient.

'Now you have all of created time to think on it, my love, while I hold you for my prolonged revenge. Your idiot servants talk of Astaroth, but you couldn't even hold Pikestaff, one of his knights. How droll, how amusing – hark . . . I must go . . . for a short while . . . but I shall be back soon, beloved, *I promise*.'

Some other hopeful magician was summoning.

A short historical and social digression now becomes necessary.

Historians generally concur that London first came into being early on in the Roman occupation of Britannia. No evidence, written or otherwise, exists to contradict this theory and so it has become generally accepted. Following its foundation, the city waxed and waned according to time and circumstances, but its general trend was towards expansion and increasing importance. Boadicea, the Vikings, the Spanish and Charles I had burnt it, but every time it rose again, irresistibly, like truth in a dark age. It became the national centre of government, and the monarch and his lap-dog parliament resided there in between intermittent plague outbursts. The mighty Universal Church also had its temporal administration there, figure-headed by the Archbishop of London. Spiritual power, headed by its own Archbishop, was tucked away in the martyr's town of Canterbury. This 'Spiritual' and 'Temporal' split was faithfully mirrored in the structure of the Church throughout Christendom.

Every large city breeds or attracts the entertainment it requires, much of which the Church would consider unfit. Therefore the more insalubrious forms of fun and merriment gathered as near as they dared without attracting the baleful glare of London's prelate, or the wrath of his legions of papal troops (answerable only to himself and His Holiness in Rome).

Southwark-across-the-water was the obvious choice of site, and a curious little community grew up there, within its own walls but attached, like a barnacle, to London's frailties. Whorehouses, inns and gaming centres of all types and quality abounded, tolerated only because of their decent separation from London proper and the lack of any alternative. An evening of 'transpontine' passed into London language and folklore.

Then, in the seventeenth century, just after the great rebellion, a well-meaning, but unworldly Archbishop of Canterbury decided that Southwark's rôle must be acknowledged and its lost souls catered for. Little dreaming he was creating a dire embarrassment for every one of his successors, he appointed a Bishop for the newly created diocese, and from his own modest wealth he provided for a small but functional cathedral. Several knocking-shops were demolished to make room for it.

Opinion within the Church on the whole approved of this move and it was thought that many sinners otherwise Hell-bound, would thereby be saved from the servitude of evil. This may well have been the case.

Most regrettably, however, the question of finance had been overlooked. A Bishopric's income, and hence status, entirely depended on the tithes it could levy. Since Southwark lacked a prosperous, respectable middle-class population (the mainstay of the Church economy), the first incumbent of the diocese had a very lean time of it indeed. The second turned a blind eye on occasion to the source of any gift or offering, in order to give himself the bare comforts of life. The third, utilising remarkable moral gymnastics, lived quite well and from then on the process snowballed, unremarked upon.

From time to time the Church applied certain ad hoc by-laws, to ensure 'transpontine' order and maintain strict insularity. Because of these and through a slow and complex historical process of legacies, seizures and appropriations, by 1976 and the time of this part of the tale, the Church had come to own nearly half of the illegal and semi-legal establishments in the township. The process was entirely unpremeditated and at first unnoticed. Later on it became profoundly embarrassing (if lucrative) but still the trend continued. Eventually, perhaps by the end of the century, Southwark would be one vast Church-owned brothel and gambling den. Even more remarkably the cathedral was packed to capacity, and beyond, every Sunday and Holy Day, unlike any other London church; however it was often an unconventional and abrasive congregation . . .

This unusual niche within the Church demanded a similarly

unusual occupant and Southwark's Bishops were sometimes faster and sharper than most of their flock. Even harder to credit is the fact that by no means all of them were wicked or corrupt men, many really did work hard to gather in the proverbial lost sheep. Nevertheless, whatever the motivation, it was a specialist job. And Londoners talked jovially of the 'mucky Bishop'.

The Bishop's staff were also far from ordinary servants of the Church; they were either recruited because they possessed the necessary qualities for the job or they rapidly acquired them in the performance of their duties. Senior members of the Church's temporal administration eventually noticed this, and a decision was made to attach a small training school for thaumaturgists to the existing Southwark establishment. In so doing they would take advantage of the observed qualities of the area to produce a small but reliable stream of magician-priests with useful specialist training. From the time of the unit's foundation, in the middle of the previous century, it proved to be of great use both in retaining order in the anarchically inclined township, and in providing suitable personnel for some of the more delicate areas of the Church's endeavours. In fact so successful, that the Southwark training programme was extended and applied to all the other great training centres in England, until eventually there was very little difference between them all. Only the unique influence of its setting remained to differentiate Southwark. It continued to be a somewhat disagreeable embarrassment, but for most of the time the 'mucky Bishop' could be forgotten or even denied.

One out-of-favour theologian had proposed that since the Church supervised most of man's activities, it was not in the least unreasonable for it to preside over man's vices as well. Privately, a number of Archbishops of Canterbury had thought he'd had a point there, but none had dared say so.

Such was the mould in which Tobias was to be placed.

Tobias' worldly possessions were few and, gathered together, fitted comfortably into a rucksack. They were by item:

2 suits of clothes, 1 black fustian for best and 1 patched-hand-me-down for everything else.
1 embroidered kerchief (a gift from his sister).
1 waterproofed cape.

1 hunting knife.

1 comb.

1 copy of *The Book of Ceremonial Magic* by Arthur Edward Waite, published in 1911 – this was a gift from Father Guido and immensely valued by its recipient.

Everything else owned by Master Oakley was on his head, body and feet, and therefore his packing took very little time.

On the day of his interview with O'Malley, Father Guido had returned and straightaway informed Tobias that he was no longer bound for Rome. The youth's spirit had plummeted like a stone, and he tried to think of what he had done or failed to do to deserve this. Surely, he thought, he was able enough? In any case a shamefaced return to Clarkenhurst was unacceptable. But where else could he go?

Then, a mere moment later, Tobias learned that he was, instead, to be assigned as a trainee journeyman and attached to the household of the Bishop of Southwark. On hearing this, his hopes rose as high as they'd previously sunk. Why did Mori sound so solemn and look so sad? The more Tobias thought about it the better it seemed. To stay amongst fellow countrymen and in such a huge and fascinating town seemed considerably preferable to the dimly grasped prospect of Rome. Not only that, but also the idea of being attached to a functioning household seemed more promising than a long period in a training school, however good. All in all he was enormously pleased with the turn of events.

Father Guido was consistently less elated though and remained abstracted and unapproachable right up to the time Tobias was obliged to leave. Even so, Tobias still felt some gratitude towards him and, sack in hand, sought him out just prior to departure from the Church's Whitehall 'Citadel'. Mori was in his room in a deep armchair, fingering through an illustrated devotional work.

'Goodbye, Father.'

Mori turned his head to look at Tobias, quite blankly at first, but then as if remembering something, with an intent gaze.

'Goodbye, Tobias. I hope you will be happy in your new life. You must always strive for that.'

'I will, Father.'

'But how do you define happiness, eh? Tell me that.'

Tobias was not going to be caught. 'I'm not sure.'

'No, I would not expect you to be; at your age you may have your own idea of it, but it will not be the correct one, so I will tell you. True happiness lies in loving and therefore serving God. It is the only way. You must be obedient to your new master . . . but never forget that there is a Master over us all and our first duty is to Him. Only through and in Him can we find happiness in this part of our story, Tobias; our best interests lie solely in that direction.'

'Of course, Father. I hope one day to appreciate that as well as you do.'

'It's an easily learnt lesson, Tobias, but it's best not to have to learn it, far better to draw on someone's experience and make an early decision on that basis – so much less painful. You see' – Mori leant forward with sudden emphasis – 'there is a right-hand path and a left-hand path and nothing in between; no middle ground or grey areas. There is right and there is wrong.'

Right is where my advantage lies, thought Tobias.

'I realise that, Father.'

He was only sixteen and this ruthless and cold attitude he had been taught was all tied up in his mind with appearing manly and stern. This was not an exclusively elvish phenomenon but a common and unappealing trait of the age.

'Good, my boy, I hope you do. In the years to come you may find it difficult to do so but you must always strain to see this truth of truths absolutely clearly.'

'I will endeavour to, Father.'

'And remember that the vigilance over you never ceases.'

'God watches over all of us, Father.'

'Precisely so; but for added security bear in mind that two others will continually consider your wellbeing, myself and another. Now go, and God be with you in all things.'

He laid his palm on Tobias' forehead and gave a blessing and a simple, symbolic warding spell.

'Thank you for your guidance and especially thank you for the book, Father.'

'I shall write to you, Tobias. Take this and now be off with you.'

Tobias went quickly out into the street and headed for London Bridge. After a few minutes he paused by a pie shop and opened the envelope Mori had just given him. It contained a brief sheet of magical geometry, expanded and put into English in places for

Tobias' benefit. A note was added beneath. 'I have found that an efficacious trigger-motivation for the power-word in this conjuration is to visualise a fair maiden staring at you in terror from a bridge. Attach this vision and the formulae above to any word you may have by you and the rite of cheerful subjugation might well be within your grasp.'

Tobias tried this using a spare and partially worked power-word he had in his memory. To his surprise and delight it almost worked; perhaps one more evening and the whole thing might be ready. It was a truly marvellous farewell gift and for the first time Tobias felt the intoxicating novelty of being one step ahead of the beginners' spell manuals.

Good old Mori, thought Tobias. He was sorry to lose him. Perhaps in a week or two he would settle down and write the old chap a letter. Meanwhile, exciting new prospects had first call on his mind. He resumed a brisk pace towards the Thames.

What had Mori meant by 'another' concerning his welfare? Could he possibly know about Joan? It was rumoured that senior magicians could read minds and hear thoughts as easily as ordinary mortals used their eyes but Tobias had never felt such a power, not even in a latent form. Even if Mori did know all the truth it was very doubtful that he would report him. After all he was a friend. Putting aside such fruitless speculations, Tobias strolled on to Southwark.

The original plan was for Guido Mori to accompany Tobias and two other young magicians, currently waiting in London, down to Dover. He would be expected to give them a modicum of instruction on the journey and in the period before their ship set sail for France. Similarly, other couriers would meet and travel with them as they passed through France, the Holy Roman Empire, Tuscany and thus at last to Rome and their journey's end. Father O'Malley, however, thought it wisest to alter this, and he allocated another man to the job of seeing the remaining two youths on their way. Instead Mori was ordered to go to Reculver and collect a young girl-magician, lately revealed and said to be terrorising her Parish. It was thought that this would take Mori's mind off things and keep him fully occupied. For, by all accounts, the girl was thoroughly enjoying herself and it was likely that coercion would be necessary.

In the event higher powers in the Church, having learnt of the

Southwark transfer, changed Mori's plan yet again. A letter from Canterbury, which found him at his prayers in his room, outlined a very much more peaceful and placid future for Guido.

CHAPTER 4

In which our hero's new home, new friends and further education are described.

Although still naïve and unversed in that form of accepted vice known as the way of the world, one walk through Southwark's streets was enough to make Tobias feel all was not as it should be.

It was midday and so he escaped any approaches or solicitations, but the people looked sharp and dressed even more sharply. Most of the men, although not nobility, carried swords and thus technically broke the law (but against so many, the watch would be slaughtered in pitch battle if they tried to enforce it). Furthermore, the taverns looked as if they had been open for many hours already and drunkards of the worst kind abounded. Pausing, he got his knife out of the pack and fixed it prominently to his belt. Any one of the proud pimps or tavern-toughs he passed could have cut him to shreds (unless he used magic), but the blade touching his flesh made him feel more secure.

This mood of orientation was soon knocked out of Tobias when he arrived at his new home, a three-storey timber building opposite the aptly grubby little cathedral. A broken-toothed man in the Bishop's livery at the gatehouse slowly read his papers of introduction and grinned at the lad like a lunatic in what seemed to be an ecstasy of welcome. Once past this obstacle, he was sent to an office at the head of a flight of stairs. Here worked the junior officer of the Southwark security staff, a round ball of a young man who introduced himself without any formality or restraint as Wally Faulkner or 'Sir, if any God-botherer is about'. He welcomed Tobias and expressed the hope he would have a happy time in 'Mucky Hall'.

'There's four apprentice magicians here (including you) plus one senior Rome-trained man called Geoff Staples, and of course Sir Matthew Elias, but you'll never see him. You're in room G2, no women in the building at any time so make your own arrangements. No excessive drinking or swearing (or at least not in public); in short, don't screw us about and we won't screw you, OK? Talking of that, watch the mercenary guard in G8 – he has an eye for young boys; otherwise he's a good bloke. I'll give you your equipment now, sort out your grub with the other witch doctors, report here seven-thirty Monday for your duty list. Best o' luck, now push off.'

All this had been said in nigh on one breath and Tobias stood mentally open-jawed trying to take it in.

Faulkner turned to a nearby locker, opened it and pulled forth an armful of objects. He dumped them on the table and Tobias mechanically picked them up and left, having said nothing at all.

Five minutes later he sat in the bare cell of G2 (bunk, table, chair and bookcase) and for the first time looked at his equipment. There was a huge (it seemed) flintlock pistol and holster with an accompanying bullet mould and lead pegs. There was a metal-capped belaying pin, an enigmatic bowl of red-coloured bees-wax, various lengths of stripped wood, some needles and a surcoat of thin cloth bearing the Bishop's insignia (two unicorns supporting a crucifix).

Tobias was bemused; just what sort of church had he joined?

Some clue was received when Tobias got his duty list. Along with the daytime programme were three evenings per week of 'Peace Promenade'. At first this was enigmatic but his three fellow journeymen eagerly put him straight. The Bishop, they explained, had a wry sense of humour; he also had a burning desire to ensure that a modicum of decorum was kept in Southwark. The old men, or bar-room boasters, of the watch were unequal to driving the township's hedonistic populace to propriety, so the Bishop undertook the task and by all accounts achieved it with characteristic singlemindedness. The peace promenades were for the journeymen to practise the skills taught during the day. If one of them from time to time got his head cracked in so doing, well that was sad and his companions would make sure that he had many people to accompany him to the infirmary (or even, on occasion, to the Chapel of Repose).

Tobias was not clear how he felt towards this side of his obligations. On the one hand he liked the idea of being able to practise the magic he already knew; on the other, his companions' bloodthirsty tales of the promenades filled him with not a little trepidation. Yet he was also aroused by the *frisson* of excitement and bravado such tales gave him. For he was a sixteen-year-old youth, away from home for the first time and bursting with untested potential.

Still his control remained with him and he showed nothing of any insecurity he might have felt. More speculation he could put aside until it bore fruit or died of neglect. In this way his increasingly incisive brain was left free for more profitable use.

His first week at Mucky Hall was made deliberately easy. With the Bishop an impossibly remote figure and Sir Matthew Elias totally absorbed in his dreamings, Geoff Staples was able to run a very relaxed and amenable regime. Tobias' duty roster was not dated to start until his second week and so he had plenty of time to 'fit y'self in and look around boy', as Wally Faulkner had instructed. He toyed with the idea of exploring the town on his own but was advised against it and for once decided to accept someone else's judgement.

One afternoon was spent at the Bishop's tailors over the bridge in the Hebrew quarter where he was fitted out in an acolyte's long gown and sugar-loaf hat in the purple that signified his possession of the talent to journeyman standard. To his delight round the right arm was stitched a design of yellow stars (a product of some past Bishop's fancy). Surveying himself in the tailor's long mirror he thought he cut just as much a dash as any papal magician and although he did not know it yet the band of stars was at least as much feared and respected in the London area as its papal counterpart of smoky red. In some areas it was hated just as much as well.

The last real conversation Tobias had taken part in was with Father Mori two days before and so he was glad to respond when the tailor proved to be chatty. They exchanged names and so Oakley met Jimmy Bergman.

Everyone distrusted the Jews, everyone needed the Jews. Several early Popes had ruled emphatically against usury amongst Christians (despite fervent lobbying by commercial vested interests) and whilst not universally observed, the ban had a smothering effect on the flow of funds available to hard-up Kings and proto-industrialists. The Jews, however, were not so bound, and moreover they were businessmen – as they needed to be in a hostile world – and generally honest to boot.

In time, therefore, it was largely left to the Hebrews to provide financial lubricant for the stirring giant of Capitalism and the ambitions of monarchs and Popes. And if, on occasion, they were not repaid on time – or not at all – they had to be philosophical about it and see the loss as the price paid for tolerance of their heretical presence.

For, as stated, they were not popular. Plague outbreaks, vanished children and sickening animals were blamed on the Jews. Beside which they had an annoying habit of becoming prosperous despite the odds against them, and in any case they did kill Christ, didn't they?

The higher and better elements of the Church enjoined Christian charity towards the Jews. There were even occasional papal Bulls and pronouncements compelling it, but to little avail.

Ugly riots and sometimes pitched battles had killed or dispersed most of the Jewish communities in the rest of England but London's Hebrew quarter survived because of the Jews' second major quality, namely that they could give battle like lions. On one occasion in the last century when the mob, enraged by the ravages of plague, had decided to deal with the 'corruption in their midst', the Hebrews had fought back to such a degree that they were effective masters of much of central London for nearly a day, during which time they took adequate recompense for past injuries. The Archbishop of London had restored the status quo using papal troops (and, to be fair, excommunicated surviving ringleaders), but the painful memory remained and the metropolitan Jews had since been left in blissful cultural isolation.

And they did not abandon their religion: neither did they seek to encompass others within it.

Jimmy was a fair example of his community but he did not make enough money to consider lending it out. Instead his skill lay in his hands and by pure chance (that is to say the working of the Bishop's mind) he received the commission for the Cathedral's clothing needs. Never being one for questioning Jehovah's beneficence (since he could so often be cruel) Bergman gave thanks and settled back to a secure and reasonably prosperous life.

Tobias knew none of this and would have held it of little account in any case. He told Jimmy (who was three times his age) of some of his life and a little of his expectations. The tailor, all the time passing measurements to his son-cum-apprentice, listened as he knew he should and put in his own thoughts when they were not controversial or specifically Hebrew idioms. Then it dawned on him that the boy had brains. And at about the same time Tobias thought, *this man's not being obsequious, he's really curious about us.*

Thus, true to the peculiar alchemy of human relationships, a certain warmth and lowering of guards ensued and the seeds of a good friendship were sown.

So Tobias left with a new uniform of which he was proud and an invitation to dine with the Bergman family, concerning which he was intrigued.

Of this curious cross-pollination, more later.

Wally Faulkner presented no front to the world; he was as he seemed through and through. To him priests were 'God-botherers' and magicians were 'witch doctors'. Lacking breeding, decorum and 'the talent', he would never be either. However, he had other talents which made him admirably suited to be a security officer in the most colourful district of England's most colourful town. Tobias heard many horrifying stories about him (the majority exaggerated or untrue) and Staples once jokingly said that he had been born without a conscience. Nevertheless his ideas of discipline and proper behaviour were immensely elastic and he and Tobias never had a cross word (for the youth was frightened of him).

Geoff Staples had qualified from the Holy Thaumaturgic College four years ago and somehow found himself in this specialist backwater. He took his priesthood seriously enough to attempt to conceal his vices but was otherwise always completely open, cool, calm and humorous. Intermittently, he taught the journeymen very well. At other times he was abstracted; Tobias never found out why. By the overall standard of the Southwark establishment he was noticeably normal.

The mercenary in G8 was a Scot who made a pass at Tobias within a week, but was not in the least offended when the lad politely sidestepped his proposal. Much to Tobias' relief he found that the man only liked willing bedfellows. Even better, it emerged that Alan Lumley (which was his current pseudonym) was a very pleasant companion. It was said he knew every permanent or semi-permanent resident of Southwark and that every one would 'shit a hedgehog rather than face his temper', as Faulkner put it.

Naturally Tobias' closest companions were his three fellow journeymen. It was the first time he'd had to face the close and inescapable proximity of his contemporaries since he'd left school some three years ago, and he was not good company to begin with. He often spent his free evenings poring over Arthur Waite's book on magic, and accordingly easily kept his head-start in matters magical. Alternatively, very conscious of his prestigious uniform, he would cross London Bridge to visit the Bergman family, his new firm friends.

Like Tobias, the three other young men had been bound for Rome at various intervals when Southwark's net had grasped them. There was a Londoner, noble by birth, and at the other end of the scale a Welshman from Swansea who was an ex-serf to one of the great Irish noblemen that ruled that area. The talent had been his passport to another, lighter, bondage and the Church had paid handsomely to free him of his feudal obligations. The third came from Derby and was a bland nonentity bemused at the turn in his life and bemused by the gift invested in him.

Between them they arranged meals and everything was amicable enough. Although all had been there longer than Tobias he was accorded some deference for he had already developed a certain presence which politely requested, if not yet commanded, respect. Besides, among themselves, all considerations of social status, strength and education were as nothing compared to the great equaliser of magical ability.

Given these heterogeneous beginnings, the four rarely had their lessons together, save for thaumaturgy. Tobias and Hugh Redmayne of Derby were roughly of a standard in education and sat at their books for long hours in a lonely classroom at Mucky Hall. After a while Tobias grew to loathe his silent bumbling companion; although he knew this was both unkind and unworthy.

Elijah Green from Dyfed had to venture out over the bridge during the mornings for he was illiterate and attended a monastery lay-school where the rudiments of letters were hammered into the sons (and sometimes daughters) of the reasonably well-to-do.

Rather unfairly perhaps, because of his good education, Simon Skillit from London was left free of elementary lessons, 'free' that is to attend as page-servant to Staples and occasionally Sir Matthew. Of the four youths he was probably the hardest worked.

Whatever their place of training, be it Rome, Avignon or one of the national colleges, the Church was determined that all its priests should possess the elements of erudition. Thus Tobias learnt Latin, a little geography (such as was reliably known), something of history (which diplomatically skimmed Europe's temporary fall from grace due to the teachings of the demon-spawn Luther) and a lot of geometry and mathematics (the basic notation of efficient sorcery). Once a week all four went to the Cathedral and were taught Church rituals, services and so on, as well as the duties of a priest to his flock. Tobias listened only to as much of this as he needed and then devoted his mind to learning the service of exorcism. He had heard that, with very little modification, this could be condensed into a very useful spell whose effect was somewhat more 'catholic' than the original service, particularly in the field of the control and summoning of unclean spirits. Anyway he felt he could afford to ignore the old priest's instruction since he already had his own idea of the rôle of the priesthood. In truth he did not really believe in God's existence; he considered that Joan's teaching had made him too analytical and sceptical for that, but the age in which he lived did not encourage philosophical debate on alternatives to belief and so he had nothing with which to replace the Christian ethos. Nevertheless he felt part of an élite, privy to secrets and thoughts which set him apart from the mainstream and their beliefs.

He would often read widely on unconnected subjects just for the pleasure of it; his mind began to bloom under the discipline and intellectual encouragement of Church education. But still he felt that magic was the path that would lead him to his as yet entirely undefined goal. At this stage he had some unruly conception of it as a state of power, status and complete fulfilment.

If there was one field of tuition in which Southwark was intended to excel it was practical magic. And this was just official tuition. Southwark was also a great school of life. Sir Matthew was a brilliant magician, both in theoretical matters and in practice; he it was who drew up the training programme and oversaw its implementation. On this point his butterfly mind was firm. He took great pains to ensure that all areas were adequately covered and would personally intervene at what he considered to be crucial points. For the main part, however, Geoff Staples was perfectly adequate to the task, possessing an above-average talent himself.

There were as many theories about the source of magic as there were magicians and so no time was wasted expanding on this. Church wizards were intended to be workmen not philosophers. To start with, a few of the basic, text-book power-words were taught so the general principle could be understood. Tobias was sufficiently advanced to skip this and only joined the class when the more difficult words were being mentally forged. Much, if not all, depended on intuitive jumps and the matching of emotional states to grasp the desired state of mind. Moreover it was a fact that people with the talent were rarely logical or dispassionate and, despite whatever Tobias thought, he was no exception. His dislike for the inoffensive Hugh was proof of this if any was needed.

The problem was to convince the journeymen of the efficacy of a power-word which Staples or Elias already knew and took for granted. The word or mental image used was immaterial, the problem lay in completely believing the spell. What a magician truly believed became fact; in effect the talent enabled its possessors to treat reality as a pliable commodity.

All of which sounds a blissfully simple proposition. However the human mind dearly loves its normal frame of reference and resists bitterly any attempt to convince it otherwise. A magician had to believe in his spells or power-words, call them what you will, just as much if not more so than a saint's belief in God. Otherwise they were just useless mutterings.

A very, *very* good sorcerer could devise a spell to deflect a bullet speeding towards him, but he would have to be entirely assured that the bullet travelling his way at 'x' miles per hour could do no harm.

Power-words were extremely difficult to construct and maintain. Few humans were able to persuade their minds that miracles were perfectly normal and predictable, and such people were said to have 'the talent'. Their mental efforts, however much they might become instinctive, were, by their implausible nature, very strenuous. Furthermore it was a recognised fact that the more 'useful' or dramatic spells tended to be more exhausting than the rest. So it would be a very exceptional magician indeed who could use a killing spell more than three or four times a day without taking to his bed in a state of collapse. On the other hand, less drastic conjurings could be performed a hundred times a day without noticeable effort or strain. There seemed to be some correlation between the degree of 'impossibility' and the drain it caused on a magician's strength but the link was not direct and defied quantification.

Individual 'magical stamina' varied just as much as physical stamina although there seemed to be no relation between the two. Similarly, as with normal strength, there was a broad average of magical 'staying power' (although there were minor variations among the journeymen) and it was to this that the Southwark training catered. Then since the power of the mind was exhaustible, all of the journeymen were also trained in the use of more prosaic weaponry such as guns, blades and fists.

The fields of demonology and ritual magic also had to be covered as useful additions to thaumaturgy. Geoff Staples mentioned the main types of demi-demons known and outlined the best way to kill each.

And in these ways Tobias spent his days for the next three years. He listened and absorbed, and learnt all that was offered him. In addition there was his private research . . .

But these were not quiet years. Tobias was about to enter adulthood and life strode in to teach a few lessons of her own.

CHAPTER 5

In which our hero goes about his new occupation and on one occasion gives way to anger.

For his first Peace Promenade Tobias did not actually venture out. A mercenary guard (not Alan Lumley, the pleasant pederast) taught him how to load his pistol and gave tips on how to fire: 'Always aim low and as if you're pointing your finger.' He was also told that if the situation grew so grave that he had to use his firearm then he was to use it to kill. The Bishop's regime was not lenient to malefactors. Tobias doubted his ability with weaponry; further-more he had never killed without magic before and was split between repugnance and a semi-guilty curiosity.

That night he lay in the warm dark, disquieted because his mental control seemed to have been proved disturbingly super-ficial. Then, just before sleep, his mood shifted to one of pleasure at the discovery that his better self remained alive and well despite all the influences weighing against it.

When Tobias awoke, he was part amused and part disgusted at his nocturnal musing – which he saw as a fine example of his mind controlling him rather than the desired contra. He had been treating the prospect of death and slaughter as an absolute certainty instead of a purely last resort. But he knew why. It was because he had been reflecting on his reaction to an event already preordained. In fact his control had not really slipped at all.

Now he was really shocked; had he always been a person who could calmly consider murder? How had this gap in his soul opened without his noticing?

The next night was quiet until ten o'clock. In the guard house Alan Lumley (alarming and strange in full buff coat, pot helmet and sword) engaged in desultory conversation with another mercenary. All four journeymen were present – it was a Saturday and so it was felt their combined presence would be necessary in the event of the pre-Sabbath bacchanalia turning sour. They were instructed to wear their journeymen gowns and Southwark-surcoats, since the patrons and citizens of Southwark would otherwise find four callow adolescents singularly unintimidating. When a member of the watch patrol brought news of the night's first trouble the party proceeded at speed to the tavern-cum-brothel in question. The two mercenaries led the way along with the patrolmen. The journeymen followed in pairs in perfect step.

Light blazed from the doors and windows of the inn and groups of patrolmen surrounded the outside. The few casual onlookers were kept at a distance by their presence (but they were few – at this hour Southwark folk had better things to do than gawp).

Tobias was excited, a little apprehensive and very busy mentally. He had already decided what sequence of spells should be used for maximum efficiency and which way he would dive while drawing his pistol. His solution merely awaited the scenario.

Inside the play had resolved itself into neat, easily recognisable sides. Representing 'good' were a number of the watch who were engaged in the dual activities of holding back the neutral side (a gaggle of curious, bemused or entertained patrons) while observing the evildoers. These were personified by a large gang of sailors who were in their sky-blue 'evening best' and hideously drunk, stationed at the very top of the long flight of steps which led up to the third floor. This was where the house's more intimate transactions took place. To Tobias the men looked very experienced, dirty and dangerous. Now that he was faced with the reality, he thought he wouldn't find it very difficult to kill.

It wasn't the sailors' occupation of the stairs that was in dispute. It was all down, explained the madame, to the fact that they had tried to escape without paying their dues, and had drawn knives and 'lady-guns' when challenged. Moreover, they'd taken several of the girls and waiters hostage. There were about twenty of them, and drink was the entire cause of the whole unpleasantness.

Lumley took charge and told the journeymen to ring the bottom of the stairs, whilst he leapt up the stairs, sword drawn, and addressed the most coherent sailor. This continued for five or more minutes during which time Lumley did not move, not even so far as to gesture with his free hand.

Meanwhile Tobias was the subject of much pointed comment and ribaldry from the ladies near his assigned post. He had thought himself hard-bitten, but their mockery passed straight under his defences and he felt a blush creeping up his face. This sign of success inspired his tormentors to greater efforts, and Tobias grew doubly annoyed with himself. But he suddenly noticed Lumley was descending the stairs and the sailors were accompanying him. All weaponry had been put away and normal conversation began to creep back. The sailors, somewhat subdued, passed into the hands of the watch, out of the door and out of Tobias' life for ever.

A relaxed Lumley called the journeymen together and they left the tavern.

Tobias was amazed – no magic, no violence, no blood. He'd been working himself up for nothing.

His sense of amazement diminished with time as he discovered this was to be the pattern of nine out of ten of his Promenades. And he soon realised that if every Southwark affray involved bloodshed, the place would be a hecatomb within a week. The Bishop's policy was a cautious, humane one within its own bounds and only the most undesirable or implacable troublemaker was injured by the official peace-keepers.

Tobias was curious as to how exactly Lumley had mastered the situation and sought him out in the refectory.

He was a tall man, rapidly balding from the forehead. Once his features might have been described as baby-like but vice, hardship and suspicion had twisted and altered them.

Tobias had to admit he looked evil, even corrupt.

'Mr Lumley – what did you say to make the sailors call it a day?'

'Why should you want to know, lad?'

'Just curiosity,' Tobias said untruthfully.

'Well, lad, you'd better learn, I suppose. You might need it yourself one day, if your black witchcraft doesn't work.'

Tobias winced.

'You see, lad, what it came down to was a matter of being *reasonable*. They were drunk and couldn't think for themselves, so I did it for them. Simple as that.'

Tobias thought for a space. 'You told them that we could summon superior force?'

'Only in a way – like I said, I had to think for them and on their level, so I just pointed out that there wasn't any way they were getting out of that place without losing three or four men and was that worth it for a few lousy shillings? I let that stew and allowed them to feel *they* were making the concessions and that they were still the masters of the situation; that way there's no panic, no hasty judgements made. Solution? Peace and light. They keep their pride and we keep their esteemed custom. No one gets scratched and the Bishop's valuable property, both livestock and fittings, remains intact. It's *reasonableness*, lad, and it rarely fails except with the worst.'

'But what would you have done if they had persisted?'

Lumley frowned, thought a while and shrugged. 'Why then, between us we'd have gutted every single one of them.'

Soon after these events Tobias went to keep his first dinner appointment with the Bergmans. It was one of his free nights and he informed no one else of his intentions. He decided to wear the journeyman apparel that Jimmy had made, as his official status was still a novelty to him, and he felt it would please the tailor to see his own handiwork. He was mistaken – Bergman was a good craftsman but when he stopped work, the thought of clothing never entered his head until the following day.

In the event the evening went very well. Tobias was hungry and the food was good. (Kosher was an unknown word to him.) The Bergman family were curious about the sallow young man and his 'romantic' profession and kept the conversation at a high level. The clan was introduced and Tobias gravely shook hands with the two sons, three daughters, one aunt and one gnarled patriarchal grandfather.

He learnt a little about the Hebrews and was intrigued. Short of Biblical references he had been entirely ignorant of their existence before. Because any Jews in the vicinity of Clarkenhurst and Reading had been removed long before, he was just as surprised to meet living specimens as he would have been to bump into a Roman or a Spartan.

The cap on this mushrooming curiosity was set by the appearance during dinner of the local Rabbi in his gaberdine and fur-rimmed hat. His eyes widened at what appeared to be a young priest of the Church Universal sitting at food with a Hebrew family. He was studiously courteous, made a little conversation, shook hands with Tobias and calmly said he would call later when they weren't entertaining.

Tobias, perhaps a little paranoid, wondered whether this was a veiled threat or expression of disapproval but the Bergman family seemed to take it at its face value and weren't in the least disturbed.

Tobias felt he was privileged to have contact with yet another 'secret' section of the world, although not as exotic or promising as Joan's. Somehow these byways of normal society had come to have a great attraction for him. His attitude was that the Southwark school would teach him all he needed to know concerning the common world but the pursuit of wider knowledge would require him to take initiatives. So he was pleased, within a week or two of his arrival in London, to be sitting in a foreign community that was within, to him, another foreign community.

Besides which he'd decided that he liked the Bergmans. He didn't know what the Bergmans thought of him but he was glad to be invited to return in the near future.

Tobias celebrated his seventeenth birthday by killing a man. It was his fortieth Peace Promenade and had seemed no different from the others when a show of overwhelming force and Lumley's persuasive reasoning had settled the monotonously regular quarrels over failure to pay dues, disgruntlement over services rendered and so on. On nine out of ten occasions the Bishop's watch were able to control any incipient ugliness but when it looked as if Southwark property, human or inanimate, was endangered the 'Promenaders' were sent for. Tobias had got used to the feel of the pistol under his gown, although he had never drawn it in anger, and more importantly to him he had got to know many of the girls and croupiers on first-name terms. His precocious maturity, recognised ability and occasional gentle wit had endeared him to the more jolly inmates of Southwark's vice dens.

Duty rosters did not recognise birthdays and so a cold March night found Tobias, Simon Skillit, Lumley and several mercenaries entering a high-class entertainment-house and hotel at the edge of the Bishop's domain facing right on to the Thames. They were all a little tipsy since young Oakley had been obliged to buy a jug of brandy to enable everyone to drink his health. They therefore set about their job with perhaps a little more than usual vigour. A man with a pistol had barricaded himself in a room upstairs, after a dispute with either a girl or the madame; no one knew which.

Lumley was in a hurry to get back to his warm guard room; in any case there were times when he seemed not to care and this apparently, was one such time. So he strode up the stairs alongside Tobias, whom fate had placed in front, and applied his left boot to the closed door. At some point he had unobtrusively drawn a pistol. The door gave way and revealed a surprisingly empty room; it was also a very shattered room and little of the furniture remained intact.

Lumley was frustrated and directed a 'bastard' at the fled occupant, before he and Tobias crossed to the open window – the obvious means of hasty egress.

Below, in a fitting irony, the establishment's solitary red beacon dimly illuminated a fleeing figure making for the bridge. The symbol of his sinning was responsible for his punishment because this poor light enabled Lumley to pick out the escapee and he whispered, horribly calm, in Tobias' ear, 'Take him out, dear boy.'

Tobias could see just as well and no time was available for moral reflections. With an almost instinctive reflex he pointed at the man and said the highly individual word unexercised since his night on the heath long ago. His aim was true and the black shape fell like a stone. Only then did he have the opportunity to wonder what he had done.

'If he hadn't smashed the fixtures, I'd 've let him off seeing as I'm cheerful,' said Lumley. 'Now let's go and look at your target practice.'

The man was not dead but dying. Just as Tobias had feared, the spell had had too little emotional force behind it to work; after all he had never met the fool before. The fool in question was a big fat American sailor (at least a bosun), and judging by the pencil-stripes of his uniform, probably off a clipper working the 'triangle'. More obviously he had haemorrhaged very badly. He was crying because he knew he was slipping away.

What they would never know was that he had been drunk, bewildered and outrageously cheated by the madame of the house. He had been lonely, far from home and had broken up the room in a piqued attempt to get his money's worth. He had also broken his ankle in dropping out of the first-floor window. They could have simply walked after him and caught the crippled fugitive.

Lumley, from some perverse idea, left Tobias and ordered him to stay until the man died.

Tobias had no words while his victim continued to cry and bleed from nose, mouth and ears for a little while and then was taken. He learnt that he was not as hard as he had thought he was. Perhaps this was Lumley's intention all along. Tobias' other great lesson was that the simulation of a power-word spell bore no relevance to its actual performance. The act had no point of contact with the exciting exercise that he had thought it would be.

That night he gained a year, and lost a piece of his defences for ever.

For several days he was sick at heart but then his remarkable powers of recovery came into play and he began to think less and less of the fat American. Lumley and Staples watched him closely for a while and then deemed that he was toughening up nicely, a very promising young magician.

During his seventeenth summer Tobias began to fill out and take on the appearance that would be his throughout his life. He was still undersized but Faulkner's regime had given some degree of fitness. After the Southwark style he began to wear his hair long and on his free evenings would have one eye heavily made-up from some little paint pots he had bought in a market over the bridge. This was the very latest fashion among London's young blades and under the Bishop's strangely disciplined rule even trainee priests could adopt it. His face was unmarked by pox or other disfigure-ment and his fathomless black eyes relieved his visage of its sallowness. Some women would have considered him handsome, some not.

Other things began to fall into place that year. Almost unconsciously he came to associate all advancement, prestige and happiness with the acquisition of magic powers and he accordingly worked at his studies like a man possessed. This is not to say that his motives were entirely selfish, magic was genuinely fascinating to him and its learning occupied the greatest part of his speculations. With Joan's initial impetus he was fast outstripping the older but less inspired journeymen.

At the same time, on what Father Guido Mori might have considered the debit side, Tobias floated in an ethical vacuum and was driven only by considerations of self. He discovered alcohol and the other pleasures of the Bishop's dens and became the sharp young man about town in his free time.

The one incongruous element in all this was that his visits to the Bergman family continued (he even cordially re-encountered the Rabbi once or twice) and on those evenings he dropped back into the path of decorum and decency. He was never drunk or boastful and this he rationalised by thinking, 'a change is as good as a rest'. However this, like most rationalisation, was not the entire truth; once again he was enjoying the *frisson* gained from living in two entirely different worlds. Moreover he still liked the hospitable Hebrew family that had almost adopted him in his first lonely London days.

Tobias' father wrote from time to time. He duly replied but there was no depth or warmth in their correspondence. Father Guido had sent him one farewell missive and thereafter the tomb-like silence of the monastery engulfed him for ever. Tobias was quite sorry about that and presumed the most active interest in his moral welfare was now stilled. At the time he held it to be of very little account.

On reaching the grand old age of seventeen and a half he found his life had fallen into a routine. During the day he worked hard at learning to be a magician and less hard at being a priest. In the evenings he either went drinking (with his fellow journeymen or the 'ne'er-do-wells' he had met in his wanderings) or was on Peace Promenade. By and large these were dull affairs and he took the opportunity to carry on his research and studying. By these means alone he had already mastered two new basic power-words. Once a week he sobered up and guarded his conversation to dine with the Bergmans and if Jimmy noticed the strain, it was never mentioned.

He also learned how to function efficiently despite lack of sleep and a hangover every morning.

By the Bishop's standards he had fitted in well. He was not sure that this was the good life but at times it seemed pleasant enough. Work was his hobby and obsession, and his leisure was left free to use or misuse as he wished. In fact there was almost no other area of the Church where Tobias could have received such a *laissez-faire*, but high-quality training. All in all, he reflected as he bestrode his little world, it could be worse . . .

Over the weeks he had formed special friendships with Jimmy Bergman's younger son Daniel, and his eldest daughter Mary. Often they would shop or explore together, for by now differences of culture were largely forgotten.

One day fate decided to speed events up again by inspiring Tobias to ask them to come and visit him at *his* home where he would 'show them all over'. Daniel was twenty, Mary seventeen; they were curious and naturally accepted.

It is apposite at this moment to bring Tobias' fellow journeymen back into the story. In the period of just over a year they too had developed and 'grown'. Elijah of Dyfed had had to work particularly hard at his studies and had reached a reasonable standard of literacy, his magical standards were similarly adequate but uninspired. He was a bluff, cheerful man with no great depth – in short, good company during one of Tobias' nocturnal forays into Southwark.

Simon Skillit from London had discovered women when he moved to live at Mucky Hall and after initial experimentation he enjoyed great success. Apart from classes or promenades, his fellows saw little of him. He too was likeable, having a dry wit and an ever-increasing well of dubious anecdotes which usually began, 'Have you ever tried . . . ?' Not so Hugh Redmayne from Derby, though. He, too, had expanded in character since the early days but this merely served to irk Tobias who thought that Hugh arduously limped through life dragging a pall of damp, foggy confusion with him.

In fact most of this existed only in Tobias' mind for each trivial encounter was poisoned by the initial dislike. For his own part,

Hugh was unaware of any enmity since Tobias sought every opportunity to avoid him. However there was no denying he was a very good magician, as good as if not better than Tobias and he excelled in producing magically endowed objects (similar in nature if not function to Joan's little wooden arrow). Furthermore he was a promising scholar and took the prospect of imminent priesthood seriously.

Tobias grew to hate him unto death and once or twice idly considered the possibility of killing him and escaping detection, but the method and impetus eluded him.

Inspiration, however, was winging on its way provided by one unwitting comment. A small enough provocation but, in the event, quite sufficient. Mary Bergman was a comely girl and Tobias had more than once assessed the chances of seducing her. He had decided against, partly because of the schism this would cause with her family if discovered, and partly because none of the Hebrews he met had shown any interest of that kind in Gentiles. Even so it was to her that he was happily chatting one day as he entered the Southwark establishment. Daniel, a large man with shaggy hair and brooding eyes, padded behind taking everything in. He felt he was penetrating the very heart of the goyims' faith, the holy of holies – he had never entered a Christian establishment of any kind before.

It was to be a remarkably short visit for, as ill-luck would have it, Hugh of Derby was waiting at the end of the entrance corridor and, even worse, he was in one of his occasional communicative phases.

Tobias was prim, reserved but civil.

'Hugh, this is Daniel and Mary Bergman, my friends from across the bridge.'

As Hugh took his religion and calling seriously, to him the Jews were simply the Christ-killers and quite possibly poisoners of wells. 'Goodness: vile Jews in a holy place' he said. 'Whatever next?'

Tobias' unconscious reaction was to bare his teeth and for once allow the glaze over his eyes to drop, and it was recognition of this that saved Hugh from serious injury. The former flicked a finger at the latter and hissed one of his words. Hugh just had time to lift his forearm to parry and to commence a warding spell, and consequently the full force of Tobias' angry incantation did not make its target. Even so Hugh's face and neck was instantly covered in a brown-purple bruise. At another time he might have looked like a comically made-up Moor; just now it wasn't so funny.

The injured journeyman decided through the pain not to turn the other cheek and a split second later his spell hit Tobias' covering arm just as he completed a ward. Obviously Hugh was better than suspected for despite this guard, the skin of Tobias' arm and hand blackened and died.

Less than a quarter of a minute had elapsed but neither party was in a condition to continue the conflict. Inevitably enough Geoff Staples chose that moment to come down the stairs and, utilising the rapid grasp of events that had gained him his post, he decided that reasoned argument could be postponed to a later date. One brief phrase was enough to freeze the two injured warriors in an unbreakable mental grip like fish in solid ice. However dangerous Hugh and Tobias were compared to ordinary men, they were nothing as compared to a good magician some years out of the Roman school.

Daniel and Mary had wisely turned and fled.

The statue masquerading as Tobias thought, *I'm sorry I did that. Next time, I'll kill the bastard.*

CHAPTER 6
In which our hero is rebuked for his energies.

However, one can't go around engaging in magical duels willy-nilly even in the Bishop of Southwark's establishment.

Neither youth was allowed out of the hall for a month save on Promenade and a stiff religious penance was levied. Finally, just to emphasise the point in a physical as well as spiritual way, both Hugh and Tobias when deemed sufficiently recovered, made intimate and excruciating contact with Wally Faulkner's fists and boots. 'Nothing personal lads, just a lesson from above.'

The experience laid them in bed for three and two days respectively. Nor was that all. It triggered something lying close to the surface in Tobias' mind and when he was about and walking again, his ribs heavily bound up, it was as though he had just emerged fresh from Joan's tuition. He saw what was to be done and the shortest way to it; emotion and cluttering contradictions had been cleared away and his mind felt clean and full of purpose once more.

He went to the Bergmans and devised a comforting explanation to cover everything and promised to call again soon. It seemed that Mary and Daniel had been reticent in explaining their early return home and so Tobias' task was not too difficult. The two junior Bergmans had come to accept his magical talent as an academic fact but seeing it in dramatic practice had nevertheless surprised them; he could see the process of re-evaluation in their eyes. In his new mood he cared little for the outcome.

He formally apologised to Geoff Staples for his 'lapse' and gave undertakings as to his future behaviour. In time Wally Faulkner got to hear of this and knowing his man decided that something was amiss.

Even more disturbingly Tobias went straight to Hugh Redmayne and begged his pardon, and proffered friendship. Hugh was at first disturbed and then, being of a forgiving nature as his gospel demanded, admitted that it had all been *his* fault and it was up to him to apologise; which he did. They shook hands, laughed over their collective bruises and breakages and offered mutual compliments on the efficacy of their own fighting methods. To formalise their reconciliation, it being a free night, they went by special permission to a moderately respectable tavern and drank the evening away in an excellent semblance of comradeship.

Directly after, Tobias went to the washroom, dipped his head under a basinful of water to wash away the alcohol and then retired to his room. On a piece of notepaper he drew up a list of the personnel of the Southwark establishment and considered each in turn, noting beside each name his estimation of their memory and degree of natural suspicion.

Over forty minutes later, after much hard thinking, he decided that six months would be a safe margin of time.

Hugh of Derby would be killed in six months' time give or take a day. Then with customary care and caution he tore the paper to pieces and put it down the privy.

Later Tobias found himself starting to analyse the wisdom of his decision. How would this help his supposedly single-minded and ruthless path to a shining future? He discovered, however, that he had no interest in mere debate any more and savagely thrust it away. The well that Joan had sunk in him was at last being tapped deep and a spout of white-hot bile was bubbling to the surface. He made a custom of spending a quarter of an hour each night meditating to formalise his rough plans.

Within several weeks he had progressed beyond the meditation stage and by the end of the six months he had Mori's 'subjugation' spell in his grasp.

He did not alter his life style perceptibly but bit by bit sought to endear himself to the Southwark 'powers' and raise himself above any suspicion in connection with what was about to arise. To Hugh he continued to show degrees of conciliation and pleasantness until they might well be considered friends.

At last even Faulkner decided that this was just another adolescent tiff that had blown over, thank God, and please Lord may neither of them bear a grudge against me. For all his professed disdain of 'witch doctors', Wally had seen too much of magic in action ever to regard its threat without fear.

In March 1978 Tobias was due to go to a dinner party organised by the Bergmans in honour of his fast-approaching eighteenth birthday. That same night Hugh was on the rota for Peace Promenade at nine o'clock.

At seven, Tobias entered a cheap hotel-cum-brothel with a garish floozy not of his acquaintance and booked a night room.

Hugh was asleep in bed in preparation for the long night ahead.

At ten past seven Tobias dismissed the girl with a half-fee, explaining that a surfeit of alcohol made further association pointless.

Hugh slept on.

Tobias put the room's sparse, cheap furniture to one side and, using chalks he had brought along in a small satchel, drew a pentagram, taking up as much of the room's area as possible. The two candles and holders provided were placed either side of the uppermost point.

For a long time Tobias stood and just stared at his creation. It had to be perfect, every line and angle firm and strong. As satisfied as he could be, he went to the wall opposite the leading pentagram point and roughly drew a rectangular shape some four foot across.

There being no excuse for delay he returned to the pentagram and sat cross-legged in the middle. From the satchel he drew a small bowl, a bandage, a tiny wooden rod, and his belt knife which he placed before him. He had wanted to bring his small library and his own notes on demonology but had abandoned the idea as impractical. Accordingly he'd had to memorise everything necessary and so now all depended on his powers of recollection.

Everything was ready. Strangely enough, despite the vast gaps that he knew must exist in his researches, Tobias felt no fear; he felt nothing at all. This was the outcome of six months' scheming and no emotion could be allowed to intervene now.

The candle flames were quite steady and the room was very still. He was pleased to find that his absorption was such that though he could hear the beginning of the Southwark revels outside, they failed to enter any conscious level of his mind.

Tobias shut his eyes and for a long while concentrated on his breathing, taking short, but silent breaths. Bit by bit he gained quietness until he could hear the unmistakable beat of his own heart. At first in his mind and then in a whisper he began to recite a rhyme. Intrinsically the words were meaningless but Tobias brought his 'talent', which was essentially power over belief, to bear on them. His mind was open, defenceless, and anything at all would be accepted. Still the rhyme remained without significance.

He carried on for another long while and then with an inward sigh stopped and snapped his trance.

A complete and utter waste of time.

But the room was cold and musty and the candles were guttering slightly. Tobias exulted: his invocation *had* reached something and he had stupidly remained in his trance, unable to notice it.

Part of him was surprised and unnerved by this success. The magician's great enemy, fear, made an appearance.

Hurrying lest his advantage considered itself ignored too long, he fumbled with the knife and rolled up his left sleeve. Slashing deeply he opened his basilic vein.

'Christ, oh Christ that hurt!'

He leaned over the bowl and blood trickled along his arm and into it. He recited the rhyme and it helped to dull his recognition of the pain. In seconds that took years the bowl was half full and Tobias was feeling faint.

'Come,' he invoked and his voice sounded as if it came from far away in a deep fog.

The bandage he hurriedly swept on to his arm, and with the rod he turned it into a tourniquet. Looking up as quickly as he could, he saw that his chalk rectangle on the facing wall had taken on the appearance of a window and greyish light was seeping out of it into the room. In pain, groggy and still fearful but growing more confident, Tobias saw that everything had gone as it should. 'Come,' he repeated.

Now he could see through the 'window' and he was transfixed. He saw what looked like moorland at dusk; across it a small road wound into the distance. There appeared to be a grey and brown town there, many of whose windows were already ablaze with light. The picture was fascinating but somehow he knew it was not a benign landscape; nor was it any earthly view. A dot set out from the town and walked along the road.

The chalk dust of the pentagram began to jump and shift. Fear really set in now; within minutes Tobias could see that the dot was a solitary man striding along and in some subtle way the road had shifted so as to pass directly under the chalk window.

When, five minutes later, the man climbed through the window and into the room Tobias was clammy with cold sweat but his mind had his body in a vice-like grip. The lines of the pentagram were slowly washing back and forth.

The visitant seemed to be an ordinary man or rather a youth, skinny, sallow and narrow-shouldered. He wore black business clothes, such as might be seen on any London street, with a somewhat 'fast' embroidered waistcoat. He had a bitter, sullen expression on his pale face and his hair was sandy and unkempt. He was even smaller than Tobias and carried a simple walking cane.

'My name is Bellaston,' he said. 'How do you do?'

Tobias had been prepared for almost anything, but not this; he was disarmed – but only for a few seconds.

'I have summoned you to perform a mission for me at the conclusion of which I will release you from my service for ever. I so swear.'

'What poor swine is it that you do not have the guts to kill yourself?'

'Kill for me in some unobtrusive manner one Hugh Redmayne, once of Derby and now in the household of the Bishop of Southwark. Do it at eight and thirty of the clock so that I may be elsewhere.'

Bellaston looked at him briefly, said 'No', and advanced towards his summoner. Within an instant he halted and a quizzical look crossed his morose face. A second or so later he raised an eyebrow at the magician and changed his mind. 'Very well.'

Tobias' control had barely survived this last incident; he was on the very verge of panic and capitulation.

The youth, or being, called Bellaston returned to the magical 'window' and climbed back in. The desolate moor and town were no longer there; Tobias saw that the demon was now in the upper hallway in the Bishop's Hall opposite his own room. He observed that the huge grandfather clock at the top of the stairs said almost eight-thirty p.m. Elijah Green entered the picture and went into his chamber, completely ignoring Bellaston. Hugh's room was at the end of the hallway and the demon seemed to know this. He entered the darkened chamber and a weird grey luminescence emanated from him in the light of which could be seen Hugh, still dozing on his pallet.

Bellaston appeared to snarl, and twisted his walking stick. The handle gave way and a needle-thin blade, glowing white-hot, appeared from the false scabbard. He drew back the bed clothes and Hugh did not stir. With one surprisingly rapid and vicious thrust he drove the sword-stick up Hugh's anus. The young priest bucked and heaved, his eyes and mouth instantly wide open but not a sound escaped him. The spasm lasted but a second and he was still again. In a most gentle fashion Bellaston closed the eyelids and composed the face out of its grimace; finally he re-placed the bed clothes.

The hallway was clear and Bellaston clambered through the portal once more. Behind him the scene returned to its previous appearance.

The whole episode had taken less than three or four minutes but Tobias was too busy and apprehensive to consider his success yet. He prepared to recite the dismissal.

'Before I go I would like to show you something, Tobias.'

Thus Bellaston interrupted the final rite and the magician watched open-mouthed as the demon crossed the room and quite deliberately wiped a whole section of the pentagram off with his foot.

Instantly Tobias knew all was lost but, showing the same characteristic that had endeared him to Joan as a child, he refused to die acquiescently. His killing spell affected Bellaston not a whit. Significantly, though, the demon's stiletto remained sheathed.

'As you can see, Tobias, your pentagram is useless, quite useless. This sort of business requires experience, knowledge and fearlessness, and you have none of these. Did you seriously think that I kill and perform at the beck and call of any and every apprentice that catches my attention? Consider yourself dead meat, Tobias – dead meat granted an unbelievable second lease of life. At the very least I require a real sacrifice, a baby or two, a virgin child or some such cliché; consider yourself very fortunate that you seem to have friends that speak to me and intercede for you.'

He turned and walked away.

'One thing, though,' he added halfway through the portal. 'In the long run it might be better for you if I had killed you today as I should have done. Good day.'

He was gone.

Tobias watched the prim figure dwindling along the road. Bellaston was dragging a reluctant, writhing figure. In that land, night was not far off and the gloom quickly swallowed the demon and his prize.

The wall reappeared.

Tobias was almost in shock. This was too much to take for the moment; he postponed analysis of the whole thing until a later date. He sat in his ruined pentagram and said and thought nothing for what seemed a long time.

I gained what I wanted: Hugh is dead. I did it myself, by my magic. What do I feel? Triumph? Satisfaction? Remorse? Pity? I feel absolutely nothing.

After clearing the room and removing all evidence of his presence, Tobias made it to the Bergmans by five minutes past eight. He had dashed into a nearby tavern over the bridge and downed two measures of brandy to stop his shaking and calm his breath. Outside the tailor's shop he swallowed a restorative potion he had bought and the colour slowly returned to his face, the nausea of fear left him. When at last he was ready to face other humans again, he plunged in.

Tobias thought he put on a consummate performance during the meal although perhaps he was a little *too* expansive in compensation. Feigning fatigue and citing tomorrow's duties he ensured that each and every Bergman realised the time (it was a quarter past nine) and then left.

This was, however, a mere mummer's rôle compared to the self-control he had to exercise upon returning home to Southwark Hall.

An angry Alan Lumley had gone to rouse the absent Hugh and instead found someone quite beyond rousing. By nine forty-five or so, when Tobias arrived, things had calmed down somewhat. The body had already been taken to the Chapel of Repose after a hastily summoned surgeon had pronounced life extinct. The Southwark household had neither the nature nor inclination to speculate idly or gossip on the matter to any great extent; most of them had a more than passing familiarity with death. Accordingly, little was expected from Tobias beyond a measure of surprise, curiosity and regret. It took all his discipline to restrain his real feelings and provide that measure. Since he was considered somewhat unemotional, no one was surprised at how little his famous equilibrium seemed to be disturbed by the tragedy.

To his satisfaction and delight no one seemed to recall the long-past feud, he saw no suspicion behind the glances that came his way. Since he could provide a 'cast-iron' alibi for his whereabouts at the presumed time of death he felt doubly secure.

At night, though, things assume wholly different proportions and Tobias could not sleep for going over that day again and again looking for faults and loopholes in his act. Worse still he was increasingly conscious of the mental wall he had constructed to hold back any immediate analysis and assessment of his deed. For the moment, survival was far more important. One week, he thought, was what was needed; if he could get through one week, then he would be clear. Everything – emotion, spirit and humanity – had to be sublimated to surviving as a wholly innocent young priest, free of sin in thought and deed, for just seven days.

So thinking, he slipped into a self-imposed trance that his tutor had prescribed for moments of deep prayer and communion and he used this as a substitute for sleep.

And he dreamed, though not actually sleeping, of Joan holding up a canvas bag which contained the body of Hugh. Hugh was an elf and then he was alive and ran screaming out of the sack and he, Tobias, killed him again but still he ran . . .

Dawn came, carrying with it a welcomely improved sense of perspective. Tobias was ready to face his week of apparently saint-like innocence. It was, of course, this subtle change to unnatural, exemplary behaviour that aroused suspicion in the many faceted, if erratic, mind of Sir Matthew Elias. The death of journeyman Redmayne had puzzled rather than upset him since he was by nature somewhat thin-blooded and little affected him deeply. Another local surgeon had examined the body at his request and confirmed that internal bleeding was the cause of death. Such things were not unknown, he said; oft-times the arteries were not resolute enough to carry their load of blood and in such cases the soul must fly to God.

Sir Matthew was minded to leave it at that, but time hung heavy on his hands at that particular juncture since the Southwark household had reached a level of training and cooperation whereby little or no routine supervision was needed.

So he turned his butterfly-mind to the problem one afternoon when his light lunch was violently squabbling with his queasy stomach (itself the product of last night's experiments). Just suppose someone had done away with Hugh, a healthy young man. Who and how? Who didn't like him? No one that he knew of; there again he didn't know the men too well, must ask Faulkner about it. Who would know how to do it and have the nerve? Just about any of the men they'd trained; pointless line of enquiry. Anyone behaving strangely? No one, but then how could you tell with this bunch . . . hold on, what about Oakley? Cold sort of fish usually, but not *this* week . . . and didn't he once give Redmayne a slight roasting? Yes, he did! *Yes*, he might have done it, not the sort of bastard to need much reason, they're all as mad as hatters . . . how to find out though? Simple, ask him.

Sir Matthew had had his room cleared somewhat and concealed some of the more dubious or reprehensible contents. Against all custom and knowledge, he shared his large teak desk with another today. This other was a woman of uncertain, but probably middle, age. She was dressed in a fashionable crinoline of quite some style. Her face was partially covered by a veil and by the shadow of a large feather-adorned hat of the type favoured by high society. This lady said nothing and gave no sign that she acknowledged Sir Matthew's presence; all her attention was centred upon a silver bowl of clear liquid placed on the desk in front of her. Once or twice she made hand passes over it and then covered the receptacle with a black lace kerchief from her valise.

Sir Matthew observed this with a cold eye and then, suddenly animated again when the woman had seemingly completed her task, he rang his desk bell.

He just had time to compose himself and assume an authoritative mien before Wally Faulkner and Tobias came in. Both men were inscrutable in expression and carriage but a sense of the guard and the guarded was very keen between them. Faulkner left without a word and, unbeknown to Tobias, stationed himself the other side of the door. Sir Matthew had told him to issue himself a pistol and bring it fully primed and loaded.

Tobias had given undivided thought to the unprecedented interview ever since having heard of it some few hours before. He was in little doubt as to its subject and in the first few moments of wild thought had considered flight. He rejected this as abject and the automatic negation of what he had achieved. Far better to take the chance offered him and call Sir Matthew Elias' bluff (if that's what it was). Initially he'd had some vague idea of fighting his way out if events took an ugly turn, but once in Sir Matthew's office all such thoughts fled posthaste. He doubted if even his most insidious and deadly spell would surprise or effect Elias, whereas it was almost certain his own head would vanish in a gout of flame if he made any hostile move. Besides, without a doubt, Faulkner or some other was stationed behind the door. *Brazen it out but try to take him with you if all is lost.*

'You called for me, Sir Matthew?'

'Yes, Oakley – yes indeed. I believe you can help me complete a line of thought I have been amusing myself with lately.'

'My duty is to serve you, the Bishop and the Church in that order, sir.'

'Quite so, Tobias. Just so. Mind you – you left God out of that list . . .'

'An oversight, sir.'

'Doubtless, lad; we all at times forget that God oversees us all.' Sir Matthew favoured Tobias with a sunny smile. 'How do your magical studies go, lad?'

'Very well, thank you, Sir Matthew.'

'Yes. So I have heard. Were you complicit in the death of acolyte Redmayne?'

Tobias was too alert and subtle to be caught out by this sudden change of tack. He put a convincing tone of surprise and conviction in his reply.

'Not at all, my Lord – how could I be when it was Nature that carried poor Hugh off?'

'Nature has many facets and servants, Tobias. You will learn this as you get older.'

Sir Matthew turned to the woman beside him, who had been studying something under a lace cover throughout the interview, and conferred in a low whisper.

Witch-bitch, thought Tobias.

She slowly shook her head.

Tobias' question master turned to face him again and rested his chin upon a cradle formed by his fingers. His watery eyes stared at Tobias and through him to some unknown place.

A long silence dragged on but Tobias felt no impulse to break it. He felt entirely in control and resigned. The genesis of a spell was mulling in his mind.

It was a bizarre scene: Sir Matthew staring through a young magician who stood to attention, his eyes in turn glazed and contemplative. The veiled, unknown woman sat with her face unseen and downcast. Time had gently seeped away from the room and only the loud tick of the mantelpiece-clock remained as evidence of its existence.

Sir Matthew at last focused on his interviewee. He had made a decision.

'Have you ever considered death, Tobias?'

Tobias instantly had some pat answer ready about it being the duty of all good Christians to ponder on the after-life, but rejected it. Elias' voice contained undisguised menace and the situation had gone beyond pretence.

'Sometimes when I see it take others, Sir Matthew, but not often.'

'Let us postulate *your* death young Oakley, say relatively soon. Do you know what an epitaph is, lad?'

'Yes, my Lord.' He was of two minds whether to try and kill Elias now and at least bow out with some pride.

'And what would you say would be an appropriate one for you?'

'I would need to give it some thought, sir.'

'Well, let me suggest one for you, Oakley. If you should die in the near future how about "A Dangerous Energy" written in large letters across your tombstone, eh?'

'I submit to your superior judgement, my Lord.'

'Superior judgement and a certain amount of prophecy in this case. Of course murderers are not buried in consecrated ground and hence don't have tombstones or epitaphs do they?'

'No, my Lord.'

'No, well let's just say that your behaviour in the remaining time up to your graduation will have a very direct bearing on whether my prophecy comes true. Do you truly appreciate what I am saying?'

'Absolutely, my Lord.' Tobias' face was frozen and inscrutable.

'Now get out.'

Tobias had the presence of mind to bow to the lady and then to Sir Matthew before leaving. Wally Faulkner was there and escorted him down the stairs without a word.

Sir Matthew was silent for a little while and then, without turning, said, 'Thank you for your services, milady. In view of the debt I owe you and the possible need I may have for your help in the future, you may rest assured that no hint of your, shall we say "unorthodox" magical proclivities will reach the ears of the relevant authorities. I will arrange for a carriage to take you to some point near your residence.'

He rang a bell and in due course the silent witch was escorted out by a Southwark menial.

Sir Matthew poured himself a generous libation of Bells whisky and studied the Thames through his window.

Who cares, he thought. *Let them kill each other. Why should I judge? Murder them all, who'd miss them? They're all damned anyway.*

CHAPTER 7

In which our hero listens to the wise words of his employer.

Almost a year to the day later, Tobias Oakley was alive and well still. On a rainy 30th March in the year of our Lord 1979 he was sitting in one of the front pews of Southwark Cathedral waiting to be ordained as a 'priest thaumaturgist' by the Bishop. Awaiting a similar fate with him was Elijah Green and twenty or thirty assorted journeymen from other schools. The 'Feast of the Magicians', as it was known, was always a great event and excuse for celebration, and the larger English churches took it in turn to play host to the ceremony and ensuing mass. This year it was Southwark's show and so Tobias and Elijah were not unduly taxed in travelling to their transition to professional adulthood. Simon Skillit should have accompanied them but after a catastrophic assessment in his priestly examinations due to overweening external interests, he was in considerable disgrace and only in the observing congregation. He would have one more chance next year, failing which a dismal career as his noble father's personal magician awaited him.

Tobias was resplendent in a freshly laundered dark red gown. The ring of stars around his arm was surmounted by a band of a different, more smoky, red. He was gaunter than was normal for him and his eyes had lost much of their previous humour. The year past had been a considerable strain to him. He had known without a shadow of doubt that Sir Matthew would have him strung up if the mood so took him and for the first time he experienced the agony of knowing that his very existence was dependent upon something outside his influence. As a man little given to relying on anyone else this was a constant goad to his spirit. Throughout, a small voice had whispered exhortations to flee this uncertainty but it was never more than an annoying undertone. Tobias felt this was a test and, lacking complete confidence, tests were as a divine command to him. He did not know it, of course, but this was one of his greatest weaknesses. So he had stayed and behaved like the model and devout, young trainee-priest. In a perverse way this worked to his benefit in that it ensured that his studies prospered and he was able to score exceptional marks in the final graduation assessments. Elias' trap was never sprung and Tobias thus felt his own courage was proven. He had arrived at the object of his ambitions and today was sitting in a house of God to bear witness to that fact.

The whole of Southwark establishment were present and in their smartest uniforms looked quite imposing. For almost the first time Tobias felt a flash of pride at being one of their number. This was a somewhat belated impulse since within the hour it would cease to be true. His subsequent posting within the Church had been known for some time, but it was traditional to withhold this information from the candidate so that the mind might have no distractions from contemplating the solemn vows about to be taken. Tobias' small number of possessions was already packed for his imminent departure to pastures new.

As the organ ornately brought the dedicatory hymn to a proper close, Tobias sat down and studied the Bishop as he mounted the steps to the pulpit. It was only the fifth or sixth time he'd seen him and they were never to speak. *For three years*, thought Tobias, *that man has shaped the world in which I have lived and thereby, I suppose, has moulded what I've become.* This of course begged the question of what it was he thought he'd become.

The Bishop was thin and very sallow-skinned. Incautious and foolhardy wits had even at times speculated merrily on his racial antecedents. His eyes were deepest black and were unkind. And although he was old, the Bishop's skin was that of a young man (another cause of wild theorising among Southwark folk). Despite or perhaps because of his singularities, when he leaned over the pulpit and addressed his bizarre congregation, they could be in no possible doubt that he was the leading figure there that day.

'God's very first vicar of Rome,' he'd said, 'the blessed Pope, St Peter, has this to say concerning those talents the Lord has bestowed upon us. "If any man speak, let him speak as of the oracles of God, if any man minister *let him do it as of the ability which God giveth.*" This is, of course, a very apposite reference considering the celebration and witness which brings us together today. To each and every man is given a range of senses that we may perceive God's creation, and a degree of specific talents that we may further God's plan as manifested in his world. This is the sum reason for man's life on this earth and there is no other. In His wisdom our Lord gives to some much and to others but a little, some will have ability in such and such a thing, and others will not. This is God's plan and there is no righteous escape from it. Furthermore it is a directive *from God Himself* as to the course He wishes us to take. If for instance it has been given to a man to be skilled in the shaping of wood as it was to St Joseph, then it is plainly the Almighty's wish that such a man should express the Lord's praises as a carpenter. Another might be blessed with a singing voice and here again it is obvious that his first duty is to use this gift to glorify its bestower.'

At this point many of the Southwark congregation became restive as they each in turn considered their own particular abilities and decided that this was probably not what the Bishop was on about.

'If this is true for the humble carpenter and chorister, how much more true it must be for those amongst us who have been granted exceptional gifts, those among us seemingly singled out for a more decisive rôle in the implementation of God's will. I, of course, refer to those young men assembled here today to pass through the first stage of their priesthood, their calling to God. You have come from widely separated areas and backgrounds united in one thing only, an extraordinary talent granted by the good Lord for the furtherance of His will; for this is its purpose, make no mistake. Just as He has enabled some men to bring beauty to simple glass,' here he waved a hand at the Cathedral's main stained-glass windows, 'in order to enhance one of His houses, just so has God granted you magical powers to aid the Kingdom of God on Earth as manifested in the Holy Church.

'So, by your heightened faculties you have the opportunity to earn correspondingly greater levels of grace. On the left-hand path, however, it is similarly true that selfish use of your gift will lead you into greater levels of sin than are possible for ordinary men. And so, my children, you will see that in your grasp is the opportunity for great good but also the possibility of great evil.

'It is for this reason that the Church Universal gathers to itself those whom it knows are singled out by God for special grace or sin. The Church can appraise these fortunates of their potential and point out to them the path God wishes them to take. It is on this path that you are about to set out today.

'*A chosen generation, a royal priesthood, a holy nation, a peculiar people that ye should show forth the praises of him who hath called you out of darkness into his marvellous light.*'

'As the first Holy Father thus tells us, you are a chosen people, chosen by God that you might have the greater might to guide yourself and others to salvation, and that along with righteous brawn you may be the strong right arm and defence of God's will on Earth, the Mother Church.

'God go with you, remember service is a virtue and a duty, and grace is earned thereby and remember pride is a sin.

'The candidates for ordination will now approach the altar and kneel while the congregation rises and sings hymn number twenty-three in your book. St John Wesley's paen to Holy service:

> "And have I measured half my days
> and half my journey run
> Nor tasted the Redeemer's grace
> Nor yet my work begun?"'

91

BOOK TWO

MAY 1982 – NOVEMBER 1985

MARGIN NOTES FROM THE EASTER
ANNALS OF ST ANSELM'S CHURCH
AT PAGHAM, SUSSEX

*(Sussex Antiquaries Association
Collections Volume 82 (1975))*

RENDERED INTO MODERN ENGLISH by LADY ELIZABETH GALE

' . . . *throughout the tragedies of that period. Readers will, no
doubt, be aware that Easter is a moveable feast the date of which is
related in a complicated way to the phases of the moon. In view of
this complexity, various learned scholars produced tables of
calculations showing the date on which Easter should fall over a
number of years. The many columns of the tables, e.g. the "Golden
Number", the "Epact", the "Sunday Letter" and so on, concern
themselves with the technical calculation of the "DIES PASCHAE"
but often a wide margin is left at the right-hand side of the text as is
the case with the St Anselm records. This provident space was often
taken up with a laconic sentence or phrase describing the most
important or memorable event that occurred in that year. Therefore, such Easter tables as have survived into our own era provide us
with an invaluable record compiled contemporaneously with the
events described therein. My attention was particularly drawn
by . . .*'

1562   October Queen Elizabeth the Wicked was called to God by
       the smallpox.
1563   Queen Mary II and her consort Henry Stewart, Lord Darnley
       did [begin to] reign.
1564   Cecil's men from Lewes took the church plate save one
       chalice which was hid.
       (A reference to the 'Protestant' rising of that year nominally
       led by William Cecil. The rebellion in Sussex attracted only
       sporadic, half-hearted support. The annals surprisingly make
       no reference to the heretics' bloody defeat in the following
       year.)
1570   A sea-calf was washed ashore. Quite dead.

1571 The King died.
(Again surprisingly no mention is made of the violent, unnatural manner of 'Henry IX''s demise.)

1575 Spaniards killed two men in the village.
(Although present in England as allies and at Queen Mary's request the behaviour of the Spanish troops was not always all it should be.)

1580 Lewes was burned.
(A characteristically brief reference to the Lewes rising and the town's sacking by an (English) Royal army.)

1588 In this year the Spanish came.
(A reference, of course, to the Great Armada welcomed ashore by the Queen herself at Dover.)

1589 Cambridge, it is said, rose against the Church and the Queen.

(Then in a different hand.)

1591 By the Grace of God the realm lay at peace. The Spanish departed to the Lowlands.

1596 A tide higher than any in the memory of the living.

1600 Queen Mary died.

1601 Fighting in London. The Lord Essex was Regent.

(Then in a different hand.)

1602 King James of Scotland came to reign.

1625 The King died. King Charles reigned.

(*Thereafter the tables are without a marginal commentary although the record runs up until the defeat of the great 'Protestant' rebellion in 1649.*)

CHAPTER 1
In which a day in the life of our hero is described.

On a drizzly 1st May 1982, Curate Oakley rose, as was his custom, at six-thirty a.m. He washed and rapidly donned his priestly garb and boots. Three years had changed him greatly and his hair, while still fashionably long, was thinning rapidly. His dark incisive eyes and bland, abstracted expressions were unimpaired, however. He crossed to the window and opened the shutters and then stood for a while quietly observing the rainy street below. Tired of this, Tobias turned his back on the view, sat on the windowsill and stared blankly at the bed. The girl was still sleeping, her long brown hair flowing over the blankets and pillow. Soon enough this view palled as well and he unfolded his arm and flicked one finger at her while whispering a phrase. She woke with a jerk and sat up instantly, eyes wide with terror, but this just as quickly passed when she saw that nothing was amiss and Diane French, spinster of the city of Rugby, bade her lover good morning.

The lover continued to stare, somewhat discomfiting the girl, but replied to her greeting in no unfriendly way.

'You must go, my dear,' he said. 'I have an early mass to assist with.'

'Yes I remember now – Tobias, stop staring *through* me. It's haunting – why do you do it so?'

'I'm reading your mind, Diane.'

Miss French looked momentarily alarmed. 'But you always told me that magicians couldn't do such things!'

'Maybe they can't, who can say? Never trust a magician's word.'

Smiling, he strode to the door and was half through it before Diane had time to digest his words.

'Do you want me to be here tonight?' she said. Tobias stopped, hand on the door knob and considered.

'Er . . . no – come Monday if you like.' With this rejoinder, he left the room.

Downstairs in the kitchen he lit a fire and heated some porridge. This, together with some fruit, tea and biscuits provided his breakfast. It was Tobias' long-established custom to make his own breakfast and eat it in complete solitude; at that time of the day he wished for company less than ever.

Once she heard him leave, the housekeeper, Mrs Coley, would come down to start the day's chores and prepare a meal for him if he was returning to the house for dinner. By the time the high-minded and disapproving Coley had established her presence in her domestic kingdom, Diane would also have gone.

Tobias had met Diane, along with her stolid artisan father and self-effacing mother, at a Cathedral-run Bible class over a year ago. She was no beauty, had no history of previous admirers (save those who had cynically flattered, loved and run) and so was desperately pleased to be the recipient of a magician's advances with all the reflected status and the associated aura of romance and dark mystery. She found Tobias a strange, introverted and somewhat cold man but there again she had found all men to be essentially like that and so never noticed anything particularly out of the ordinary. Not far below the surface, she thought, lay a kind and warm-hearted nature and indeed he had been both affectionate and considerate to the girl and had gone a long way towards reviving her sagging confidence and self-esteem.

The reality, alas, was somewhat more prosaic on Oakley's side. He had particularly liked her very long and silky hair; this was the initial attraction. Secondly she was undemanding, sweet-tempered and relatively sparing in speech and thus formed a well-matched partner for him. The clinching factor was that despite being plain (no sin, thought Tobias, I'm that myself), she was compliant and had a tolerably attractive body.

As time wore on he had occasional impulses of affection for the girl and sometimes went out of his way to bring her a little happiness (as he knew anyone so easily could) to convey his gratitude for their stressless relationship. This was as far as it went. As for her feelings for him, he knew nothing and declined to speculate on the matter. When the time came, as it inevitably would, to break with her, he had resolved to do it in a manner involving as little hurt as possible by concocting some cock-and-bull excuse. It was, he thought, the least he could do.

Mr and Mrs French were not entirely pleased at the intimate relationship between their daughter and the magician, but the guilty party was too far up the social scale and was too unpredictable and powerful a man for any mere artisans to amend the situation. Even so, Tobias was no longer wholly welcome at the French household; and yet it had come to his ears through his many and varied contacts that Mr French the carpenter was still capitalising on the considerable, if unconventional, kudos his family had accrued because of the association. Tobias thought this a touch hypocritical but he was less and less inclined to judge people nowadays since he had only his own sense of right and wrong as a guide and he felt this was too wildly individual and lax to be a useful reference.

He heard Diane leave via the back entrance as he washed and wiped the breakfast things. When finished, he had merely to snatch his priestly sugar-loaf hat and umbrella, and he was ready to face his working day.

Rugby was a cramped town surrounded by a semi-ruinous wall and ditch, whose upkeep (in contravention of myriad statutes) had been neglected in the last fifty years or so. Beyond the town, in easy view from most parts, were cultivated fields owned in almost equal proportions by the Church or local small farmers of long standing. This land was protected by a barrage of ancient privilege and usage (not to mention considerable political influence) and only very rarely could any of it be appropriated so that the beleaguered town of Rugby might let out her corsets a little and expand. In consequence, the streets were narrow and buildings tended to aspire upwards rather than horizontally. Dominating this snug little community was a castle rising on an artificial mound; since its Norman conception, however, its profile had softened and made some concessions towards aesthetic appeal and human comfort. Nevertheless, it was still, in essence, a functional citadel for times of trouble. Nestling into the castle mound and yet surpassing it in architectural splendour lay Rugby Cathedral, Tobias' destination that morning.

Besides these manifestations of past endeavour, Rugby was obviously a thriving modern community. Several major railways met there, thus ensuring that Rugby had the best turntables and depots in the Midlands. This in turn attracted trade, commerce and a large and easily exploitable passing population. Thus around the terminal, hotels and warehouses abounded.

Another corner of the town boasted a university with a small number of students but a very high reputation. Tobias was occasionally called upon to lecture there.

So much for a guided tour of the salient points. It was just after 7 o'clock on a Saturday morning and in the rainy narrow street in the mildly insalubrious part of the town where Tobias had been given a house, a steady stream of people were proceeding to their places of work: apprentices, labourers and the like – whose Trade Guilds had insufficient bargaining power to get them a shorter working week or free weekends. Tobias raised his umbrella and set forth to the Cathedral, head down and taking care not to splash his long gown. In this way he was prevented from seeing that he had joined a company of people until some time after he had actually done so. Lost in idle considerations, he was shocked out of his reverie by hymn singing close at his ear. Looking up, he immediately recognised the open and virtuous faces about him – *the Avon Street Group, of course, of course. Oh no – don't say they're coming to the service*.

Indeed they were. A group of twenty or so men and women in artisan-black were striding along in vague formation singing a rousing hymn as the rain pitter-pattered on their umbrellas. Leading both the advance and the singing were a tall young man and large, if not fat, young woman.

Tobias faltered in his step and then stopped. *Let them carry on, and put some distance between you and those cranks*. None of them had noticed his presence at the back. Just then he realised that it was necessary for him to reach the Cathedral vestry before any number of worshippers gathered, and so feeling rather foolish, he broke into a hurried pace which soon brought him level with the singers. His dark-red priestly gown and hat made him conspicuous, to say the least.

'Good morning, Father', cried the tall young man; he was thin and curly-haired and his eyes burned with an eager earnest light.

'Curate actually,' said Tobias, lowering his umbrella and nigh-on smiling despite himself. The innocent remark had touched his shrinking sense of humour. Prior to their second ordination and the passing of their final priestly exams, priest-thaumaturgists were termed 'curates' for ease of identification within the context of the church's hierarchy. In terms of position and sacramental duties, however, they were priests in all but name. In due course Tobias would be ordained 'full priest', be entitled to be called 'Father' and deemed ready to move on to higher things.

'Oh it's you, Mr Oakley – pardon me, I didn't recognise you with that brolly covering your face.'

'Good morning, Curate Oakley,' said his plump female companion; she had a pleasant friendly face, Tobias thought, a little less 'other worldly' than her husband's.

'Hello,' he replied. 'I hope to see you all at early Mass – you won't disappoint me I trust?'

'Assuredly not, Brother', the man said. 'We gathered early this morning to pray together in preparation for it.'

'Jolly good, very commendable,' said Tobias. 'Well: I must precede you, I'm afraid, to prepare the sacramental instruments for that very service. I'll no doubt see you there.'

'Assuredly, Brother,' said the woman. With this, Tobias increased his pace and quickly drew away from them. *Bloody fools*, he thought.

The Avon Street group were a constant bane to the Bishop of Rugby. They were so open, so pious and honest that they could hardly be persecuted or publicly disapproved of in any way. However, this very religious fervour was a grave embarrassment and goad to those of the faithful in Rugby who had in the course of time made acceptable compromises between their desires and their religion. Their leader was the lanky young man who had greeted Tobias – an ex-army officer from Bristol who had liquidated his meagre possessions in order to buy himself out of his regiment when religion had first claimed him body and soul. In church they sat together in a body and their sheer fervour of prayer and singing made them as prominent as a Holy visitation. No one had any real deep objection to them save the Dean Spiritual of the Cathedral. He had conceived a deep and abiding hatred of the devout brethren, for it was said (and this was the source of his ire) that in their private meetings the Holy writings and Church teachings were discussed and analysed in a disgracefully free manner. Such musings and interpretations were entirely the business of the Church and more specifically, in the context of Rugby, himself. He had despatched an experienced and trusted deacon to attend one of these meetings but his report had been disappointing. They had given him a most cordial reception, he said, and while discussion may have transcended those limits he considered to be entirely safe, he had found no fault or heresy at all. Indeed, the deacon continued, he had found the whole evening quite touching and uplifting.

The Dean Spiritual had raised a surprised eyebrow at his old friend and had left the matter at that. Even so, on those days when his gouty leg was playing up he found his thoughts turning more and more to those damn sanctimonious upstarts of the Avon Street group . . .

Tobias' job that morning was to assist one of the priests attached to the Cathedral in the early mass. A properly trained magician was supposed to be present at every celebration of communion but since Curate Oakley was the only person answering that description within the jurisdiction of the Diocese, it was impossible for him to be at every mass. Magicians were in short supply and so this stipulation of service rubric was quietly ignored save when a Church-trained man was available, in which case the mass was invested with a special solemnity. With characteristic efficiency and concern for detail the Dean Spiritual had, in consultation with the Bishop, drawn up a rota of services at which Tobias might reasonably be expected to attend. To show willing and to expand his knowledge of Church ritual in preparation for his final priestly examinations in two years' time, Tobias tried to attend at least a couple of extra services each week and so together with his multifarious other duties he was kept a busy man.

He swept hurriedly past the front portal of Castle Waith and gravely acknowledged the salutation of the liveried musketeers stationed there. Passing round the Cathedral via the graveyard path, he entered the vestry at the back and found the presiding priest, a young Surrey man with whom he had a passing acquaintance, already begowned and preparing the communion vessels. Since they were equals in Church status, Tobias merely nodded a greeting and went through the motions of composing himself in prayer. Magicians traditionally did not wear special vestments for conducting services and Tobias approached the chalice, paten and corporals on the priest's bench. The thaumaturgist's rôle in this concelebration was firstly to perform a magical exorcism over the vessels to remove any possible taint of evil or ill-will that might have become attached and, this done, to conduct a test to see whether the instruments of communion were as they should be – plain base metal and linen, or whether they were still imbued with some extraneous force in which case they could not be blessed. Happily Tobias' training had given him the means ('spells' as others called them) to fulfil both these functions. In a passing of hands and a muttered phrase he ascertained that as usual the vessels contained some form of residual power; emotions and memories of those who had touched them, perhaps. His exorcism cleanly swept this away and a further test confirmed to him that the objects before him were now fully inanimate as they should be. It was the work of a few moments and, by now, second nature. He crossed himself and withdrew and the priest stepped up to bless the instruments.

The service was in the small Lady chapel of the Cathedral and went as usual. Since it was known in advance to be a concelebration with both full priest and magician, the congregation was slightly bigger than usual. Once the initial cleansing of the vessels was done the magician had but a slight rôle in the service. There were certain silent prayers ascribed to him at certain parts of the process of communion but other than this the rubric stated that, 'throughout the celebration the thaumaturgist will stand beside the celebrant silent and contemplative, his arms held such as to prominently display his badge of office in order to evidence to the faithful gathered there the dominion of God as manifested in the Church Universal over all fields of endeavour, spiritual and material, natural and supernatural.'

Tobias had of course read this and strove to maintain an air of awesome power (albeit harnessed to the Church's will), a stance which at first had made him feel acutely ridiculous. The passage of time, however, had made the act familiar to him and he considered that he now carried it off with considerable aplomb, although he did not take this to the point of vanity. Safety, the best way he had decided, lay in moderation and the concealment of his abilities.

By eight o'clock mass was completed and Tobias gave the blessing and the dismissal.

By a quarter past eight he was waiting outside the office of the Dean Spiritual, one Obadiah Cocroft, to report to him his intended programme for the day. This done and since the Dean had no alterations to make on it, he proceeded next door to the Dean Temporal and related his plans to him. Dean Alan Banks saw no fault in these and quickly released Curate Oakley to go about his business.

It was a moot point exactly to which Dean Tobias owed the greatest allegiance and to whose staff he should be attached. In theory the magician's primary rôle was to add additional nuances of meaning and efficacy to a whole battery of Holy services and functions. In practice, magic was found to be of inestimable use to the more materialistic areas of Church operation and influence. Therefore, the Curate found himself being drawn more and more into the web of the Dean Temporal whose staff regulated those parts of Rugby life not already administered by the Crown through the Waiths of Castle Waith. In so far as he thought of it at all, Tobias was not unpleased at this general tide of events; at best his spiritual duties were a mere means of learning necessary ritual and dogma, at worst they were a sheer waste of time. More practical activities seemed to him to hold far greater opportunities for advancement and mental stimulation.

By nine o'clock he was able to leave the Cathedral and fulfil what was, to him, his first agreeable appointment of the day – his weekly report to the Bishop. The Bishop's relatively modest residence, somewhat incongruously termed a palace, was one of the few large buildings permitted outside the city walls, and the somewhat epicurean Bishop who was responsible for its present form had landscaped its surroundings and spared no expense to make it probably the most aesthetically pleasing structure in the area. Normally the visit would have entailed a journey of twenty-five minutes since Tobias was not yet able to afford to maintain a horse. Yet due to a fortuitous series of meetings made during his sojourn in the town, it was not always necessary to make this long slog. Skirting the base of the Castle he entered by the main gate and asked one of the guards for Haraldsson.

The Waiths were said to be one of the oldest noble families in the country. Certainly they had survived the Spanish pogrom of the Protestant nobility as well as Essex's equally bloody pogrom of suspected collaborators, but even so stories of their pre-Norman origin were dubious. Nevertheless with longstandingness of this degree comes seemingly boundless respect and grandeur and, the Waiths being pretty decent people as the nobility went, they were duly awarded it by the people under their sway.

Lord John Waith, nearly sixty now, was the head of the family. He had had an adventurous youth fighting abroad and serving in several of the crusades in eastern Europe, it was said, and upon returning home he became the moral and political tutor to the young Prince Charles who was now King Charles IV, King of England and Wales and Lord Protector of Cornwall and Scilly. The young king-to-be had evidently loved his teacher well, for now Waith was called in to advise on the highest matters and had the ready and affectionate ear of the Crown.

Tobias had only met him once when the Bishop had formally presented him as the new incumbent priest-thaumaturge of the diocese. Lord John had struck him as a very large shaggy-haired man with none of the air of gentle nobility that Tobias had expected. Despite his age he still appeared powerful, and his eyes were wild and bright. Tobias thought him capable of any enormity.

That may or may not have been a correct assessment for direct evidence of Lord Waith's personal rule was scarce. Despite a well-known professed love for home life and the town of Rugby, he spent much of his time in London presumably engaged in high-level politics. His shadowy wife, Lady Priscilla, and his two daughters Elaine and Susannah (his only surviving children), were occasionally seen about town but in Waith's absence town rule was somehow jointly agreed upon and regulated by a body of prominent town businessmen elected by their peers, the staff of the Dean Temporal, Lord Waith's private secretary George Paxton and his 'Castellan' Maurice Fidelio (a Florentine). Although the seeds of discord were heavily sown in this arrangement they never seemed to come to germination. Somehow, invisibly and inaudibly, the decision-making process made decisions and the great bargain of Church, state and people was kept, and flourished in the little microcosm of Rugby.

It came to Tobias' attention that the only other professional magician in the area, a freelancer of non-Church training by the name of Phillip Chitty, was employed by the Waith family. In due course Curate Oakley officiously sought out his company and thereby met Harald Haraldsson, a Swede, a sometime-mercenary who had served the Waith family as guard-commander for ten years and more.

Haraldsson was quite prepared to lend Tobias a docile old mare for the morning and so in less than ten minutes he was handing the horse over to one of the Bishop's stablers. Since the honourable gentleman would be expecting him, he wasted no time and strode through once a lackey had let him in. Pausing only to straighten his gown he knocked sharply on the relevant door and went in.

Soon after his arrival in Rugby Tobias and the Bishop had struck up a close rapport. In many ways he reminded the magician of Father Guido Mori, save that he seemed to have none of that man's graveness and solemnity. Whereas the two deans (being Tobias' only other superiors in the Rugby establishment) were wont to stand on their rank and dignity, the Bishop was far more approachable, or so at least Tobias had found. If evidence was needed, his greeting that morning was sufficient.

'Ah, good day, Tobias. And how are you this fine God-given morning?'

Tobias bowed deeply. 'My Lord Bishop, good day to you. Since you ask, I am well and refreshed from this bountiful rain that the Lord has generously provided.'

The Bishop half smiled at this gentle rejoinder. 'Remember it is good for the crops, Tobias. Take a chair.'

The Bishop was seated behind a large desk, its surface entirely concealed by a thick pelt of documents and letters. He was small and white-haired, and his eyes were humorous. However, Tobias had sensed right from the start that a spirit of hard steel lay not far beneath the surface in this man: in no other way could he have risen to his present exalted position. As far as possible, however, the Bishop kept his deep streams of necessary darkness hidden in reserve and allowed the lighter, more pious side of his nature free rein. Certainly he was more happy with this face presented to the world; that was how he would have been through and through if the dictates of survival had not dug out some elements of his character better left unexcavated. According to his lights he was a sincerely devout man.

Tobias had taken his seat and, the respectful formalities completed, he was now very much at ease. He was studying the ornate panelled and tapestried room until the Bishop finished a particular piece of correspondence.

'It is my custom to take a cup of coffee around this time of the morning. Would you care to join me?'

'Very gladly, with your permission, my Lord.'

The Bishop rang a small bell he kept in a prominent position on his crowded desk.

This was equally a custom, acted out nearly every time they met – the Bishop's was one of the few households in Rugby to be able to afford to serve coffee at all regularly. Tobias had a great partiality for the drink that he had discovered during his stay in London with Father Guido and the Bishop had somehow become apprised of this.

A few minutes later a servant brought the beverage in and both men leaned back, savouring the opulent smell.

Meanwhile downstairs, the under-cook was enjoying his own cup of coffee that he had wrung out of the beans allotted by the store-master for two people only. The Bishop had guessed that some such thing was going on when the coffee began to decrease, almost imperceptibly, in strength. The thought of his lowly under-cook enjoying the same standard of living as a Bishop of the Church Universal never failed to amuse him, and so long as the brew did not get so weak that it had to be helped out of the pot he would not make a fuss.

He poured coffee for both of them, then asked, 'What do you have planned for this week, Tobias?'

'My Lord, I see that the Dean Spiritual has allotted me five masses – that is four mid-week services and high mass on Sunday. In addition I hope to make it to a couple of morning masses if I can raise my weary head in time.'

'Fine, Tobias. Excellent. And, since we touch upon early mornings, how is Miss French?'

Despite himself, Tobias blushed: how did the crafty old fox know about that? 'She is well and bonny, my Lord.'

'Good, I'm glad to hear it – convey my greetings when you see her next.' He smiled broadly. 'And I think perhaps you ought to squeeze in a period of confession into your weekly programme – don't you?'

'As you say, Bishop; I'll see my confessor on Sunday.'

The keeping of concubines was a commonplace, if rarely mentioned phenomenon among the supposedly celibate Holy Orders. It would take a man of far greater power and influence than the Bishop of Rugby to stop the practice and somehow suspend a basic urge of mankind.

'As for the rest of the week, well, I've got open lectures at the University to conduct on Monday and Tuesday as usual. Wednesday, I'll spend with Father Hartgroves, studying, and the inbetween times I will probably be dancing attendance on the Dean Temporal solving the more unpleasant items on his list of problems.'

'That seems fine, Tobias. One other thing: I'm receiving a delegation of Chapter and Warden-Committee officials on Thursday. Just a routine exchange of views, you understand, and perhaps a little grievance-airing. There will be a private mass in one of the side chapels afterwards. I'd be obliged if you'd be here early on that morning to act as my officiating curate – those earnest tradesmen do so appreciate some good old-fashioned church pomp you know.'

'I'll be in full regalia and look as stern and powerful as possible.'

'Good. Well, that's all we need cover officially I think.' He drained his bone-china cup and leaned back again. 'How goes things in general?'

'Well . . . pretty good as usual, my Lord. Er . . . I think I've got the Church rituals almost beaten now so my final exams shouldn't present any great difficulty. My development of magical skill technically finished when I graduated from Southwark of course, but I study for myself a lot and the university lectures help me to clarify my thoughts in that direction, though how much gets into the heads of my victims I'm not sure.'

'Quite a lot I should imagine – the university has spoken quite highly of you to me.'

'That's heartening, my Lord. As a magician I never know just how much those without the talent appreciate what I'm trying to describe. To be honest, and at the risk of sounding arrogant, the only people who can truly appreciate the nature of magic are going to be magicians themselves. I mean, it's like trying to describe a taste, in that you invariably end up desperately grasping for comparisons that are far from exact.'

'That's well put, my boy. Incidentally – are there any magicians among the philosophy people you take?'

'Well . . . I've looked quite carefully and there are several who *might* be, judging from their attitude or the questions they ask afterwards. Even so, they're going to keep quiet about it for obvious reasons and I suppose they'll learn what they can and merely practise secretive "hedgerow" sorcery. A waste of talent. Do you want me to hunt them out?'

'No; the last thing I want is a bevy of recalcitrant and press-ganged magicians. If any have real ability I have no doubt they will come to our attention whether they like it or not, as did our own Master Chitty from the Castle, in which case the Church can come to a separate . . . understanding with them.'

'Just as you say, my Lord.' Tobias was wondering exactly how much the old man knew of his circle of acquaintances. There had been a humorous glint in his eyes when he'd mentioned Chitty and he therefore presumably knew of Tobias' friendship with his titular rival. As the Bishop obviously knew about Diane as well, someone, somehow, was reporting on Curate Oakley's entire life style. This was no danger at the moment since he was leading an almost faultless existence, but he filed the information away for reference. Half his mind explored the none-too-alarming ramifications of it while his interview slowly drew to an end. They discussed a programme of Bible studies to be conducted in the Mechanics Institute for the largely illiterate artisans of the town, and Tobias touched upon his own readings. At some unspecified point the Bishop must have decided himself satisfied with his Curate's progress and their talk drew to a close.

'I will see you at High Mass tomorrow – and don't forget Thursday, Tobias; you are to represent the strong yet paternal arm of the Church to the vastly impressed Church-wardens of our little Christian community.'

'I'll conjure a demon to bring with me, my Lord.'

They both laughed, although to Tobias demons were very far from a laughing matter. He made a final bow and left.

The rain had stopped and so Tobias had a pleasant, easy canter back into town. The Bishop's gently chiding comments had turned his thoughts towards Diane and female companionship in general. Some eager spring sunshine revived his spirits and by the time he crossed the town ditch he had decided to change his mind and to summon Miss French over to accompany him this evening.

At the Castle he met Haraldsson again and thanked him for the loan of the horse. He asked after Chitty and was informed he wasn't in. No reason was proffered and, presuming some activity in the Waith interest was the cause, he enquired no further.

As it was a free point in both of their days, Haraldsson challenged him to a game of chess, a game which Tobias liked although he played abominably. The young priest always enjoyed the mercenary's company and so readily agreed. They withdrew from the comparative hubbub of the outer courtyard which served as a trading area, market and general social centre, into Haraldsson's small guard room, a place which during his decade-long sojourn he had converted into a comfortable haven from the strains of duty.

Haraldsson, a gentle and slow-witted man, originally came from a small and primitive village on or near the Arctic Circle. His size and strength had marked him out for an extraordinary career from the start, and when both his family and the village had fallen upon hard times, he had been persuaded to present himself as a volunteer to the armies of the Emperor of Sweden in lieu of some back-taxes. In such a manner the family had managed to struggle on to face a new year at the cost of one son. For ten years or so he had served in various garrison towns, fought the pagan Lapps and East Prussians and generally preserved the integrity of the expansive and prosperous Swedish Empire. At the end of this time, as reward or punishment, he never knew which, he was transferred from his unit into a specially raised regiment of foot destined for one of the mini 'Crusades' waged at regular intervals against the sophisticated but pagan inhabitants of the Crimea and Ukraine. It was here that he met the future Lord Waith who was a volunteer in an English troop of horse, earning only their food and grace by involvement in the campaign.

In the burning ruins of a Ukrainian village, John Waith somehow acquired the impression that Harald Haraldsson had saved his life. This may or may not have been the case but Harald could never remember the incident; there'd been so many corpses about that day. Anyway, Waith had told him he was a famous nobleman and offered to buy him out of the Swedish Imperial Forces and give him a post as personal bodyguard in a place called Eng-land. To Haraldsson this seemed a chance to escape the intolerable spiral of killing and violence and he'd accepted the proposition with both hands. Things had worked out far better than he had dared to dream, and in the ten ensuing years he had barely had to kill or hurt anyone. True, he was still a soldier but Eng-land was a safe and settled place compared to his experience of the rest of the world. Also, a genuine bond had grown between the Scandinavian and his wild master and now Harald felt that Lord Waith was the sole person he would still use violence to protect or save. He had found himself a very nice niche which should, with any luck, carry him gently and safely through to his old age without having to hurt anyone any more.

Over a couple of cheroots and a mug of beer, Tobias won several times at chess (the only company in which he could do so). Around midday he said he must be going home for dinner and proffering his regards to the Waith family he took his leave. Home was a brief walk away, the sun had dried the streets out and the concourses were busy with people enjoying their leisure. He bought some apples and chocolates from a small shop and within minutes was entering the homely confines of 23 St John's Street. Tobias heard Mrs Coley in the kitchen and shouted through to her that he was in.

A short while later he was seated at the plank table facing the street window and eating the meal that the housekeeper had had ready for him: lamb chops, potatoes and peas. He gave her the apples when she brought in a suet pudding and announced he would be in his study that afternoon and only at home to the more important callers.

When dinner was finished and Mrs Coley was washing up, he put his boots on again and sallied out into the street, only going so far as the door of the next house. A youngish, dark-haired woman answered his knock. She carried a baby and a toddler was firmly attached to her skirts.

'Good day to you, Mrs Keen. I wonder if I might ask you a favour?'

'Hello, Curate Oakley – yes, surely. What do you want?'

'I wonder if your little Phillip would run another errand for me?'

'Of course, he'll be happy to. It'll get him out in the fresh air for a while. I'll send him round.'

The door closed and Tobias returned home. He took a scrap of writing paper and an envelope from a folder on the table and with his pen scratched out a hasty message to Diane. He sealed the envelope just as the door was knocked and Mrs King ushered in a black-haired boy.

'Hello, Phillip,' said Tobias in a friendly tone. 'I wonder if you'd take this letter round to the nice young lady in the little red house you've been to before for me. Would you do that, eh?'

Phillip was shy and not a little frightened of the magician but his mother had told him that he was a kind and safe man just so long as one was polite. He nodded, eager to please.

'Jolly good. Now tell me, do you have a piggy bank, eh?' He knew very well that he did.

The boy nodded again, and willingly accepted the Curate's threepence.

Upstairs in the room next to his bedroom, Tobias had constructed a study and whenever possible he spent his afternoons there. Through his rich variety of contacts he now had access to the three best book collections in Rugby – the libraries of the Cathedral, Castle and University. As a person in a position of trust he was even allowed to remove books and take them home. Therefore he never wanted for research or reading matter and his magical studies had wandered off into quite arcane and esoteric fields. He had reached the point where basic thaumaturgic primers could teach him no more and anything he learnt now was not part of common community knowledge in magical circles. Currently the perfection of demonological lore was his particular interest. He was determined to explore and appreciate this branch of the art after his near-fatal experience in London with the demon whose name he did not dare to mention outside a pentagram.

He made a pot of tea and took it upstairs with him. Passing the afternoon buried deep in a large tome from the Castle Waith collection and sketching pentagrams in coloured inks, Tobias found the hours went quickly.

When the study clock struck six he was roused, and noticed that he had forgotten to drink his tea.

Tea of another sort was awaiting him downstairs; a large plate of Mrs Coley's sausages and mash. Afterwards he retired into his parlour and sat reading the Bible. His studies at Southwark had given him an excellent facility with Church Latin and thus enabled him to peruse the great book of his religion. In a world ruled by the Church this was no small consideration or power. Copies of the Holy Writ in the vernacular did exist but all dated from the time of the great Protestant heresy and so by now were aged documents. Even so, the inherent danger in possessing such a book had not decreased one whit.

Diane arrived at half past seven and Tobias' working day was over. He drew the curtains and they were alone, Mrs Coley having retired to her own room.

The evening passed convivially enough. He read and she occupied herself with one of her interminable pieces of knitting. They talked. Tobias made notes from Johnson's great *Lives of the Magicians* until 10.30 pm when, both a little bleary-eyed, they had a glass of wine and a biscuit or two to pass as supper. Tobias then turned out one of the oil lamps and proceeded upstairs with the other, closely followed by Diane. While she was combing out her hair he returned downstairs to make sure Mrs Coley had locked up and thus assured, he returned to his bedroom.

And later, in the bedroom, they undressed each other and made love. Tobias was lucky in that Diane was a willing partner; he had always detested it when a woman regarded sex as an offence and lay there like a martyr. To him that was a distasteful experience akin to necrophilia, and belonged to his less choosy Southwark days. After they'd lain entwined together for a while, Tobias closed his eyes and was very soon asleep. His Saturday, 1st May, 1982, was now a matter of history and would never return.

Such was the agreeable rut Tobias found himself in at the grand old age of twenty-three.

CHAPTER 2
In which our hero provides a friend with breakfast.

Phillip Chitty, master magician attached to the retinue of Lord John Waith, having uncharacteristically risen early took it into his head to go and visit his friend Curate Oakley. He rather hoped Diane would be in evidence, but in this he was disappointed as Tobias was the sole person as yet out of bed in 23 St John's Street. His Church rival was trying to pull his other boot on.

'Oh, it's you, Phillip.' Tobias suddenly remembered the hour, 'Is there anything wrong?'

'Nothing at all. But I thought I'd pay you a visit, seeing as you're always an early bird.'

'And why not? I was about to make breakfast – you can join me along with Diane; mind you,' he added hastily over his shoulder as they proceeded down the hall, 'it's my habit and general preference to eat alone.' Tobias had no intention of allowing this to become a custom.

Doffing his broad, befeathered hat, Phillip settled down in the kitchen and busied himself making some tea. Tobias went to the stairs and called for Diane. By the time she had roused herself sufficiently to come downstairs in her nightgown a simple meal was ready. An unexpected exotic sight in his gaudy silks and embroidered dress-coat, Phillip smiled a wolfish grin at her while she gaped and let out a small whimper of surprise.

'Tobias, you did not tell me you had a guest, I would have dressed. Good morning, Master Chitty – how are you?'

'Just fine, mistress. Just fine.'

Phillip continued to smile at her fixedly. As far as Tobias knew he was like this with all women and according to Diane he had tried to proposition her three or four times. His lascivious ambitions were only barely concealed when Tobias was in audible range. Tobias supposed that he ought to be offended but he was nothing of the sort. In a way he enjoyed Diane's obvious discomfiture although this was a petty and ignoble pleasure. Diane might be one of Phillip's favourites but he was liberal with his affections and Chitty's name often cropped up in the confessions Tobias took as part of his training programme. Sometimes he worried for the safety and honour of Lady Priscilla herself.

Diane considered the advisability of retiring to put some more substantial clothing on, rejected the idea for a variety of obscure and undefined reasons, and took a seat at the table.

'Give me a moment and I'll get breakfast for you both,' said Tobias and then, lost in thought, he turned his back and gave his attention to the kitchen range. Diane looked up cautiously, met Phillip's stare and casually disengaged her eyes to take in the room.

'What brings you here so early, Master Chitty?' – this to break the uncomfortable silence.

'In truth, mistress, I was sore stricken by conscience in the night and at the first sign of dawn felt impelled to seek the guidance and reassurance of my friend Curate Oakley who knows my struggles with sin better than any man.'

Tobias either didn't hear or declined to rise to the bait and Diane couldn't formulate a suitable reply. If Chitty had any religious sense, or concept of right and wrong, this was its first manifestation. Diane on reflection felt somewhat slighted at Phillip's mockery. Indeed, she concluded he was treating her like a common drab instead of, well, one half of a serious relationship.

At length Tobias brought over some bowls of porridge and mugs of strong tea but declined to break the silence. To that extent he was determined to keep his established custom. Thus, Tobias abstracted, Diane slighted and Phillip uncaring, the repast passed in perfect quiet.

At length Diane felt that her proper presence had been sufficiently established and rose to go. She and Tobias confirmed the date of their next liaison. Then without a farewell she swept upstairs to dress and eventually depart before the formidable Mrs Coley was present to express wordlessly her profound disapproval.

Tobias began to put dishes in the sink and resumed the conversation as if fifteen minutes had not elapsed. 'What *does* bring you here at this inconvenient hour, Phillip?'

'The opium has arrived – all we wanted and a bit more.'

Phillip Chitty was a minor scion of an equally minor but honourable noble family who owned a swathe of good farming land near Bagindon and a lot of property in Coventry. His magical faculties had been noticeable, indeed unavoidable, from a very early age and his father, seeing in him the revival of past family fortunes, reared him as a golden youth. No expenditure of money, affection or patience had been spared on him. Indeed, to save him from the clutches of the Church, a magician-tutor had been procured for him (from Church sources, with Church approval, of course) at exorbitant expense, whereby he might remain under the family eye and influence.

Sad to say he proved a poor investment, for when he had learnt all his tutor could teach he left – along with a portion of his father's cash and such readily disposable assets as he could carry, including a few obscure and rarely read volumes from the family library. Two things he left behind: a note expressing 'thanks for everything' and the family name. His new identity was selected almost at random from the first piece of printed matter that crossed his path. In this manner he disappeared into the commonwealth of everyman and never again surfaced to trouble the dreams and aspirations of his ancient lineage. His father's search efforts, at first inspired by fury, then by a spirit of conciliation and finally by fury again, proved at every turn fruitless. At last despairing, he turned his attention to his eldest son, up till then somewhat neglected, whose propensity for unquestioning obedience might mark him out for a career in the military.

This obliging dullard rose to command a foot regiment and on the 23rd day of his new appointment was fatally wounded by a crossbow bolt directed by a 'free Wales' insurgent. And so, save for Phillip's unguessed-at illegitimate progeny, the family line died out – the disappointed father having died insane in Coventry some years previously.

The first two years of Phillip's new life seem destined to remain forever mysterious. Even deep in his drink he would refer to them only in enigmatic and often contradictory terms. It seemed apparent to Tobias that some of it at least had been spent in Scotland, in the environs of Loch Lomond to be specific, and that during that time his magical talents had reached a very high degree of development. Something had also happened in that time to make Phillip mature at unusual speed for when he'd first presented himself in Rugby two years ago, he was but sixteen summers old, and yet had acted like a man of considerable and varied experience. This was all Tobias had been able to glean from Phillip's occasional disclosures and popular Rugby knowledge, and he saw little point in pursuing speculation further.

At any rate it was undeniable that he'd arrived as a young lad of unknown provenance, possessing only whatever was crammed in his backpack. His obvious breeding and refinement alone would have marked him out had he not made his magical abilities widely known. It was rare that magicians of obvious skill were free of commitments and available for employment, and Paxton of Castle Waith had already toyed with the idea of engaging the youth as part of his Lord's extensive retinue when Chitty saved him the effort and made the approach himself. His opaque, not to say entirely invisible, past was a factor capable of oversight – subject to a probationary period.

To Paxton's relief, Chitty turned out to be a model retainer and, as a magician, a considerable source of kudos to the name of Waith. He was invariably polite, deferential and eager to serve, and since the Waith household had no means of knowing what went on in his head they were well pleased with him.

In his turn, he was grateful to Lord Waith and his family for their generosity and until such time as something better occurred to him, he was content to serve them to the best of his ability.

Phillip met Curate Oakley soon after he joined the Cathedral establishment and, as the two acknowledged magicians of the town, naturally they formed an acquaintance. Chitty immediately sensed a kindred spirit and before long a friendship existed between the two.

Obviously, due to his position in society, Tobias had to be circumspect in his associations and his public behaviour, and so most of his entertaining had to be done in private dwellings away from passing scrutiny. At times he held soirées in his St John's Street abode, at others he visited friends who understood behaviour perhaps somewhat less restrained than that expected of a good churchman. By and by, with a little thought and organisation, he did not lack for high times and raucous enjoyment, an indelible taste he had acquired in Southwark. Phillip Chitty was in a good position to provide the same since he was by inclination a bon viveur and, more importantly, had illicit access to the Castle wine-cellars. Also, from some unspecified source, he regularly obtained quantities of high-grade opium powder, some of which he consumed himself and some of which he furtively sold. The presence of a man of Curate Oakley's calibre presented him with the opportunity to expand this enterprise in a way that he had been planning for some time.

Narcotic drugs first appeared in Christendom soon after the great Wars of Religion when overseas exploration was resumed. From Venice, Rotterdam, London, Marseilles and even Rome, they came via trade routes of quite unbelievable tortuousness. Their arrival was hotly followed by a growing battery of Holy dicta outlining quite horrendous punishments to be visited on both the body and eternal soul of those possessing or using such infernal substances. Of course they continued to be available, sometimes in abundance, at other times only in a trickle, and for a person of daring, with suitable contacts, presented an obvious area of exploration with a view to a large and quick profit.

Phillip and Tobias admirably fitted the criteria and between them were on the way to becoming moderately prosperous. The first main problem was that of supply, but in some unguessable way which Tobias forbore to investigate, Phillip overcame this. The second barrier was safe distribution and this was where Tobias came in. As an officer of the Church Universal he was nominally above suspicion of wrongdoing and moreover came into frequent contact with people able to support this expensive habit. Setting up a network of buyers had been difficult, not to mention dangerous, but Tobias had not been so crass as to reduce the exchange to a mere merchant-and-customer transaction. In various ways he had seen that susceptible characters had been exposed to the powder as an experiment, free of charge, without himself being visibly involved at all. Thereafter it was relatively easy for him to 'discover' this indulgence via the sacrament of confession, or personal conversation, whereupon he could offer, albeit reluctantly, to support the continuance of the practice so as to preserve the user's 'mental stability'. For this he received only his 'expenses' and thus grew rich on a show of Christian charity. A small but significant number of Rugby notables were now in a narcotic servitude that was maintained by an obliging and sympathetic priest. Each, of course, thought themselves the only such person in the area.

Tobias bought rare and arcane volumes and stockpiled the rest of his earnings in preparation for the next stage in his advancement, while Phillip purchased women, wine and flamboyant clothes.

Things were going well for them both.

And so the next evening Tobias made some excuse to visit Haraldsson in the castle, afterwards calling in to see Chitty in his rooms in the inner courtyard and shortly left again after a decent interval with a parcel neatly concealed beneath his heavy great-coat. He made his way under the intermittent light of the gaslamps to where, with trembling hands and desperate anticipation, one of his penitents was awaiting his arrival.

CHAPTER 3

In which a summary of our hero's missing years is provided, together with a description of how he fails to renew an old friendship.

All in all Tobias had found the last three years both rewarding and instructive. He felt he had learnt, developed and advanced. Southwark, instead of the massive hurdle he had felt it to be at the time, was a dimming remembrance of necessary but elementary groundwork. The few contacts he had made there took little time to dissipate; occasionally when he was feeling vaguely nostalgic he would write to the Bergmans outlining his progress; from time to time he received a rambling homily in return, but the memories were fading fast and this habit would soon cease. He never heard from any of his fellow journeymen again, nor ever felt any impulse to initiate contact himself. Like a painter, he had learnt from an experimental painting and then wiped the canvas clean for more accomplished re-use. His Rugby canvas was now quite full. He had had to set magical studies to one side for a while so that he might fully learn the intricacies of Church Universal practice and when this dogma, ceremony and mode of life had been fully assimilated he had had to work doubly hard on his 'talent' to ensure he had not fallen behind. His success in this period was confirmed by several examinations conducted externally by the See of Canterbury, but his masters allowed him no respite. The Church had carefully moulded a suitable tool and now had work for it to do. He took services and confessions, taught, gave advice on matters magical and so on, and was generally glad of his bed at the end of the day. He had made several long journeys on his Bishop's service, accompanying parties to Church gatherings at Nottingham, Chichester and even London (where, being in a misanthropic and abstracted mood, he had hidden himself away and visited none of his old haunts or companions). He had met other Church magicians (they were comparatively few and always conspicuous) on these odysseys, and so bit by bit his name and face were becoming known in their tight-knit and incestuous little world. Indeed, in the field of demonology he was considered (in some circles) to be a promising researcher. Among the eccentric and bizarre family of magicians, he passed as a normal, amiable chap.

One lingering cloud was removed from Tobias' mind when he attended a High Mass in London (held to celebrate a great naval victory over the Mamelukes) at which Sir Matthew Elias was present. Part chance and part the dictates of etiquette threw them together after the service and Sir Matthew looked straight through Tobias and walked on without a word. The young magician took this to mean that while Elias still considered his actions reprehensible he was prepared to hold his peace so long as no further bad reports reached his ears. Once he realised this, Tobias breathed a mental sigh of relief; his immediate future was not threatened and one day he would rise above Elias both in ability and position – at which point, if necessary, Sir Matthew and his secret could be silenced for ever.

In fact, as so often in the field of personal relations, Tobias was quite wrong. The truth was that Sir Matthew Elias had failed to recognise his one-time pupil, having completely forgotten him some two years or more back. Elias' life was sufficiently full of morbid humours and memories to allow such a comparatively minor misdemeanour to fade away unnoticed.

Other than this, Oakley's life was topped up with the usual continuing commitments of existence: a small number of women discreetly passed through his clutches; he studied for his remaining priestly examinations; he drank, made friends and as easily dispensed with or lost them . . . and so on.

All about him unseen interests, pressures and eyes enveloped this exceptional yet ordinary, this kindly but amoral, young man.

*

'What do you make of Curate Oakley, Father?' enquired the Bishop of the Dean Temporal.

'A pit beyond the Church's fathoming,' he replied, for he was in a poetic cast of mind that day, ' . . . but reliably useful.' His practicality had reasserted itself.

'A most promising young priest,' replied the Dean Spiritual on a separate occasion for, paradoxically enough, he really only ever saw the superficialities of life.

And if the Bishop had chosen to ask others?

Phillip Chitty: *A man after my own heart – dangerous and wouldn't trust him an inch.*

Diane French: *So kind and strong and yet shy and gentle; he's deeply in love of course.*

Harald Haraldsson: *A good honest man – for a priest.*

Mrs Coley: *A gent.*

Phillip Keen (aged six): *A good bad man.*

As many opinions as people.

In the summer of 1981 while a member of the Rugby diocesan contingent at a conference in Chichester, Tobias had grown bored with the apartment in the Cathedral annexe allotted to him, and similarly bored and puzzled by the magical texts he had brought with him as reading material. It was early evening and quite light. He leaned back in his chair and considered alternative entertainments – for instance smoking a pipe of tobacco or even one of opium (a recent but very occasional habit acquired from Chitty) – but his mood was suited to neither. Being away from home territories precluded any serious drinking or whoring, and so he was left to his own resources. The earnest business of the conference was infinitely above his status and any intrusion on his part would have been considered an impertinence. This was a closed gathering for Bishops and Archbishops alone.

Diane would appreciate a letter but at this distance she seemed insubstantial, a matter of mere hearsay and fallible memory. Nevertheless the thought of Diane, her uses and inherent possibilities, did nothing to settle his mind. In time the boredom became Chichester itself and dispelling the one meant physically getting out of the other. So, he snatched his saddlebag and cape and went downstairs to the stables for the horse he had been allocated for the trip.

Once he had cantered past the city gates and the sentry had saluted him out, Tobias felt renewed and curious again. On pure impulse he set out for the coast.

In times to come this evening would always occur to his memory as a series of small vignettes rather than a continuous narrative. For instance:

Himself: scattering a flock of sheep – riding to the very head of Selsey Bill and surveying the bland sea below, no one else in sight.

Himself: hammering his horse at full gallop through the one street of a dirty, impoverished little lobster hamlet called Selsey in order to frighten the peasants.

Himself: in solitude again, at Pagham dismounting, tethering his steed and then firing twenty or thirty shots at a tree with the pistol he had taken when he left Southwark. He liked such target practice, and thus amused himself whenever a suitably unobserved occasion presented itself. In so doing he had improved leaps and bounds but would never be more than a slightly below average shot.

Finally when it was almost dark he drew near Church Norton where he had heard there was an interesting chapel of considerable antiquity with an attached monastery. He thought he would have a glance at both, mumble a few prayers for form's sake and then ride home fast to exhaust himself. There were no habitations nearby, and so the monastery was easy enough to locate, many of its oil and rush lights already blazing. The building in question adjoined the chapel at the top of a low hill which rose out of a stunted copse. From high on his horse Tobias could see a party of monks laden with bales of faggots, their day's labour, toiling up the wide path.

He sat awhile and gazed: content, young, predatory and at the height of his wellbeing; well dressed and equipped. A compact unit of strong energy: physical man, magical man and strong horse. A neat force to be directed at his merest whim.

At length he moved and, the chapel being his objective, he proceeded along the path into the copse – slowing down as he caught up and was about to pass the work party, mostly humble dog's-body novices he noted, led by an older monk who, dutifully enough, was bowed down under a load as heavy as that of any of his charges. Tobias pulled up at his side to give a civil greeting to this fair-minded brother as befitted the due of youth to venerable age.

Then he recognised the man as Father Guido Mori.

Tobias had been informed by Mori himself that he was to take monastic vows and had thought little more of it, presuming that he meant an abbacy or the like, at least.

This Mori was aged, weary and hollow within. He bore no sign that under the humble brother's cowl was a first-rate Church-trained magician. From being Tobias' recruiter, he had descended and become an old man under a pile of sticks.

And now Tobias loomed above him, majestic and sleek, armed and rewarded, clad in finery and held in esteem – high on a horse looking down at a good old man.

Mori squinted up through the gloom at the stranger.

But Tobias was off at charge speed, splattering the party with flying dirt and gravel as he went.

This pace was scarcely relaxed until he reached home and the horse was played out. He sent out the stable boy for a bottle of whisky and retired to his apartment where he drank half of it. Bed would be like the tomb, so instead he dozed fitfully in the wicker chair by the window. For once he set no guarding spells around himself prior to sleep.

His behaviour was inexplicable even to himself, but Tobias felt a nothingness more profound than that which had seized him the evening he had killed Hugh of Derby.

The movements which had put spur to his horse were but the very last twitchings of a corpse. It would not rise again and the grave was now sealed.

In later years he always dated to that evening the final closing-down of a large section of his soul.

Tobias, twenty-one, asleep with a half-empty bottle of whisky, before an open window.

CHAPTER 4
In which our hero dines out and is benevolent to his fellow men.

It was a universal phenomenon among the more enlightened hosts of Rugby that wherever Curate Oakley was invited young Miss

French was coincidentally, and separately, invited. It was in this way that the two young lovers were seated together at dinner one December evening in 1982.

In the Mediterranean, renegade Christian and Mohammedan pirates had harried the coastline of the papal states and destroyed some superlative villas – the creative apex of joint European artistic endeavour – but most of the galleys had been intercepted by Neapolitan ships on the way out and sunk with ruthless thoroughness.

In Poland the Governor of the Holy Roman Emperor was ordering out the vast noble retinues of armoured cavalry to combat a joint Magyar and Tartar incursion.

Outside the towns, apostate bands roamed the night competing with non-human predators. And yet trains steamed constantly across the European network. Whilst on the main roads (maintained in good order by Church labour-gangs of criminals, bankrupts, heretics and pagans brought from 'Crusades'), night scarcely abated the blood-like movement of goods, raw materials and people. Slowly but surely, the restrained, distrusted energies of industry were forcing the pace of life and change.

A darkly rich, richly dark tapestry. Yet in safe, civilised Rugby sat the priest and his mistress at the home of a prosperous haulage magnate lately grown secure and respectable on railway holdings. But all the share certificates in the world could not smooth the rough corners left on him by the initial scramble for the capital to *buy* those shares. The first ten thousand pounds was always the toughest. Tobias was the confessor of this man, Samuel Wiltshire by name, and he was often invited to dine with the family and their circle. Tobias felt any influential friend was an asset; Diane was flattered simply to be present; Wiltshire felt some of the Church's boundless gloss would rub off on to his reputation. And so every party had something to gain by these evenings.

Samuel had a big, new house, richly and recently decorated, in a part of the town where residences were still decently spaced apart and patches of green were visible between them. In fact the only thing that house, household and householder needed for acceptance was a patina of age. However Samuel was impatient and loath to let any son reap his bountiful crop, and so he contributed generously to Church and charity and endured many snubs in his path to the next goal in his insatiable climb. And after that? Maybe ceaseless strivings towards a title or a royal monopoly . . . then on yet higher until the grave put a stop to him.

And yet Wiltshire was no mere philistine. If so, social mechanisms designed for the purpose would have confined him within the rest of the frantically aspiring and yet unencouraged mercantile classes. He had a broad and charitable view of man so long as his own interests were not at stake, which – coupled with a permanent taste for humour – made him an often charming host. Besides which, his food was good since he had employed the disgraced ex-cook of the Laird of Dalriada on the principle that so long as what came out of the kitchen was of a high standard, he didn't care how effeminate its creator was. Tobias was, of course, of the same viewpoint.

So, drawn by culinary delights and glamour respectively, Tobias and Diane were chez Wiltshire that night. Also present were Mrs Wiltshire, simple and silent, a child-bearing machine, her two generously favoured daughters and the giant, hearty son. As well as Evelyn Purcell, a consumptive-looking warehouse proprietor who was much tied up in the Wiltshire family fortunes and, finally – a gamble this – a don of Loyola College, Oxford. (This being part of the protracted negotiations to ensconce Wiltshire's son firmly in a seat of learning, however precarious his subsequent posture might be.)

Tobias felt abnormally expansive and cooperative and, like little presents, he made gifts of conversation to each person of interest.

Wiltshire, Purcell and the don were the pertinent characters, the rest toy-soldiers to be deployed when and if needed.

'In Rugby,' said Tobias to the don, catching his attention. 'In Rugby, Dr Meerbrook, we have a number of small prayer-congregations who hold meetings of a religious nature separate to official celebrations . . . '

'Yes, I have heard of your flourishing Avon Street group even in Oxford.'

'Oh, news reaches that far afield does it?'

'Rest assured – only to those who look for it.'

'I see; well as I was saying, do you have similar groups in the university town? I thought the gathering together of so many intelligent, burgeoning young minds would be conducive to religious enquiry . . . '

'Indeed so, Curate Oakley, a number of such societies exist, but so far as possible we endeavour to bring them under official guidance and leadership since young men at that age have an unhappy tendency to discover unorthodoxies and heresy. I don't imply any repression of course, but I do feel talent unbalanced with experience cries out for direction. Indeed it demands it.'

'Well, I can see that, but Master Wiltshire was telling me earlier that the college authorities have not always been so tolerant.'

'Not until Vatican Two's terms were implemented in England in '66,' interjected the son Wiltshire. He was no great scholar but he had an extensive knowledge of Church history, liturgy and dogma. Tobias had touched upon this in conversation with him over aperitifs earlier.

'Well, on the whole you're correct in saying that,' replied the don. 'But surely . . . '

Soon the two were deep in conversation and vistas of academe's groves began to become more substantial before Mr Wiltshire's eyes.

One favour. Tobias smiled at the elder Wiltshire and received a wolfish grin. It then occurred to the Curate that this man had no illusions or misapprehensions about him. A good judge of character.

'Mr Purcell, I don't believe you have had the honour of meeting Miss French before – am I right?'

'I'm very much afraid you are, Curate, but I hasten to remedy this lamentable lapse.'

'Miss French is assisting me in cataloguing my library and research notes prior to my submission of a thesis to Canterbury, whereby I hope to gain my first degree in Thaumaturgy.'

'So you are a scholar as well as a beauty, Miss French. *Enchanté* – and where have you been hiding from Rugby society all this time, eh? You answer me that, my dear . . . ' And so on.

Tobias again withdrew and refilled his glass. Another cheap favour.

Mrs Wiltshire was complimented on the standards of her table and the daughters on their charms (a cliché and somewhat risqué this, but effective nevertheless). And so like a St Nicholas, the priest hopped round the table delivering his presents to people who were two-dimensional to him: want and ambition, influence and character. So easy to influence – but could they pat him on the head and influence him just as easily and imperceptibly? He thought on this awhile.

The table was buzzing with conversation. Everyone seemed

happy. Meerbrook was displaying his wisdom on nuances of Church belief and Master Wiltshire was offering support and scoring incidental points. Purcell had a young woman to talk to and Diane was being flattered. Samuel Wiltshire was basking in contentment and mentally drafting a letter to Dr Meerbrook at Loyola College, dated, say . . . about three weeks from now. Mrs Wiltshire and her daughters were thinking about husbands although not from the same perspective.

And Tobias? Well, he liked to see people being happy even if he couldn't join in himself. He felt free to lean back and quietly, unnoticed, have a lot to drink. And everyone there assembled thought *what* a good priest he would make.

In sixteen months' time, Tobias, still the same man but accelerating further along his chosen path, will acquiesce in mass-murder and shoot a man he admires.

And in eight years' time, he will descend, one sunny morning, down a grassy bank into a lane full of dead and dying men. To one side sits a group of survivors, bound and helpless. With the help of his unit of musketeers, Tobias will murder these men and then set about despatching the wounded.

At the door, the party being done, Samuel asked Tobias and Diane if they required a cab or sedan.

'No thank you, Mr Wiltshire. I'll see Miss French safely home; from there it's but a step to my rooms so we'll walk, it being a brisk, dry, evening and all that.'

'Very well. I hope you enjoyed the dinner; you must come again.'

'Yes, indeed,' echoed a smiling Mrs Wiltshire.

'It's been a wonderful evening,' said Diane who had cast all propriety aside and was hanging on to Tobias' arm. Her eyes were glowing with her pleasure. 'Thank you so much.'

'Yes,' affirmed Tobias, 'and I shall no doubt see you in the near future in my professional capacity.'

'As soon as I sin I'll be round to tell you,' replied Wiltshire jocularly.

'In which case may our parting be a lengthy one.'

More jokes, thank-you's and good-nights and then off.

'You *were* joking about escorting me home weren't you, Tobias?' said Diane.

'No, I'm afraid not. Tonight my dear you sleep at home.'

For although he would have been quite pleased to sleep with Diane, it was good policy, he thought, to keep her uncertain and on her toes.

CHAPTER 5

In which our hero goes hunting and sees some old friends.

The restrictive prohibitions that went hand in hand with Tobias' chosen career were such that he sometimes had to undertake his diversions in a discreet or hidden manner vis-à-vis Diane. So that one still July morning, early enough for the day's weather prospects to be unresolved, Tobias let himself out of 23 St John's Street almost furtively, certainly in a way not normally associated with Curate Oakley's straightforward and confident approach to life. Under his cape he was wearing a layman's suit and he carried a travelling bag. No one was visible at this early hour.

· Tobias made fast time to the top of the long Castle Approach, the street which effectively joined the Castle and the West gate. Here, already waiting, was Haraldsson – ready mounted, dressed in buff-coat and waterproofs, and with a spare horse.

With little or no formality Tobias slung his luggage into the saddlebag and within the minute the two were cantering towards the gate. One hundred years ago this would have been made fast until dawn was fully broken but now that man's hold on the land (that is to say civilised and Christianised man) was gradually strengthening it was considered quite safe to open town-gates several hours earlier to accommodate transporters of market produce and other assorted early birds. So long as they were guarded.

Just prior to coming in sight of the wall and gatehouse, Tobias pulled his broad-brimmed hat well down over his eyes and sank into his cape. The two men passed by the militia pikemen at the gate at some speed but did not neglect to shout a good morning.

'Ten to one that was a priest with Haraldsson,' said Private Mark Bracegirdle (by normal trade, a baker) to his friend, Michael Sque (a banking-clerk).

'I don't doubt it – I think it was the magician one. Nasty type, I don't like him.'

'Why not? You've never met 'im.'

'Maybe not but all his type are the same – not natural, creepy, not quite *human*.'

Mark was tired after his night-duty and not inclined to question or dispute this bigotry.

'Well, I reckon they're off to do some very human whoring.'

'Dirty bastards, they ought to be setting an example.'

'Would you follow it?'

'Well, maybe not but . . . '

Harald and Tobias were intent on a weekend of fun which had included a great deal of planning and premeditation; there could be no spontaneity for the exalted. The Swede had waited until his master and mistress were away and even then had gone to great lengths to ensure that the lowest and dullest member of his retinue knew precisely what to do in almost any eventuality, from a noble visitor to a Mameluke assault, in his absence.

Tobias, by comparison, merely had to wait for one of the odd weekends when he did not have a Sunday mass to conduct, to drop a letter to Diane and to give Mrs Coley the time off. It was quite simple really.

And now both were ready to kick the traces and pretend they were young and uncommitted again (a fallacy, for neither had ever, apart from the briefest of childhoods, had any years of liberty).

Accordingly, Haraldsson who had planned the itinerary of the jaunt had come well equipped: two boar spears for hunting; two carbines, pistols and short swords, also nominally for hunting but conceivably for more catholic uses. In a separate pannier were bottles of brandy and port (Harald's favourite drink when consumed in bulk), and a small drum of cigars and cheroots. This was his contribution. In return it was agreed that Tobias was to provide the 'loose change' for the trip, that is to say, the hotel and drink bills, and so he had brought along a small purse of gold and silver coins. This and his company was to be his contribution.

Once out of sight of Rugby the jollity could begin. The hunting weaponry was doled out and Harald shared the fiery contents of his hipflask. Tobias could for once abandon caution and in between swigs he lit up a cheroot.

By the time they ambled through Long Lawford, the sun was out and they could be at ease and laugh together. The incongruity of their friendship, a magician of Mother Church and a mercenary of the far North, did not strike them for their experience had led them to expect life to be thus bizarre. Only the ordinary could now seem strange.

They took rooms in an inn at Brandon and hired rods to fish in the Avon. Then, in the early evening, paradoxically enough, Harald went to mass in the nearby church while Tobias took his pistol into some woods and murdered a few trees by way of target-practice.

Later in the evening the two took horse for nearby Coventry and found an inn low enough for their tastes (and in so doing inadvertently rode by the house that was the birthplace and childhood home of Phillip Chitty). Here they drank heavily and as always this made Tobias progressively more taciturn and introspective. Harald saw and recognised this, and seized the opportunity to go and fetch a couple of tarts who had been patrolling the pub. Tobias was in that fortunate stage between desperate adolescence and grateful old age when a degree of selection and fastidiousness can be exercised and he chose not to get involved. Nevertheless, he retained his girl, bought her a drink and questioned her on low life. Haraldsson's companion offered to lift her skirts for him outside for ten shillings. He accepted and had her in the shadows of a nearby church. When he returned, Tobias' lady friend was gone and the disguised priest was considering picking a fight with a loud-voiced lout up at the bar. In the end he decided not to because magic would have to be employed and this involved too much of a risk. They drank more and then, both satisfied in their own way, rode noisily and unsteadily back to Brandon.

Understandably, the next day they rose late, but it was a fine Saturday and promised good sport. Nearby were some deep woods that ran undisturbed to the outskirts of Coventry and after a fine breakfast they entered them and found and killed a boar. Harald was the expert in this matter, but it was Tobias who made the kill. Haraldsson had thought they were on the track of a deer herd and Tobias, seeing nothing, bowed to his superior knowledge. Accordingly they had primed their carbines when, Harald having dismounted to look at some tracks he fancied he saw, a smallish and unwise boar chose to hurtle out of the bushes like a bullet. As chance would have it the Swede had his back turned, and the distance was too short to use the carbine.

Fortunately, it was a relatively simple procedure for Tobias, still on horseback, to drop his carbine and make a passing of hands at the beast. It was all happening too fast for Haraldsson. He turned to see his friend drop the gun and heard Tobias say something horrifying – not in any literal sense since the phrase was gibberish to him, but nevertheless Harald forgot the boar and had to cope with the fear that emanated from his companion. For the very briefest of intervals existence became so disgusting as to be entirely intolerable. His mind blanked for a while, sank, and then by force of will clambered back to awareness. Harald had caught the backwash of the spell; he was gasping and wide-eyed with terror.

Meanwhile, the boar had sunk like a stone in mid-charge and was lying on its side, legs working frantically while all its orifices pumped blood. The reason for its wild charge was then revealed and this had Tobias diving off his horse, clawing for the fallen carbine.

Five leathery, naked figures had emerged quite silently from the trees and shrub bordering the path. Names for them varied from country to country and even region to region – bogles, goblins, Disva. In a semi-secret Church tome, Tobias had read that they were called demi-demons and were classified as of the party of Hell but soulless. For all this they were somewhat like men if a foot or so shorter on average. Their skin was a dull wrinkled dun-brown and their eyes – milky, oval and pupilless – glowed. With clawed feet they moved absolutely silently save for the swish of the heavy flint blades they carried. This last detail carried no particular message for the Disva and their myriad kin were already known for their all-consuming antipathy to other forms of life.

After the event, it might have been said the Disva were slaughtered with ease; that Tobias and Harald's impressive actions were indicative of the violent history of each. However that would be to ignore the moments when the fight could have gone either way.

Tobias landed in a most dramatic manner in a kneeling position. He grabbed the carbine and fired it from under the horse and between its legs. This was hardly conventional but effective; one of the Disva folded over his groin trying to grasp an improbably large hole and pitched forward. The shot was hasty but true.

The noise of the shot caused the horse to rear and Tobias had to rise rapidly and back off. But Harald had whirled round and, if anything, was even quicker than Tobias. Still gasping, he shot from the hip with the carbine he had been clutching when the boar made its entry. Another Disva was struck and thrown back by the force. It lay still, with an elegant scarlet buttonhole. Another fortuitous hit.

Harald dropped the gun and reached behind him. He had fought long years and would know the layout of a cavalry saddle in a coma. As it was, his instinct and experience did not play him false; his groping hand found the pommel of his sword. The weapon came cleanly out of the scabbard and flew down in an arc to crush the skull of a Disva who had been poised to strike.

Just then Tobias reappeared and killed again with the spell called 'anathema'. It took the Disva unawares from behind. One of them burst out in pallid blue flames and fell writhing.

Another, possibly slightly younger than the others, and certainly smaller, looked from human to human as if casually debating. This lasted for only a wink until he opened his mouth showing row upon row of tiny highly pointed teeth and *hissed*, an incredibly bitter and angry sound. So doing he leapt for Haraldsson, blade swinging, and was helpfully met halfway by the Swede's charge. The courageous creature was impaled, wriggled and then expired on Harald's sword.

The violence once reserved for enemies of his Imperial Swedish majesty had briefly reasserted itself. He grinned and boomed, 'What a bag, eh, Tobias?' So strong was he that he could hold the Disva aloft on his sword in one hand.

The Curate did not reply but rushed to pacify the horses.

'We've made a pretty penny, boy!'

This was true, for town governors were authorised to pay a bounty of five sovereigns for a Disva head. Unfortunately, bounty-hunters generally had a short life since the Disva usually only emerged from their underground habitations in groups large enough to hunt or raid. Even individually they were a match for most armed men. Tobias and Harold were not just 'most' men; more important, they were lucky.

Harold rested to catch his breath and then fetched a large butcher's knife from his saddlebag.

Tobias spoke, 'Harald – give me your pistol – *quick*!'

Tobias had noticed that the horses were frightened and were staring into the forest. He looked long and hard and then reached for the pistol which still lay holstered in his saddle.

Just visible in the depths of the woods were a number of tall humanoid figures. Tobias' eyesight was excellent. He could see their dun-coloured clothing, broad hats and spears. They were standing perfectly still and staring at *him*. Across a gap of fifteen years, cold yellow eyes appraised him and raised many memories.

Harald came up and handed him his pistol. 'What's up – more?' He followed Tobias' glance. 'Heath folk!'

'Harald, gather the horses' reins and hold them fast but remain behind me; that's the only way you'll be safe.'

'Okay.'

Tobias suddenly raised a pistol and fired it at the watching figures. In a blur he transferred the remaining loaded pistol to his right hand and fired that as well. Although no great shot, at that moment he felt inspired. A faint but clear cry of pain came from the forest and Tobias grinned in pleasure. No spell he knew of could reach that far and so he had to rest content.

'Stay right behind me, Harald.'

Halfway through this sentence two or three arrows flew out of the wood. One struck a horse which died instantly. Another barely missed Harald's head (he was nearly six inches taller than Tobias) and thereafter he abandoned his dignity and crouched low.

Tobias' grin abated not a bit for he knew they would not harm him. He saw the figures hurriedly retreating, dragging one of their number with them.

'Haven't I learned my lessons well,' he shouted at them. 'Run, you bastards, you . . . pixies!' Then he laughed and laughed and laughed. It was a great moment for him.

Soon enough Tobias announced it was safe for Haraldsson to emerge from his foetal crouch. They both looked at the dead horse, from which a black feathered arrow protruded.

'Never mind, man – the Disva bounty will cover the cost of a new mount for the Castle.'

'It was my own,' said Harald.

'Oh – well, *still* never mind; you can buy an even better one and still not be out of pocket.'

Haraldsson was not by nature a curious and contemplative man. He forbore to ask Tobias for an interpretation of what had just happened. Somehow he felt the answer would disturb his peace of mind. In his slow-moving thoughts various impressions of his friend were circulating. Tobias' courage had never really been in doubt but still Harald was impressed at his rôle in the fight. The spell's backlash had appalled him not a little and it brought home to him in a physical sense just exactly what his friend was. However, he had experienced magic before, once when a Ukrainian warlock had tried to kill him and once when a Jesuit-magician had gently put him to sleep so that his appendix might be removed. What bothered him was Tobias' finale with the pistols and the laughter; with a man of such elemental violence neither he nor any other normal human could have any point of contact.

But, true to Harald's nature, his memory of this mental debate faded in the succeeding weeks and their friendship did not suffer long.

It started to rain very heavily and, being a touch squeamish, Tobias left Harald to behead the Disva and gather their blades as trophies. After putting his cape on, he busied himself struggling to remove the saddle and harness from the dead horse. He managed to extract the flint-tipped arrow whole and kept it – it was a revered and highly significant memento for him.

In time all was done and, Tobias sitting behind Harald, they rode slowly back to Brandon where later that evening they would celebrate most uproariously. And on the morrow they would fish.

CHAPTER 6

In which our hero has a productive evening and asks some questions.

'More tea, Toby?' said Diane, and Tobias could not prevent himself from smiling broadly. He had heard that phrase or permutations of it so many times at discreet and refined afternoon tea-parties given by stalwart old ladies, in black and lace (as befits pillars of the Church), that it had become a private joke among the clergy of Rugby and for all he knew, all over tea-drinking England.

'What's so funny about that, Toby?'

'Nothing at all. Yes, please, I'll have another cup.' 'Toby' was a recent addition to Diane's vocabulary as she grew more confident, and Tobias saw no burning reason to correct her although he didn't particularly like the name.

It was a Saturday evening early in February 1983, and a rest day for Tobias which he had chosen to spend with Diane. They had both had a very pleasant time. In the morning they had walked, well wrapped against the cold, to the Cathedral and around the nearby hamlets before a cosy fireside lunch in an inn. Back in Rugby in the afternoon, they had done a little half-hearted shopping and as an extravagance Tobias had bought a large iced fruitcake for their tea.

Just as they were preparing this meal, a courier knocked on the door and delivered a crinoline which Diane had been admiring that afternoon, and which Tobias had covertly purchased. It was no great sacrifice since between his stipend, opium income and other less regular sources of revenue, he was now reasonably secure. However, Diane's reaction was not the expected one since, half-tearful and half-joyful, she tried to correct any implication that she consorted with Tobias purely to receive such presents. Accordingly, he had to convince her that no such idea had ever entered his head (this was true). This was done at length and, her point clearly made, she could give way to delight. Tobias was deeply untouched by such tedious explanations but on reflection felt himself lucky to have found such an honourably minded concubine.

· They had been together for fifteen months or so, sufficient time for any gossip (such as might be provoked by shopping together) to die down, and long enough even to dull the edge of Mrs Coley's disapproval. Tobias had never anticipated a relationship of anywhere near this length, yet partly because no one else had caught his eye and partly because of her undeniable sweetness, they had gone on and on until it was an effort to conceive of life without her presence. In some vague sense he felt this to be somewhat threatening – to what he could not be sure, but it seemed incongruous to the main flow of his life. Yet he was loath to end it.

He brought out the whisky decanter which was always the sign that he planned a domestic evening, and since this was Diane's greatest delight she had grown to take a quite irrational pleasure just in the sight of the unremarkable glass vessel. Besides which, like Tobias, she had a great liking for alcohol, both in moderation and occasionally in excess.

As they drank, he smoked and she (as ever) knitted – though Tobias had rarely seen a finished product of her labours. The fire glowed and the small parlour was warm. Tobias and Diane separately thought that at this moment, misgivings and anxieties forgotten, they were happy.

Later on when silence began to pall, Tobias asked Diane to read aloud for a while (this was a way in which they often passed the evening), and she selected Waugh's 'The Temple at Thatch', (which she knew to be a great favourite of his), from Tobias' growing library. She had a pleasant enough voice and a good reading manner, derived from many desperate Sunday afternoons as a Sunday school teacher – a vile, cold memory.

Tobias sprawled in his chair, satisfied and unneedful of defences. 'Life,' he considered, 'or my life, is a very rich thing.' He looked at Diane and she smiled.

Later, after a particularly successful swiving, they lay in the bed that Diane now considered to be 'theirs' and studied the ceiling.

'I'm very, very happy, Toby.'

'Good.'

There was a very pregnant pause.

'And you are too, aren't you?'

Tobias was silent for a while.

'Yes, I think I can honestly say that I am and I'm very thankful to you.' For once Tobias spoke from the heart. Diane rolled over and clasped him very tight.

'Careful, you're hurting me.'

'When you're with me, just us, you're so different, so gentle and nice, not like when you're out in the world.'

To please her he agreed, but he knew which was the real Tobias.

Tobias sat in his study enjoying a cup of tea and some biscuits. His attention was engaged by the pentagram he had just chalked and painted on the floor. He had been checking this for fully ten minutes and was already satisfied with its completeness. Nevertheless he would allow another five minutes by the study clock, as he had previously decided, to make absolutely sure nothing had been omitted or incorrectly done. In the field of demonology, caution was Tobias' master now.

During his initial researches he had, needs must, used his Southwark notes and, to a much lesser extent, Sir Arthur Waite's *Book of Ceremonial Magic*. But his subsequent work went beyond such sources, surpassed and corrected them. He had found that much of the elaborate ceremony which surrounded demon-summonings was superfluous and could be safely abandoned. At the same time some of the protective and dismissive rituals could be reinforced to give greater security to the magician. His greatest work was, however, in the field of naming the myriad spirits and powers available for help and consultation; by painstaking delving into confused, contradictory and always dogmatic texts, he had been able to abstract a number of concrete ceremonies and namings which were pared down to the necessities. With Diane acting as his secretary and typist, he had put his findings into a small monograph which, when he finally submitted his degree thesis, the See of Canterbury would be good enough to issue in a small print order thereby bringing Tobias' name to a wider, and on the whole, appreciative audience. Needless to say he did not tell all that he knew or suspected as a result of his studies.

On this April morning in 1983, he was putting his efforts to practical use. He finished his tea and using a taper he lit the candles which stood at each point of the pentagram. This done, he crossed to the door and made sure it was secure. Mrs Coley had been impressed with the news that he was not to be disturbed for any cause whatsoever. 'Even if the house is burning down.' Underneath her guise of unflappability, she had a deep and profound dread of magic; she took the hint and found an excuse to put off the upstairs cleaning until the next day.

He chalked the customary square on the opposite wall and, since he valued comfort above dramatic effect, he took his desk chair and placed it in the middle of the pentagram. When he felt at ease, he took a small tin case from an inner recess of his gown and removed from it five thin circles of unleavened bread. Tobias had appropriated these blessed hosts (at great risk even to a priest) during his last mass and, despite himself, had to admit the awe which these holy sacraments generated in him out of their proper context. He set them down in a semicircle by his feet.

At Southwark he had been taught a spell which, while ineffective in itself, was conducive to inducing a magical 'atmosphere'; a catalyst to greater events as it were. Tobias had developed a version of this specifically applicable to demonology and he used it now.

Little more was needed; the elaborate and wordy summonings that he had been forced to memorise at Southwark were unnecessary. All the requisite symbols were already on the pentagram and so those forces which he was confident were now observing him, knew precisely who and what was being summoned.

'Barrow, come. You are required,' he invoked.

At once a tiny part of his brain flicked awake and was filled with something, or someone, that was not entirely Tobias. He had been noticed. It was a distinctly unpleasant feeling.

'Come on, damn you. You'll have to come eventually.' Tobias leant forward in an irritated manner, picked up one of the hosts and ate it. 'The longer the delay the less you get.'

This seemed to be effective, for his mind returned fully to himself and the chalked square facing him began to show something that was more than wall.

When the mist had cleared, Tobias could see a quite charming scene; the inventiveness and vanity of these unguessable forces never ceased to amaze him. He could afford to relax as this was but a minor summoning and quite safe to a man of his abilities and thoroughness.

A windy, grassy cliff top had been revealed; white flowers dotted the thick lawn, while far below the sea was choppy and dark. Wherever this was, it was sunny and probably very early morning.

A girl came into the angle of vision and walked along the cliff top towards him. She stopped just short of the 'window'.

· Barrow was undoubtedly very pretty and smiled most disarmingly at Tobias.

'Hello,' she said in a sweet manner.

'Hello,' replied Tobias with his nicest smile.

Her hair was very red and long, but he noticed it was dark at the roots – henna dye? Her teeth protruded and her eyes were slightly too large for her small round face and, as so often happened, these small faults combined to make a most pleasing whole. Barrow was very short and dressed in a long claret-red dress.

'What do you want?' she asked.

'The usual bargain, sealed by your solemn vow according to the black eminence in return for four bodies.' He indicated the hosts by his feet. She seemed disappointed.

'Oh; you know the bargain well, do you?'

'Backwards and in mirror language, my dear, so I'm afraid truth must be your master for a while.'

Barrow smiled again, seemingly reconciled.

'OK then, three questions.' She leant over the frame into the room and appeared completely at ease.

Tobias stirred in his seat. 'One: A Miles Bostok of Rugby, England, an opium addict, has been forcibly confined to a private bedlam by his family, where presumably he is undergoing agonies of withdrawal. What I want to know is whether he has revealed or will reveal my name as his supplier?'

'He has not, and will not, as he hopes to leave his captivity and renew his addiction. However, he is very sick and weak and an infection will take him and cause him to die in twenty days from now.'

'You vow as I have directed?'

'I vow.'

'Second: have I now got the necessary ritual and bindings established to summon in safety and then control and dismiss your kin, the demon known to man as Bellaston?'

'Your researches have revealed to you the measures necessary to fetch, control and dismiss the force known to you as Bellaston, without risk to yourself, so long as all precautions are observed.'

'You vow as I have directed?'

'I so vow.'

'Third: is Diane French of Rugby, England, truly pregnant and will the babe be born alive?'

· 'Your seed has grown, Tobias, and Diane will bear you a live, bonny boy in seven months' time. Congratulations.'

'Thank you. You vow as I have directed?'

'I so vow, bring me the bodies please.' Barrow once again fixed him with an innocent and winning smile.

'Good try,' said Tobias, 'but I think I'll stay in my nice safe pentagram, thank you.'

Barrow blew him a kiss.

Tobias replaced the four hosts in the tin box, tossed it through the window in the wall and as she bent to retrieve it, and so disappeared from view, he said the spell of dismissal. The window disappeared.

Tobias felt pleased and satisfied that the summoning had gone so smoothly, but the news it had brought was mixed. Two heralds of good tidings and one of inconvenience.

He would clear up, and then root out Mrs Coley from her hiding place in order to procure another pot of tea and then settle down in private for a long think.

And later as he sat in the transformed study, considering what was to be done, he found his eyes and thoughts more and more dwelling on the black-fletched arrow which hung opposite his wicker chair, and all that it represented.

CHAPTER 7
In which our hero helps a friend in need.

'Any chance of enlisting your assistance in this venture?'

Phillip Chitty, at his most predatory and excited, was talking to Tobias who had come to visit him in his room at Castle Waith.

'Why? Do you reckon you'll need it?'

'It'd help.'

Tobias settled back in his chair and studied Phillip through slitted eyes. He was having to do some serious thinking quickly. At the end of it, everything was evenly balanced between yea and nay; when he added his personal inclination this just tipped the scales in favour of affirmative.

'OK.'

'Phillip grinned broadly and slapped Tobias on the shoulder. 'Good man – we'll do a grand job on those bastards.'

The illegitimates in question were a section of the small but highly regarded University College in Rugby, with whom Phillip had fallen into dispute and he proposed nothing less than their physical extinction.

Chitty could not be said to be a violent or vindictive man, but he had very set views of personal honour, which when breached could bring him to a state of quite savage rage in which all restraints were set aside.

The story was relatively simple. Several weeks before, Phillip had been in the company of one of his lady friends in a quite respectable eating house in town. Also present were a number of university hearties who formed a loose club which they termed 'The Beau Monde'. This association of worthies were known for what was charitably termed 'boisterous behaviour', although when sober their tastes were known to extend to more cultural and commendable activities, such as political debates, poetry readings and so on. Some of the noblest-born undergraduates were known to patronise The Beau Monde. Surprisingly enough the unacknowledged leader of the group was a tutor at the university, a Professor Goring, whose lugubrious presence often graced some of their more discreet meetings. The University Senate, in its time-laden majesty, approved of this, seeing his influence as beneficial and restraining.

Unfortunately this was not so. Goring was quite a young man by the standards of his profession, thirty-five or so, but had already rid himself of all his more worthy characteristics. Not that this in any way inhibited his career or social interaction, since his undeniable ability and natural propensity for ingratiation (when necessary) guaranteed rapid professional promotion and this in turn always assured him the supply of a certain type of friend. Within the university, and among certain members of the town council, he exerted a great deal of influence and in a wider sphere his unparalleled knowledge of the intricacies of Homer was greatly respected. This left him free to be as drunk and gratuitously offensive as he liked to those without similar repute or influence. In Phillip Chitty, however, he met the barrier that was destined to halt this charmed progress.

The Beau Monde contingent, Professor Goring among them, were very drunk on the evening in question, but Chitty was no stranger to this state himself and paid them no attention. Later on, however, he had no choice but to do so when an empty bottle glanced off his head. The desire for destruction had mounted to the level where various pieces of crockery and cutlery were taking to the air (the weary manager was used to this and had retired to the safety of his kitchen where he would put an inflated estimate for breakages on the party's bill).

Phillip was in no such philosophical frame of mind and strode, incandescent with rage, to remonstrate with The Beau Monde. Sad to say, his protests were met with laughter which – his companion completely forgotten – Phillip chose to quench by upsetting their table and piling in with boots and fists.

The manager, observing this, decided that his tolerance was exhausted and a kitchen boy was sent scurrying for the militia.

Phillip had neglected to calculate the odds against him and when three officers of the militia arrived, they found him in a deep sleep. Of the six men he had fought, two were damaged. Not so Professor Goring, however, who was quite *compos mentis*, having quickly withdrawn from the fray. He was a known and respected town figure to the militiamen and such was the glowing tale he spun that when Phillip woke up he found himself surrounded by the uncompromising walls of a prison cell. He was not in the least surprised to discover that none of his foes was suffering the same fate. When his headache had abated somewhat, he managed to convey who he was to the duty officer and earned himself more deferential treatment.

By the time he was due to appear before the Magistrates with other unfortunates and undesirables that afternoon, he had had time to despatch a letter to the Castle. To his relief Paxton and Fidelio were present in court and gave fulsome character references. Phillip was just grateful he had resisted the temptation to use magic in the battle, otherwise he would have been facing altogether graver charges. Lord Waith's name had a greatly soothing effect on the three be-wigged Magistrates sitting on the Bench, but matters were not helped at all by a personal letter of complaint addressed to the Court from Goring at his most respectable and proper.

Accordingly, Phillip should have been grateful that he was merely bound over to keep the peace and fined five shillings, but such warmth was far from his emotions at that time. Nor were his troubles over. George Paxton was severely chastising once they returned to the Castle, even when the true course of events had been explained and Phillip had to promise to bear 'the good name of the Castle' in mind at all times.

It was the unfairness of it all that really rankled with him. Goring's word had been accepted above his in Court and the nature of Phillip's company that evening left him vulnerable to a one-sided view of events. That is to say, his female companion was not of the sort that could be produced in Court to make a favourable impression, and the restaurateur was too intimidated to stand for the truth. Phillip was in no doubt that if he had not been protected by the name of Waith, Goring and his cronies would have been able to secure his lengthy imprisonment. Deep and bitter poison was implanted within him.

But Goring's seemingly frivolous vindictiveness did not stop there. It transpired that he had sent letters roundly condemning Phillip to various town figures. The town council received one, so did the University Senate and the Dean Temporal at the Cathedral. Worst of all a letter from Lord Waith, away in London, made it clear that he had been contacted as well. Waith demanded clarification. It became clear that an effort was afoot to displace Chitty from his career and his home.

Fortunately, Paxton felt somewhat slighted by the undue harassment of his protégé and despatched a furious defence of the magician together with a request for Lord Waith to exercise his power to rectify the situation. Lord John had never had too high an opinion of academics in general and Rugby University in particular; and, too, he sensed a vague attack on his own name. He reacted by broadcasting his faith in his magician in no uncertain terms. And the strength of his desire to hear no more of this 'ludicrous and exaggerated incident'.

Goring had bitten off an overlarge mouthful and there the matter should have ended. But Phillip had very different ideas.

Tobias was not inspired to cooperate solely out of friendship, but he was anxious to secure Phillip's trust and gratitude in connection with several loose threads and plans that were coming together admirably. There was a risk of course, but it was mostly on Phillip's part. If Professor Goring met a suspicious end, attention would naturally focus on Phillip, but suspicion could mount to whatever improbable levels it liked as long as nothing was provable. This last factor was to be the subject of many long discussions between the two magicians until, at length, they felt they had a scheme which was as safe as thought could make it.

One thing that Tobias had not mentioned was the personal motive that had tipped the balance towards his participation. He had frequent dealings with the university; he lectured there as often as twice a week and once he had been introduced to Professor Goring who was drunk at midday. Tobias' friendly greeting had been met with a sneer and a snub. In the normal order of things he would have done nothing about this, but he was not the type to forget it.

Goring had made one enemy too many at last, but he remained blissfully unaware of the dark clouds edging into view. A blackness of his own creation was sweeping in towards him; perhaps unlikely tools of divine justice were being manipulated. At any rate the black would shortly cover him and when it moved on he would no longer be there.

It was no armchair summoning. Tobias and Phillip stood in a large and particularly detailed pentagram in Phillip's room at the Castle. Chitty had spent nearly two hours drawing the design according to a pattern Tobias had given him and, even then, Curate Oakley insisted on spending twenty minutes or more checking its every detail. The door was locked and only then were the candles lit and the final preparations made.

Together they recited the spell of preparation. Only Tobias had the specific demonological version of this but their joint effort was sufficient. Straightaway, the sixth sense that constituted their 'talent' informed them that they had been heard and that something was stirring in response.

Bellaston answered the call. He walked down the moorland path, from his town, taking several minutes, but at length his sallow and sullen face was peering into the room.

'Oh, hello – it's you is it?' The demon looked down and critically surveyed the pentagram. 'You've been studying since we last met, I see.'

'Perhaps,' said Tobias. 'At any rate I still have need of you.'

'But,' interrupted Bellaston, 'I thought that at our last encounter you had sworn to release and renounce me for ever?'

'I know the ancient bargain better now. Don't prevaricate and waste time – you know what we have for you. Now listen to what we want you to do – '

Chitty spoke for the first time. 'Proceed to the apartment of Professor Goring of University College, Rugby, England, where a party is in progress. Kill all there save Goring himself – do not harm him in any way. Then depart the scene but maintain the bridge. When we have finished our part of the business, you may return for your reward.'

Bellaston stared at the pentagram again as if unconvinced. 'Very well; I have little choice.' At which, he turned his back to them and drew the blade of his sword-stick.

Phillip and Tobias tensed.

Quite abruptly the scene through the chalk window changed. Instead of the desolate moor, there appeared a small dining-room where a noisy meal was in progress. Goring was there as well as three undergraduates from The Beau Monde in the garish frock-coats the group affected. A serving-maid had just entered the room with a decanter and apparently a very convivial evening was under way. To the startled Goring, it seemed as if an assailant had walked through the wall, but on closer inspection he could see an inexplicable 'hole'. Through it, he could see another room which should not have been there and, worse still, two grim figures who, without hyperbole, had death in their eyes. Two of the students had their backs to the wall and one died, thrust through, before he knew anything was amiss.

Meanwhile, Tobias and Chitty were busy. Tobias seized Goring's mind with a spell and held him absolutely rigid; the professor could not move any more than to blink in terror. It could have been a fair fight between opposing forces, but Goring's mind had been weakened by years of self-indulgence and unhealthy ponderings. Tobias' will was iron-strong and Goring's had but the strength of a child.

Tobias immediately appreciated his total victory and smiled at the victim. At the same time Phillip gestured wildly and cast a spell of silence. Backed by his anger and resentment, it was a strong enchantment and so the slaughter proceeded in absolute quiet – mouths opened to scream or protest, but no sound emerged. Both magicians hoped no one else in the house would notice the sudden quiet from the dinner party.

Bellaston was quick about his work as he killed the students and the maid. They fought and ran to no result, the brief resistance served only to wreak silent havoc on the furnishings. The demon straightened up from despatching the young girl and looked at Tobias. 'I will be back shortly,' he said and disappeared.

· Phillip broke the silence spell, took a deep breath and bent his will to reinforce the spell on Goring.

Like a reluctant marionette, the professor began to move at the behest of two magicians of very high standard. Tobias and Phillip grinned in triumph at the unfortunate man in the last stage of fear. It was this sight, of two merciless faces, that he was to carry with him into the grave. First he walked stiff-legged to a chest of drawers in one corner, from which he took a sheet of writing paper and a fountain pen. He was made to sit down at the table. Here he gained second strength and resisted in earnest; beads of perspiration broke out on the magicians' brows but they were still more than equal to their task. Goring wrote and then, helpless as the magicians made a final effort, he snatched up a table knife and planted it firmly into his abdomen. He was crying and obviously in enormous pain but still he could not speak. Phillip seemed minded to spin out this entertainment but Tobias made it clear that a speedy end was needed. Goring accordingly took the knife in both hands, pulled it up in the wound and thereby died. He fell forward on to the table in a pool of gore which mixed most distastefully with the scattered food.

The spell was ended and Phillip and Tobias knelt briefly to regain their breath. A mere moment later, judging themselves sufficiently resolved, they arose to implement the final and, from Phillip's point of view, the most dangerous stage of their plan.

Tobias held himself ready to launch counter-measures should Bellaston unexpectedly return or someone enter the scene of carnage.

Phillip picked up a bundle from beside his feet, hurriedly left the pentagram and via the magical window he climbed into Goring's room. There he unwrapped his package and took out a sword-stick that was a passable copy of that wielded by the demon. He thrust this into each of the students, and the maid, and then laid it on the table by the professor. The other item in the package was a small wooden box containing a moderate quantity of adulterated opium. He found a clean saucer and put some of the powder in it; this he left by the suicide note.

The room now contained everything necessary to tell a story which despite being astounding was far more credible than the truth.

Phillip regained the safety of the pentagram with the empty bundle.

Swiftly Tobias summoned the demon again and, as if impatient, Bellaston reappeared instantly. His background was the moor at dusk again.

'Did you enjoy yourself?' asked the demon.

'Yes, very much,' said Phillip. He felt relieved now the path to the murder room was sealed. In one sense they were safe.

'No time for talk – take your present and depart.' This was Tobias, who knew their work was far from over. He stooped and picked up the remaining parcel lying within the pentagram. It was a babe in swaddling, a few weeks old, and fast asleep – having been liberally dosed with laudanum ever since Phillip had smuggled it into the Castle. Chitty had bought the infant from a drab in one of the crowded tenements of Rugby's slums for a few pounds and such was the value of life in such quarters that it had been a matter of the utmost ease.

Tobias lightly tossed the bundle through the window and Bellaston just as lightly caught it.

'Begone, Bellaston.' He had no wish to see what would happen. With Phillip, he recited a spell of dismissal and the wall became comfortingly blank again. It was almost over.

There was no time for rest; as previously agreed, Phillip was to proceed to see Lord Waith who was in residence again and thereby establish an unassailable alibi for most of the evening.

Tobias would hurriedly clear up and then meet Haraldsson with whom he would play chess all evening and so have some form of defence should suspicion unaccountably fall upon him.

Even the most hostile examiner would have to admit that it was impossible to be involved in what was obviously a drug-induced massacre and suicide some three quarters of a mile away *and* be at the socially impeccable Castle community within two minutes of the time the tragic event would be presumed to have taken place. Suspicions would doubtless abound but, lacking substance and roots, would, like everything else in its good time, pass.

Tobias merely felt the 'nothing' that was increasingly his companion these days, but Phillip hurrying to his alibi felt impelled to find time to turn and say, 'You know, I've got to admit it – that was more deeply and honestly satisfying than having a duchess.'

Concerning which Tobias was lost for comment.

CHAPTER 8
In which our hero receives help from the friend that he helped, and a problem is solved satisfactorily.

On the 14th of May 1983 Tobias had occasion to call upon Phillip's apartment about business that he considered as important as Chitty in turn had considered his own request for revenge. In the last four weeks they had deliberately eschewed each other's company so as to deny suspicious minds food for thought. Now, however, it seemed as if the storm had passed. The town coroner had ruled the Goring case closed when the highly entertained jury had returned a verdict of suicide and manslaughter committed while in a state of diminished responsibility. More astute and enquiring minds found themselves less convinced by the 'facts' of the case but the simple truth was that the late and little-lamented Professor Goring lacked any true friends to investigate or revenge his death. In short, Tobias had been lucky again and Phillip was in the clear.

A new problem was requiring pressing treatment and Tobias sought to draw upon the balance of gratitude. So, over a decanter of brandy, he and his friend set to hard talking, although the gravity of the discussion only gradually became clear to Phillip.

'You've always desired Diane haven't you?'

Chitty ceased toying with the lace of his cuffs. 'Oh lor, you've not decided to take offence have you?'

'No.'

'Good.'

'How would you like to have her?'

Phillip was more or less shameless. 'A hell of a lot, when . . .' There was a hesitant pause as his enthusiasm died down. ' . . . and the catch is?'

'She's three months or so pregnant.'

'Oh.'

Phillip decided to fight for time while he thought. 'You used the normal contraceptive spells?'

'Of course, but as you know none of them guarantee certainty. It certainly is my child, though. I know she's not been unfaithful to me.'

'You trust her?'

'Yes – but I checked as well.'

'Just as well, I suppose.'

'A summoning confirmed to me that it's mine; it's going to be a boy and will arrive in October.'

'How about abortion?'

'Firstly, Diane would not agree' – here Phillip shrugged his shoulders in a dismissive gesture – 'and secondly I'm not prepared to let her run the risk of injury and infection among ham-fisted abortionists.'

'You're being sentimental, Tobias.'

'Perhaps.'

'And you're asking me to take her over for you and claim the child as mine?'

'Precisely.'

'You're asking a lot.'

'I know, Phillip – and there's little I can offer you in return except for the enjoyment of Di for a few months, so really I'm appealing to your friendship. The point is that I want Diane to be looked after by someone I can trust and I want her to be able to keep the baby, for that's what *she* wants. So what we need is an acknowledged father; it can't be me because of what I am. Not only that, but I also need someone who is going to be around a few years to look after her and see her parents or whoever don't prise the babe off her. I'll supply funds to you to keep them and as an initial gesture you can have my stock of opiates for resale – about two hundred pounds' worth, so you're not going to lose financially. I become a full priest in a year's time or so; soon after I'll rise in position so that I'll be able to send for her and the child. We'll be above, in hierarchical terms that is, any moral reproach and I can have as many "nephews" and "nieces" as any other Doctor of Thaumaturgy, or Bishop. You see my plan?'

'It won't help my position in the Castle very much.'

'Does that worry you?'

Phillip considered and shortly decided.

'Tobias, my dear friend, I owe you a great deal – you rendered me a great service, at risk to yourself when you needn't have done so. If I refused you this I would be a bigger bastard than I'm assured I am. I'll do it gladly.'

'Undying thanks, Phillip, I always assumed you would.'

'And knowing you, you've already worked out the means of effecting this transfer, haven't you?'

'I'm afraid so.'

'Well?'

'Here is the opium for starters and there's a list inside the box of the people who require supply. There'll be no difficulty as we've got a small and discreet circle of about four wealthy addicts – very secure. Also here is a letter to Diane in which I explain what we've agreed upon today. Show it to her when she's brought to you.'

'Suppose there's a little difficulty, shall we say, in actually persuading her to join my retinue?'

'There won't be. I know her well, and there's a "crusade" spell in my repertoire. She'll do precisely as she's ordered for about four hours; after that she'll accept the inevitable – believe me, I know her.'

'I'd hate to have you as an enemy, Tobias.'

'You're impressed?'

'Very.'

They refilled their glasses and Phillip rather dramatically proposed a toast. 'To a mutually satisfying agreement.'

'Absolutely,' echoed Tobias with a broad smile.

And thus all the loose threads and plans were joined at that moment, leaving Tobias outside, free, safe and victorious.

That very evening, Diane French was led zombie-like to Phillip's rooms and there embarked upon the first night of her new career.

Tobias, upon returning home, could not deny himself a small private celebration to underline his deep satisfaction at the fruition of all his intrigues, and so he opened a bottle of an expensive Scottish single malt.

As he sat in his study, he considered the sum of things. It was true he had lost a girl who was honest and honourable, who had many uses and whom he rather liked, but on the other hand many problems were thereby resolved. His progress to priesthood was now unthreatened; the path was clear again.

For a year he would keep his bargain and see that his son and Diane were provided for; but after that he intended to be free again and they could look for him in vain. Tobias' letter to Diane admitting parenthood would be of no avail to Phillip for it was typed and unsigned. The same applied to the list of opium addicts.

· All in all he thought he had handled matters particularly well. Once, he remembered, he had vowed to abandon Miss French in a gentle manner even if inconvenient to himself, but now he felt forced to behave otherwise. Adverse circumstance was the only wind strong enough to propel Tobias' ship of state. If he felt any unease at all, a black-fletched arrow was facing him to show how stupid that was.

And the next day Mrs Coley was told that Miss French no longer had right of entrance to the house, nor was she to accept any correspondence from her. And so when Diane duly made her arrival in the afternoon she found the fort barred against her. Tobias happened to be in his study at the time and heard the indefatigable Mrs Coley take charge. What a pity, he thought, that his spells and charms against conception should have proven fallible – perhaps they were capable of improvement in some way and he wholeheartedly researched the problem for the remainder of the day.

On the 7th of October in the year of our Lord, 1983, Tobias became the father of a fine, healthy son who was already a good image of his sire. Even more unfortunately, inspired by Diane's memories and Phillip's perverse sense of humour, the baby was subsequently christened Tobias, 'in honour of a friend of the family'. As luck would have it, Curate Oakley was not called upon to preside at the christening.

And in December 1983 Diane fell or leapt from a third-storey window in her parents' home and died instantly; and thus Tobias' final betrayal of her and Phillip was never put into execution. The child, aptly enough, was placed into Church care and soon passed out of Tobias' knowledge for ever. The opprobrium attached to Phillip's name and the sympathy extended to Diane's memory in popular opinion was soon dispelled – although Chitty's absolution was somewhat arduous.

To Tobias, Phillip quite truthfully disclaimed all responsibility and Tobias also quite truthfully assured him he bore no ill will. Events had been tragic but preordained.

Soon only Mr and Mrs French retained any bitter or suspicious sentiments but they were old and without influence.

CHAPTER 9
In which our hero is busy about God's work.

In February 1984, almost a year to the day since he'd conceived his son and thus sealed Diane's fate, Tobias was fully behind the reins again. Any lingering difficulties had been safely settled and in a state of tranquil order he was gliding through his last few months prior to becoming a full priest of the Church Universal. His typed thesis and degree papers had been submitted to Canterbury and he had sat his final priestly exams; to his mind, they had gone well and he was confident of a favourable result. That is to say, of becoming Father Tobias Oakley BA (Thau) by May. Once these elementary prerequisites were achieved, only the extent of his ambition could limit him, and that seemed to be, like the Church, universal and boundless.

After these labours he was available to the Deans Temporal and Spiritual once more and Obadiah Cocroft, after a thorough briefing, instructed him to become involved in what was developing into the 'Avon Street Group affair'.

Characteristically, Tobias felt matters would best be served by proceeding straight to the heart of the matter in only a quasi-official capacity. He went to see the two leading lights of the group at their decidedly humble home one evening and more or less invited himself in for dinner. Mr and Mrs Cherry were as hospitable as their religion could ask and were content to allow companionable chat, despite the obvious fact that Tobias was enquiring into things other than their home cooking. He was wary of any talk of 'pure' religion since it was an endless obsession with people like the Cherrys and far removed from the deeply practical religion known to himself. However, Tobias at length managed to steer matters on to the Church in Rugby rather than the general nature of prayer or transubstantiation. He adopted the manner of the Dean Spiritual, authoritative, condescending and corrective. This was a disastrous failure.

'So, you see, there is a growing disquiet about the direction your group is taking; in fact there are misgivings within the clergy about its very existence, Mr Cherry.'

'James.'

'Er, yes, well: as I've said, just what concrete assurances do you think you can give the Church Universal that your meetings, conducted outside the Church's auspices, are not conducive to error and unorthodoxy?'

'Or heresy?'

'It hasn't gone that far has it?'

'*It* hasn't gone anywhere at all, dear Curate Oakley, except perhaps a little further in the footsteps of Christ; more tea?'

This rejoinder served to throw Tobias off his mental balance just when he'd been getting to grips with James Cherry's sweet reasonableness. He accepted another cup and thought about another line of approach.

The fool's being truthful in what he says, thought Tobias. But he's no milksop. In what Cherry thought was right Tobias considered that he'd probably be unbreakable. He had seen that light in other eyes.

Emma, his wife, was out of a different mould but strong enough in her own way. She had taken just as much a part in the conversation as her husband, declining to speak only when an air of controversy crept in – (duly confirming Tobias' original opinion that of these two leaders of the group, James Cherry was the fountainhead of inspiration). It seemed clear to Tobias that it was she who would be more open to persuasion, or seduction, being a warmer, less spiritual soul than her spouse. From time to time he caught nuances of look or speech that suggested the spirit of the flesh was not yet laid in the plump, friendly Mrs Cherry. The ribbons on her dead-black dress served to confirm the notion.

He had to admit he liked the couple, religious lunatics though they were, probably because they were also everything he, now, would never be. They were everything Tobias purported to hold in no regard. They clung on to the qualities he had relentlessly dug out of himself and thus he should not have been surprised at the attraction of different poles. Perhaps on a more simple level, Tobias was charmed by their display of openness and motiveless friendship – a rare commodity in his circles.

At any rate, despite this attraction, Tobias felt a very great, if illogical, desire to end the evening as soon as possible and to eschew the Cherrys' company. To do so, he abandoned subterfuge and stated his case honestly.

'Look – listen to this, you two – the path you're following, you're going to be smashed, scattered and probably killed. You've built a separate Church and you're holding private services in it and the Church, the real one, is not going to tolerate it – do you understand? They're . . . I am . . . going to break all of you if you carry on. A small prayer group was just about tolerated – just – but a separate Church! You're signing your own death warrants!'

'I can't see how, Curate,' said Emma Cherry. 'We told the Dean's deacon and we've told you – there's no harm or wickedness in our little chapel, we just meet there to pray and sing.'

'That's just so', confirmed James, 'we all of us go to mass as regularly as ever before, save that now we meet in our chapel as well – there's no harm in that is there?'

Tobias sounded almost angry in his eagerness to get his message across. 'You don't understand, listen – *The Church Universal will brook no rivals* – however small, however sincere, however innocent. We will destroy you regardless . . .'

James Cherry attempted to interrupt. 'But . . .'

'Shut up – look, the Dean's man obviously didn't make anything clear to you, so I'm stating things in terms even you in your virtue can understand. You have formed a prayer group which makes such an exhibition of its piety that you've come to the notice of the Dean Spiritual – you've survived that – because of public indifference and because we have a good Bishop. Where I was trained, the Bishop would have had you arraigned for blasphemy before your third bloody meeting. Never mind – you survived – but now your group has bought a shed, decorated it and called it a chapel; you all meet there several times a week for services – because you say our services are lacking in certain spiritual fields. Well that may be, I don't know, but with true Christian tolerance the Bishop still hasn't moved against you, *despite* pleas from many church quarters. No – instead he's sent two churchmen telling you to stop and you haven't. Now I'm here – I think it's the last visit you'll be getting – of this sort at any rate. Will you *please* do as you're told and save yourselves.'

James seemed lost in thought but spoke all the same.

'Curate Oakley, you've given us some very straight talk, delivered out of good intentions I think, but with no conviction behind it. You seem to wish to preserve us from a danger I did not know was so great, but your good wishes stand unsupported by anything stronger. We, too, have opinions, firm ones based on truths above mere good intentions. I'll speak as straight to you as, perhaps ill-advisedly, I did to the Dean's deacon. We, the group that is, worship in our chapel to supplement the Church worship that we think is weak and incomplete. For all your ceremony and dogma, material aids to heaven and relics of saints, you're worshipping a shrunken God; we can't see Him fully for all the human-imposed obstacles in the way. So our group supplements this worship by trying to perceive God completely, looking Him in the face without need of intercession from the Holy Mother, from saints and angels. All we're doing is spiritually enriching ourselves according to our own perception of things, Curate. Do you see?'

Tobias no longer felt motivated. 'Did you tell the Dean Spiritual's man all this?'

'Yes.'

Emma entered the conversation; of the three she was the only one who did not seem to believe in the inevitable wrath of the Church.

'The Church wouldn't persecute and destroy us, would it, surely not if we remain good churchgoers all the time?'

'I'm very much afraid it will, Mrs Cherry,' said Tobias with a hollow laugh.

Although his desire to flee was growing stronger by the minute, he saw one last avenue of negotiation open. 'James Cherry, will you not consider others out of charity? If you insist on bringing doom on yourself, don't you see that it'll descend on a good many others as well – consider them, balance in your conscience a recantation on your part and the consequences of your actions to others; surely to God you can see the sense of that?'

With this, Tobias got up to leave. He expressed his regrets and noted Emma glancing in bewilderment, and something more, between her husband and himself. There was hope there at least.

At the door Tobias turned, 'Mr Cherry, James, consider one other thing – the Bishop may be a soft man but he'll have to move on you before news spreads, otherwise the Holy Office will be in Rugby. That's the choice he has to face you see. What decision would *you* take?'

'I take your point, Curate,' Cherry shook Tobias' hand. 'Thank you, Tobias, I will consider what you have explained tonight and we shall all pray on it.'

Tobias sighed and walked off. As he strode home through a light misty rain, he realised what had been wrong with him during his meeting with the Cherrys. He had been sickly jealous of the evident bond between the two, their inner security and selflessness, and was reminded that he had unhesitatingly destroyed just such a relationship not a year ago. Now, however, a date had been irrevocably put upon the Cherrys' happiness and that of his own past meant nothing to Tobias.

In March of 1984 the world was as busy as ever:

Young Master Wiltshire of Rugby finished his first year at Loyola College, Oxford. Academic life had shown him to have a mind of quite unsuspected ability. He was heading for an outstanding degree and supported by his father's railway holdings, profitable as ever, he would go on to write many, vastly respected, books on liturgical development. Wiltshire senior, as he moved on into his dotage, felt this to be both a source of pride and of disappointment. True, the name of Wiltshire became known in the very best circles just as he had once wished, but could a theologian safeguard his expansive haulage concern? Already, several highly dubious sharks were scouting round his daughters always looking to the old man's demise. It was a great worry to him.

The day before Tobias' twenty-fourth birthday his father died; the news would reach Tobias a few months later. His mother had died several years earlier but no one had bothered to inform him. He celebrated his birthday by getting terribly drunk in Coventry with Haraldsson and Chitty.

A papal legate, no less, was ambushed and killed along with his escort by 'unincorporated' Aborigines in Australasia Secundia. To avenge this unprecedented insolence, regiments of neatly uniformed incorporated Aborigine infantrymen were sent out to wreak promiscuous destruction in the bush. News of the murder and the ensuing pogrom reached European newspapers seven months later.

Whether James Cherry's prayers had any issue at all, Tobias never knew, but the meetings in the Avon Street Chapel continued and so their fate was sealed.

Curate Oakley reported back to the Dean Spiritual and the Dean Temporal; they in turn reported to the Bishop and he with heavy heart began writing explanatory, moderating letters to various authorities above his head.

Tobias felt impelled to dash into the threatened, smouldering building and pull at least one person to safety before the edifice collapsed; perhaps two could be saved if his plan worked well – all the better.

Why he felt so is unanswerable; perhaps it was one of his occasional impulses to good, perhaps sympathy with other people caught up in the Church's stern duty. It was undeniable that even now he sought to express some of the little good left in his own self.

He went to the Cherrys' house again. James was at the Bishop's palace, receiving formal notification of impending anathema proceedings. He would be gone some hours. Emma Cherry was pleased to see the Curate, who was, she felt, their one terrestrial ally in a world of enemies.

He was conducted into the parlour and provided with wine and small-cake.

'They've pronounced anathema against you all, effective in two days unless you make public penance before the Bishop – any chance?'

'Curate, I don't rightly see how we can . . . '

'I'm talking in terms of saving skins rather than honour.'

'Probably a half of the group will recant, family people and so on, plus a few faint hearts.'

'It's a stupid thing to die for and it mayn't be quick – the inquisitors might be here to enforce the notice, you know.' But Tobias knew this to be a lie; the Bishop had prevailed on the Archbishop of Canterbury to stave off the Holy Office wolves.

'Curate . . . '

'Call me Tobias, please.'

'Tobias, I don't think you believe at all, do you?'

'Frankly, no.'

She looked shocked and gestured at his gown and general person. 'Then why all *this*, why help us?'

'It is a very long and improbable story. As to your second point – it should be obvious to you of all people that the Church is very far from having a monopoly of human kindness – my experience suggests quite the opposite. *Please* recant.'

'I cannot – I cannot deny God.'

'You needn't, just say what they want, all the while believing something else – who cares?'

'God cares.'

'Oh,' Tobias sighed, 'Yes – well, maybe. Strangely enough you're probably more qualified than me to judge that. My dear, it's very sad. You're going to die the day after tomorrow.'

Put this baldly, the abstract idea that Emma had been steeling herself against was suddenly before her eyes and became master of her mind. 'Oh Tobias – help us!'

'I've done everything I can – you *must* recant and then forget this ever happened: a closed chapter in your life rather than the closing chapter.'

'But James will never recant.'

'We shall see; I will speak with him.'

Emma was still undecided and gently tearful.

'Recant and I will see that no retribution is taken against you, I have some influence with the Bishop. Who knows? A man as good as he might protect your whole group from harm.'

Emma, fully tearful now, hurled herself at Tobias and wept copiously on his shoulder. He held on to her by the backlaces of her bodice.

'I really don't want to die, and leave the world behind but . . . what will be left of me if I recant?'

'Everything safe and sound as I have explained.'

She raised her reddened face and, collected, now said, 'Not the priest at all are you, Tobias? A man first, magician second and nothing after.'

His consoling embrace became more intimate, he looked into her face and raised his eyebrows in an inquisitory manner.

She nodded and they went up the stairs together.

Emma Cherry was a woman on a mental knife-edge and accordingly Tobias found their coupling somewhat demanding and dramatic, but not without a bizarre sense of enjoyment – and, as always, there was the cold joy of conquest.

He calculated that James Cherry would be home in a half hour or so and so had time for some conversation with Emma as they dressed and she rearranged the room.

'I think James is going to be very disappointed in me.'

Tobias was genuinely astonished and paused in mid hair-brush. 'God's teeth woman, you're not going to tell him are you?'

Emma looked surprised. 'But of course!'

Tobias made as if to say something but changed his mind. He continued brushing his hair shaking his head in a disbelieving manner. It saved him a lot of bother of course; he had planned on staying till Cherry arrived back home and informing him in plain terms of his wife's adultery. This he hoped would sow sufficient discord to break the filial bond that was the core and strength of the Avon Street group's recalcitrance. One or perhaps two recantations would ensue and thereafter the flock would probably follow. If Emma was so truthful then all the better – it would save Tobias a distasteful interview with a man he liked and admired.

Accordingly he left with little further ado. And the next day Mrs Coley brought a letter up to him in his study where he was quizzing an early medieval manuscript of spells. The note read:

Dear Tobias,
    I freely forgive you as I have my wife, as the Lord has always forgiven me. Thank you for all your attempts at succour – both conventional and otherwise; alas we continue staunch in the Lord.
Bless you.

It was signed 'James Cherry'. A postscript in a different hand read, 'I now understand; we will pray for you – EC.'

Tobias fell into a black temper and that evening had recourse to the bottle.

And so it was that Tobias found himself, one dull, cloudy morning in early April 1984, standing before a converted stable and coach-house just off Avon Street. It was this shaky building that the group had sacrificed much to lease and for which they were now to sacrifice much more.

About half of the Avon Street group had recanted yesterday, just under twenty people – clad in penitential black and the paper-cone hats of the heretic, they would have to do the same again, in public, before the Bishop and higher clergy of Rugby tomorrow. The recalcitrant balance had gathered together in their chapel to see the matter draw to an end. This made things much easier for the Bishop's forces and saved the group's face. Far better to await the end together than to be routed out individually like rats from a hole – they thought their cause deserved better than that.

The coach-house-cum-chapel was set in a little patch of what was once garden; standing around this were the forces of orthodoxy – Tobias and twenty of the Dean Temporal's Cathedral retinue under an officer. Despite expecting no trouble they had, by custom, come fully uniformed and armed. However, the musketeers stood easy – they knew there would be no demanding work today. Tobias was nominally in command of the detachment, being the senior operative of the Temporal Staff, but he was happy to let the foul-mouthed officer (an ex-Marine) take charge. For once he felt dejected and stood staring morosely at the chapel door, taking no part in events which he would normally have found interesting.

Some distance in front of the door, a trestle table had been set up and on this the Dean Spiritual and two acolytes were performing the rite of anathema popularly known as 'bell, book and candle'. Several priests were dancing attendance. On the very perimeter of this exciting event was a contingent of Castle retainers whom Waith had provided, at the Bishop's request, to maintain public order. With half-pikes they held back the gathering crowd of the curious, the morbid or the sympathetic. Haraldsson, despite his inclinations, was present, but he saw and recognised Tobias' mood and steered clear.

Dean Cocroft was drawing the ceremony to an end and in a loud if not very sincere voice (his gout was tetchy today), he called upon the heretics one last time to recant and flee to God's protection.

Five people, including an old man and his wife, availed themselves of this offer and rushed out of the chapel; a priest and several of the retinue took them to one side while they muttered hysterical confessions. From certain sections of the crowd a dismal howl went up, both disappointed and accusatory. Tobias shot them a baleful glance but they were too far away to see it.

The Dean Spiritual rang the bell once to show that the anathema was complete and dipped his hands in a bowl of water held by an acolyte. He nodded to Tobias who instantly conveyed the signal to the retinue officer.

Bales of staw had been piled all around the chapel save at the door. This gap was now plugged with more combustibles by two guards, and the officer lit a taper from a musketeer's match-cord. Proceeding round the building, he lit the bales at strategic points. He looked at Tobias for approval.

'OK, put ten men round the building to watch the windows, you and the rest come with me to the door.' He indicated the space vacated by the Dean and his trestle table. 'Right, prime and stand ready, wait for my word of command and mine only.'

The fire was taking rapidly now and the straw was almost consumed. The chapel's wooden structure was well ablaze. Even from thirty paces away, Tobias and the retinue-men could feel the heat. Obviously those inside could as well, for two young women and a young man leapt the fiery barricade at the chapel door and rushed out – shrieking incomprehensibly although their meaning was clear enough. One woman's gown had caught alight during her escape bid.

'Fire,' Tobias said in an even voice.

Most of the retinue men fired and the three figures slumped. The soldiers began reloading quickly.

Soon afterwards a few shots sounded at the back of the building. From within the sounds of a hymn could be heard.

At which point a familiar face appeared at the chapel door. Standing still with no intention of escape, James Cherry found and caught Tobias' eye; he looked pained and scorched but still his message was unmistakable – 'forgiveness'.

This was intolerable and Tobias hastily drew both his pistols from his belt and fired at the chapel. One shot hit James neatly in the temple, more by luck than judgement, and he fell back into the building. Soon after, the flames leapt up too high to see the interior any more and so the closing scenes remained thankfully obscured from view.

The singing that could just be heard above the sound of the fire and the crowd's mumbling ceased, and was replaced by screams.

From behind him Tobias thought he heard raucous laughter and, turning, he saw a group of young apprentices who had come as near to the scene as they were permitted. He spoke to the officer of the retinue. 'You and two men come with me – the rest of you fire at will until I return.'

He led the three men near to where the dozen or so crop-headed apprentices were capering in their heavy boots. From this angle he could see the cause of their merriment – at one window a hand could be seen trying to prise open a shutter. However, by now, the metal frame and fitments were obviously intolerably hot and the hand would swoop, struggle and quickly withdraw, only to try again, equally fruitlessly, every few seconds.

The lads stopped laughing as soon as they saw the priest and his three guards approach.

Tobias pointed at one of them at random. 'Officer, arrest that man, I distinctly heard him shouting heretical slogans.'

'Yes, sir.'

The officer and one retinue-man bundled out the man they assumed Oakley had indicated, an under-sized, ill-favoured lout with fair hair. The others were too surprised to offer resistance even if they had been so minded. Tobias signalled to a Waith guardsman nearby and shouted, 'Escort these filth away! Right out of earshot. Tell Haraldsson they should spend a night in the Castle lock-ups.'

'Yes, Curate.'

Tobias strode back towards the blaze and waved the Cathedral guard away. They were at a corner of the site, not directly visible from the Dean's position, nor could most of the crowd view them.

'Officer, I want you to take personal charge of this prisoner; if he tries to escape kill him.'

A shot rang out at the front of the chapel.

'I'm just going round to the chapel door to finalise things and I'll send a man back to relieve you in ten minutes.' He lowered his voice somewhat. 'You know, looking at this man, I would not be in the least surprised if he tried to escape in the next ten minutes; do you take my meaning?'

'Yes, sir.'

'Good. Carry on.'

Tobias walked along the building. The fire was past its peak now; in front of the door were a few new bodies, all badly burnt. Emma Cherry was not among them.

The Church had no further business here and the Dean Spiritual's group was preparing to head off. The Dean addressed Tobias, 'We can do no more here, Oakley. The Bishop will want to see us both after lunch for a full report; I expect to see you then, just draw off half of the retinue and you're free to go.'

'Thank you, Dean – but I think I'll stay here to supervise the burial detachment and crowd clearance. I want to see the job is properly done.'

'Very well, then – until this afternoon.'

Tobias turned and went back to the fire which was rapidly dying down now. Here death was everywhere and dominant, while life in the form of the crowd and retinue-men going for water was drifting away; and here Tobias felt at home.

CHAPTER 10
In which our hero's advance is checked.

'I asked to see you simply to say that you will not be ordained as a full priest this year.'

'I see . . . ' said Tobias slowly. 'Am I allowed to know why not?'

· 'It is a matter of readiness, Tobias,' said the Bishop. 'Now, I don't deny that you have proved yourself a very competent churchman. Indeed, the two Deans' reports and your examination results confirm that. Nor do I doubt your magical ability – I hear your degree papers were very enthusiastically received at Canterbury and various members of my staff testify to your practical skills in this field – so you may well ask, what is the problem?'

'Do you not think me a fit person to be a priest?'

'Precisely. Frankly Tobias, I do not. You were once and you will be again, but at the moment – no. I'm sorry, lad; perhaps it's through no fault of your own, but you're not ready.'

All of this was something of a bombshell to Tobias, for when he'd received the Bishop's summons that morning he had anticipated only a pleasant chat concerning the impending ordination ceremony. Now, in this familiar and friendly study he felt his future slipping through his fingers.

'Could you be more specific, Bishop? Also, what do you plan regarding the continuance of my vocation?'

'Your second question is easier to answer: I've arranged for you to spend a year at a monastery which is headed by an old colleague of mine. Under his guidance I hope you will find yourself again. At the end of that year, pending favourable reports, I will recommend your ordination, I promise you.'

A weight of indecision flew from Tobias' mind – so his ambition was not to be unrealised – merely postponed. Nothing, save time, was lost.

'So it's merely that you feel more time is required for me to reach the proper, considered condition for priesthood?'

'Not exactly, my son. Time, in part – yes, certainly; but mostly I want to place you in a situation that is conducive to good in the broadest sense of the word. I feel, having followed your training extremely closely, that the events of the last year or so are not those which I would choose for you to have in your mind as the initial influence for your future career.'

Tobias felt moved to protest at last. 'But my Lord Bishop, I really do feel that nothing in my duties or actions over the last years has affected me in any adverse way at all.'

'And that, my son, from your own mouth, is the reason why I have postponed your ordination.'

CHAPTER 11
In which our hero is given a new home and goes for a walk.

'And this, Brother, is where you'll sleep.'

'I see,' said Tobias. He did indeed – he saw a tiny cubicle of stone with a plank bed protruding from one wall. There was just enough space left for a tiny table and chair. The room was lit by a tiny window high up near the roof. What he would have liked to have said was, 'You must be joking.' But he was long used to making such honest comments only to himself. No cosy study and afternoon cups of tea here.

'Of course you'll only be here to sleep, morning and evenings will be occupied by religious observances and work; the afternoon, as you know, is your own and for that purpose we have decided to make the Abbey library free to you.'

'Yes, Brother; the Abbot more or less outlined the terms of my residence when I arrived.'

'Fine, fine, when you've settled in, come along to the refectory for a bite to eat. After that there's a sung mass at six-thirty.'

'Thank you.'

'Don't mention it, I hope you'll be happy in your stay here, Brother.'

Tobias declined to reply and the monk scuttled away into the bowels of the monastery. Unpacking took scarcely a blink for most of his possessions were in storage at Rugby. He had brought only a carpet-bag of luggage: books, writing materials and various priestly gowns.

This done, he sat down on the bench or bed and noticed several blankets and a chamber pot underneath it. Although it was May and the sun was bright outside, the stones of the cubicle seemed to radiate a chill of their own.

He would have liked to lay back, calm and contented, having reconciled himself to a year of quiet introspection and research, but such a mood was far away from him. Tobias sat, his elbows on his knees, and glowered at the opposite wall three feet away. Outside he could hear birdsong and the mysterious, uninterpreted noises of the monastery population at work; the window was too high to see through.

· In his imagination and his arrogance he pictured all the monks hurrying along the corridors and paths of this building, all of them anonymous and indistinguishable in their innocence and weakness, while he sat perfectly still in one little room, a pinpoint of contained power and energy. He was a wolf among sheep and for a while he would have to bleat and answer the shepherd's call like the rest: but the wolf would store his savage energies until his own good time.

This vision was of little immediate comfort to Tobias as he rose and went in search of a meal that was, he discovered, of characteristic frugality.

At first he threw himself without respite into his priestly and thaumaturgic studies, but in conjunction with the demanding monastic routine this made for an intolerably spartan existence. Tobias was unsure to what degree his afternoons were 'free' and, after a few weeks, bored beyond measure even with his beloved magic, he decided to put his liberty to the test.

One of the benefits of monastic life was that possessions, few as they were, could be left unattended and so he merely tidied up his library desk and resolutely strode out, leaving behind his notes and manuscripts neatly stacked.

The few monks present that afternoon, too old and infirm to work, looked up cautiously from their Bibles and works of devotion, saw that nothing dramatic was in the offing and resumed their half-slumber.

Outside in the cloisters, Tobias could see and feel the sun and he began to have vague inklings of returning life. But this was not enough; passing the few old monks shambling round the walk he came to the gatehouse and, via this, the outside world. No one challenged him or rushed to report his 'escape', although it had not missed the beady eye of the gate-keeper.

Like the feeling of release he had once felt on galloping out of Chichester, so now he felt instantly recharged. With no purpose at all (for once), he set off at a fast pace down the metalled roadway that joined the monastery of St John Wesley to the ancient main road between the somewhat less antiquarian towns of Royal Tunbridge Wells and East Grinstead.

For a hundred yards or so around the monastery the monks had cleared the undergrowth and felled the trees, but at the outer extent Ashdown Forest began again with man-made abruptness. Although Tobias was by upbringing a country lad, he had never had to harden his hands with serfish agriculture and a large, unmanaged forest was a novelty to him. He had seen some suggestion of its extent on the morning the stage-coach had delivered him. One road alone crossed it and settlement was sparse; hence, presumably, the monastic house.

He walked along the old Roman road for a while and peered into the forest. Wild, in the sense that it's left alone, he estimated, but probably not wild as in dangerous.

The South of England had long been the most prosperous and cultured part of the island. It was here antiquarians presumed that man first set foot in the isles sometime shortly before the Romans arrived. (For the Bible proved that the creation took place in 4004 BC and Adam's descendants therefore had little time in which to drift from Eden to this less idyllic land.) Tobias had always been taught, that refugees from the fall of Troy had first colonised Britain and he saw no reason to doubt it. And it was here, despite the coughs and splutters of impending industrialisation elsewhere, that most of the population was gathered. Accordingly, over the centuries those forces in the area inimical to man were gradually displaced and exterminated. Ashdown Forest might shelter a few wolves or boars, perhaps even a bear or two, but it was unlikely that anything more than a small nest of 'demi-demons' remained. In the nineteenth century, at papal command, vast numbers of yeomanry and armed citizens had combed the deep forests of civilised western Europe (thereby earning grace at a level deemed equal to crusading) and had dealt a heavy, if not mortal, blow to the forces of darkness, Nature's first-born. In the North and more primitive areas, however, it was a different story and in some parts control was contested with man on an equal basis.

Not in safe and civilised Sussex; even so, in memory of older times the monastery still maintained a store of weapons and armour; to the ungodly ones no other cheek would be turned.

At any rate, Tobias felt entirely at ease and after a while he decided to strike off the road and enter the forest proper. A convenient track offered itself for this purpose and he took it – presumably beaten by foresters, it wound on and on probably without objective. In a similar frame of mind Tobias followed. At both Southwark and Rugby there had always been tremendous demands on his time and energy as well as his own private commitments to pursue – a book to be read, a woman to be seen. Now, in his afternoons he could study or he could not; there were no alternatives to make him feel uneasy and guilty about inactivity. It was the bizarre and paradoxical freedom of the prison or asylum, but refreshing for all that. For the first time Tobias felt the faint stirrings of hope that there might be something to be gained from this year.

For a while his way dipped and was shaded despite the pruning which revealed that the path was obviously used on a regular basis. In the furrows muddy water collected, quite deeply in parts, and Tobias had to skirt the track completely; then suddenly he came upon a steep hill and puffed his way up it to find himself in a clearing created by the foresters. To one side, vast pyres of prepared timber were weathering or perhaps awaiting collection. In the centre the ground was uncommonly lumpy and Tobias supposed it betokened one of the old Roman iron-working sites which the monks assured him littered this area of the Weald.

He wondered whether the path carried on at the opposite side of the clearing and ambled over. It did not. Nevertheless his curiosity was rewarded by a beautiful view. On the far slope of the hill there must have been a quarry at some time or perhaps the ground just folded naturally. The dramatic depression in the slope meant that the trees on that side were sufficiently low to allow a panorama of the countryside below to be seen and Tobias could see back towards the road, a grey ribbon stretching left and right. Two houses were visible, set off the road in their own clearings and linked to the world of man by private tracks. There was no village or hamlet in these parts, not till Hartfield some four miles off where the woodsmen mostly lived. Such population as there was lived in lonely and often grandiose houses such as these two. Here the wealthy and the solitary were wont to retire. Tobias had been told there was an almost equal presence of elderly nobility and persons of evil reputation.

He could see no clues as to the occupants of the houses below him; one, the further, was a plain squat block of the type popular at the turn of the century – suitable both for defence and habitation. It looked empty.

The second house showed signs of life; what looked like ducks and chickens were wandering round in front of it, and several chimneys were smoking. The house itself was multi-period but contentedly so, time having reconciled the tastes of different centuries from the fortifications required in Reformation times to the more relaxed possibilities of the present. Once it had no doubt been set in extensive gardens painstakingly wrestled from the forest, but now only a small cultivated area was discernible; incipient jungle claimed the rest.

Still in an uncharacteristic mood of relaxation, Tobias lay on the ground, hands behind his head. Then it occurred to him that he still had his pipe and baccy pouch (a gift from Diane) in his gown pocket from the previous night. He filled and lit this and so his contentment was complete.

And when absolute quiet grew wearisome he amused himself by peopling the houses below. Alas, his imagination was such that generally some very dark and tragic speculations emerged.

In one was a venerable magician, a doctor of magic once of Oxford University, now shunned and mistrusted for his strangeness and unpredictable temper. Here alone he whiled away the lonely blank hours till death, devising more and more arcane spells, never to be used. Here he lay alone in bed, fearful, listening for taps at the window and creaks on the staircase and no natural fire ever cheered his house.

In the other lived a once-respected nobleman, now long fallen from court and Church favour and hopeless and bedridden – all dignity gone, he was attended at last only by his once-beautiful, consumptive daughter. Servants fled when money and prestige fled and so, alone, they lived, a burden of labour or guilt to each other, reduced to growing their own vegetables in what were once flower beds.

All of which was quite untrue, of course, and a terrible presumption to boot.

After a while he heard the monastery clock faintly striking four; there was plenty of time but he felt minded to get back. Unless any repercussions occurred that night concerning his jaunt, he knew he had established a certain degree of freedom. The afternoon had raised his hopes; if he knew he was free *not* to, he would devote himself to research more wholeheartedly, to his visions and ideals. To his destiny.

The ever-watchful gate-keeper saw him return and enter the library and he wondered (as did all the monks) just what it was that this personable and polite young magician had done wrong. A minor heretic probably, come to be straightened out; they had had a few such before. But the door-man was gloomy by nature and he leant back and mentally charged Tobias with horrible murder and the death of innocents.

CHAPTER 12
In which our hero's progress is described.

At a quarter to five in the morning, a horrified Tobias, although still deep in sleep, heard the monastery bell. In the fleeting irrationality of interrupted repose he would have given his talent away for another half hour's sleep but his body, obedient to habit, started to move and he rolled out of bed, his eyes still tightly closed. Getting up was like physical pain to him but once his feet were on the floor the battle was won again for one more day.

Dimly he saw a bowl on his table; he lumbered forward and plunged his face into the freezing water therein. The shock of this and the effort of containing a scream reminded him he was alive. Tiredness left him slowly to be replaced by a false glow of energy as his metabolism was deceived into believing it was daytime. From experience Tobias knew this would fade by mid-morning to be replaced by nausea and taut nervous energy. It was a miracle he had not killed someone yet.

He slid his gown over his head, strapped his boots on and combed his long hair into a semblance of order. This done he stood for a moment to compose himself and then grimly strode out of his cell.

Having a captive magician-priest meant that nearly all of the monks' ceremonies could be concelebrations and they eagerly seized the chance offered. It was as well Tobias had learnt his liturgy and observances so thoroughly at Rugby, for he seemed to spend many of his working hours using them.

He crossed the cloistered central square, negotiated lengthy corridors, and finally swept into the chapel annexe where several senior brothers were preparing the communion vessels. Through long practice they were wide awake and disgustingly cheerful despite the hour. Tobias' reply to their greeting was less than wholehearted. He numbly waited until everything was laid out and then purified the chalice, paten and corporals. Try as he might, he could not stop yawning even as he joined the procession out in the chapel where the congregation of monks were waiting for the first religious observance of their lengthy day.

The magician's rôle in a concelebration was largely a symbolic one; he only really came to the fore at the beginning, in the greeting, and again at the end during the dismissal. At this point in his life Tobias could have wished for a more active involvement for he lived in fear of relapsing into sleep and tumbling over the altar. In truth he wished he were not there at all since he doubted the necessity of displaying the might of the Church in its temporal guise to a horde of its firmest captives.

Even worse it was a sung mass and while Tobias had a deep and impressive voice in conversation, in song it turned into a grating rumble. He had learned to keep his responses moderately pitched and soft to avoid pained expressions from those nearby.

On that chill June morning Tobias thought that his one bit of useful research would be to ascertain if it were possible to sleep with one's eyes open.

'The Lord be with you'
'And also with you'

*

After four months at the monastery, early mornings were no longer so painful. One of the beauties of monastic life was that any demands it made were compensated by the allowances made for the weakness of the flesh. In this way five o'clock eucharist was mitigated by compulsory early-evening retiring. At first Tobias found nine o'clock bedtime irksome and unnatural but after a week he found it absolutely essential.

By August 1984 Tobias was beginning to find his feet and life had become less intolerable – hard it still was, but bearable. He was beginning to feel the benefits of a regime of regular hours, abstemious diet and little stress. To his surprise he found himself leaner, fitter and even happier. His waking life fell into three neat compartments: religion, work and free afternoons. The first was empty of meaning to Tobias but the ceremonies brought some comfort as a safe and unchanging routine. Work was arduous but beneficial. His free-time research was proceeding wonderfully; he could not know but the seeds of his future masters degree and Ph.D were sown and started to grow in that dry dusty library; he had probably covered more ground and coined more ideas in the last four months than in his entire last year at Rugby – no mean feat in itself.

Sometimes, however, he needed to clear his head and in this mood his feet took him into the forest. He rarely met anybody on these jaunts, an odd forester or tinker perhaps, but he did not seek company. A woodsman he'd encountered had spread the word of a wicked magician abroad in the woods and the other foresters, duly cautious, kept an eye out and therefore generally avoided him.

He found numerous obscure paths and slowly, bit by bit, parts of the forest became familiar to him. It was not love of Nature that particularly inspired him to walk so, although he found his surroundings pleasing and conducive to mental repose. Rather it was the lack of human company and therefore the lack of need to maintain reserve and to raise shields. Temporarily he could once again be the boy of some seventeen years ago: open, relaxed and careless. But these were only in the nature of holidays, a temporary indulgence. Back at prayer or work or study the same old mind still ticked away, restless and energetic. He was in no danger of losing sight of the real Tobias.

Very often he would return to the hilltop clearing he had

discovered on his first afternoon out. He found it an ideal place to smoke a quiet pipe, read, or simply gaze at the view. Piles of timber appeared and disappeared in between visits so the place was obviously frequented, but Tobias was never disturbed there.

It was in this way that Tobias passed his twenty-fourth summer and he was not discontent.

Every so often the Abbot called to see him or asked Tobias to come to his office. He was under no illusion about these interviews; they were by way of a progress assessment, the reports of which were doubtless despatched to Rugby. In his efforts to impress and deceive, Tobias was up against a problem, for the Abbot – the Bishop's friend – was no fool. Abbot Milne was a short wide man of obvious peasant stock and with all a peasant's cunning. Bright beady eyes behind a lumpish nose gave a predatory impression which even Tobias found disconcerting. He would have given much to know exactly what the Bishop of Rugby had said of him so as to ascertain what starting point the Abbot's opinions were founded upon. The man himself gave not even the vaguest indication of what he thought; he was all friendship and solicitous enquiry, but he engaged in verbal sword-play.

'I do hope your stay here is seeming beneficial, Curate.'

'Oh yes, Abbot. You have a beautiful setting here – it's a welcome change from city life.'

'I suppose your life in Rugby was something of a strain?'

'No more than to any other long-suffering townsperson – it had its compensations you know.'

'Of course. To be sure. Still, I've always felt a righteous life was just that mite harder in the hustle and bustle of a town.'

'I bow to your superior knowledge, Abbot.'

'We are most concerned that you do not become bored with our painfully slow way of life, Curate. I was wondering whether you'd like to pay a weekend visit back to Rugby – just to reassure yourself that life goes on y'know.'

'That's uncommonly kind of you, Abbot. I'm very tempted to accept but I've settled into the routine here and my work is going so well that I'm loath to leave it.'

'Oh dear . . . well, feel free to visit any other area if you wish. I was not trying to limit your movements.'

'Not at all, Abbot. Now my parents are passed on there's nowhere else that would attract me other than Rugby. I have many dear friends there but just at the moment I feel my time is most profitably spent here.'

'Just as you wish my boy, but I have some letters for you which your old Bishop has forwarded from Rugby.'

'Actually Abbot . . . '

'Two have the Waith family insignia – most exciting; you obviously moved in high circles, my boy. And there's one which seems to be from London, quite a bulky letter too.'

'I mean no disrespect, Abbot, but since I'm supposed to be in a year's retreat here I'd just as soon leave the letters until I move back into the world when their tidings would be more appropriate. If it was anything urgent I would have been told.'

'Oh. Well, that's most commendable, my boy. You're obviously very much into the spirit of things. _I_ can never resist reading my personal letters straightaway, but of course they get fewer as you get older. Anyway, I will put your correspondence in a bundle and keep it safe for your day of departure.'

'Thank you, Abbot.'

And so Tobias passed his ordeals of temptation and firmly told the Abbot to 'get thee behind me'. But he knew these were only the surface ripples of an implacable campaign which he was powerless to influence or subvert. An intellect too adroit and shrewd to be easily deceived was devoted to examining his state of mind and so all Tobias could do was maintain a front of such honest good as he could muster. Whether this would satisfy his examiners he could not say; he just had to hope so.

All of which was rather a pity because although Tobias quite liked the old Abbot, whom he associated in his mind with Mori and the Bishop, there would always be a barrier between them and Tobias had to forgo any idea of his usual easy-going relationship with authority.

In his heart of hearts he felt assured that if he did exactly what he was told for a year and subdued all but his most innocent inclinations, then the Church Universal would never dispense with the services of so valuable and talented a hireling.

And of course he was entirely right.

CHAPTER 13

In which our hero has a dream and meets a new friend.

For the third time in a week Tobias started from sleep and jerked into a sitting position in bed. He was sweating profusely despite the cold of his room. Wide awake, he slid out of the covers and placed his feet on the floor and his head in his hands. His teeth were bared because he was furious with himself.

When he had calmed somewhat he fumbled in the dark for his gown, from which he drew a box of matches. Striking one, he sought his pocket watch.

Ten past twelve.

The match slowly burned down and darkness returned. It would have been reasonably simple for him to produce a light spell giving some pallid illumination but a lighted window in the monastery would be unduly conspicuous at this hour.

The hours loomed long before him, for there was little prospect of further slumber that night and so instinctively he lit another match and searched for his pipe. Soon enough he was puffing away although without any contentment.

It had started about a month before, infrequent at first but growing stronger and more regular. In his dream he would be before the Avon Street chapel again. It was merrily ablaze and over the fiery bales at the door could be seen the puzzled and gentle face of James Cherry. After this the dream varied. Usually Tobias would fire his pistols again and again at the face, never missing and never reloading, with horrifying and bloody results – save that Cherry never fell but stood horribly and increasingly mutilated yet always recognisable. At other times two hits would knock the figure backwards, yet no sooner had Tobias reloaded than the apparition would reappear, miraculously restored and unwounded, and so the massacre would continue without alleviation. Even in his sleep a part of his mind knew this was but a dream yet this did not make it any the less horrible. It inspired in him a composite feeling of fear, sorrow, hate and sickness which increased as the dream prolonged itself. Until, at last, a point would come when he was catapulted into painful wakefulness.

For Tobias it was intolerable that he of all people should suffer from such a feeble commonplace as a recurrent dream. Here was something he couldn't rationalise away, something beyond the savage reach of his cold, heath-born mentality and he didn't know what to do. It meant acknowledging that, even now, he was not the master of his ship – a bitter pill.

Only when the pipe was dead and most of the horror had left did he slip back beneath his blanket and invoke the dozing trance learnt in his student days. It was a comfort but no substitute for sleep; the long day before him would be a severe trial.

When part of his researches had reached a particularly satisfactory point Tobias took the opportunity to have an afternoon off, partially to celebrate and partially to give his mind a rest.

It was a pleasant sunny day for a walk and because he was feeling energetic he decided to eschew the forest and walk straight along the road to the outskirts of East Grinstead, see the fabled city from afar and straightaway return. Perhaps that would tire him sufficiently to escape another dream-ridden night in favour of real slumber.

But Tobias was profoundly unimpressed by his view of the sedate, commercial town, rested twenty minutes and began the return journey. It came on to rain quite heavily, and so he quickened his pace; however, with such a long walk before him, he was destined to get soaked.

An hour later, completely drenched and in low spirits, he was drawing near the monastery when a covered pony-trap sped past him. As bad luck would have it, Tobias was passing a submerged rut in the road at the time and from this the trap's wheel sprayed him liberally with mud and cold water. Under this provocation even his famed self-control cracked and something reasonably incomprehensible was shouted to speed the vehicle on its way. However its way was not far since a few yards on the trap slowed and turned into a drive which Tobias in his damp misery had not noticed.

At the head of the drive it stopped and a face peered out from the side cover. A hand beckoned to him.

Tobias took three deep, calming breaths and then squelched his way to the trap.

The hand belonged to an old lady wrapped deeply in a cocoon of shawls and blankets. Beside her was the driver, a young ginger-headed man. Both looked at the muddy apparition before them with interest. The horse, impatient at being delayed in the rain, fretted and steamed.

'Good day, madam,' said Tobias.

'I am so sorry – I feared we would splash you when we passed, but it is so difficult to slow down on a rainy road, isn't it Ambrose?'

The driver nodded earnestly.

'I insist you join us, Father, and I will have your clothes dried – it is the very least I can do. I will be dining shortly; perhaps you would like to eat?'

At that moment Tobias felt very low and the immediate prospect of food and warmth was temptation beyond endurance.

'Ma'am, I would be most grateful; you are too kind.'

'Not at all, Father – now follow on in haste before you catch your death.'

Tobias stood back hastily as the trap lurched forward and thereby narrowly avoided another barrage of mud.

And so it was that in half an hour he was seated before a generous fire inside one of the two houses he had noted on his very first walk in the forest. Clad in servant's clothes and drinking mulled beer, he couldn't help but feel cheerful. But with returning normality came more mundane considerations.

'I'm much obliged to you ma'am, but I'm afraid the monastery expects me back for dinner; so, alas, I must decline your offer.'

Much had been sorted out in the last thirty minutes. The old lady was much older and feebler than her voice and his brief glimpse of her face had given him to suspect. A young dark-haired maid had been awaiting them at the door with the old lady's stick and had helped ensconce her in a high-backed chair before the fire. The frail old personage was then laden with yet more shawls and scarves. At least, this was what Tobias presumed for he had been led away by the coachman to a room where he divested himself of the sodden gown and put on a spare 'Sunday best' livery that smelt of mothballs.

Returning to the old lady and served with his hot drink, introductions were duly made and so he met Lady Susan Warrilow. He corrected the misunderstanding that he was a priest and explained his presence in the area; for good measure, before his returned gown made it all too clear he confessed his status as a magician.

Lady Susan fixed him with a quite remarkable gaze. Once, long ago, she had been beautiful and powerful, thought Tobias.

'How old are you, my boy?' she asked in a voice without the least hint of a quaver.

'Twenty-four, ma'am.'

'I see . . . I'm eighty next birthday.' She added this as an afterthought.

'Then you are to be congratulated, my lady.'

'Yes . . . yes, it's a fine old age but I feel a good few years in me yet.'

'I'm glad to hear that.'

'Thank you, Curate; they do say a priest's good wishes are worth any number of dedicated candles.'

'Well, begging your pardon, I'm afraid I must take issue with that view.'

'Good; so do I.'

Tobias had begun to take a liking to this tough old bird. 'I presume you church in East Grinstead, my lady,' he asked her.

'Sometimes my boy, but in my state not as often as I should perhaps.' She paused awhile. 'You're a priest as near as hang it – why don't you come and give me communion of a Sunday – eh?'

Tobias had to think quickly. 'But of course, madam, that's an excellent idea; I will ask my Abbot for permission this evening.'

'Good. It would save my poor old bones a bumpy cold journey every week and it would give poor Ambrose a Sunday lie-in; Lord knows he works hard enough around this place. Yes, it could be a Godsend meeting you, lad.'

'Perhaps God works even through the medium of flying mud, my lady.'

She smiled brightly.

'Well, we're told he moves in mysterious ways aren't we?'

Tobias smiled back.

'Indeed so.'

'Where were you trained? Rome, Avignon?'

'Southwark, ma'am.'

'A rough school so I've heard.'

'I think most of the stories are exaggerated.'

'Probably so; you don't seem the type that they would produce.'

'Thank you, ma'am.'

'But of course, I could be wrong', she added absentmindedly.

Tobias could not think of a rejoinder to this but none seemed expected so he remained quiet.

Emerging from her reverie, Lady Susan returned to the subject.

'There's not many magicians are trained in England are there?'

'Just at Southwark, Westminster and an establishment in Liverpool, so I'm told, ma'am.'

'And Glasgow.'

'Yes, there too, but that's Scotland of course. Forgive me for asking but are you interested in the magical arts? You don't seem to have the talent yourself.'

'No; it was once thought I had but they were wrong.'

'Just as well perhaps, my lady, I believe female magicians were not looked on with favour until recently.'

'There you're talking about the Church alone; I've always felt that magic is a feminine art.'

Tobias declined to pursue the matter any further lest he provoke the old lady to any serious heresy. Lady Susan perhaps saw that she was treading on thin ice and the matter was dropped. They talked on other subjects until the silent young maid entered the room with Tobias' gown, now dry.

'Ah, thank you, Amy,' said Lady Susan. 'Perhaps if you'll excuse me, Curate Oakley, I'll retire to take some food. You may change in here where it's warm, no one will disturb you. It may be that we shall see you again shortly in your religious capacity but in any case I insist you call again in what free time your vocation gives you. It is high time I got some value for my subscriptions and taxes to the Church.' With that, she hobbled out of the room, accompanied by the maid, and the door was closed.

Tobias quickly changed. His gown was warm and reasonably dry but heavily mudstained. As he was replacing his boots there was a gentle knock at the door and Ambrose the coachman entered.

'I've come to drive you home, sir.'

'Don't bother – it's only a few minutes walk.'

The servant looked momentarily pleased and then remembered something.

'It's still raining heavily, sir.'

'Oh – well, have you got an umbrella I can borrow?'

Mr Ambrose brightened again.

'Of course, sir.'

'Well, that's that settled then isn't it?'

Tobias walked with him into the dark and cavernous hall. Ambrose leaned into the shadows behind the great double door and reemerged bearing the promised umbrella. Then he struggled with the monstrous door-latch, a relic from the area's more lively past, until, at length, the way to the outer world was cleared.

The rain was slight but constant, sullenly set in for the night.

'Much obliged to you, sir,' said Ambrose. 'Thanks for saving me turning out.'

'What? . . . Oh, that's OK but as a favour try not to splash me next time or I'll have to burn you with magic.'

'Oh my God, no, please!'

'It's a joke Ambrose, just a joke.'

The servant mopped his brow, his eyes narrowing with something far from humour.

'Oh I see, sir, yes, very good, very droll.'

'Goodnight.'

'Goodnight, sir.'

Ambrose directly went to celebrate his survival with oblivion in what the Church called the curse of his class; scrumpy cider.

As he walked home through the dusk and drizzle, Tobias reflected that after all it had been a well-spent afternoon. His soaking apart, he had made a social connection, however tenuous, that might help him beguile away his monastery days. Beside which, Lady Warrilow was plainly from exalted stock and Tobias welcomed such contacts so that the remaining rough edges of his petty artisan upbringing might be smoothed off.

Just to be safe he would go and see Abbot Milne that evening and report his visit to the Warrilow abode in case the news reached him from other sources. At the same time he would seize the opportunity to put Lady Susan's request to the Abbot – two birds with one stone.

Of Tobias' days at St John Wesley monastery there was nothing the Abbot did not know. In between what he observed himself, learnt from others or was freely informed of by Tobias, there were no gaps or grey areas to fuel possible suspicion or existing prejudice.

Tobias felt sure he had little to fear but declined to relax his guard. He made rigorous orthodoxy and obedience the arbiters of his every waking action and allowed nothing to chance.

CHAPTER 14
In which our hero earns his doctorate.

All through the morning Tobias had felt that he was nearing a breakthrough, a feeling that made the regulated pace of the monastery seem interminable. All his free time in the last week, either in the library or sleepless in his cell, had been dedicated to work. Dinner was consumed with as much haste as seemed decent and he would then stride to the library where his books and notes had been left, neatly stacked, from the day before. By and by elderly monks would shuffle in to join him but this was a regular occurrence and disturbed him not at all.

He thought he had an answer to his debilitating insomnia. A spell to put others to sleep had long been a feature of many magicians' repertoire but so far as he knew no one had ever constructed a sleeping spell effective on the caster himself. It seemed a simple proposition but in fact the absence of such a useful conjuration arose from the fundamental nature of magic itself, practical thaumaturgy depending upon belief for effect. That is to say, if the magician's conscious mind did not have absolute faith in a spell it would fail.

Philosophers and erudite practitioners of magic found there was a hidden depth to this proposition. Few, very few, sorcerers could cast a spell to make themselves stronger, more attractive, resilient, or anything else the human mind might conceive as desirable.

Understandably the first magicians, of a thousand years ago and from out of the East, found this very disappointing for those were the very things they wanted most. Alas, the vast majority had to content themselves with spells that affected only other people and objects. It seemed as if self was the one point of material reality that magic could not render plastic.

This point naturally became the lynch-pin of several interesting new philosophical stances and heartened the few remaining solipsists in their hiding places.

Philosophy apart, the consensus of educated magical opinion took this to show that there was a part of the soul or mind that could not be reached by rational processes and which knew that magic was a mere figment of itself, that is, the magician's will. This seemed to cover the point nicely and, by and large, not being of a philosophical frame of mind, the magicians and their organisations left it there. Theologians, however, suffered from no such restraint. In man's resistance to his own magic, they said, lay the proof of faith, of obedience, of spirituality beyond taint of earthly corruption.

All of which, broadly speaking, may have been true, but there were exceptions.

Throughout the history of the profession there had been people who could reach into their own being and somehow convince it in its entirety that nothing at all was true and unchangeable, not even itself. If this could be done on a regular basis then self-inflicted magic was practicable. Such people often accordingly became leading lights of their trade and aspired to high places.

It is not surprising, then, that such a possibility had captured Tobias' imagination at a very early point in his studies, in Southwark in fact. He had compulsively read what little literature was available on the subject, and had initiated a programme of experiments which had entirely and completely failed. In all probability nearly every apprentice and journeyman undertook the same experience in their youth and, faced with absolutely no prospect of success, gave up. Later on they were taught a few charms and power-words that could calm the mind and body but these were mere clever catechisms and not magical at all.

And so the matter rested, until Tobias took the subject up again in his second year at Rugby. Here he compiled fuller notes and in a purely academic sense made some progress because of the excellent reference collections available to him. However, at length, the more rewarding and practical field of demonology drew him away and once more he conceded defeat.

Such was the measure of his lack of success that the matter would have rested for ever if pressing need had not impelled him to act.

He felt that he could not go on very much longer without sleep. He was not a weak man but his stamina and endurance was not unlimited – the monastic routine was quite demanding. Yet he could not ask the Abbot for a sleeping draught or the aid of a magician since this would be fatal to the settled and untroubled image he had to maintain at all costs.

Only one solution, save blind fortune, presented itself: the physician had to heal himself and so the research project began anew.

He had brought his notes with him and several of his magical tomes might be relevant; the monastic library, however, was next to useless for it was designed for a very different type of reader. Still, it was a convenient place to work.

His research had at least progressed to the point where he was clear as to the objective. He had devised a statement, or formula of intent, in the magical algebraic notation taught in Christendom which seemed logical and self-consistent. In ordinary circumstances this and a power-word were all that was needed to construct a spell for a competent sorcerer.

In this case, however, he was beyond the bounds of conventional magical practice and its strictures did not necessarily apply. As an experiment he flicked the embryonic spell through his mind and, as expected, nothing happened. The same had been true yesterday when he had finally completed it but there was no harm in trying again.

And there most researchers left it, for many had reached this same level of progress; but today Tobias had thought of a new approach. During the early morning hours of reading, in despair he decided to abandon such work as he had done and look at the problem as if it were new to him. At the time this revealed no fresh insights and he saw the impasse to which he, like all his predecessors, had come. But then, as so often happens, the answer came to him unbidden, as if from an exterior source, when he was piling timber in the monastery workshop. He had convinced himself that his magic was a reality, a physical force like gravity; that was why it worked. The task was not to try and further convince the sceptical, unreachable part of his mind, rather it was to undermine this scepticism. If he was to introduce further doubt and suspicion, might not the stubborn core of disbelief be induced to doubt even itself? Such was the metaphysical formula that Tobias deemed worthy of experimentation. Furthermore he felt he might just be particularly qualified to pursue this approach. Chasing the idea round and round his mind all morning when he should have been concentrating on prayer or ceremony, he had let his eagerness and hope grow.

Sitting in the library, he collected his rough ideas together. Essentially what he proposed was a sustained assault on his ego and his natural grip of reality; a course of action fraught with apparent dangers. To do it he need do no more than call to mind those times in the past when that great numbness and cold, his 'nothingness', settled upon his soul; in the grip of which, everything was meaningless and therefore permissible and which thus served as a perfect tool for the purpose in hand. In the back of his mind he was loath to descend into the icy fog but he was possessed and persuaded by the possible rewards. The precise recollection and holding of emotional states was the very cornerstone of the magical arts (in this it was akin to poetry) and so he envisaged no difficulty in producing the required passions. The more he sat and silently considered, the more he excitedly felt that – just perhaps – experience had provided him with the key to a rusty and disused lock.

At Southwark he had been taught to induce a slight contemplative trance suitable for deep or difficult thought. By now, with frequent use, they had an almost magical effect on him: it was with these he wiled away his insomniac hours. Now he would employ one to enforce his inner campaign of disbelief.

He jotted down a simple notation of the mood that he required so that it could easily be held in his mind. Then Tobias arranged himself comfortably on his chair, invoked his mood of unworried despair, and passed into a twilight reverie.

None of the sleepy or studious monks also in the library noticed the young magician and his inactivity. By now they were used to his presence, his long silences and sudden movements. Yet when dinner at last came around, the last old man filing out realised that their visitor was still seated at his desk, eyes fixed and glassy on the book before him. He crossed over to the table, mildly alarmed that his approach evoked no response at all, and shook Tobias by the shoulder.

Tobias started awake and stared at the monk who fell back a pace, deeply shocked by the look of limitless despondency and hatred he could see in Oakley's eyes. The old man had been in Holy Orders since youth and the force of evil was known to him only by repute. At that moment he felt himself in its presence. It was a disconcerting experience.

But the moment passed so quickly it was difficult to believe it had happened, for Tobias recovered himself immediately and was his normal imperturbable self again.

'Time for dinner is it, Brother? Thank you for reminding me; I was quite lost in thought there.'

The monk eyed him suspiciously for a moment and then

recovered his manners. 'Not at all Curate, please don't mention it.'
He turned and hurried out of the room with much to think about.

Tobias had forgotten him already. He tried the spell again.
Nothing. It was still mere lifeless words.

Somewhat sickened by his long dark reverie but still undaunted,
he proceeded to dinner.

The measure of his determination was such that he felt impelled to
ask Abbot Milne for temporary release from his work and most
religious observances, pleading a need for prolonged and sustained
meditation over the next few days.

Pleased at this show of enthusiasm and motivation, Abbot Milne
freely granted his charge three days 'retreat' as he termed it.

Tobias studied him closely as he did so for signs of doubt or
suspicion but he could detect none and therefore felt his gamble had
paid off.

And so day after day after day Tobias sat in the library (it was too
cold in his cubicle). A simple learning device taught to all
magicians formed a reliable alarm clock to rouse him at meal times
and at the end of the day. While the bulk of his mind wrestled to
grasp nothingness, one small part alertly watched a stone tower
slowly succumb to the powers of time and ivy. It tumbled brick by
brick until only a shapeless pile of rubble remained at which point
Tobias would 'awaken'. The speed of its decline could be exactly
judged and so formed an excellent clock. The image was, of course,
a purely personal one. At Southwark his fellow journeyman,
Skillit, once confided to him that he used the vision of a nun
disrobing; perhaps this was so, for each individual had to utilise
that which he found most evocative.

Tobias had no measure to tell how well his work was going but he
knew that he was, at last, on the right lines. Of course it was a sickly
and debilitating thing to court insanity and he found the only
release from the aftermath was sleep. Fortunately his repose
chanced to be relatively undisturbed during his retreat.

And so, somewhat haggard and pale, he came to the end of his
third day of meditation. During that time he had disciplined
himself to forgo a premature attempt at the spell itself. Now at five
o'clock on a dark November evening the attempt would have to be
made. He could not risk asking the Abbot for further time and he
could not face the self-inflicted pain very much longer.

To avoid procrastination and thus a loss of mood he immediately ran the spell notation through his mind. In an inexplicable way it joined, matched and merged with the nuance of emotion he had been exploring and the two became something more than their sum. Tobias could not explain how or why this was so, or how he *knew* that magic had just been created; it was simply undeniable.

No immediate joy awoke in him for he had travelled too long in the shadow of oblivion just recently. All the same a faint glow of triumph made its presence felt. He knew, now, that come what may he would go far in his chosen profession because, due to fortune and an unsuspected ability, he had succeeded where almost all had failed. In the time it took the library clock to strike five he had gained his Ph.D. The spell would work!

He prepared the sleeping spell he had been taught, set his tower to tumble in ten minutes and placed the spell on himself. With a little resistance the mind accepted its reality and Tobias gently slid forward on to the desk.

When he woke precisely ten minutes later he found himself in somewhat different circumstances. Two of the younger monks were carrying him rapidly through the corridors of the monastery. Their faces carried expressions of concern. Behind them Tobias could just see from his undignified position an elderly monk hurrying along in equal perplexity.

Tobias let them know, in a voice of thunder, that he was *compos mentis* and felt much put upon. He was gently lowered to the cold floor.

Dignity and feet regained, he was told what had happened.

His experiment's timing had been bad. When Tobias was missed at dinner, a messenger had been despatched; he had found a coma-victim and, much alarmed, enlisted help to bear the casualty to the infirmary.

At any other time Tobias would have been amused but after his ordeal he felt drained and lacked humour. The monks were all solicitude.

'Bless me, Curate, but for the life of me I thought you were dying.'

'Are you well, Brother? Should you be standing?' And so on.

Tobias started an explanation of his admittedly bizarre behaviour, but rapidly appreciated that a credible explanation was beyond his powers of invention.

'. . . merely an unusually deep trance, Brothers; nothing to be concerned about, but thank you very much for your prompt charity.'

Nobody was convinced. The monks drifted away puzzled and disturbed, and the wealth of 'Curate Oakley and his strangeness' stories received a further handsome endowment.

Tobias was fully aware of this and another diplomatic visit to the Abbot was called for.

CHAPTER 15

In which our hero is very ill and reads the 'Book of Ecclesiastes'.

Waking for early mass the following morning Tobias began to have some inkling of the measure of his achievement. He checked and in some instinctive way *knew* that the potential for the spell was still there and permanently fixed into his experience. Once learnt, like any other skill, a spell was very hard to lose.

Getting up, however, knocked some of the ebullience out of him. His joints were stiff; he felt burnt out and weariness was gnawing at him.

Not tonight though; tonight he would have hour after hour of luxurious uninterrupted sleep. This would be but the first of the many and varied prizes that his discovery would bring him. But it was a prize, the presentation of which he barely survived.

Retiring at the normal hour of nine-thirty p.m., he set himself a six-hour 'tower'. That would give him a margin of time before breakfast in which to consider the experiment's result. Then he placed himself to sleep.

What followed was probably the very worst night of his life. Sometime not long after his artificial dropping-off, the nightmare started and Tobias went through his paces again and again. At length he reached a point where his alarm and distress were such that he would have woken up. However the tower was still some two-thirds complete and accordingly there was no such escape. A part of his awareness knew that he was trapped in a mere dream but self-imposed iron bonds firmly held him and the agony continued and continued.

Time has little meaning in the confines of sleep and dreams and

Tobias endured an infinity of discomfort. Somehow he knew it would have an end and at first that was comforting but then as whole epochs seemed to pass and waking memory faded, he ceased to believe in any form of existence other than his current tribulation. Again a part of him knew he was sweating profusely and writhing wildly but that was in a physical world remembered only dimly.

His shrieks at length roused the monastery but neither the Abbot nor Physician brother could do anything to allay his torture. Unbeknown to Tobias a sad and solemn exorcism service was held over him that night but to no immediate avail.

And then his resistance ended and his eyes opened much to the delight of the monks who were in vigil at his bedside. However this release brought little relief for, sorely damaged, he lay speechless and with dulled eyes. The soup which they gave him he vomited out immediately. Only when one of the monks made to leave the room did he show any sign of life for Tobias had no wish to be left alone with his imaginings at that moment. Thereafter it was arranged that the room remained crowded and a light shone in it throughout the dark hours.

And in this manner Tobias celebrated his entry into the higher ranks of practising magicians in Christendom.

Recovery was slow and for days he lay in a stupor. His condition was not so bad as it outwardly appeared to the monks, however, for a day or so after his ordeal Tobias gathered enough strength to push his mind into the meditation trance and there he rested, regathering his personality and energy. To inform the monks of his partial recovery would have been to dissipate vital resources and so he remained recumbent and passive. The one positive development was that, perhaps burnt out by dreadful repetition, the dream did not return. He was rid of that particular demon at least.

After four days he was sure of his identity again, his soul once more well back from the dark edge to which it had been dragged. Eventually he opened his eyes and in a hoarse voice announced his return to the world of man.

Several days on from that, fully himself again, up, dressed and active he had a very difficult interview with the Abbot in an attempt to explain away what had passed. Tobias had long observed that all the best lies used a plating of truth and he thus pleaded an unusually appalling dream. He then hinted at grim secrets learnt in selfless service of the Church. Milne was most understanding but at their meeting's end remained suspicious. This young man was the most worrying and opaque character he had had to deal with in all his long years of handling the lives of the Church's chosen. He had not ruled out demonic possession and pondered at length as to whether his exorcism had taken. In the succeeding week he fired off salvos of letters to those of his contacts who might be able to help in his assessment. Their replies brought him little comfort for their opinions were almost equally divided.

And so the matter dragged on until at length and quite reluctantly, Abbot Milne was obliged to give Tobias the benefit of the doubt.

Meanwhile, feeling the power of increased scrutiny upon him, Tobias buried himself in religious duty so that not even the most critical of judges might find any fault. But all the time, despite the initial setback his mind was bubbling with excitement at the new vistas before him.

The way ahead was clearer than ever before, now brightly illuminated by the torch of abnormal ability that he bore. Yet even this light could not reveal the end of the road.

All of which was a far cry from Tobias' humble occupation on Christmas Eve in the year of our Lord 1984 when he, along with two other monks, was seated in the refectory kitchen peeling a mountain of potatoes in preparation for the morrow's dinner.

The last few weeks of recovered health had served him well and his physical and mental strength were now back to their normal level. He had conserved himself and had therefore done little in the way of research, and had curtailed his jaunts outside the monastery. Such efforts as he had expended had been directed at re-establishing himself in the eyes of the monastic community. To some extent this had been successful and whispers of the possessed magician had diminished and lost their initial power.

At any rate on this day of festival with the snow falling lightly outside, Tobias felt inclined to be expansive and thought he might serve the cause of his reputation's rehabilitation by conversation with his workmates.

He knew them vaguely by sight but this was the first time that duties had thrown them together. Both were considerably older than he and, having nothing else to go on, Tobias selected the least taciturn-looking to make his opening. He leaned forward and briefly eyed his prey before starting.

'It looks as if we'll be some time,' he gestured vaguely in the direction of the potato pile.

The monk looked round in mild surprise. Tobias had made the wrong choice; he could see no intelligence behind those eyes.

'That's true,' the monk replied.

Tobias turned with hope to the other peeler seated to his right.

'Still, I find repetitious work only occupies a small part of the mind after a while and thereon your thoughts are free, is that not so?'

Monk number one got in first, however. 'Most true, Curate – so long as my work doesn't suffer I call to mind the psalms in number order. I'm trying to learn them by heart you know.'

'Really? How interesting.' Tobias tried to look fascinated.

'It's taken me many years, eight to be precise. That's as long as I've been here.'

'How far have you got?' Tobias was mildly curious.

'Number Twenty-three; my memory is rather poor but I can remember bits of the rest.'

'How singular.' In case that had sounded a little acidic, Tobias hurried to redress the impression. 'What about you, Brother: to where does your mind wander?'

The second monk turned his head slowly to regard the magician. He had a lined and expressionless face. 'Nowhere in particular, Curate: I find even potato peeling can take up all my attention if I so wish.'

'You so wish?' said Tobias brightly.

'Oh yes, most definitely, I try to bring all of myself to everything I do however small and insignificant.'

'Even potatoes?'

'Even potatoes.'

The psalm-learning monk was edging to enter the conversation but couldn't quite think of the method.

'What on earth for?' said Tobias. He was quite curious; the tired looking monk had spoken with a voice of intelligence and education. His answers seemed to be the tip of an interesting iceberg.

'Well,' said the monk slowly, 'I don't want to sound fatuous, and forgive me if I do, but the answer to your question is "Why not"? Potato peeling is an honourable and valuable task and not fit to be despised.'

Tobias was intrigued. 'Valuable certainly, I'd not dispute that. But outside the context of this monastery, it would hardly be a fit occupation for a gentleman of your evident breeding and education.'

The monk smiled gravely. 'Thank you for your compliment, Curate; I must concur with your comment but I think that is the outside world's mistake and not ours.'

The psalm-learning monk saw the opportunity for his entry to this interesting conversation, saying, 'Brother McCrone was at Oxford and was set to be a fine lawyer before he heard the higher call; is that not so, Brother?'

'All true, Brother,' he replied.

'In what way do you feel this to be the higher call?' Tobias had hardly uttered the last syllable before he realised what a faux pas he had committed.

Brother McCrone turned to face him with the faintest element of surprise in his eyes. 'But surely you already know the answer to that one, Curate?'

Tobias thought on his feet and regrouped quickly before he did his reputation more harm than good. 'Well naturally, Brother; I just thought it would be interesting to hear your assessment of the vocational call.'

'It is that state of mind which allows me to think nothing of the outside world's vanities and clamour and, hard as it may be to believe, a gift that allows me to see God's service in preparing a humble vegetable.'

McCrone was not actively participating in the process of argument, his statements were issued, calm and definite, from an inner stillness that could not be whipped into storm by Tobias.

All of which was dragging from cover, bit by bit, the arbitrary intemperance which Tobias kept from view. 'In my particular field of service to the Church, and thereby the Almighty,' he said, 'much emphasis is placed on good works, although not at the same time discounting faith. Given this, we also perceive that the greater the developed talent, the greater the range of good works possible. In my humble estimation an Oxford-trained lawyer could have a great capacity for the propagation of good abroad in the secular world, Lord knows there's enough that do the opposite; and yet you tell me there's greater right in bequeathing your talents to the kitchen tasks which any scullion might do. I don't see it, Brother; I just don't see it.'

'The Son of the Lord Himself did such things; he did not shirk the humblest tasks.'

'But, thanks be, he did not make them his career.'

Once again the monk turned to face the proto-priest but his busy hands did not cease for a moment. His voice was heavy with weariness.

'Read *Ecclesiastes*, my friend. It succinctly deflates all the worldly vanities which you so admire. That is all I can say to you.'

To this Tobias had nothing to say and with all Christmas spirit defeated, he turned his attention to his task in order to dissipate his anger.

That night, as the monastery clock chimed in Christmas Day, Tobias read as McCrone had suggested and thus perceived the basis of the monk's detachment. It was his second reading since Tobias had, some time ago, made it a point to read through the Bible from cover to cover. However, it became apparent that on the first occasion his concentration had gone amiss and the words of the Prophet had not registered at all.

Now, on this day of festivity, Tobias had to admit that the writing was of some philosophical merit but found the reasoning therein was characteristically at fault. Whether McCrone took his opinions from *Ecclesiastes* or found that his own experiences or opinions concurred with it, was immaterial; either way he was misinformed and deluded. Tobias was cynical in many ways but had a naïve and passionate trust in temporal power which it would take more than a defeated lawyer and ancient writings to dispel. Far more convincing teachers had shown Curate Oakley what was vanity or not.

He decided to retire for a few hours before the first service at which his presence was required and as he lay down his empty, cold head, the strains of Midnight Mass still in progress wafted on the night air as a soothing lullaby. That night, contrary to custom, he slept well.

CHAPTER 16
In which our hero hears an interesting confession.

Tobias had been as good as his word and had sought the Abbot's permission to take the blessed sacraments to Lady Susan Warrilow and this was gladly given. Having had much practice, the Curate was swift and adept in his duties and there was considerable time to talk and dally without being away overlong and thus arousing suspicion.

He came to respect the old lady's active mind which belied her spent body. On occasion, when he had given her communion, lively discussions would arise and sherry, wine and wafers would be served by the ubiquitous and silent Amy. He came to look forward to these little holidays and increased their frequency from occasional to regular weekly events thereby presumably earning Ambrose his much-needed lie-a-beds.

On one particular Sunday morning in May 1985, a week or so after his birthday, Tobias was called upon to perform another religious function. He always thought that Lady Susan treated his spiritual ministrations in a decidedly off-hand way but among the ranks of the laity this was not entirely uncommon and he did not think it of any great moment. That morning was no exception and he obligingly jollied the ceremony along so as not to impose unduly on his fidgety congregation's patience. Once done, they repaired to the main living-room (with due respect to propriety, communion was given in the tiny chapel constructed in a usually shut-down wing of the house), and Amy armed Lady Susan into her high-backed chair beside the roaring blaze. When the maid had left and Tobias was settled comfortably on an ancient chaise longue, the old woman fixed him with a gaze of quite startling intensity and spoke in a voice as clear as a bell.

'Why do you think I have you come here, Curate?'

'Well, madam, to . . . '

'None of your false prattle, Oakley – I can see you through and through to the very core; or lack of it should I say.'

'I'm sorry, ma'am, I don't know to what you refer or what you wish to hear.'

'Please, Curate – Tobias – on this one occasion give an honest opinion, I beg of you.'

He regarded her coolly, quickly checking back through his past impressions of her to see if he could remain one step ahead of whatever revelation was to come. 'OK . . . I'll be honest, I've no real idea why you have me come here to celebrate communion. For the benefit of your soul?'

'To send me to my Maker in peace.'

'Confession?'

'Just so, my dear Tobias, and you're just the man for the job.'

'But why all this melodrama? You must know that as a magician-priest at my present level of training, I am empowered to hear confessions just as I am allowed to celebrate communion.'

'Of course. What I meant was that you are precisely the man to hear this particular confession.'

'Why?'

'Because with almost any other priest what I am going to tell you would bring my life to a premature close.'

'I am curious to know what makes me special, ma'am.'

'You're nearly empty, boy; you were full once but it's all been syphoned out and now you're a husk. There's not an ounce of religion in you, so anything I might say won't worry you an iota.'

'My lady, I don't feel I deserve this — '

'Oh hush,' she interrupted, 'do you take me for such a booby as not to see you for what you are? Calm down. I mean no insult – in fact I know you well enough to realise that you're secretly flattered by my description – is that not so?'

Tobias casually shrugged his shoulders.

'Anyway,' Lady Warrilow continued, 'I think I know how you came to this pass so I attach little blame and Lord knows I'm hardly one to judge. The existence of a priest of your type serves my purpose.'

'So you wish me to hear your confession since I'm not likely to be shocked or outraged.'

'And thus report it to your superiors – and please don't foul your mouth with lies about the sanctity of the sacrament of confession because I'm knowledgeable and cynical enough to know better.'

'In the light of these opinions one wonders why you feel the need for the remission of your sins, my lady.'

'Because, my boy, I'm old and where once I was strong I'm not any more, and where once I didn't care now I'm fearful.'

Tobias leaned back and outwardly relaxed..

Lady Susan smiled and narrowed her weary eyes. 'Oh Oakley, there you sit all smug and unconcerned but just you wait till you're old, feeble and friendless – *as you will be* – and then you'll lie awake at night waiting for the last breath. By God, I warrant you'll be clinging on to the last useless remnants of your earthly span with a desperation born of fear. And that's just if there is nothing to come after. If what you preach is *true*, then you and I should be doubly frightened.'

'My lady, what on earth can you have done to bear such pain of conscience?'

'Conscience has nothing to do with it. Like you I had it once and like you I was instructed to leave it behind. So you must accept fear as my motive for repentance. You will hear my confession and keep it safe?'

'I will.'

'Praise be. Y'know, Tobias, you and I are very close versions of the same story. I'm right in saying you're elf-trained?'

'That's correct.'

'I thought so from the first hour of our first meeting. You have their mark on you; not so clear as might be, but good enough to bind you. I never had much dealings with elves, although I was present at meetings with them once or twice. The teaching was that they were our temporary but untrustworthy allies, not held in the same eternal esteem as the Master holds for us.'

'I *see*,' said Tobias. 'The inverted Church – is that it?'

'What else, Curate Oakley, a good enough sin as they go and quite sufficient to propel even such an honoured and venerable old lady as I to the stake.' Her mind wandered. 'Hard masters the elves would be, I imagine, as hard as ours were.'

'Doubtless.'

'And they've done well with you – you must be very useful.'

'Alas no; I go my own way by and large.'

Lady Susan smiled indulgently at him. 'At any rate *I* was useful, very useful, and in my prime I could have broken you, Tobias. Here, touch my fingertips.'

He got up and stepped forward to do so. The minute their fingers touched, he jerked back and then shook his hand vigorously.

'My lady, I must bow to your appraisal of our relative talents. Do you have some kind of shielding spell?'

'Of course – you didn't even know I had the talent did you?'

'No, I didn't.'

'Well that's no shame on you as I've had long years and much need to perfect deception. I daresay now, abandoned by my colleagues as I am, that you could kill me in duel.'

'Yes, I think so.'

'But that's all gone now, even if I can't forget it. I'm alone and final obliteration is very close.'

'Where is your Church, my lady?'

'My dear Curate, our Church has no time for passengers and old invalids.'

'Doesn't that anger you?'

She gazed at him with real animation in her eyes.

'But that's how it *should* be; it's entirely right and justifiable.'

'Even when it's you that is cast off?'

'Like your Church, ours teaches that the individual is as nothing to the pursuit of the greater aim; it's just that *we* really believe and practise it.'

Tobias pondered this a little, then nodded his head. 'Yes, I can see that.'

'. . . and yet at this late stage I have doubts. I've lived too much in the supernatural and amassed a lot of information and it seems to me that *perhaps* you're right and we were wrong.'

'You mean the balance of power and the final victory?'

'Yes.'

'I find that very interesting.'

'I only said *perhaps*.'

'It seems to me that I come out all right either way – either my calling or my behaviour saves me.'

'You jest at this serious juncture in my life; but never fear – you'll survive and prosper. But I can see as clear as spring water that you'll end as I have, except that you're a mite more strong-minded and stubborn than I so the outcome might be different.'

'Is this use of talent or reasoned guesswork?'

'Talent.'

'I see. I will store it in my memory; thank you.'

'Don't mention it, boy. And now I've prattled enough – will you do me this favour?'

'Yes.'

And so the ancient penitent levered herself out of her chair and tottered across the room. Tobias placed a kneeling stool in the centre of the chamber and helped Lady Susan on to it.

And thus as a light shower pattered at the window outside, the faithless priest prepared to hear the last and crucial testimony of the believing diabolist.

Tobias made the sign of the Cross and Lady Susan followed.

'In the name of the Father, the Son and the Holy Ghost, Amen.'

The old lady bowed her head and sent her memory down nearly sixty years of active iniquity.

'Bless me Father for I have sinned . . . '

CHAPTER 17
In which our hero mixes with the nobility.

Prolonged exposure to benevolent and uncompetitive society was a disconcerting experience for Tobias. Since his entire outlook was based on something completely alien to it, he had begun to feel something akin to a tool without use or function. A few years before, such beneficial monastic incarceration might, given time, have awoken seeds of goodwill and charity in him. Alas the soil was now sterile and any good influence merely served to puzzle and discomfit.

However, from time to time intimations of normality drifted in from the outside world, over the monastery wall and into Tobias' daily round. They were few enough in number but sufficient to convince him of an outer reality where all was well and as it should be. Quite clearly his present abode was the oddity, the unrealistic mirage.

Lady Susan Warilow had been one such zephyr. Another, instead of drifting in, rode quite openly through the gates.

Part of the monastery's rôle and an occasional source of revenue to it, was the provision of overnight shelter to travellers, rich and poor alike (although the degree of service might vary accordingly), who found themselves on its lonely road between two towns at nightfall.

Only a month or so before Tobias' anticipated departure, the monastery was obliged to receive its most exalted guest for many a long year.

Curate Oakley had not noticed any arrival but on making his way to Vespers he observed a large travelling coach, minus its team, parked beside the diminutive monastery stables. Looking closer he saw a noble but unfamiliar coat of arms painted on the door. His curiosity was mildly aroused but the caution within which he had deliberately cloaked himself during his year of trial precluded further direct enquiry. The matter was soon forgotten in the complexities of the ceremony in which he was obliged to serve.

After the service, however, when he was reading and making notes from a missal in the monks' common room a messenger sought him out and conducted him to the Abbot.

'Curate Oakley, would you be so good as to oblige me in a small matter?' It was a perfunctory request requiring no answer.

'Our guest for the night requires company and speech. I'd be grateful if you'd go along and entertain him as best you can.'

'I'd be glad to oblige, Abbot.'

'Good. It's Baron Philby, Arthur Polybius Philby. From the Canterbury region I believe, or at least that's where his family lands are. I seem to remember, however, him mentioning a long period spent abroad – I had little speech with him,' the Abbot said by way of explanation.

'Judge for yourself, but I think you'll see why I chose you for this rather than one of our more scholarly brothers. Doubtless he'll be fascinated by your particular vocation.'

'I'll endeavour to amuse and distract him, Abbot.'

'Fine, be about it then – oh and by the way, come and see me when you leave him.'

'Regardless of the hour?'

'Whatever time it is.'

Arrayed in his full priest-thaumaturge gown bearing both the marks of Rome and Southwark, Tobias entered the guests' wing at about a quarter past eight. The air was unseasonably close and clammy that evening and not for the first time he was minded to flout Church fashion and wear his hair short in the monkish way; for it was too hot and the vanity that prompted his preenings at Southwark had ebbed away. Besides which he was prematurely thinning on top anyway.

He walked quietly to the door of the best guest-suite and listened for a moment or two. No noise at all. A last-moment adjustment in dress and then three loud knocks.

A voice that could only be described as 'fruity' or 'juicy' made some noise within and so Tobias entered.

Behind a large table a man was sitting and Tobias made a low bow to him. A lifetime of profound shocks and surprises, the occupational hazard of a magician, allowed his face and eyes to remain neutral and blandly normal as he rose.

The fruity voice said, 'Oakley, I'm obliged to you for your company. I damned well thought I would die of the tedium – you won't let me down will you?'

'Not so far as it lies within my powers, my Lord.'

Baron Philby paused a breath and studied Tobias before drawling, 'Yes, just so. Sit man, and take a drink.'

Tobias was given a balloon glass and the baron tipped into this a more than generous quantity of the venerable brandy which he had beside him. It was thick and treacly and not at all to Tobias' taste; however, he supposed it to be a highly valued product and thus to be respected.

The voice, which Tobias suddenly compared with this rich syrupy liquid, said, 'And these are my two nieces.' A white-gloved hand was waved imperially at one wall where Tobias now saw two little girls were seated on a low bench. He doubted they were more than ten or twelve years old; both were very pretty and dressed in the height of fussy childish fashion. They looked precocious but incurious.

The baron, speaking again, drew Tobias' attention back.

'Lovely, aren't they, unripened fruit y' might say, my sister's children; she died of the flux, or pox more like it, in Italy last year.'

Tobias nodded in acknowledgement.

'I expect you wonder why I wear this,' said Philby delicately touching the purple velvet operatic-style mask that covered his face from mouth to forehead. The bright lights of his eyes shone from two slits hemmed with a yellow cotton design.

'It had crossed my mind, my lord.'

Philby turned to the girls. 'Shall we tell him, pets? Yes, why not; you tell him Poppea.'

It occurred to Tobias that the baron was already far gone in drink but carrying it particularly well. Only a very few signs betokened his state.

One of the girls rose from her supine state. 'The baron caught an awful disease in Italy, in a big town. It pocked his face awfully so he wears a mask.'

The girl's accent was very far from what Tobias had expected from the progeny of a baron's sister. It was more like artisan London, he thought.

'And so,' the baron announced in a triumphant tone, 'the ravages of Mother Nature oblige me to don this little protector – protector, that is, of my vanity and the public sensitivities.'

'Misfortune is no respecter of birth. Does it become easier to bear as time goes on?'

'Not really,' replied the baron, 'but I've always felt it my destiny, or some such claptrap, to be marked out in some way; *marked* out, d'you see, Curate, *marked* – a joke.'

Neither party laughed, however, The baron leaned back in his chair and replenished his glass. He was a stocky, heavily built man of perhaps forty years. He was also dressed in what Tobias presumed to be the current Italian fashion with (he thought) absurdly exaggerated shoulders, lapels, cuffs and collar. Above the half-ludicrous, half-sinister mask, his hair was thick and black and curly. For all his size he did not give any impression of strength but sat with a graceless sense of bulk.

Silence reigned for a while but this never worried Tobias and perhaps perceiving this, the baron (as in strict etiquette was his prerogative) initiated conversation again.

'I hope the girls' presence isn't bothering you, Curate?'

'Not at all, my lord; they seem quite delightful children.'

Philby smiled without the slightest element of mirth. 'Just so – but I think it is time they retired. Poppea, Persephone, to bed; I shall be in to say goodnight in due course.'

After their silent departure a further period of quiet followed, until the baron said, 'I see you are a magician, Curate – what are the stars?'

'Southwark College, my lord.'

'Ah, that gives you a different outlook on life than if you were trained in, say, Rome or Avignon, does it not?'

'Conceivably, my lord; the basic training is the same all through every college in Christendom but each one tends to specialise in certain areas, deliberately or otherwise.'

'My dear Curate, your remarks cause my brain to foment with unanswered questions.'

'Forgive me, my lord, long association with users of magic instinctively leads me to assume the same esoteric knowledge in others. Feel free to question me in whatsoever arouses your curiosity; my meagre learning is at your disposal.'

'Hmmm . . . well, for a start what was the specialist area as taught by Southwark College?'

'Something I once saw defined in a manual as "temporal enterprises management".'

'Which you would define as . . ?'

'Taking care of Church affairs in areas where trust in God alone is not always sufficient.'

'What a glib, forthright man you are, Curate; I do believe you've worked out these answers beforehand.'

'Perhaps, my lord, but not in the way I think you mean. It is just that I have given these matters considerable private thought.'

'I would suppose you have ample leisure to embark on such inner examinations in this lonely place, a lot of opportunity for contemplation, yes indeed . . . but why a magician-priest here in a monks' house? Why aren't you busying yourself in fields where simple faith isn't enough?'

'I was entrusted here by my Bishop, my lord.'

'Evasion, Curate Oakley, your glibness fails you. *Why*? That's what I'd like to know.'

'To be honest, my lord, I'm not really sure; I think he perceived in me some deadness of conscience unbefitting one due to take Holy Orders.'

'Poor old Oakley, eh – "deadness of conscience" was it? Well, I can certainly sympathise with you on that. I've travelled a lot, as you might guess, with very few ties. My disfigurement is not conducive to settling down in a fixed place and the strange thing is that as time goes on, what I see and hear impresses and affects me less and less. I model myself quite a lot on Byron, you know, save that' – here he chuckled a little – 'no poetry has emerged from my ramblings.'

'What is your impression of Rome, my lord?'

'Go hang Rome, Curate; I've not let you off the hook about your conscience yet. Here, have more brandy.'

He refilled Tobias' balloon.

'Not being my confessor, my lord, there's little more I can tell you.'

'Watch your tongue, Curate. Remember yourself!'

'Your pardon, my lord.'

'We'll return to that; meanwhile . . . well what about the colleges *outside* Christendom?'

'How do you mean, my lord?'

'Do *they* have magicians?'

'It's hard to say. No one really knows the whole truth concerning such places and more than half of what one hears is drivel. I had a friend once, however, who fought against Crimeans, Tartars and the like and *they* had sorcerers, apparently good ones.'

'So magic is not a Christian preserve?'

'I can't answer that dogmatically. Certainly the Crimeans are pagans but it could be that their magicians are renegade Christians like their artillery-men.'

'In Sicily I once met a negro sorcerer, no Christian I think; he was burnt.'

'That proves nothing, my lord; in Sicily he would have access to Christian culture and thus, indirectly, the magical arts.'

'No, I think not – he spoke, under torture of course, of other tutors. He babbled about them quite a bit in fact, but there again, talkativeness is encouraged by such savage racking. I expect he was talking rubbish, all about . . . ' Here he spoke an elvish word – one of the few that Tobias had been taught, meaning (roughly) 'Us with you'.

Quite convinced by now, Tobias answered with the variant form: 'Me with us'.

'Brother,' said the baron, and held his glass aloft.

'Brother,' replied Tobias, and they clinked glasses.

'Is your trouble insuperable, Curate?' said Philby.

'Doubtful, my lord, merely an annoying obstacle.'

'What Bishop?'

'Rugby.'

'Very well: such influence as I have will put to clearing your path. Prepare yourself for rapid advance, Curate; my family's name is now behind you.'

'That is more than I could have hoped for, Brother.'

'By your training you now owe me a similar boon.'

'I agree; it is your due.'

'Have you magic for my face?'

'I'm afraid not; not a cure, that is; if it pains you . . . '

'No, no – might such magic exist somewhere?'

'I very much doubt it, and any illusion I could cast would be only very transitory.'

'This is what the other magicians told me, but from you I have no choice but to believe it; your debt is discharged. Well, Brother, it seems my travels must continue. Here's to them and to elf-chosen everywhere; us especially.'

'Here's to me and you,' said Tobias raising his glass.

After long hours of talking, Tobias left the baron and, as instructed, sought out the Abbot. No need, now, to court such favour since far more exalted patronage was his. Thus Tobias simply conveyed the baron as being a burdened but essentially upright man, and the Abbot had to be content with that. In part he was relieved since his charge seemed to have taken no obvious damage from the regrettable intrusion on his retreat. Perhaps no ground had been lost. Tomorrow their vile and notorious guest would be gone, presumably for ever. The Abbot would remember both men in his bedside prayers when he retired.

Tobias now felt sufficiently confident to undertake a mild risk so as to satisfy his curiosity. He returned to the guest wing and at the entrance he put a spell of silence upon himself. Entering, he slowly made his way in the dark to the two doors of the rooms occupied by the baron's party. On top of the silence Tobias cast a sensitivity spell he had been taught at Southwark and then placed his hand, fingers outstretched, and his forehead on one of the doors – no people. He repeated this on the next door – three people.

Equally silently he left the building and, smiling slightly, moved across the cloisters to his solitary bed.

At the same time the Abbot finished praying for the souls of Philby and Oakley and snuffed out his bedside candle.

CHAPTER 18
In which our hero sets off on a journey.

' . . . and what after Rugby, Curate, or should I say "Father" Oakley?'

'Technically it's still "Curate" 'til the ordination on the 22nd, Abbot,' said Tobias. 'After that I can't say – it rests in the hands of the Archbishop's staff. Presumably a period of residence in London while they're making up their minds.'

'And then a master-of-magic post, I suppose.'

'Oh no, not that for many years yet, unless something unforeseen happens.'

The Abbot leaned back and sipped at his mug of mulled beer. He looked over the rim of his tankard at Tobias sitting in the opposite chair.

'I have written to the Bishop concerning your stay here – have a glance at a copy.'

He casually tossed a sheaf of paper to Tobias and watched intently as the magician read.

'Thank you very much, Abbot; you praise me more than my deserts.'

'Not at all, Tobias; you've given me no cause for concern here so what else, in all fairness, could I report to my friend the Bishop?'

'I have endeavoured to please, Abbot.'

'Quite so, Tobias, that was well noted. Would you care for another mug? It's a cold day and a long journey you've to make.'

'No thank you, Abbot, I drink but little nowadays.'

'Wise my boy, very wise, temperance and moderation in all fields of life is a very great virtue.'

'The practice of magic contains a tendency to aesceticism I've found, my lord.'

'Really? Then how alike, and yet unalike, it must be to monastic mysticism.'

'Doubtless, Abbot.'

'*Doubtless.*'

An acidic silence fell; the Abbot wished to question, to reach an elusive truth but he knew he had lost and his influence was at an end. Tobias merely wished to go as soon as decently possible. In an attempt to signal this he put down his empty tankard.

'Perhaps you'd be so kind as to convey my best wishes to Lady Warrilow when I've gone, Abbot.'

'Of course, Curate; now you've pointed out our duty we should be only too happy to continue to keep Madame Warrilow in regular communion but I don't doubt she will miss you.'

'Perhaps, but for the important task in hand one priest is as good as another.'

'There, my son, we must differ. Rise and I will bless you for the journey ahead.'

Tobias stood and bowed his head, and the Abbot pronounced a brief benediction over his thinning pate.

And then there was nothing left to delay his departure. Tobias picked up his carpet bag and made his way to the waiting coach in the monastic courtyard.

There was no one about on the chilly November morn save two novices hurrying across the yard in pursuit of some domestic chore. The Abbot waved a final farewell from the door of his apartment and after that there was no one else to see Tobias' final leave-taking.

His time of preparation was finally over. He was by now fully equipped in both training and character for the greater life beyond. His employers had belatedly given this fact recognition and so the last restraining thread was broken and Tobias, the complete and final man, stepped forward to the hired conveyance that was to take him to his reward.

If the wraiths of history were present in the courtyard that morning he did not notice them. He felt entirely and eternally alone and this was as he would wish it.

Tobias was dead, he knew; his unregarded body lay somewhere in some London brothel or Rugby gutter. However his invulnerable and clever cadaver walked on, its stride all the more light and sprightly for having shed its cloying burden.

With Tobias safely ensconced, the coach trundled off along the dead straight road before it.

BOOK THREE

AUGUST 1990

From: 'AFTER THE AWAKENING; A NEO-CHRISTIAN RECONSIDERATION.'

Edited by Neo-Cardinal Francis Ludwin
Avignon Ecclesiastical Consolidated Publishing Co.
First Published : The Year of Our Lord 2423 AD.

' . . . although in most parts the feudal machinery of government still existed. In this respect England was little different from other parts of Europe; increasingly the old way of life grated and jarred with the barely suppressed economic and cultural aspirations of the larger cities.

Human settlement was restricted to isolated outposts dropped in the vast, ancient forests that had stood largely undisturbed since the end of the last glaciation. In these pockets of civilisation, progress was regarded with deep disapproval and distrust. The social order, the world as it was, was seen as a manifestation of God's will; therefore any potential agent of change, be it spiritual or temporal, was suspect and actively discouraged.

Yet, despite these self-imposed restraints, man continued to make progress, albeit slowly. Out of the remnants of the high-classical civilisations of Greece and Rome came fits and starts of advances in philosophy and even science. During the flowering of thought that we now recognise as active in the Fifteenth Century many great figures (mostly, it must be said, churchmen) increased human understanding in huge leaps and bounds before incaution led to heresy and heresy to suppression.

Therefore, despite the imposed conservatism of the age, it could eventually be said that mankind collectively possessed a large store of knowledge regarding his place in the world. However, every man, from great philosophers to the humblest churls, knew that the sum of the unknown had far more relevance to life as it was lived than any snippets of information held in the cities and universities of Europe. The alarming fact of workable magic, and the dark discoveries to be made thereby, was proof of this if any were needed.

Small wonder, then, that in the face of all these uncertainties and threats, man gave his allegiance to the one sure thread and feature in this disturbing montage. Inhuman in its monolithic size, invincible, ancient and eternal, the Church Universal offered reassurance and consolation in a stable but dark world. The price for this service was simple; obedience to the one true God and to His representatives on Earth.

There were, however, the occasional acts of rebellion . . . '

ARCHBISHOP OF LONDON'S LIBRARY
ENCYCLOPAEDIA BRITANNICA 2020 EDITION
CRUSADES: this term was originally applied to the great movements of Christian arms against the heathen in the Holy Land which occurred between the 11th and 17th centuries prior to the great and abiding success of the so called 'Enterprise of Richlieu' in 1635. [*See index for individual expeditions.*] In modern parlance however a Crusade has come to mean a course of action, problem or area for concern declared to be a particularly valuable opportunity for the earning of grace. Such a Crusade may be declared by a Pope, a Church Council speaking ex cathedra or, in certain circumstances, a 'provisional Crusade' may be declared by an individual Archbishop where a situation of emergency precludes time for contact with proper higher authorities.

In essence the defined doctrine on the modern Crusade states that any effort made by one of the faithful to aid the said course of action or solve said problem earns grace and indulgences at a rate equal to that gained in a freely undertaken and sinless pilgrimage to the Holy Sepulchre. It can readily be appreciated therefore that participation in a modern Crusade is of inestimable value to the soul's salvation. [*See: PILGRIMAGES; ACTS OF FAITH; HOLY LAND; HOLY LAND MILITARY ORDERS OF; See also: ARMIES – SERVICE IN: BOSPHORUS, CRETE, MALTA, NEW MEXICO, THE PAPAL STATES, RHODES.*]

The present doctrine on Crusading was first laid down by the Council of ABERLEMNO in 1848 . . . which stated that . . .

. . . therefore it comes as no surprise to see that most causes declared to be of Crusade status have been able to call upon the services of myriad volunteers from all over Christendom. It is because of this phenomenon that it is said of the Holy Father: 'his conquering armies are raised from empty air'. And 'he topples Empires by proclamations'.

Anyone who wilfully opposes or hinders a matter of Crusade status is deemed excommunicated.

By far the most common use of the Crusading phenomenon has

been either in the defeat of heresy or in the alleviation of suffering caused by famine or natural disaster.

One may convey some idea of the power implicit in the Crusading ideal by quoting the example of the great Phillemian heresy current in the 1930s. In this case over 100,000 volunteer troops assisted the King of France's armed forces in stamping out the dangerous, dualist heresy which had been declared by Pope Constantine 111 as: 'the secret army of Satan in Europe' (1939). [*See: COMPIEGNE, BATTLE OF.*]

Even in Britain, a nation not known for producing heresiarchs [*But see: PELAGIUS*], 40,000 volunteers flocked to the joint papal-royal banner to suppress the levellers of the Thames Valley in the summer of 1990 . . .

LEVELLERS: a heretical and subversive movement current in England since the closing days of 'the Great Civil War' (1642–1649), but at its most widespread and active in the middle-to-late 20th century. The Levellers' belief was formed during the final years of the great 'Protestant heresy' and if this enormity lives on anywhere it is among the underground activists, or 'pastors' as they call them, of the Leveller groups. For all its egalitarian dogma, the Leveller heresy was and is sustained and propagated by an intensely secret and tightly knit group of these pastors whose numbers are never very large.

Their undeniable organisation and high degree of motivation, from time to time, allowed them to take advantage of discontents and grievances among the people and thereby transform their élitist heresy into a popular assault upon proper orthodoxy and the divinely ordained status quo. By far the worst of these attempts was the so-called 'Thames Valley crusade' of 1990 [*See cross-reference*] where Leveller elements cleverly took control of what had started as a minor breakdown of public order (caused by unpopular troop levying for service in the Ukraine). The situation so deteriorated that by the summer of that year much of the Thames Valley was avowedly 'Leveller' and several major towns were in their control, including Reading. Two separate detachments of royal troops had been soundly beaten in the open field and the rebels (for such they were) had framed a number of impudent demands regarding desired changes in the Church and State, and the system of taxation.

Anticipating such a serious turn of events the Archbishops of

London and Canterbury had jointly called for a Crusade to restore proper order and religious freedom to the faithful in the area. This was confirmed and ratified by Pope Simon Dismas when the news reached Rome in the early summer, whereupon volunteers from all nations . . . '

CHAPTER 1

In which our hero is briefly reintroduced whilst about his business.

'Cease fire and advance.'

Thus saying, Father Tobias Oakley, BA,MA,Ph.D, stepped from his hiding place and edged his way down a steep grassy bank, replacing his fired pistol as he went. Already the musket smoke was dispersing and the bright sunshine shone through it in distinct beams. If he'd cared to look, the town of Reading was clearly visible to the North.

At the bottom of the bank was a small roadway and adorning this were the bodies, both moving and not, smitten by the still-resounding volley. Five or six of the enemy were still standing but had dropped their ill-assorted weaponry in a show of surrender.

The two files of musketeers under Oakley's command had followed him down into the lane. They outnumbered the survivors of the ambush two to one and it seemed as if the action was over as quickly as it had begun. Tobias had his men bind the enemy – those that still lived – and shove them into a sitting position by the edge of the lane.

'Sykes – send two men each up the lane north and south. Make sure we're not surprised ourselves.'

His file captain set about this while Tobias took off his broad-brimmed clerical hat and swept his lank hair back. He was hot and thirsty, and eager to push on before he and his men were trapped and exterminated in this rebel territory.

He squatted down in front of the first man in the line of prisoners and fixed his eye. 'Was there an officer with you?'

The man, a shaggy-haired yokel, stared back sullenly and uttered not a word.

Tobias flicked a finger and a phrase at him, and the man slumped back, dead or dying.

Father Oakley moved on to the next man in line but saw no difference in his eyes nor the probable response they betokened. He stood up and surveyed the prisoners.

'I don't think any of them are officers. They're just farmboys – what do y'think, Sykes?'

'As you say, Father; don't reckon this bunch was officered.'

'No. OK then: dispatch them and when you've done, send the men up to join the picket of two at the South, recall the northern picket and have them finish any wounded and search all the bodies.'

'Sir!'

Tobias looked briefly around him. None of the dead yokels were likely to be carrying anything worth having and their armaments were largely improvised; – no, nothing here for him. He strode on up the road, stepping over the bodies, and left his soldiers to their work.

CHAPTER 2
In which our hero goes to see a prince.

Once his party had returned to the comparative safety of the main camp, Tobias directed them to that part occupied by the baggage train where they might remain relatively inconspicuous. There for the first time in over forty-eight hours he had the opportunity to get some sleep other than a fitful doze. Sykes was ordered to requisition a small pack-wagon, straw was placed in the bottom of this and on it Tobias slept.

When at length he arose, it was getting on for dusk. Still lying prone, he took some deep breaths which inadvertently made him aware of his unwashed state. Then when he felt sufficiently aware, if not awake, he sat up and looked around. His musketeers had stayed by the wagon as ordered. Several were still asleep but others had somehow procured some food and were brewing up a stew of sorts. All around them the hectic bustle of the commissariat continued, ignoring their little island of stillness.

Neither Tobias nor his soldiers were at their best. During their raid into enemy territory they had not had time to pay any attention to appearances, but even before that the tough opposition they had met almost as soon as they lost sight of London had taken a toll in terms of smartness as well as lives. The men's standard-issue blue Army coats were heavily and variously stained and their original uniformity in headware (broad-brimmed straw hats dyed black) was lost. Even Tobias' black fustian clothes and heavy buff coat showed signs of dirt and neglect, and across the front of his chest a particularly heavy scythe-blow had opened up a pale-coloured cut in the dark rawhide coat. Each soldier had days' worth of beard-growth. All in all they looked a rascally crew, not the popular image of men on crusade.

Tobias noticed Sykes squatting by the cooking fire, a character-istically blank expression on his brutal face, and beckoned him to come over.

At the same time he delved into his heavy canvas pack which lay beside him and withdrew a spy-glass from it. Opening the little telescope he surveyed his broader environment.

In the distance he could see the town walls of Reading; lights were already lit within, clearly visible through the rubble-strewn gaps. A few matchstick figures moved on the fortifications.

In between the camp and the town stretched an expanse of open terrain on which all the trees had been felled, undergrowth fired and any structures pulled down. Trenches, emplacements and other assorted instruments of siege cut and delineated this dead ground. More stick-figures were at large while here and there still figures could be seen lying in the open.

While he looked Tobias talked to Sykes. 'What news?'

'Just what you might 'ave expected, sir. The apostates have been pouring into the town all day from the North and little we could do to stop them save pepper 'em with the big guns. Then Lord Pearce got back with the cavalry this afternoon and made such a slaughter of 'em as you never did see – bags of prisoners too, most of 'em barely armed at all, just ploughboys with more heresy than sense.'

'Did I sleep through all that?'

'Yes, sir. It's no shame, so did I. I only heard about it from a waggoner who was carting our dead back.'

'When were the breaches in the wall made?'

'Yesterday far as I can tell, seems that the gunners have been giving 'em a foretaste of hell for two days and nights but they're saving it now for the assault.'

'Which is when?'

'Tomorrow if they've any sense, before the townies throw up covering walls; but we've not been told anything yet.'

'Very well; stay here Sykes; use my name if anyone questions you. Also, we've *just* arrived – understand?'

'Sir.'

'If needed, I'll be at the prince's tent, OK?'

'Sir.'

From the town a cannon fired and both men looked round in time to see the ball hit, bounce, roll and come harmlessly to rest not twenty yards away from them.

Tobias moved from the chaos at the edge of the camp where he had slept to regions where some military discipline prevailed. On the periphery in no discernible order were tents and vehicles of all descriptions belonging to the volunteers who had positioned themselves and their gear with little reference to others. At the centre of the camp in a small circle of organisational sanity were the bivouacs of the seconded regular foot and horse regiments.

At the very middle, around Tobias' destination, lay the camp of the Prince of Wales Footguards laid out with meticulous precision and surrounding the command pavilion.

Whatever the soldiers' grasp of military decorum, the Army was at this moment of one common purpose and in pursuit of this small fires were starting up everywhere as the evening meal was prepared.

Even the gaudy headquarters pavilion, Tobias noticed, showed signs of campaign weariness; a long plain patch which heavily contrasted with the patterned tent material showed where an enemy artillery-team had been either exceptionally accurate or lucky.

Tobias straightened his clothing, plucked some of the more obvious pieces of straw off himself and then stepped forward to the presence of his commander. It was, however, considerably past the commander's bedtime (the Prince of Wales was only nine) and he was nowhere in evidence. At the door of the pavilion, two resplendent halberdiers relieved Tobias of his sword and pistols and then allowed him to pass.

Inside there was a motley collection of ADCs, high-ranking officers and waiting messengers. Tobias stood distinct from them since his attire was starkly militaristic; only his collar and a smoky red armband decorated by the Southwark Stars spoke of his clerical status. In contrast, the assembled gentlemen had made few concessions to their warlike occupation and the baroque fashions of the current London season were well represented. Ordinarily Tobias would have looked the same but his raiding mission had precluded cutting any sort of a stylistic dash.

His eyes sought out and at length discovered his immediate commanding officer who was browsing through a book while eating bread and cheese. Tobias made his way over to him and executed a perfunctory bow.

Their relationship and relative standing were hard to assess; between a wealthy knight and a priest who was also a respected and high-ranking magician there were many subtle nuances of rank. However, since Tobias was technically a soldier, albeit temporarily, and Colonel Sir Joseph Hartley-Booth was a senior officer, it seemed as if a certain deference on the former's part was the simplest solution to the problem. But there was no question of Father Oakley being subjected to the various indignities occasionally visited upon junior officers (and then generally transmitted with interest to the men under their command): his cloth and profession carried a high degree of respect.

Colonel Hartley-Booth was in normal times a landed gentleman of leisure as well as an amateur writer of the saints' lives. The crooked logic of the military and the inventiveness implied by this hobby had led him to be appointed as 'Master of the Special Retinue' – a rag-tag unit of specialists increasingly common in European armies. To him were sent those thought to have particular talents and it was Sir Joseph's job to find a productive use for them.

In defence of his beloved faith, Colonel Hartley-Booth was as a man possessed. He spent long hours in prayer asking for inspiration in his task. Nor were his pleas denied.

He coined the idea of calling in one of the Crusade's magicians to assist with the interrogation of several captured 'pastors' and the Army-trained inquisitors were left speechless with admiration at her tricks before death brought an end to the prisoners' gibbered confessions.

He scoured the volunteers and Army regiments for crackshots, ex-gamekeepers, poachers, huntsmen and the like. Out of his own pocket he purchased expensive long-barrelled rifled fowling pieces for them and then sent them out into the dead ground before the town with two days' supply of food and drink, and plentiful ammunition. Collectively these snipers were a grievous thorn in the side to the enemy until, aggravated beyond measure, the Levellers sallied out one night and caught a dozen of them whom they then put in cages and lowered over the walls to discourage further artillery bombardment.

At great personal risk Colonel Hartley-Booth led a party of priests (not including Tobias) right up to the town walls at the dead of night and the last rites were whispered to the cages. The following morning the bombardment started again.

Again the Colonel's snipers took the field but this time when the Levellers sallied out he was waiting for them with a hand-picked group of the toughest and most brutal men in the Crusade who were armed with axes, picks and half-pikes. A grim and ferocious mêlée took place until the ambushed Levellers broke; a few reached the town. Thereafter the snipers continued their play uninterrupted.

With the proffered services of a pious-minded duelling-master the Colonel also tried to arrange a trial-by-personal-combat with the opposing general. However this scheme came to nought for the general was a man of humble origins and so did not share Hartley-Booth's views on 'honour' and the challenge and acceptance ethos.

More successful was the Colonel's idea to send out a large number of small parties, led by men of particular resource and zeal, into the heart of enemy territory which the campaign had not previously penetrated. Tobias led one such group. A few of them did not return but the rest took a very heavy toll of the callow and unprepared rebels. A senior officer had suggested offering a bounty for each pair of rebel ears brought in so as to increase the soldiers' enthusiasm, but a genuinely shocked Hartley-Booth had successfully argued against this. Had they forgotten, he'd said, that they were on Crusade?

The Colonel dressed in a slightly archaic ornate frock-coat and silken breeches; somewhat incongruously he ensconced his feet in heavy and far from aesthetic military boots. His countenance could only be described as 'rakish', an effect heightened by his long curled moustache and elegantly ringleted hair. He looked perhaps somewhat less than his forty-five years. It was well known that he was a man of great natural piety and his presence on the mission was a sincere one.

This could not be said of all the other volunteers on what was to become known as the Thames Valley Crusade. A sizeable proportion of the free-booting elements in European society had rushed to aid the none too enthusiastic King of England in his problems. Crusades always offered the opportunity for good plundering and free licence for behaviour normally only approved of when exercised on the infidel. In the camp, then, were elements of the

pious and the lawless from France, the Empire, Poland, the Swedish
Empire, Burgundy, Spain, Ireland, Florence–Tuscany, Naples and
the Swiss Cantons. If King Charles of England's anguished prayers
were unanswered and it proved a lengthy campaign, then contingents from the Americas and the Christianised East might begin
to arrive. Arranging their departure would not be such an easy
matter.

Over the edge of his book Hartley-Booth noticed Tobias' bow
and he gave a courteous nod in return.

'Ah, Father Oakley, I'm glad to see you safely back; when did you
arrive?'

'I've come straight to you, Colonel.'

'Good; excellent. But you and your men must be very fatigued by
now so I'll excuse you and them from further duties until the
morning – all right?'

'Thank you very much, Colonel.'

'How did it all go?'

'Very smoothly, we encountered elements of the enemy five
times and prevailed in each case.'

'Casualties?'

'Certainly fifty and possibly ten or fifteen more, plus two of our
own.'

'Prisoners?'

They had to pause as a six-horse gun limber thundered by,
shaking the pavilion's silk and velvet sides.

'We took none, Colonel; there were none worth having – such
leaders as they have all seem to be in the town. We were just picking
off the latecomers.'

'Quite; most of the other groups report a similar picture.'

'Also we cleared and burnt a particularly hostile village.'

'Called?'

'Clarkenhurst.'

'Very well; I'll tell the map-master and he'll record it. The next
thing, Father Oakley, is the matter of the assault on the town. I can
tell you under conditions of strict secrecy that it's been arranged for
tomorrow just after dawn. The Crusaders will be informed an hour
or so beforehand.'

'Thank you, Colonel.'

'And the thing *is*, Oakley, that my Special Retinue have been
allocated responsibility for one of the main breaches.'

A hail of gunfire and shouts broke out at that moment. It sounded quite far away, but Tobias raised an eyebrow in enquiry.

'Just a diversion attack, Oakley, to keep the heretics alert and sleepless. They'll be happening at intervals throughout the night; one of my humble ideas.'

'A very good one, Colonel.'

'Thank you, thank you; but as I was saying it's been given to me to take and hold the big gap in the wall by the Silchester gate – number 4 breach – and I've asked for you to be one of my chosen team. Are you agreeable?'

'That's fine by me, Colonel.'

'Excellent; I may say Oakley you've been a not inconsiderable help to me. I shall not forget it.'

'You are too kind, sir.'

'Not at all, now to practical matters; I'm bringing half a hundred men – do you want your two files with you?'

'Yes, Colonel, I think that would be for the best.'

'I'll not deny that to all intents and purposes you'll be leading once we reach the breach tomorrow, I'm only along to supply the legitimate authority – too old for proper fighting you see, not like you.'

'What about briefing, Colonel – that is to say do we follow any particular plan?'

Colonel Hartley-Booth smiled absently. 'No, not really. I've organised a few things but nothing that needs consultation; what I really want is for you to get up there and deal death, that's all.'

'Very well, sir.' Tobias turned away.

'Oh, by the way,' the Colonel called after him, 'we'll assemble by the camp south gate about four and since you'll be the only priest present I'd appreciate it if you'd say a few words over us just beforehand. There's no preparatory mass, y'see, in case the heretics spot it and take warning. That will be all, Father. We'll meet again at four.'

'Very good, sir.'

Hartley-Booth had already forgotten him. Lord Onslow of Guildford was asking if he needed any of his 'Surrey-Puma' fanatics for tomorrow . . .

CHAPTER 3

In which our hero goes for an evening stroll and his recent history is recounted.

Straightaway Tobias went to a provisions tent that catered for men of his rank and ate a meal of bread and chicken washed down with a quart pot of porter. He dined alone on a bench at the side of the tent; the area was crowded with gentlemen volunteers and the odd Army officer, but people had come to shun his company.

That is often the lot of priests, for they remind others of God and mortality, but in Father Oakley's case he had also gained the reputation of being morose and withdrawn. He cared nothing for this. The meaningless babble of fops would only serve to enrage him if one of them were unwise enough to cultivate conversation. It was sufficient that they feared him.

When he had finished eating and drinking he leaned back and smoked an elegant cigar (one of a case he had rescued from the dead body of a Crusade officer). Not twenty-four hours ago he had been killing and that frame of mind was still upon him so he smoked and stared coolly at the assembled gentry and officers to intimidate them.

They were all dead or vanished, everyone who had known him. When he had burnt his childhood home the day before yesterday, he had vaguely felt that it would resolve or provoke something. But there was no one to recognise him. His parents, Allingham, Todd-Williams, Pegrum, Fitzsimmons were all dead, his brothers and sisters were gone. So, even, was his first woman, buxom Betty Lockwood. Tobias had been too disappointed to make detailed enquiries and his ensuing thoughtful mood ensured for the villagers a relatively moderate treatment.

Though he did not know it, he still retained the self-image of a Tobias ten years gone, dapper and impressive and had not yet adjusted to the image that others perceived. At the age of thirty the only impressive thing about Tobias was the armband sewn on his tunic. His hair had become spare and lanky, his face was pouchy and sallow. At times his eyes were hot and burning, at others they were boundlessly abstracted.

It was commonly said that the souls and bodies of magicians were quickly used up, but poor Tobias was ahead of his time.

An even more common belief said that burning eyes were the product of the priestly obligation of celibacy. This, however, could not be said to apply in Tobias' case.

What remained and would not depart from him was the aura of power and energy inseparable from Father Oakley, whatever his physical state as a man. This was what Joan had told him was reality. He had believed, indeed still did, and so now he had an abundance of reality.

If the sensitivity and open mind of the old Tobias had still survived he might have reflected that it was a strange sort of 'reality' that so set him apart from everyone else and left him to eat his meals in solitude. As it was, he didn't, wouldn't, perhaps couldn't, see the paradox.

In fact he was consumed with a great disgust and anger at himself and the world, and his place in it. It was an easier thing to vent this anger on heretics than to think . . .

And it was a luxury for him to allow such free rein to his feelings. In the five or so years since his ordination Tobias had maintained an icily level temperament which had served him well. With Baron Philby's invaluable patronage, and his own undeniable ability, no barriers could be raised against his rapid advancement.

With letters of recommendation and introduction preceding him at every step, his passage through the records and appointments office of the Archbishop of London had been mercifully short; within a couple of weeks his path had been directed westward.

In the establishment of the Bishop of Llandaff, a turbulent part of the world, Tobias' quiet, unquestioning efficiency had been readily appreciated. To the over-worked and over-stretched department of the Dean Temporal a man who would quietly accept orders and then not reappear until they were fully carried out was a godsend.

Tobias earned his spurs in the slave plantations of the Gower peninsula. With a tiny number of troops he put down an embryonic rising by the Welsh-speaking bonded workers and restored the area to peace and proper order with what was, by contemporary standards, a remarkable degree of moderation. He was voted a donative sum by the grateful Irish shareholders of the Plantation companies and when he returned to Llandaff his promotion to Assistant Master of Magic was assured. But before he fully and exclusively devoted himself to single-minded advancement, a vista he thought to be boundless, he felt the need for one final and thorough purging of his pent-up energies.

It was all terribly illogical but true for all that.

Therefore the news of the unrest in the East leading to the declaration of Crusade had been the answer to Tobias' prayers. He had applied for leave of absence and the Dean Temporal and Bishop, although surprised at such a move from a man who had never declared any enthusiasm before, had had little alternative but to release him.

Thus at the height of his outward success and the maturity of his plans, Tobias had travelled back east on a pack-horse to vent his unadmitted self-disgust and frustration on his fellow man.

Within a few years he knew he would reach Master of Magic rank and any number of indiscretions bar heresy would then be forgiven him; but until that time he must perforce be a model of orthodoxy as at the Wesley monastery. This holiday, this indulgence of his grossest tastes and more violent longings should last him until his position made him entirely beyond human reproach.

So thinking, he watched the press-ganged butchers from Wantage and Earley and the volunteer sadists from among the Crusaders moving within the prisoner pen where several thousand heretics were being kept after their capture by the cavalry that day. Since they were too expensive to feed, they were being led out one by one to have their noses slit and right hand removed. (What about left-handers? Tobias thought.)

A few brave or cowardly souls refused to come out and so were shot down. In the pen were the rank and file; Army pastors or gentry-cum-officers had already been weeded out to be mind-mangled by Tobias' kin or bodily abused in more conventional ways by Army inquisitors.

The noise arising from the pen beggared adequate description but fell on the deaf ears of the captors who lacked imagination enough to stand in their victims' shoes. There were a number of women in the pen and these were sorted out, for they had a practical use. However such usage would but delay their fate; in matters of heresy, punishment in this world or the next could not be mitigated on grounds of sex. Tobias saw none that he wanted, nor was he in the mood. After finishing another cigar he wandered on.

In due course he relocated his musketeers. Ignoring his promise to Colonel Hartley-Booth, he appraised them of their rôle for the morrow; they were old soldiers, life-service men and so displayed no emotion at the regrettable turn of events. Sykes was told to go and get some more useful hand-to-hand weapons for his men in preference to the cheap swords of government origin they already carried. Tobias was adequately equipped with an expensive broadsword courtesy of a recently deceased Florentine Crusader.

When a number of pick axes, sharpened spades and the like had been assembled he gave the men a blessing and told them to sleep. He did not feel the need for bed, mainly because he had placed one of his unique self-affecting spells on himself. Until a twenty-four-hour tower had finally decayed it would be impossible for him to enter into sleep. He was utterly determined to savour this experience to the full.

He returned to the command pavilion and acquired a long-barrelled carbine from the commissariat officer who dealt with the weaponry requirements of the command staff. Then like a black-clad death's head he crept into the trenches outside the town, darkened his face and hands with mud and spent the night carefully sniping at any light which showed on the town walls.

CHAPTER 4
In which our hero delivers an uplifting sermon and enters a town.

' . . . and though our minds and bodies will undoubtedly be fully engaged today and at times we may forget the all-pervading presence of God, let us pray that, in all of what is to come, God will not forget us. In the name of the Father, the Son and the Holy Ghost, Amen.'

Tobias had neither the time nor inclination to prepare an original address to the Special Retinue and so had cobbled up something he dimly remembered as the words of one of the generals in the Great Civil War.

At any rate it had seemed satisfactory and as they rose to their feet none of the officers showed any signs of recognising it. He doubted in fact whether any of them had listened to him at all; Colonel Hartley-Booth certainly had not, he was still on his knees mouthing a fervent, if silent, prayer.

They were a most motley group of soldiers representing most of the regiments, groupings and races in the crusading Army. Tobias' musketeers could be said to be the most coherent group amongst them if only for the fact that they all came from the same regiment. Hartley-Booth had obviously scoured the Army for the most robust and ferocious for his group and they brandished a great variety of weapons. The Colonel himself retained his dandy, old-fashioned costume and carried a short-sword in one hand, a furled banner in the other.

Behind them the Army was stirring and moving to position prior to the artillery opening up on the town; it was essential for the half dozen storming parties to be at their posts before then. It was still half dark.

Perhaps realising the need for a degree of urgency, Colonel Hartley-Booth rose from his prayers and strode wordlessly forward; Tobias fell in beside him and the rag-tag force followed on.

They entered the sappers' trench where Tobias had been employed a few hours before. Some of the veterans grabbed handfuls of soil from the sides to rub into their faces and hands. This was an eminently sensible precaution because the defenders of the town had already noted the unusual amount of noise coming from the besieging camp and some of the more nervy heretics had been firing wildly into the dark.

The Special Retinue trudged on in single file, keeping low; in time they came to the large hollow scooped out a few days previously and where a file of musketeers were already in residence. These they relieved.

Tobias peered over the lip of their refuge. In the distance he could see the very first light of day twinkling on the Thames, but he had lost his appreciation for views. His attention was wholly given to the town now only a couple of hundred yards away. Directly opposite him the wall had been severely battered by the artillery and it was nigh-on down in one place. The heretics had tried to fill the gap with timbers and the like but that would not last for long.

For days now he had hardly felt anything but, freed at last from years of restraint and maddened by war, all his animal impulses suddenly broke loose. Weakness was death. If he could rouse some strength then there was no reason whatsoever for him not to indulge it to the full. He had no scruples and such was freedom, he thought. He could just as happily, in other circumstances, have killed Crusaders. As it was he looked with eager eyes to the town for his pleasure.

By way of contrast his commander, the Colonel, was profoundly sad, although grateful for the opportunity to serve. To him, it was woeful to have to take lives, especially those of heretics with no hope of salvation and he took advantage of the waiting period to ask for mercy for their souls.

A mile or so back in the camp a massive bronze bell had been erected on a high timber frame. There had been a bell and cannon foundry at Wantage until the Crusade had passed through it two weeks ago. Five men heaved on a rope attached to its clapper and then loosed their grip. A booming high note like the transubstantiation peal was emitted and thus the day's work for nearly a hundred and fifty thousand men and women was started. As the Crusade's batteries of culverins, demi-culverins and sakers began to speak, soon enough they received a reply from the town and a lively conversation ensued.

Unaware of the sea of soldiers for miles around, Tobias lay on his back and tried to spot the cannonballs flash overhead. The noise was quite astounding and he felt his animal madness begin to heighten. With just the sky to watch and this apocalyptic accompaniment he could not but feel unreal; he was more than ever convinced of the validity of his nihilistic views. The laws and moralisings of man were flimsy façades at the best of times, weak to the point of transparency for those with the strength of will to see. In such a mood, every edifice of propriety was blown flat to the ground and Tobias found the resultant wind of freedom exhilarating.

Such second-to-second living was as exciting as it was animal. It was for what the real, underlying, Tobias had been chosen, groomed and trained. This was *his* time.

Thought was no longer needed, now, even if he were capable of it and an enormous explosive energy occupied him body and soul. If he could make sense of anything he could at least destroy and perhaps *that* was the sense of it.

He turned over and tried to peer through the smoke in front of the town. The gunners' aim seemed to have been good, for the barrier at the breach in the wall had been blown apart and unidentifiable mangled remains lay unevenly in its place. From within someone was screaming in a horribly calm and level tone.

Around him Tobias heard some of the men mumbling at their rosaries. He felt possessed, his fingers twitched, he gripped his broadsword again and again, and felt capable of bounding the distance to the town in a couple of steps.

A hand was laid on his shoulder. Colonel Hartley-Booth had quietly come over. He signalled to his timepiece so as to say 'soon' and Tobias gave him his first uninhibited, broad grin for years to serve as reply.

The retinue grasped their various weaponry and tensed, preparing to go.

They could not see it, but the other forward-positioned storming parties did likewise.

In a vast semicircle round the town the Crusaders stood to arms. Myriad brief prayers fled to the Almighty.

Again the great bell sounded and the Crusaders' artillery ceased. Most of the Levellers' guns had been silenced by the bombardment but a few carried on, punctuating the ensuing tension.

Unknowingly, Tobias resumed an adolescent mannerism and bared his teeth in a half-grin, half-snarl. He was quite unaware of anything but his fury.

Again the bell tolled and nearly fifty thousand Crusaders moved forward with one accord.

Hartley-Booth unnecessarily whispered 'Go!' and his retinue sprang over the edge of their shelter. In a ragged mob they sprinted for their objective, all but the most stupid feeling hideously exposed and vulnerable. The town ditch had been allowed to fall into disrepair and the Crusading Army had arrived too soon for this to be remedied. Now it was a mere rubbish-filled dip in the ground and most of the men did not even notice crossing it.

The heretics up on the wall were firing downwards. Once Tobias felt the rush of a ball passing by his cheek and several times he heard brief cries behind him, but by and large his party reached the approach to the breach intact.

Then, when they were a mere thirty yards or so distant, he noticed a plank which was lodged drunkenly on the rubble and which blocked the breach. He saw it being pushed forward from the inside. It slid clumsily out of the way to reveal a close-set line of musketeers. The Crusaders were too far distant to use their pistols or grenades so it was to their credit that after an almost imperceptible hesitation they rushed on rather than flinging themselves down.

Tobias felt that every musket was directed straight at his head and a chill feeling washed over him, but independently his legs kept moving and his fury spurred him on.

Horribly, he could see an officer behind the musketeers with his arm raised waiting to give the order. With his sharp eyes Tobias could see the man clearly: he was pudgy or so his head and shoulders seemed to indicate; his face was dirt-smeared and alternatively drawn or screwed up with anxiety. Then his arm dropped leadenly.

Amid the resultant popping noises and smoke, incredulously, Tobias found he could continue to run. He was in the van of the retinue so he did not see a round dozen of men fold and fall behind him.

Then a steep slope inhibited his further progress and one step later he found himself near the top of the rubble mound blocking the breach and towering above its Leveller defenders. Several men detailed for this task were still with him and they delicately lobbed hissing spherical grenades into the enemy ranks. Wisely, Tobias ducked.

Rising after the bombs had gone off, he found the problem considerably simplified. There was a lot more smoke about but it seemed there were precious few people left behind the breach where he jumped down, landed, recovered and saw a smoke-wreathed figure to his left. He shot it in the stomach and it grunted and fell backwards. Roaring madly a large man rushed at him with a half-pike and Tobias dropped him with an incantation and a flicked finger.

All around him members of the retinue were similarly plying pistols and every type of edged weapon; by the time Tobias had finished off his next opponent with his sword only Crusaders were both in the breach and alive.

Tobias looked round inside the town. In a semicircle around the breach was a hastily assembled barricade of cases and timbers. Beyond this stretched a longish street bisecting two rows of mean-looking houses. At the bottom of this street a mob of figures was boiling with frantic activity and purpose. He pointed to the inner barricade. 'Take and hold.'

The sixty or so survivors ran to comply. Somewhat more leisurely, Tobias strode forward sword in hand, looking around. How remarkably easy it had all been! Colonel Hartley-Booth came up and clapped him on the back.

'Well done.'

'Nothing to it as yet.'

'Time to give the signal.'

'Thorpe – signal!'

There was no answer until someone yelled, 'He's dead!'

'OK – Mepham go up on the breach and wave your tunic till you're sure the infantry have seen you.'

Mepham never did so. Tobias heard several simultaneous gasps of horror from the soldiers and looked round in time to see a large cannon muzzle being poked out of a hitherto invisible hole in the side wall of one of the dingy houses. It was not twenty yards distant. Simultaneously, crowds of yelling heretics emerged from the nearest houses.

It was a very clever trap.

When Tobias tried to shout 'Back!' his word was drowned and lost in the tremendous roar of the Leveller saker. But once again he was spared, as was the Colonel, and so they were able to see a whole section of the barricade and the men behind it thrown up in the air to disintegrate and fall in oddly shaped pieces. The cannon had been charged with grapeshot ready for their coming.

Fortunately the Levellers pressed their charge home in wild order, they had grown too excited during their wait in the houses to think of anything but closing with their hated opponents. They surmounted what was left of the barricade like a wave and within seconds they and the Crusaders were irretrievably mixed, which happily prevented the saker from speaking again.

Having lost their fighting ranks to engage in individual duels, the Levellers were robbed of their considerable advantage since the Special Retinue were men specially picked for their suspected or known propensity for this kind of scrummage. Moreover the heretics were not élite troops by any means; these were on the walls, dead in the breaches or waiting in reserve deeper in the town. The Retinue's present enemies were town volunteers, militiamen, idealists and young bloods keen on excitement; all very good in their way but an unsuitable match for their brutalised opponents. At first they pushed the Crusaders back, but by weight of numbers this rate of retreat slowed and finally ceased.

None of which was apparent to Tobias for he was engaged in a sword fight with a man of far superior ability, perhaps a duellist or the like, and his mind was too occupied with increasingly desperate and graceless parries to be able to construct a spell to save himself. This was eventually done by another Crusader who, just at the point when all seemed lost, found himself without an opponent and obligingly hacked down Tobias' tormentor from behind with an axe.

With the realisation that he was still alive, Tobias also saw that they were victorious. The remainder of their ambushers were slowly retiring over the barricade and down the street. The ground was unseen beneath a carpet of the dead and a few Crusaders who still had the energy wandered around to ensure that this was indeed the condition of the fallen.

Hartley-Booth was still there; like a bizarre vision he was waving a bloody axe.

Tobias saw what he was looking at, 'Saker,' he screamed. 'Saker—get that fucking saker!'

While shouting, he ran forward towards the cannon that had done so much damage before. (He had not thought to question the wisdom of so doing.) He dimly appreciated that others were following him.

As he drew close he could see how the trick had been done; the bricks in the wall of the house had been loosened and then replaced, presumably leaving a spy-hole. Now enough bricks had been displaced to allow a view into the house. Beside the cannon muzzle one man was watching Tobias approach. Less clearly visible, another man was sighting the gun, moving feverishly fast and another was approaching it with a glowing taper.

One of Tobias' pistols had not been fired – he had not had the opportunity. Now he drew it from his belt. Judging by the sounds behind him, he was a good few yards ahead of his nearest compatriots. The black muzzle of the cannon beckoned him on and illogically enough he felt sure he was going to run into and down it before being spat out rudely. Even at such an inappropriate moment several sexual comparisons occurred to him.

Then with a degree of relief he was never to experience again, he reached the wall of the house and was out of the field of fire. He would have been happy to stay there for ever, his fighting mood having passed when faced with the actuality. However he was not allowed to remain uninvolved. He looked inside and four gunners looked at him; then one moved to apply the taper to the touch-hole. Another raised a half-pike but, moving faster than he knew he could, Tobias clashed his sword with the haft below the blade and thrust the danger aside. With the other hand he raised his pistol and shot the taper-man through the head. As befitted a crisis, his aim was true.

Then some idiot buffeted into his back and he tumbled head first through the hole in the wall and into the room beyond.

Once again, he was lucky. In falling he had stuck his sword out in the faint hope of warding off blows. Instead he felt it hit and sink into something. He landed in a confused heap underneath the muzzle of the gun beside one of its wheels, his face painfully rammed into his armpit. A heavy body landed on him and they wrestled. Something cold and sharp slid across Tobias' forehead and blood began to trickle into his eyes. Made strong by fear, he freed his arms, found what he thought to be his opponent's head and in a smothered voice shouted a brief phrase. The aggressor's body gave a couple of spasms and then was still. Tobias heaved the dead weight off and sat up. Through a thin sheen of blood he surveyed the ghastly scene, the focus of his attention, naturally enough, being the surviving member of the artillery team. In his turn this man found Father Tobias of similarly consuming interest. They stared at each other for a long moment. What the priest saw through a red haze was a shock-headed youth who had the look of a dare-devil, but at this moment a panic-stricken one. The instantaneous destruction of the gun team before his eyes had perhaps been the final straw in a day of mounting horror. He held a sword and could have skewered Tobias with it for the priest was bloodied, confused and jammed into a helpless position. Instead, somewhat jerkily, he turned to his left and walked briskly out of the room.

Something of the full gravity of the moment had also communicated itself to Tobias, although he was less afraid of death than most men since he attributed no value or sense to life. He scrambled up, his hair matted with blood and all over his face, his clothes pale with rubble-dust. Somewhere deep down in his vast coldness was a tiny spark of human panic, something he was unaccustomed to and fearful of. Today he had clearly seen the awful random quality of existence.

No one had the right to exist, all were likely to be penetrated by blade or projectile and die from it. In a few seconds a room full of men, individuals all, with minds aware of their aloneness, could be swept clean and each of those stories terminated. Therefore a man's all-pervading sense of self did not increase his prospects of survival or prosperity against those of his contemporaries.

The sum effect of which was to knock some of Tobias' boundless confidence out of him because it meant the universe would continue to function quite happily without his presence.

Somewhat chastened and a touch more cautious than hitherto, he swept his face clear of hair while recovering his sword from the floor. He was grateful for the feeling of security given by the walls that remained solid. But he became conscious of a wider world again and looking behind him he saw through the holed wall that the Crusaders still held the breach. A fat, bald-headed man with an axe, presumably the one who had knocked him into the house, was about ten feet away. He waved at Tobias and shouted some incomprehensible message of congratulations.

Further away by the ruined breach the surviving men of the retinue were standing in skirmish order with apparently no enemy to worry them. And Hartley-Booth was standing at the base of the mound filling the breach. He waved his sword, yelling his approval of Tobias' exploit.

On top of the mound a nervous figure was signalling wildly with Hartley-Booth's banner so as to call in the waiting Crusader infantry. Occasionally leveller snipers attempted to still him.

Tobias felt a trifle calmer now. Sword ready, he skirted the gun and the corpses, gingerly advanced through the door and thus into a dingy hallway. There was a stair on his left and a few open doors gave glimpses of empty rooms.

Time for a breathing space, he thought, returning to the original room. Already he could feel his normal calm returning. He noticed the taper still glowing in the dead hand of the gunner he had shot. He ground it out beneath his boot to ensure this particular heretical gun would remain silent.

Somewhat limp, he stood still for a moment and observed the world through the hole in the wall. Suddenly he saw the faces of his companions register indecision and fright in turn, but could not see the cause of their alarm.

Some of the Crusaders fired off hasty shots and then all turned and ran. They had barely covered twenty paces when the cause of their precipitous retreat came into Tobias' line of view: Leveller pike-men, at the trot, in good formation and all of them uniformed in green, and fully equipped with pot and plate armour. There seemed to Tobias' aghast eyes to be an endless stream of them. Obviously a full regiment of foot previously kept in reserve had been committed to this area. In the time it took to appreciate the fact, Father Oakley's line of retreat was blocked by a solid phalanx of enemy soldiery.

Quite rightly the much depleted force of Crusaders had realised that they stood next to no chance against such a superior force and every man had turned to save himself by returning over the wall. A few, slow-witted, were trodden down in the Levellers' original rush. A couple more, unable to summon up a sufficient burst of speed, were despatched by pike thrusts to their unprotected backs. The rest scrambled up and over the mound in the breach and disappeared from Tobias' knowledge. He recognised Hartley-Booth taking part in the ascent. At the top the old man paused, looked back at the enemy and was for a moment undecided. Cautious counsel seemed to prevail for at the last moment he turned to flee over the breach. At that instant God saw fit for a cannonball, presumably a Crusader one, to strike the Colonel and neatly remove his head. The divorced remainder of his body was flung like a stringy doll into the advancing enemy.

Nothing daunted, the square of pikemen trotted on to the top of the breach a mere moment before the first wave of Crusader infantry reached the gap they had thought secured. Tobias heard the two forces mix in distant battle.

He had been entirely absorbed in the spectacle of the Colonel's demise but when his eyes turned to look for fresh diversion, several things immediately struck him as relevant to his predicament. Firstly the musketeers of the Levellers reserve regiment were following the dense phalanx of their pikemen. They were scattered around the area in loose formation looking for something useful to do. Before long some of them would notice the cannon emplacement and classify it in this category.

These were the heretics' doughtiest troops, men trained in secret in preparation for an uprising and, moreover, fully convinced of the dogmas for which they struggled. That such bodies of men existed and waited for their day was long known to the Church, which occasionally caught and made examples of a few. However the degree of strength and organisation of their present manifestation in Southern England shocked all observers.

These regiments of disciplined troops must have been the fruit of innumerable dangerous and secretive gatherings in out-of-the-way places and 'safe' houses. They were the creations of pastors who obstinately refused to despair at the weary round of travelling, writing, organising, cajoling and suffering. Each soldier, each musket, each piece of armour was the product of near-infinite patience and endeavour. Each soldier killed was the irredeemable loss of a massive investment. How reluctant therefore the Levellers must have been at last when it came to committing their legions. Or perhaps not for they were, for the most part, fanatics. Or spiritual men who found it difficult to reckon things in terms of earthly values.

The next thing Tobias noticed was that the cannon so obligingly loaded by its now deceased or departed crew was temptingly pointed at the plug of Leveller soldiers in the contested breach. He envisaged the poetic justice of discharging its load of grapeshot into their densely packed ranks. Hotly following this agreeable vision was the thought that he had put out the only means by which the cannon might be fired. He had little time for self-reproach or even the devising of a means to relight the taper, for the enemy were approaching.

In many ways he felt that enough had been asked of him for one day and extreme discretion suddenly seemed an entirely proper course of action. He scurried out of the room and after a moment's indecision proceeded up the stairway he had noticed a few moments before. Upstairs he found a door ajar and, seeing no one through the gap, he went into the room beyond.

Obviously it was a bedroom but the occupant had failed to stamp their personality on the space, which suggested an austerity more likely born of poverty than taste. Tobias viewed it as a rotten place for his final stand. He closed the door and leant against it so that he might hear what transpired downstairs. For comfort he held his sword at the ready.

At length he heard some disturbance below and a number of voices. He could catch the sense of only a few words:

' . . . peace . . . '

' . . . on . . . '

' . . . no time or . . . '

At one point he heard footsteps in the hall and what sounded like a single boot being planted on the stairs. After a while the footsteps receded, at which point he considered he could stop living from moment to moment and think properly. He failed miserably because he felt like a trapped rat.

He went and sat on the bed. It was unexpectedly comfortable. Laying his sword close beside him, he reached for his pack and methodically reloaded his pistol. He wondered where his other one had got to; he had probably dropped it in the cannon room.

The window which looked on to the street now called his attention. Sidling across the room, he peeped through from one side.

Nothing much had changed. Levellers still held the breach and, as he watched, files of the regiment's musketeers were being led back to reserve positions as the danger gradually passed. Some fighting continued by the wall but it was clear who had the upper hand. A heavily bearded musketeer was going through Colonel Hartley-Booth's pockets. *No valuable pickings there*, thought Tobias; *these people will be here the rest of the day. Now is as good a time as any to go.*

Before picking up his sword he placed a spell of silence upon himself for safety's sake. Then rearming himself he edged open the door and stepped on to the landing.

A surprise awaited him: at the base of the stairs was sitting a Leveller pikeman in the dark-green uniform of the regiment in the breach. He seemed fully absorbed for his head was in his hands and Tobias could detect no motion. Across his backplate was a splay of blood, presumably not his own. He seemed to have abandoned his helmets and weapons. Magically silent, Tobias slowly descended the stairs and delivered a death-blow with his sword.

Which was a pity, for Tobias was in no danger whatsoever and at any other time would have found the young pikeman, seven years his junior, entertaining company. His victim's membership of the Levellers sprang from a fundamentalist Christian belief which had been his joy and support since his very earliest years. His name was John Scott and he had tried to externalise his faith by joining the organisation which led to his demise, but what Scott had seen in the breach that day was not Christianity he had realised. And when he had impaled a man on a pike that afternoon, it became clear to him that his relationship with Christ, so essential for salvation, was at risk.

So he had flung away his weapons, retired from the fray and sought out a quiet place in which to seek forgiveness for his culpable error and lack of love. Here Tobias had killed him.

Stepping over the body, Tobias saw that the cannon room was

empty once again but that the open space visible beyond its broken wall was still in enemy possession. It occurred to him that if all the Crusader attacks had met the same fate as the Colonel's then he would be faced with the ironic task of trying to get *out* of Reading at any costs – as opposed to his wish of not so long ago. Looking around, he saw that the downstairs passage had a back as well as a front entrance and after a cautious exploration he found that the back door opened on to a jungle-like walled garden. Through here, he thought, he could make his escape. Retaining his sword in hand as reassurance, he forged a way through the massed vegetation and scaled the wall at the bottom of the garden. He became aware again of the active and nearby sounds of battle, though whether the noise originated from inside or outside the town he could not say. At least the issue was still being contested. Having landed in a similar if slightly better kept neighbouring garden, he drew his pistol from his belt and cocked it. Much of his old confidence was back and the noise of battle was cheering him. He booted open the door at the end of the garden path and strode into a hall leading to a street door as in the building he had just left. Passing through, he saw a large family gathered in their living room behind an improvised barricade of tables and chairs. They seemed to offer no resistance so Tobias merely scowled at them and left them even more frightened and perplexed than hitherto.

He saw himself out and emerged into a street that was deserted save for a few corpses. He realised he must be only a road away from the site of the retinue's defeat and so decided to head towards the other side of the town in search of friendly forces. It seemed bizarre to be an enemy soldier walking unhindered through a besieged town with only the occasional body and battle noise to remind him of his predicament. The unexpected respite meant he was relaxed when four obvious Levellers pelted round a corner and made straight for him. If anything they seemed more surprised than he. Tobias had ample time to rest his pistol across his straightened arm and take careful aim at one of the figures when it became apparent to him that none of them were armed and that they were shouting for quarter. Since four to one is not good odds even for a magician, Tobias was glad to hold fire and thereby intimate his willingness to accept their surrender. If need be, he could dispose of them later.

The four stopped ten paces or so short of him. They looked all in. On closer inspection Tobias could see that two of them were women, or rather girls. One of whom had dropped leadenly to her knees and in an exhausted voice spoke again and again.

'Recant . . . recant . . . recant.'

The others by various signs showed that they, too, were not prepared to offer further resistance that day. Tobias wondered at their enthusiasm for capitulation but did not need to ponder long. Around the same corner came a mob of men howling madly, obviously Crusaders. Tobias should have felt a surge of hope or triumph, but he did not.

His captives cast anxious looks at their pursuers and then placatory glances at Tobias. Obviously they had been in search of a sympathetic party to whom to surrender.

'Please, Father . . . save . . . '

'Recant . . . recant . . . '

Some of the mob, perhaps a hundred men, came down the road towards them, the rest spreading out through the town. Those leading, a heterogenous mix by the look of them, were a storming party of Central European volunteers and regular soldiers. They saw Tobias and greeted him with a ragged cheer. He could see no officers and so naturally took charge.

'Where are you from?'

A bland-looking musketeer undertook the rôle of spokesman. 'Number five breach.'

'How goes it?'

'All finished by looks of it, we're all over town.' He looked at the prisoners. 'The prince has sounded the no quarter and sack signals.'

'I've come from Number four breach,' Tobias explained. 'There will be prolonged resistance there, I suspect, and at the town centre where the heretic reserves are. As acting officer I therefore temporarily suspend the sack signal. Pray consider yourselves under order once more and follow me.'

'What about these?' said a runtish man of Irish appearance, pointing to the captives with his sword.

'Father please . . . please,' said one.

'No quarter as ordered,' replied Tobias, 'and that includes the wenches; time enough for fun later today.'

While his order was enthusiastically enacted Tobias mustered his troops and proceeded forth, impelled by no great emotion, to avenge his fallen Colonel.

CHAPTER 5

In which our hero covers himself in glory and considers what to do next.

As the later morning and then the afternoon drew on, Tobias found himself with no lack of employment. He had gathered several bands of exultant Crusaders together and led them to attack the unbroken Leveller regiment at his own, Number four, breach. Ironically enough, at one point he found himself struggling for possession, along with another five hundred men, of the very house he had hidden in a few hours earlier. At length and at cost they took it but it was not until the artillery pieces (including the Leveller cannon well known to Tobias) were brought up that the firm if diminished heretics were scattered. The cavalry pranced through the gaps in the ranks torn out by the cannons and, soon after, any effective resistance ceased.

Father Oakley had the good fortune to be noticed at the van of one particular charge by a member of the prince's personal staff who at this juncture dared to venture into the town. In this way Tobias' part in the battle was officially noted – to the considerable benefit of his future career.

Ignorant of this, Tobias waited until the green-coats were finally broken and then took leave of the officer in charge of this particular struggle. He was commended for his prompt action in rallying forces to a part of the field where battle was still in progress and reminded that the proper chain of command could be temporarily set aside in the absence of higher authority. Tobias thought that his rag-tag bands of Crusaders and the artillery he had had brought up could have done perfectly well without this booby and his troop of gentlemen cavalry and, moreover, *he* deserved the medal that this effete old fool would undoubtedly receive for the bloodbath. However he said nothing and took his leave in search of fresh diversion.

Of the military sort there was little to be had. Tobias arrived in the centre of the town just in time to see the final collapse of the Leveller reserve regiments which, according to later historians, marked the end of the Battle of Reading. This was not quite the case, for individual houses and blocks full of die-hards continued to

234

hold out to the early evening. However, the noise produced by their suppression was largely indistinguishable from the horrendous row of the town being put to the sack and Tobias saw no more fighting that day.

Save for the few units involved in the mopping up and the prince's regiment, who considered themselves above such things, the Crusaders were allowed to stand down and seek whatever entertainment most appealed to them. Like a Cinderella, Tobias had until about ten o'clock of that evening in which to do as he wanted. By that time his twenty-four-hour tower would have fallen completely and he would be assailed by a massive fatigue.

Age and status had given him a degree of fastidiousness and so he did not think just in terms of personal enrichment or simple rutting like most of his compatriots. Instead he decided he would wander and observe some of his fellow men at play for his own amusement and experience. Then he would retire to his well-earned repose after, he thought, a highly worthwhile day.

Such were his thoughts as he sat on a bench facing the town square. All around him corpses were piled and men driven half-mad by relief and the lack of restraint were rushing hither and thither. It had been a turbulent day for them all and Tobias found it easy to accept the temporary bedlam.

It had also been a fine, hot day and even in the late afternoon, brassy sunshine continued to pour upon the town. Tobias considered the possibility of removing his heavy, buff coat, but found that he couldn't be bothered. He sat there abstracted until the Cathedral clock at the other side of the square solemnly struck five. The Cathedral itself had been used as a barracks by the Levellers in order to show their lack of esteem for such grandiose pomp. When the tide turned against them, impelled by no other reason than desperation, they had used it as a citadel and in the process had caused even more destruction.

However, some pious or practical soul had contrived to keep the great clock going and thus Tobias was reminded that it was time to go about his business.

CHAPTER 6

In which our hero assists a damsel in distress, removes her from danger and is thereby enriched.

In the hours left to him before he needs must sleep, Tobias intended to look for experience and entertainment in that order. As a man of intelligence, education and some refinement, and with a whole city and its surviving inhabitants at his absolute disposal, he was amply able to satisfy his requirements. In material terms, by the time he was obliged to return to camp he was richer by the acquisition of a ruby necklace and two (pure gold, he suspected) ankle chains. Needless to say these were of little intrinsic use to him and he very soon disposed of them for a rather large sum to a Jew in London.

However the means by which he came to own them was to prove a rich memory for a number of years to come and this he accounted the greater gain for he already had money sufficient for his needs. Otherwise, though, he often found his mind prey to a poverty which manufactured boredom; hence his lust for life of a sort.

Sometime in the late afternoon he entered a wealthy-looking house not far from the central square to find a file of royal troops pillaging the residence. Evidently they had not been there long, although the damage to furnishings was copious, for they had only just embarked upon the interrogation of the occupant. He was a huge man, soberly dressed, with an implausibly resolute jaw; perhaps fifty years of age but not old as yet. Even so he showed no signs of resistance save a lofty disdain. In a level voice he told the blue-coats the location of his money box and then that of the key.

Tobias was half-heartedly inspecting some of the surviving china figures which had decorated the room before the Crusaders' acts of vandalism. There were none he particularly wanted and he replaced them neatly, then turned and looked coolly at the tall man held between two soldiers and towering a head above them. His gaze was returned sternly.

Tobias was looking somewhat more priest-like now for he had removed his buff coat and thus revealed his clerical gown (tucked into his breeks). And he noticed that the captive's eyes flicked for the barest of instants to his armband.

Although the man had been both courteous and cooperative some of the soldiers had drawn knives to torment him further since they were a little drunk and had grown accustomed during the battle to the free exercise of their wilder natures.

Tobias said quietly, 'No – halt!' and the soldiers desisted. After their initial abashment they had ignored his presence but his relative position in authority was far from uncertain. They had been hoping he would drift on as noiselessly as he had come and so leave them to some uninhibited fun, but they knew their master's voice even in this anarchy.

Tobias felt that there was something wrong with the vignette before him, in the sense that the principal actor was not playing the part one would expect. The householder did not have the appearance of someone given to easy capitulation; certainly he had faced the prospect of physical torture without undue fuss. As if to confirm Tobias' thoughts, two soldiers suddenly reappeared carrying an open strongbox between them. It appeared to be full of banker's notes and gold coinage.

There was no figure of rank present so Tobias made his question general. 'How many of you are there?'

Everybody pretended to be engaged in counting, typically waiting for someone else to act as spokesman.

'Come on, come *on*.'

'Six, not counting him and you, Father,' said a tubby, begrimed soldier with a Surrey accent.

'That's all, no more searching the house or whatever?'

'No, Father.'

'Hold him for a moment.'

Tobias closed his eyes and envoked his sensitivity spell, restricting it in his mind (and therefore in reality) to the physical confines of the house.

Each person present appeared *and* felt in some subtle way like a shimmering cone of light behind Tobias' eyes. Others would have marvelled or speculated upon what this represented, but he had lost the faculty to find his own abilities interesting. Thus without any undue curiosity he counted the cones: nine; he recounted, nine. Tobias opened his eyes.

'There is another person in this house, probably in a secret room of some sort. I am interested to see who it is.' He turned to the householder. 'I don't suppose you'll tell us will you?'

'I have no idea what you're talking about.'

'I thought not. Very well – kill him and then search the house. I'll wait here.'

Hearing his doom pronounced, the man began to struggle and rapidly threw off his two captors. It would have been both troublesome and dangerous to engage him in hand-to-hand struggle and so one of the soldiers shot him at point-blank range with his musket. The noise was surprisingly loud in the smallish room and the smoke hung for some while.

While one man made sure of the heretic with his knife, Tobias ordered the rest about their search. Some were plainly reluctant to leave him with the strongbox, but none had misgivings powerful enough to make them mention it.

Tobias decided to wait because he thought the episode had possibilities and since, for the moment, he felt a little fatigued. He noticed a cigarette box and filled his pocket with the contents. While he waited he sat in a deep armchair, chain-smoked and thought of nothing.

From all around him came the noises of frustrated soldiery and methodical destruction until after about a quarter of an hour his patience was rewarded by the resonant boom of a gunshot from upstairs. It was immediately followed by a loud grunt and the sound of something heavy striking the floor.

As he climbed the stairs he could hear a cacophony of voices but no further sounds of struggle and so he did not bother to draw his pistol. It was easy to locate the source of the disturbance, a large bedroom to the left of the stairhead. Entering, he saw a most eloquent cameo.

The first thing that caught his eye, naturally enough, was a woman. Less naturally, she was dressed in plain men's clothing: white linen and a black suit, surmounted by a clerical collar. A mixed look of hatred and fear occupied her rather ordinary face. In fact, he mused, she was not in age and features unlike Diane of fond memory, although infinitely more determined and Amazonian. Two soldiers held her none too gently by the arms and hair. The reason for their strength of feeling was clear, for one of their compatriots sat on the floor bewailing his arm which had been shattered by a bullet. Another leaned groggily against a chest of drawers trying to staunch a heavy flow of blood from a deep sword-cut across his forehead.

Firmly fixed now as the acknowledged spokesman, the tubby soldier gave voice. 'Hellish fucker, look what she done. Leveller *bitch*, we're going to *damage* you!'

'Where was she?' asked Tobias mildly.

'In there,' said another, bearded, soldier pointing to a cupboard-like cavity concealed behind the headboard of the bed which they had pulled away from the wall. Obviously they had detected a hollow surface and smashed it in with their musket butts – at which point the occupant had retaliated.

'Let us deal with her please, Father.'

'Alas, no,' said Tobias firmly 'Orders are quite clear in this respect, even if a "No prisoners" call has been given. *All* captured pastors, especially female ones I would imagine, are to be conveyed to the general staff headquarters for interrogation.'

'But Jack here is like as not to lose his arm 'cos of her!'

'And my pretty face is spoilt for ever.'

'Bloody right, no one 'ud know.'

'Let us 'ave her!'

Tobias sensed that feeling was running high enough for the situation to get out of hand so he decided to make a concession while all the while his imagination raced.

'So you shall – providing no permanent damage is done; after which she'll be taken for questioning and you know what happens *there* so the end result is the same.'

While they paused to consider this he pressed ahead in getting his own way. 'Is she fully disarmed?'

'Yes she is.'

'Right, wait downstairs until I've finished questioning her myself, then you can do what you want.'

'But what about — '

Tobias interrupted with a shout. 'Those are bloody orders, not a topic for discussion, now get out – move!'

Perhaps realising the rashness of their last few exchanges, the soldiers hurried to comply, leading the wounded with them.

'We'll be seeing you, *lots* of you,' growled the tubby one to the woman.

'Besides,' added Tobias mildly, 'your strongbox is downstairs unattended.'

With this added incentive the men left and Tobias followed them in order to shut the door. This done he turned to face the woman. 'I should state now that if there's any attempt to escape or injure me on your part I will kill you immediately.'

She seemed to think about this and in the ensuing pause Tobias studied her more closely.

There *was* a passing resemblance to Diane but not much more than that. This woman's features were naturally stern and cold. Her longish black hair was drawn firmly back into a tight bun and it seemed probable that this was not just a campaign measure but a habitual practice.

'By magic I presume you mean,' she said in a high-pitched, yet fragile voice.

'Probably – though pistol or hands would serve equally well.'

'Doubtless.'

'I presume I'm right in saying you're a pastor, I mean that collar's not just something you've put on for some obscure reason?'

'Deaconess actually; my pastor exams await me.'

'Or not, as the case may be.'

She did not answer this.

'I have a bargain to offer you,' said Tobias. He moved across the room and sat on the bed.

'I will not betray friends and brothers, nor will I divulge any secrets to which I am bound by oath; I'm ready to face your filthy tortures . . . Crusaders . . . phah!'

'Please don't bluster,' said Tobias, 'I am not in the least bit deceived. In any case that is not the nature of my bargain, please be seated.' He indicated a wicker chair and proceeded to light up another cigarette, all the time keeping a wary eye on the woman.

'I'm not afraid of you, priest. I count myself as dead now and what more can you and your crew do to me beyond that?'

'Quite a great deal I should imagine, for we are rather an inventive lot. You see, there are different means of departing this world, some quick and easy, others . . . less so. And at the time the means is so terribly important. Don't get me wrong, please; I don't wish to deal in crude threats. However as you so rightly say, you are to all intents and purposes as good as dead, which is where my bargain comes in as a means of reviving you.'

Obviously the woman was less than totally committed to the inevitability of her forthcoming demise. Her eyebrows rose and her attention, hitherto lacklustre, was fully sparked.

'What does that mean?'

'My part of the bargain is to ensure you escape to fight another day as it were.'

Try as she might, the woman could not keep the signs of renewed hope from crossing her face.

'Alive? Escape? Out of this town?'

'Absolutely – look will you *please* sit down.'

She failed to hear this, being somewhat dazed at being reborn. However, humans are notoriously ungrateful creatures and soon her natural pugnaciousness began to reappear.

'And what do you receive in return?'

Tobias pulled on his cigarette and raised his eyebrows. 'What do you have?'

She considered this and then reached inside her tunic, at which Tobias instinctively stiffened, ready to kill her, and pulled out a handful of jewellery. He could see a necklace of red stones and some gold-coloured chains.

'Rubies and gold, priest. I had thought to use them to finance our activities should I escape from here. Now you can have them – quite appropriate really, they're pillaged from a rich, papist bitch. Render unto Caesar you know . . . '

'The "papist bitch" – young and pretty?'

'She was.'

'I see.' Tobias was revelling in a quite exquisite fashion over her unjustified confidence and arrogance. This was going to be *so* sweet; he was able to feel again. Old disused nerves too coarsened to appreciate anything less than the extreme came into use.

'Will they do, priest?'

'Yes,' said Tobias.

'Excellent – here!' She slid them across the floor to him.

'In part,' he finished.

'What! But I have nothing else, priest, take that or . . . No, please . . . why are you *playing* with me?' She almost broke down.

'You have the immaturity of the fanatic, madam,' said Tobias. 'Either you are all puffed up with confidence or an abject little girl. Remember your situation; I hold *all* the cards to use a metaphor and you must bargain with me in order to survive.'

As hoped, he had disorientated her now, and watched her swing from despair to hope and back again.

'But, priest, I have nothing more to offer – can't you see?'

'I beg to correct you, madam: there is your first and most precious possession – your body.'

And there she is, he thought, a trainee priestess in an underground, persecuted Church. A proven warrior, probably spent all day up to her hocks in blood and gore and yet she reacts like a frigid mother superior at the suggestion that she has a usable carcass. St Paul's got a lot to answer for.

When her mouth ceased gaping, she spat out, 'Never!' and looked downwards. Then, recovering fire, she stared at him again. 'I really would rather *die*!'

Tobias lit another cigarette and took a deep breath.

'Possibly. But listen.' He proceeded to count using the fingers of his left hand. 'One: the soldiers downstairs, and probably your interrogators and executioner, will take you anyway so your fate in that direction is sealed. Two: your decision is a selfish one; if you continue to live I presume you feel you'll be continuing to do God's work. At the moment you're putting personal pride, a sin, before the chance to continue that struggle. Three: your choice amounts to suicide – that is the sin of despair and presumption, a burning offence I'm told. And four: under our interrogation you will not be able to help betraying your comrades or "brothers" and the organisation you serve. Once again, you are putting pride before the best interests of others. Think on this.'

At last, the woman slumped into the wicker chair as she waged a war in her head.

Tobias knew the precepts of virtue well and had mustered his arguments skilfully. It was hard to use truly good people but he had met few enough of them (Cherry, what about Cherry? – *forget*) but these half-moral, half-human types could become like putty as they tried to reconcile two conflicting ideals.

When she looked up, he knew he had won; her eyes were hollow but just the *smallest* bit expectant.

'What do you want, priest?'

'Oh, about an hour should be sufficient,' he said brightly, 'an hour of absolute free access to your body in which you will cooperate in all I wish to do. You may speak and express any opinion during that time; in fact I would welcome such comments. In return, when I have finished I will take you to the London gate and secure you a horse and a passage past whatever guards are there. After that you are dependent on your undoubted ability to survive.'

'Why all this fuss, priest? You could have taken or bought any woman in this poor town. Come to that you could have *taken* me.'

'The point is valid, deaconess. However, for what I have in mind I want a pliant woman, not only that but a special *type* of woman. Your type gives me an especial *frisson*. So?'

She put on her strong and resolute face. 'Very well.'

'Good. Get on with it then.'

Very slowly at first but then speeding up, she undid her belt and lowered her heavy corduroy trousers. She had nothing on beneath them and Tobias appreciatively noted her nicely shiny thighs and bushy pubic mound. But halfway through her undressing she paused, rather ridiculously with her trousers partially down, and looked at Tobias.

'But can I trust you, priest?'

'There is no guarantee I can offer bar my word – and that, frankly, is worthless. Ironically enough you just have to trust me. Please proceed.'

Without going into more technical details it can be safely said that Tobias thoroughly enjoyed the Leveller woman during the following forty-five minutes or so. As a young man his attitude to sexual relations had been more or less orthodox. However in later years his researches (particularly in demonology) and, strange to say, his Bible readings had introduced him to more unusual avenues of obtaining satisfaction. Reading had led to curiosity, curiosity to further research, further research to fantasy and, Tobias being the man he was, fantasy naturally led to practice.

Throughout, the woman seemed to be in a mild state of shock, coupled with vociferous disgust; although she remained compliant and obeyed his, often complex, instructions. This was exactly what he had hoped for, since a cooperative and yet unwilling partner brought nuances of domination and submission which were a major part of perversion's appeal. His previous experiences with harlots and the like had lacked this element and had therefore been less sweet.

The Leveller woman had been a virgin and once this was discovered her deflowering had been Tobias' first, swift action. Thereafter it might be said, looking on the bright side, she gained in less than an hour the equivalent of the accumulated lifetime experience of the most accomplished of courtesans.

When Tobias came for the second time and was finished, he hauled himself off her and began to rearrange his clothing. Even at that moment the memory of her pale face with downward twisting mouth and wide, glassy eyes, had the power to excite him and would continue to have this rare quality for a long time to come.

The woman, however, did not move but remained as she had been left, naked and bent over the bed staring at the opposite wall, eyes awash with hate.

Tobias could often be, when no material self-interest intervened, a man of his word and so, ignoring the woman, he left the room and went downstairs to the waiting soldiers. A couple more had now joined their number. Briefly and firmly he told them that they could proceed upstairs and take her as promised, on the strict condition that she was neither visibly nor permanently damaged by their attentions. He would give them half an hour by which time they must be finished.

It seemed that their long wait had not cooled their ardour at all for the men fairly rushed upstairs, even, Tobias noted with amusement, the wounded man with his injured arm in a rough splint which was obviously causing him enormous pain. Tobias wondered how on earth he would contrive to do anything; another anecdote stored in his head which due to a lack of desire to amuse or impress, he would never tell.

While the soldiers were about their business he resumed his place in the armchair, smoked and idly flicked through a book belonging to the room: a geographical acount of the southern Americas, largely fiction he thought. By his feet he saw the strongbox, now empty; obviously the share-out had already been made. He did not even consider demanding a portion for his own labours; let the common sort have their small rewards for their obedience.

His attention slid away from his bogus geographical tome and he listened to the noises he had been ignoring up to now. From outside the clamour was at much the same level as it had been for hours now, a blended mixture of human misdoings reflected in speech and cries and odd sounds of destruction. From upstairs he could hear the noise of his particular band of 'the common sort' enjoying themselves; there were various bumps and cries, and occasionally the woman screamed. Tobias found that he was thoroughly enjoying the situation. It was sufficiently far removed from his normal experience that it seemed endowed with an exhilarating freshness and novelty.

At length he consulted his timepiece, stubbed out his cigarette and from the bottom of the stairs, called time on the soldiers.

When they brought the Leveller woman down with them

(seemingly unharmed in body), she appeared to be almost surprised to find the priest still there. Then her eyes glazed over once more and her mind withdrew from the whole affair.

In fact the unfortunate girl now expected nothing but death; in part she almost wished for it. She felt as though dirty hands had dabbled with her soul.

However, to her mounting astonishment, Tobias dismissed her soldier ravishers and led her, not to the Crusader camp and thus torture and death, but through the town to the London Gate as he had promised. Several times they were accosted on their progress by officious or rowdy Crusaders but a few brief words and stern looks dispersed them. Apart from these incidents Tobias seemed oblivious of her existence or anyone else's for that matter, but she was bound to him by cruel necessity. She felt low and animal-like.

Before the heavily damaged London gate he bribed a cavalry trooper to give him his horse. She was unable to see how much this cost him but it seemed as if a large number of coins changed hands. Thus provided, and her clerical collar covered by a blanket from the saddlebag, she was waved past the half dozen drunken and sullen guards at the gate who were full of resentment at having the ill-luck to draw guard duty at such a momentous time. Tobias had not bothered to concoct a story other than to hint at a necessity for secrecy. It did not matter – no one would know, for the guards did not care and the words of a magician priest were not to be lightly contradicted.

And so, hardly crediting it, the woman went free and rode off along the road like thunder and out of Tobias' life.

However, as he had intended, in one sense they never parted – for each was to recur frequently in the other's mind, although cast in very different roles. In some obscure way which he did not bother to rationalise, it was necessary for him to know that the Leveller woman continued to wander the earth somewhere. In this way his memories of her and what he had done to her would be living things. It also pleased him to know that someone, somewhere was thinking of him, long and often.

In fact the woman successfully escaped from the area and after an initial period of confusion resumed her underground activities with one of the fanatical Gideon Groups which the surviving members of the Levellers' command council had formed subsequent to the Reading debacle. Comprising men and women who had survived the uprising or who had not been called into service, these small groups practised assassination and sabotage ostensibly as a means of destabilising Babylonian society. In reality the council members used them as instruments of angry revenge on behalf of their fallen comrades and to punish the world for not seeing the blinding truths of the councillors' beliefs.

After the shattered chains of command were reconstructed and the scattered brethren regathered, the frustrated anger of these essentially pious men began to be felt in the towns and villages of England once again.

But serious and widespread consideration of the earthly equality of man, the morality of wealth and one Church's monopoly of the means of salvation were things that awaited a more relaxed and gentle future era. When it eventually came, in a form no one suspected, all the protagonists in the Levellers' tragi-farce were dust and bones, long forgotten by all bar God.

At first the Gideon Bands achieved some measure of success; then they provoked too far, and the drastic repressive measures destroyed most of them. The survivors bided their time, reorganised, became a power again, were smashed . . . and so on, and on and on.

The Leveller woman enjoyed by Tobias became a leading light and eventually 'pastor-leader' of a group that operated around Guildford and whose trademark was the capture, castration and killing of priests. While attempting the assassination of the Bishop of Farnham, she and a number of compatriots were captured and sentenced to be burnt at the stake.

Awaiting sentence in Guildford Gaol, she went mad; but she was burnt anyway, howling and wailing just like the sane ones, on the 2nd of September 2000 AD, aged thirty.

CHAPTER 7

In which our hero refreshes himself in a tavern.

That was not the last of Tobias' exploits that day. In another house he found and had a pretty boy, although the use of brute force was necessary in this case. This was another practice he had long been curious about and he found it not unpleasing.

His physical energies at last sated, he sought and found a tavern back at the town square. The original landlord, although much battered and abused, had retained possession by the dispensing of his stock to the victorious Crusaders. His tavern maids and his wife had also been plied into service but the owner dared not protest, for at any moment these animals might decide to slit his throat and help themselves. There was no reason why they should not. His one hope was to keep them all befuddled with drink and so far he was succeeding.

Accordingly when Tobias edged through the door he entered upon a riotous scene. Soldiers of all type and degree were there, ranging from a small group of frivolously drunken English gentlemen-volunteers to the survivors of a double file of Irish gallowglasses who had reached a stage of maudlin religion. The latter crossed theselves when they saw Tobias.

The tavern was tightly packed with people at, or under, long benches. A great number were very gone in drink; some had captured local girls, most of whom seemed not unwilling partners. A few, all sense of propriety gone, rutted away quite heedlessly on the floor; no one seemed to notice unduly save to urge them on occasionally. The noise was enough to drown out the sound of the greater entertainment outside.

Moving regally through the mob, Tobias raised his hand to signal the harassed landlord. When at last the man arrived, he said, 'A table alone, cigars and a bottle of good whisky if you please.'

A small table slightly raised on a small dais at one end of the room was found, and Tobias used his rank and profession to order its two Welsh bowmen occupants away. Shortly after, he was nicely settled with a large carton of cigarettes ('All I can find, Father'), and a reasonable bottle of single malt. Tobias thought it would be ungrateful to cavil at the provisions and so thanked his host gravely. 'If you find yourself in serious peril, landlord, call upon me for help.'

'Much obliged – God bless you Father, thank you.'

The man felt a tinge of hope; perhaps he would see tomorrow and if so, he swore before Mary and all the saints he would never swerve, not a single inch, from the Church's path, not ever again.

Tobias relaxed, leant back and mulled over the events of the day. He watched the soldiers at play – drinking, swearing, shouting, screaming, fornicating – and he thought them the lowest of the low. Because his pleasures were taken in a calmer and more considered way and because they were, he thought, of a more discriminating nature, he felt very superior to the cavorting humans before him. And yet much of what *he* had found pleasurable today would have struck the common soldiers as base and bestial. Tobias now entirely lacked self-doubt and the ability to appreciate other viewpoints. He was truly the single-minded man he had wished to be.

After a while he drifted off into reverie, rousing himself only once when he saw that the landlord was in great danger of his life. Tobias caught the eye of the principal offender and an impatient gesture was enough to halt the dangerous horseplay.

In fact Tobias' vacant, brooding eyes, roaming over the scrum, acted as a considerable dampener on the collective spirit so all were glad when he decided that he had drunk and seen enough, and he stepped out into the early evening. Or nearly all.

Soon after, the unfortunate landlord was seized, bound and put to cook on his own roasting spit.

CHAPTER 8
In which our hero ponders upon the nature of things and arrives at two great truths.

It was early evening when he emerged and he envisaged returning to the camp rather earlier than originally intended. However as he walked on, his attention was caught by a large crowd in and around the Castle and the nearby abbey. He went to investigate.

Unlike Rugby, Reading was (or had been) a 'free town' without any feudal patron. Therefore the Castle was already in a state of advanced decay before that day's savage fighting. A disciplined, élite group of white-coated Leveller soldiers holding the tumbledown gatehouse had had to be destroyed almost to the last man before the stronghold fell. Inside had been a newly raised regiment of Leveller sympathisers, mostly townsfolk who, largely lacking proper weaponry, surrendered after some token resistance. Faced with so large a number of captives, five hundred or more, the senior officer at the scene had suspended the no-quarter signal, partly for practical reasons and partly through a personal Christian dislike for killing. 'Lord knows,' he'd muttered, 'there's been enough of that today.'

Later, however, he had been obliged to move to another part of the town and was succeeded at his post by a man of much coarser moral sensibilities whose religious drive was less demanding. More prisoners were crammed into the Castle and after a cull of the fittest-looking men, deemed worthy of service in the Mediterranean galleys, the slaughter began.

The remaining men (and some women) were forced on to the rampart walk of the Castle and thence into its highest surviving tower. From there, they were prodded out of a high window with a pike to plummet to the ground, perhaps seventy or eighty feet below. At the bottom of the tower, outside the wall, a group of unsolicited volunteers made sure, with dagger and spear, that the process was completed.

Tobias came upon the scene when it was already well under-way and the setting sun's weak beams were making the painful sight less stark. A constant low keening arose from the con-demned, peppered with the occasional scream. The audience buzzed with conversation, ironic laughter and applause at the failed flights.

Tobias stood at the back of the crowd for a while and watched unobtrusively. Humans constantly amazed him; how could these people just *stand* there patiently waiting to be led to their death? Why not attempt a break-out, however hopeless? Try and take a few of their killers with them and perhaps die wounded from the front like a man: that's what he would do. Pathetic milk-and-water sheep; not the same men who smashed us at breach four, and contested the Cathedral and town square until we were pleased to give the survivors' quarter. They were all dead or escaped and Tobias wished them luck in either case.

However, as always, death drew him, helpless to resist, like one of his opium addicts to their pipe and he ordered his way through the crowd to the front of the Castle. There was a heavy guard of regular soldiers at the gatehouse. For the most part the remains of the previous Leveller detachment remained in their posts also, an honour they well deserved prior to being flung into the communal lime-pit along with all the rest. The living garrison declined to challenge him and Tobias strode through into the Castle yard.

A junior officer looking very calm and collected spotted him and came over. 'Good evening, Father; can I be of any assistance?'

Tobias looked him up and down and did not like what he saw at all. A mere youth, but all puffed up with the arrogance born of lifelong privilege. He affected to be a dandy as well and had adorned his blue line-infantry uniform with gold lace and silks. Tobias put on a look of utter disgust and distaste.

'Name, rank, regiment and senior officer.'

The young officer was quite abashed and dropped a portion of his self-satisfied look.

'Timothy Savage, junior officer, Sir Malachai Ferry's regiment of horse, Colonel Sir Henry Melrose, Father.'

'Right, expect to hear more of me very soon, Savage; in the meanwhile, get me an escort through this mob and up into the tower.'

'Yes, Father.'

That should deprive him of a bit of sleep thought Tobias. Upper-class puppy.

Four musketeers were found, rather needlessly, to club a path through the horde of captives for Father Oakley and very soon he was ascending the circular steps of the tower. A curious scene at the place of execution greeted him. Two heavily bearded characters, probably pikemen in normal Army life to judge by their clothing and armour, stood at the door and ferried the individual unfortunates to the gaping window. Two more brutal-looking types stood by and wielded the half-pikes that persuaded the doomed to advance their last one or two footsteps upon this earth. Soldiers with muskets or pistols standing ready were ringed all around the walls and continued in a line down the staircase.

Supervising this efficient operation were two officers seated in comfortable armchairs pillaged from the town. They had obviously ceased to watch the process of death as the novelty wore off and were chatting lazily to each other. Both sprang up as they noticed Tobias' entrance, but he wordlessly waved them back to their seats and watched, entranced, the unfolding and repetitious drama.

In the twenty minutes or so that he stood there, abstracted, he came to see (because the lesson was hammered home again and again in a way it had not been before) that the prospect of individual extinction was only real to humans a few brief moments before it actually happened. Hence the surprising passivity in the courtyard below. He further came to appreciate that once the awful realisation *was* made, humans either found life inexpressibly beautiful (too late to appreciate their enlightenment) or were consumed with fear at the prospect before them. In either case amazing things were said and done in order to live perhaps a few seconds longer.

Tobias found this experience enormously valuable, perhaps more so than anything else that day. Life was not the cheap thing he had always thought; it was priceless – irreplaceable, mystical and unique.

However, this revelation did not make Tobias baulk at the prospect of future bloodshed. Quite the contrary: it endowed the idea with a profound significance, a 'thrill' that was now his closest approach to emotion. Killing a fellow man, he could now see, was not an occasionally necessary expedient and perhaps pleasure, but a great cosmic act of the will.

Tobias felt very much the richer for this knowledge, but he was so far gone in his blindness that he could not see that the whole thing, a lesson so expensive in human life, could be interpreted in an entirely different way.

After watching Grimes, a very cool individual and supposedly the chief heretic General, being prodded off the wall, a contemplative Tobias descended the stairs. Perhaps a quarter of the way down he noticed a captive somewhat different from the rest, a relaxed young man with long hair tied into a pony-tail and an ugly battered face. He sought and caught the priest's attention.

'Do you happen to have a cigarette you could give me, Father?'

Tobias eyed him for a moment and could see no trickery or mockery, and so said. 'By all means.'

And he lit and gave the man one of his stolen smokes. Unusually enough, he felt sufficiently curious and at ease to pursue the conversation. 'You're very unperturbed considering, young man.'

'Am I?' he replied politely and in a naturally melancholic voice, 'Yes, I suppose I am, surprisingly enough.'

'Were you active in the rebellion?'

'Yes, as a volunteer dragoon.'

'Then are you still heretic?'

'Never was, Father; just starved of excitement that's all.'

Obviously this struck a chord with Tobias, 'Then you are still true Church?'

'Would it save me if I was?'

'No.'

'Well, I am anyway.'

Tobias made the sign of the cross over him, 'Then I absolve you from all your sins so you go to death pure as at baptism, if God wills.'

Several others became agitated, some hurling basic theological abuse and others pleading similar shriving. Tobias ignored them.

'It seems strange,' said the man, 'that this is the end of me. I went to university you know. Ronald Butcher, BA, late of Oxford. All that time educating me, my parents raising me, having me for that matter: all that painful growing-up. What a waste of time.'

'Is that what you feel?'

The man shrugged.

'Well,' said Tobias in a profound tone, 'nothing lasts for ever, that's for sure.'

Then he gave the man another cigarette and set off down the stairs.

CHAPTER 9
In which our hero admires a view.

Back at camp Tobias waited patiently in his wagon-cum-bed until the last brick of his tower tumbled and then he slept the clock around. Just as unnaturally, he awoke with a start and for a moment thought himself back in time before the great assault. As then, Sykes the file captain was squatting before a cooking fire and several soldiers he recognised were also lolling around. The difference which at last re-established his sense of time was that there were a lot less soldiers than hitherto and one was swathed in bandages.

Any hangover he might have deserved had come and gone during his oblivion, but still Tobias felt stiff and generally rather grim.

'Hello, Sykes; you survived then.'

The stumpy man looked round. 'Oh, hello, sir – yes, I'm OK. I see you got scratched.'

Once mentioned, Tobias' wound began to throb.

'Have you got a mirror of some sort?'

There was a pause. 'Er . . . not really sir, but try this.'

Sykes came over to his officer's wagon with a battered morion helmet full of water. In his shimmering reflection Tobias saw there was a disfiguring mark across his temple.

'Ugly,' he said.

'But harmless, sir, so long as you washes it.'

'Permanent do you think?'

'Probably.'

Tobias swung out of the wagon. From his pack which he had hidden under the straw he took a cut-throat razor and using the water still held by Sykes he began to shave.

'What's happened and who's left?'

'Town's been under sack all night and day, sir; I think the order is to fire it now – leastways, the people are being driven out.'

'Heretics?'

'All dead or fled, they've been killing and maiming prisoners all night, sir. I 'ear tell that some regiments who escaped are making a fighting retreat across the chalk downs; only two or three at the most, mind you. Lord Pearce 'as gone after 'em.'

'Our file?'

'Ten left plus me, sir – not too bad considering the rest of the retinue.'

'I see; did you have a good day, Sykes?'

'Not bad, sir; we moved to five breach, 'twas a mite easier there, once in we split up and I enjoyed myself for a while.'

'How so?'

'Just drink and a pretty plump girl, sir, beggin' your pardon.'

Sykes had come to know Father Oakley reasonably well and so was not abashed to offer this sort of information.

'And pillaging no doubt.'

'A little, sir – just looking out for my wife and kiddies.'

'Doubtless; in that case how much do you want for a bottle of whatever drink you stole – bearing in mind I could order you to *give* it to me.'

'Er . . . a fine Bordeaux from a gentleman's cellar . . . a pound?' He offered tentatively.

'You're a bloody thief, Sykes, a pound it is and don't go for it till I've done shaving.'

'Right, sir.'

'And go and get a chair for me, comfortable mind you, and a decent wine glass too. You wouldn't understand, but this is a beautiful and important night and must not be spoilt in any detail, however small.'

'Just as you say, sir.'

The Army, Tobias discovered, was still in a state of chaos although enough troops remained under order to implement the command to fire the town. This was done partly to make an example and punish, and partly as the only conceivable means of ending the sack and thus reuniting the Army.

As usual in such events, senior officials attached to the Crown were beginning to rack their brains as to how to persuade these now unwelcome guests back to their own countries.

As it was, save for the regular Army units, troops were scattered all over the countryside and coming and going much as they pleased. Therefore, Tobias thought, there was plenty of time yet before he need report his experiences and his continued existence to a commanding officer.

And so by ten-thirty p.m. on the day following the fall of Reading, Tobias was settled comfortably in a large high-backed chair (late of a well-furnished home) with a glass of fine wine in one hand and a constant succession of cigarettes in the other. Like a barbarian chieftain, he had his (diminished) warriors seated just behind him round a large fire. To his front was a fire on an altogether more massive scale. It was an impressive panorama that Tobias had for his amusement that night. A large part of the town was merrily ablaze and in the rest tiny points of light moved as the Crusaders went about their business or the townsfolk sought escape. Similar dainty fireflies picked their way to and from the town. In the inky blackness beyond, individual farms and villages went up in flames, so that the resultant wasteland might be an eloquent warning of the dangers of heresy. In the night sky the stars twinkled merrily so that the whole earth and firmament was both burning light and deep darkness.

Despite himself Tobias was quite moved at the beauty of the dying town; the noise of the surrounding baggage train and its animals ceased to reach him. From the burning ruin he seized great truths and a rare stimulation of mind. Not a bad day or two at all.

It was a glorious thing, he thought, thus to sit in comfort, not to mention luxury, and watch the whole world on fire knowing that it was, in part, your own handiwork.

So reflecting, he sat, smoked and drank and watched Reading burn. However after a while his thoughts dulled, although he continued to raise glass and cigarette to mouth mechanically. His eyes glazed over and he fell into the even, frigid trance in which he was to spend much of the rest of his life.

BOOK FOUR

NOVEMBER 2003–NOVEMBER 2026

From: THE BOOK OF CEREMONIAL MAGIC

By Sir Arthur Waite
Published London, Auto-da-fé Press, 1911.

. . . Since I am most mindful of my moral duty to my readers and aware of the impetuosity of youth under instruction, I feel it apposite to close this volume with some words concerning an aspect of the magical arts but lightly touched upon above; namely *Demonology*.

I say straightaway it is entirely correct that the laiety, the uninvolved, be taught that such creatures are part of the Hierarchy of Hell, as named and enumerated by the Church since earliest times. The only duty of the faithful is to know, to fear and to leave well alone; subject to the very gravest penalties in this world and the next. Even to breathe the relevant names is both perilous and a sin.

The deeper truth, however, is that such powerful princes of the Enemy's realm are happily beyond the feeble summonses of man. Those who answer to our call are some lesser breed, inimical to be sure but oft-times useful. Their professed ignorance of our theological universe and their ultimate Master is, of course, a dastardly lie and only to be expected.

If on occasion we suborn Satan's footsoldiers to the cause of good, then that is a laudable thing, sanctioned by Mother Church and a fitting use of the strange talent given, in His benevolence, by God to some of the sons of Adam.

However, and I beseech you not to skip lightly over these words, the work of which I speak is not for novices. If this volume has been of any use, if its most difficult exercises have not been the merest child's play to you, if you are not shielded by the armour of virtue and steeped in long years of the deepest magic, then you are not ready.

Those who prematurely seek the company of demons will meet only one – and then spend all eternity in its company.

A.W.

London, Bognor, Jaffa. 1902–10

CHAPTER 1
In which an impressive gathering is described.

Practical considerations aside, magicians' conventions were first and foremost an excuse for socialising and dressing up. Even Tobias felt a slight surge of pleasurable expectation as, stepping on to the speaker's dais, he saw in the audience a number of old acquaintants with whom he might wish to exchange a few words. Like the rest of the glittering array gathered there, he had taken the opportunity to put on his full regalia and devote more care than usual to his appearance.

Physical middle-age had come upon Tobias early but thereafter his decline had stabilised somewhat so that he looked only a little older than other men of his age. His bald crown was today concealed by a fine scarlet sugar-loaf hat. Its shadow hid the curious broad scar which transversed his forehead while, behind, his remaining hair protruded, grown long and waxed into a fashionable stiff pigtail. He wore a matching scarlet gown of good quality cloth as befitted his Master of Magic status and it was further dignified by two medals, gleaming brightly. (One was a common award to all senior participants in the Thames Valley Crusade, the other was an award for conspicuous bravery in the field during that event – Tobias had been most surprised to receive it.)

Along with all the other worthies, he took a seat on the platform behind the long oaken table and looked benignly into the middle distance. In front of him the large lecture room was nearly full to capacity, perhaps three or four hundred people, many as highly qualified and resplendent as himself.

Outside it was bitterly cold (it was mid-November) but within the lecture hall a line of old, red painted boilers kept the temperature agreeably mild.

He realised the conference would not start for some time yet as a number of people, too exalted to be rebuked for their poor time-keeping, were still entering the room. Some kind soul had shown great consideration and prior knowledge of the speaker's habits by putting a large ashtray by his appointed place at the table. Duly reminded Tobias lit up a cigarette. He smoked constantly, mostly cigarettes, though he had a passion for cigars and pipe tobacco as well. He always held his cigarettes in a curiously distinctive manner with his palm facing outward. It was accounted to be another of his mild eccentricities and it came to be a widely known mannerism; in due course of time it was even copied by young magicians seeking to emulate an illustrious figure in their profession in every detail.

Through the large side windows Tobias could see the impressive and gloomy bulk of Westminster Abbey to which the lecture theatre (kindly lent by the Archbishop) was attached. Judging by the clouds he would not be at all surprised if it snowed in a short while.

All of the conference organisers and participants had just marched in solemn ceremonial order from the Abbey where a special mass had been conducted in honour of such an important occasion. Once this was out of the way everything became much more informal and up to a point the finer elements of rank and seniority were forgotten in an atmosphere of professional expectation. Rumours were about that this conference was to be a particularly significant one and, in pursuance of raising such hopes, Tobias had deliberately chosen a striking title for his initial address. He could see people reading this in the conference programme, raising their eyebrows, drawing their neighbours' attention to it and then gazing at him in a vain attempt to seek further clarification. Obviously his innocent ploy had worked, although its success or failure mattered not a jot. Perhaps, on second thoughts, it was a touch on the vulgar side but neither did this worry him; magicians were renowned for their supposed lack of 'good taste' and could be safely relied upon not to notice any such minor skirmish with propriety.

A depressed-looking Aborigine steward came round bearing a tray of coffees for the speakers. It was to be presumed that he was the same man who had thoughtfully provided for Tobias' incendiary habits and so he was favoured with a polite smile as Tobias took his cup. Coffee always made him feel a slight tinge of cheerfulness. Even after all these years it still had all the properties and associations of a rare treat to him although his kitchen never lacked a large jar of it (of the one and only type he favoured), now that his fortunes had so improved.

He placidly stirred the beverage and studied the audience as they buzzed and hummed and shuffled to their seats – several bishops, perhaps a round dozen masters of magic, maybe twice that number of assistant masters. In fact they formed a very imposing group if a speaker happened to be nervous, which Tobias was not.

Also scattered about the room was a handful of black-gowned elderly men whom Tobias took to be dons of theoretical magic from one of the universities. And there were a few magicians from the Army and Navy distinguished by their extravagant blue uniforms. In practice the Forces did not attract magicians of high calibre or learning, and very often His Majesty's Army or Navy served as a safe refuge when some professional or social indiscretion came to light. One man, to judge by his dark-red suit of military cut, was attached to the papal forces stationed in London; therefore one could presume he was not English (it was strict papal policy to station troops in countries other than that of their origin), and that he was a man of exceptional talent.

Also present, unknown to Tobias, were observers from the great teaching schools at Rome and Avignon. There at their own behest were individual Church magicians from The Empire, France, Ireland, Scotland, the Duchy of Cornwall, 'Free Wales' (unbeknown to the organisers for, of necessity, the man in question was masquerading as a Breton for the duration of the conference) and a host of other, lesser, nations. The brotherhood between magicians, born of a common search for knowledge, could, on occasion, transcend Christendom's hobbling sense of nationalism.

The rest of the gathering was made up of contingents from the English teaching centres, London (Westminster), London (Southwark) and Liverpool; both teachers and pupils. Tobias was pleased to note a short row of journeymen who bore a ring of stars on their armbands similar to his own, but he did not recognise the two senior magicians in charge of them.

A large number of freelance magicians, nearly all Church-trained but now working in secular fields, completed the gathering, their occupations and apparel being too diverse to recount. They were either men of ability but dubious reputation, akin to Phillip Chitty, too good for the forces but too degraded for the Church or of insufficient ability to be required by either.

It would be more correct to say that these 'Jack-magicians'

almost completed the gathering for at the last moment, when the chairman was clearing his throat as a means of requesting silence and Tobias was meaningfully shuffling his notes, two most unexpected guests entered the room and the conference was unquestionably delayed until the new arrivals were ready.

It was a rare thing for a Grand Master of Magic to travel at all, let alone attend conferences where, surely, he could learn nothing new. And yet, here, the conference – and indirectly Tobias as chief speaker – was honoured by the presence of the Grand Master of Magic of the South-East. This grossly corpulent man was responsible for all matters magical and all related 'political' interests of the Church in an area greater than that presided over by England's grandest noblemen, although he was but the son of an illiterate fisherman from Newhaven. From such humble beginnings, Baxter had risen to a position where it was quite within his power to strike off the heads of all those who exploited and burdened his father. Yet he forbore to do so because he was, or had become, a very practical man with whom such passions as revenge and snobbery had not even a passing acquaintance. It is a paradox of power that it is often necessary to renounce some of the more stimulating emotions, the indulgence of which is one of power's major attractions, in order to attain it in the first place.

Men like Baxter usually remained ensconced in their palaces, fully absorbed in the myriad complexities of their little kingdoms. In theory they were answerable only to the King and the two Archbishops.

However, for this unusual occasion he had brought his assistant along with him, himself a high-ranking Master. In great contrast to his master, the assistant was an abnormally thin man, emaciated to the point of being skeletal. His skin had a bluish tinge to it although that might have been a trick of the light.

The two men unhurriedly made their way to vacant seats in the very front of the concourse acknowledging no one and leisurely settled themselves.

At once the atmosphere was charged with a new excitement, since this was a great portent. To magicians, such a man as the Grand Master carried more weight than any other of their spiritual superiors; as professionals they respected his implied expertise over and above the respect due to any other person. His presence was a great commendation to any enterprise.

Once arranged to his own satisfaction, the corpulent Grand Master indulgently waved a beringed hand as a signal to proceed.

With his self-assurance only slightly diminished, the chairman (Master of Magic to the Bishop of Lincoln) rose to give the initial address.

'Your Grace, Brothers, esteemed guests, it is my honour and privilege this year to welcome you to the one hundred and thirteenth Annual Thaumaturgical Conference of England. May I say how gratified I am to see here so many senior and renowned members of our vocation gathered together in a common enterprise of enquiry. This laudable spirit makes us all look forward to a profitable exchange of views and knowledge this week and therefore I will delay the start as little as possible by my introduction. As you are all aware our general theme is that of Demonology, a field in which there has been surprisingly little research in the last century or so. It is therefore with great pleasure that I introduce Father Tobias Oakley, who is currently Master of Magic to the Bishop of Reading, and who is undoubtedly well known to you all through his widely acclaimed publications. As senior speaker, Father Oakley's first paper is entitled . . . '

The chairman picked up his agenda sheet and quizzed it through his pince-nez (an affectation – they contained clear glass).

' . . . is entitled, "Demonology – An Over-elaborate Art". A most intriguing title I think you'll agree. Your Grace, Brothers: Father Oakley.'

Tobias stood up to an encouraging round of applause. He bowed politely to the Grand Master.

'Your Grace, Ladies and Gentlemen.' (Here he scored a point, for perhaps a third of the more junior magicians present were women. The Church had recently relaxed the rules on such matters, for as its Empire grew larger, more and more possessors of the talent were required and those thus gifted could not be passed over solely on the grounds of gender.)

'I hope I am not being over-ambitious in my plans for my address but, to be blunt, my intention is in the course of this conference to diminish the demonological art radically. Hence the somewhat sensationalist title I notified to the Agenda Committee, for which I hope you'll forgive me.

'To be specific, I intend to show that around one fifth of the ceremonies described as "essential" in the standard texts for the ten major summonings are unnecessary elaborations and can therefore be safely dispensed with. I hasten to say, however, that my task is not entirely a destructive one. Alongside the proposals I have just outlined, I also intend to describe new spells or ceremonies of my own design which reinforce or improve existing formulae for summoning, subduing and dismissal.

'In short, brothers and sisters, I hope to offer you the basis for a wholly revised standard demonological manual.'

Those who knew him or had read his works appreciated that he was not a man given to hyperbole and so Tobias was gratified to hear a low hum of reaction in the hall and to see the Grand Master's eyebrow arch in mild surprise.

He drained the dregs of his coffee to provide a suitable pause and then continued.

'Of course I cannot hope to accomplish this in one day, in fact I'm not entirely sure how long it will take. However if you will bear with me I believe your tolerance will be amply rewarded by the end of this conference.'

He cleared his throat – another timely pause. The audience readied their inksticks and pads. A number of the younger delegates had the exhilarating sense of being present while magical history was being made. The older and less impressionable hands entertained hopes of a conference that was going to be profitable in both professional *and* social terms; usually only the latter could be relied upon.

Tobias' voice was not unpleasant, it had come to be deep and even-toned. He spoke in a relaxed, conversational manner that at times seemed almost like a soliloquy. Thus, although this was not the ideal voice for delivering an address, its very calmness made the listeners concentrate all the more to grasp its meaning.

'Perhaps I should begin by a concise summary of the art today and thereby point out the subtle inconsistencies which first prompted my researches.

'As you all know, Demonology and its associated practices was first codified for the Church by the Spaniard Ibarra nearly eight hundred years ago. Liguori's masterful work in the 1790s, built on the great Corbishley Codex, allowed us to dispense with the previous artificial divisions of demons into "good" and "evil". For in practice such distinctions were found not to exist. His three-volume work published posthumously in 1815 gave the major details of the ten major and ninety-seven minor summonings which remain substantially unchanged up to the present day . . . '

CHAPTER 2
In which our hero delivers a lecture.

Tobias spoke and drew on the blackboard with coloured chalks; he gave what he knew to be a good performance. Each session of the two and a half days for which he lectured was attended by more and more magicians, many of them very senior, as the news spread.

It was, however, all very stale stuff. He was merely relating that (larger) portion of his researches at Rugby which he had been too cautious and close-lipped to reveal in his first, small-circulation publications. It was only now, years later, that he realised there was more to gain in sharing his acquired knowledge over and above the advantage of keeping it to himself. During his years of practical experience he had effectively carried the framework of a complete revision of the standard Demonological texts around in his head. Therefore when invited to speak on the strength of his previous publications, he decided to unburden himself of this hard-won knowledge and dispense his wisdom to a wider audience. If the theoretical stuff was peppered with a few impressive anecdotes from his practical use of the research, then he felt sure the resultant lectures would be very well received.

Every so often the conferences saw breakthroughs in theoretical magic and in each case the instigator's reputation was raised very high. Even Tobias could not call his work a 'breakthrough' but the revision of a long-established textbook was an achievement which lingered lastingly in the memory of magicians. Tobias was not interested in such longevity, but in the advancement to magical studies which accrued from it. In part this stance showed that the years had matured him somewhat. He could now see that secrecy and the pursuit of purely personal advantage were not necessarily the best policy.

But it was, as has been said, all rather stale stuff. Tobias thought he had perfected his demonology, when he had not, and considered his researches at an end, when they were not. For a number of years he had worked instead for revived sensitivity to the ordinary human pleasures for which he now so desperately craved.

CHAPTER 3

In which our hero attends a party and renews an old acquaintance.

All and sundry were agreed that the conference had been memorably successful. Aside from Tobias' *tour de force*, other speakers had delivered addresses which neatly complemented his by expanding certain areas or filling in points of detail. Towards the end of the week a bright young spark called Fuller, an intense, pale Assistant Master of Magic from Portsmouth, had revealed some quite stunning research work. This seemed to point the way to a new, hitherto-unknown minor summoning and in the subsequent discussion session it was agreed that a team of more highly qualified practitioners would follow the matter up and see if there was anything in it. In which case Fuller's complete disregard for his safety in having pursued such a project on his own was amazing. Bereft of proper, tried and tested ceremonies, 'summonings were suicide'; so ran a piece of doggerel that Tobias' instructors were fond of reciting and he was well placed to appreciate its essential truth. If the investigating team of Masters found Fuller's hypotheses and tentative experiments to have any solid basis, then there was certainly a doctorate in it for him with sure promotion in its train.

And yet Fuller's suspected triumph in no way detracted from Tobias' greater one. On the contrary it added to it, for the conference would be remembered as the one where the principles of the fourth revised edition of the Demonological Manual were laid down *and* where the search for an entirely new minor summoning was successfully initiated. In the glory accruing from this joint achievement, it was Tobias' name that would be remembered and which would find immortality on the cover of the manual over which future generations of students would toil.

So, at the end of the week's conference, Tobias had every reason to rejoice and, after his own manner, he did. Yet it was a cold and arid satisfaction that he felt. His success was seen only in terms of the pursuit of his chosen path and plan and nowadays he was unsure that this almost-lifelong obsession of his had any value at all; certainly, to date, it had afforded him precious little enjoyment. However, lacking any alternative that seemed even vaguely attractive and meaningful, he would carry on. He reconciled himself to the fatalistic thought that it was too late in the day to consider any change now, and therefore any further debate was useless.

Such reflective moments came to him quite often, usually prompted by some obligatory event or action which gave him no pleasure or peace. In his especially black moments he felt he was spending his life doing things not to his inclination. But all such sloughs quickly passed, and before long he would be treading his lonely path, unreflectively, once more.

Baron Philby's patronage could carry him no further forward; therefore his career needed an extra fillip, such as he had achieved at the conference, if he was to ascend to the greatest heights. So Tobias was pleased.

With every rose, however, there are thorns and one of the penalties he had to endure as part of his success was to be present at the semi-formal reception which traditionally ended each conference. Tobias had seen all the people he wanted to see: a few prominent theoreticians whose brains he wished to pick and two acquaintances of his from his days at Llandaff and the Gower campaign. Now all he wished for was to be removed from this wearisome babble, alone in some locked room with a book and a drink for company. After all the talking of the last week he had nothing more to say to anyone. However, he clamped on a fixed polite smile and wandered among the colourful chattering throng of magicians, making the right impressions.

The reception was being held in one of the many large chambers in the Archbishop's palace, which would have been called ballrooms but for their situation. Most of the invited guests had turned up and so the room was quite full. A number of those who, for various reasons, had not been invited (including the incognito Welshman) appeared anyway and so leavened the gathering with their less conventional personages.

Outside it was snowing yet again, but the room was pleasantly warm. The Archbishop's servants wandered around distributing mulled wine and beer. Coffee, tea and hot chocolate were also available from a table at one side of the room on which there were plates of savoury delicacies. At the door everyone was handed a tulip-glass of very fine sherry; Tobias took the first opportunity to covertly dispose of this into a convenient bowl of trifle because over the years he had found that this was the one drink that not only tasted unpleasant but also gave a strong hangover without providing any prior state of intoxication as an inducement or consolation.

Instead, he armed himself with a mug of hot, spiced beer, and thus fortified, moved randomly through the crowd to exchange a few, meaningless, words here and there. At one point, rather suddenly, he found himself facing the Archbishop himself. Their eyes met, locked and thus there was no alternative but to go up and present himself. Tobias made a knee and kissed his spiritual Lord's ring. He had seen him quite often before but only from afar; now, close up, he was less than impressed. The Archbishop was a very small, bald man, with tiny, almost Asiatic eyes and a trim goatee beard (a fashion of perhaps fifty years before). Tobias had heard that he was a man of political ambition first and foremost, with a mind unencumbered by convention and yet blessed with subtlety. Their conversation went some way to confirming the former, if not the latter report, for after a brief phrase of congratulations concerning the conference, the Archbishop went on to ask a number of probing, knowledgeable questions about the distribution of real authority and power in the Reading diocese – which Tobias did his best to answer. Beside the Archbishop stood a tall, thin secretary, who was quite openly noting down the replies. Then after commissioning Tobias to draft him a precis of the conference's findings, the Archbishop made it clear without actually saying so that the interview was at an end and Tobias bowed himself away.

Even he found this treatment a trifle brusque, and more sensitive souls would have felt violated. However accomplished this prelate was at playing politics he had no knack for making friends. Probably at his exalted level he thought there was no necessity to do so, considered Tobias, also estimating that, if so, such an attitude would be the Archbishop's downfall, and serve the silly little man right – playing at being cold and ruthless, what did he know? People who saw complete obedience as the only form of behaviour due from a subordinate were destined never to go very far. There are stronger human bonds to play upon, but clever-clever idiots like this one ignore and despise them because they're so wrapped up in their pose of cold-heartedness.

Having retired out of the Archbishop's sight, Tobias found a safe place by the wall where he could stand and drink with a good chance of being left alone.

How much less proficient ordinary humans were at devising and doing evil of their own accord compared to tutored people such as himself, Tobias concluded. They lack style and imagination because they don't have any ideology and faith other than the pig-like pursuit of their own material interests. When they assume a ruthless philosophy without the moral grounding of some greater belief, they are merely shallow and base. In this strange inverted way Tobias had become morally squeamish.

His thoughts were interrupted by a tall middle-aged man, perhaps ten years older than Tobias and of Master of Magic status judging by his apparel. Tobias thought his thin sincere face somewhat familiar but it was hard to say because of the heavy black beard which concealed much of the lower features. He had stopped opposite Tobias and was holding his hand out in a friendly manner; for all Tobias knew the man could have been there some time while he was lost in his dark spiral of thought, so he hastened to shake the proffered hand and composed a greeting.

'Good day to you, sir; I have a feeling I should know you, but I hope you'll forgive me if I can't quite place . . . '

'Staples . . . from Southwark. You surely remember Mucky Hall, Tobias?'

'Of course . . . please forgive my poor memory for names and faces – so many years have passed since I last saw you and you have changed somewhat. How do you do, Father Staples?'

'Very well, thank you; and may I be allowed to congratulate a former pupil on his progress in the world? You've done credit to Southwark, Tobias!'

'Thank you so much, Father Staples.'

Geoff Staples dimly remembered that Tobias had been a quiet and reserved boy but had not expected this cold formality; he had even caught a glint of offended disapproval in Oakley's eyes the second time he had called him by his christian name. Accordingly he rephrased his next address.

'Your conference address was quite masterful, Father, but I don't ever remember you specialising in demonology during training.'

'It was an extra-curricular interest, Father Staples.'

A liveried Abyssinian flunky stopped to offer them a tray of sweetmeats. He was probably there voluntarily, a freeman in service to pay for a Church education; for Rome had long ago set its heavy hand against all forms of slavery.

Tobias waved him away before Staples had the chance to indulge.

The conversation died and as the silence stretched, Tobias felt obliged to continue the exchange.

'And do you still work at Southwark, Father?'

'Until three years ago when I was transferred to the school at Liverpool — '

Downgraded, thought Tobias absently. ' — where I run a course specialising in developing the talent in those where it is weak or marginal, or even periodic as in one or two cases.'

'I see,' said Tobias and then was lost for something else to say.

'Sir Matthew Elias and Wally Faulkner are both dead, you know,' said Staples, gamely persevering.

'Oh . . . and how is that?'

'Sir Matthew by food poisoning about ten years ago (he never took care over his food you know), and poor old Wally was stabbed in the back by some street assailant five years ago.'

'I'm most sad to hear that.'

'Did you ever keep in touch with your fellow journeymen, Father – how are they?'

'I'm afraid we rather lost track of one another and so I'm sorry to say I'm unable to inform you, Father Staples.'

'I see. Well, I must be going. It was pleasant seeing you again. While I'm in London with the Liverpool contingent, please come and visit me and we'll dine together. We're staying at The Saracen in Cheapside.'

'Thank you, Father Staples', said Tobias, most insincerely. 'I will certainly do so. Until then . . . '

And so, considerably hurt and slighted, the normally amiable Father Staples moved off. Unmolested once more, Tobias was sufficiently misguided to think that he had handled this bore rather well, having concealed his lack of desire for conversation very cleverly.

And so, lost in directionless thought and drinking moderately, he was sought out by Grand Master Baxter and his assistant, Hillaire, who had only just arrived at the reception. In heading straight for Tobias, they delivered a calculated snub to the Arch-bishop at whose behest the function was being held. Spotting their approach, Tobias hurriedly put his glass down and made a bow.

'May I have a word with you, Father Oakley . . . ?' said the Grand Master in a pleasant, calm voice.

'By all means your Grace, my time is at your disposal.'

'Thank you. I'll be brief, I'm a man of few words. Anyway – heard your speech; I've read your publications: I liked them. I've taken references and for the most part I approve of your career as well. Do you want a job in my establishment? Pretty senior. What do you say? Yes or no?'

Tobias had only heard scant rumours about the Grand Master and so his abruptness took him by surprise. To give himself time to think, he tried to stall him. 'What would be the nature of the post, your Grace?'

'My present assistant, Mr Hillaire here — ' He indicated the tall Master of Magic beside him. ' — has cancer, rapidly entering the terminal stage, and so does not have long to live.'

Only slightly shocked or embarrassed, too caught up in his own need to make a decision, Tobias could not help but turn to look at Hillaire and directly saw the proof of these words. The unfortunate man's skin was almost translucent and, beneath it, bluish conglomerations were visible. He returned Father Oakley's stare in a steady, not unfriendly manner. Thus satisfied, Tobias turned to look at the Grand Master who in his corpulence looked the very opposite of Hillaire's ill-health. He noticed that Baxter had the entirely expressionless, inscrutable eyes that he associated with those who were untrustworthy.

Still, Tobias could hardly believe it. For a few brief seconds of weakness, he wished for a friend with whom he could share the good news. Was he really being offered an Assistant-Grandmastership on a plate? His self-belief was second to none but, even so, it took some adjustment to see himself as the second senior magician in all of South-east England. Besides, the assistants were the ones who really *ran* things, they were the ones in the seat of power.

'It would be the very greatest honour, your Grace, but at present I am — '

'That presents no difficulties; transfers can be arranged.'

'In that case I wish to accept your offer, your Grace.'

'Good; you will be hearing from your superiors about it.' Baxter half turned to go, but then remembered something. 'By the way, I don't think Fuller's hypothesis will come to anything, I spotted a significant error in his thaumaturgical geometry quite early on in his address. The effects he reported were probably incidental sub-stream from some existing summoning. Could be wrong though. Thought you'd like to know.'

With that the two men bowed perfunctorily at the Archbishop and made their exit.

At last Tobias had something really interesting to think about and he seized upon it hungrily, so ignoring the curious stares of his professional brothers. Later on, as soon as seemed decently possible, he left as well and thus became prey to more open speculation than hitherto.

CHAPTER 4

In which our hero is pondered upon by his new employer.

That evening Grand Master Baxter dictated a letter to his superior, the Grand Master of London. Ordinarily this responsible job would have been entrusted to Kenneth Hillaire but early on in the evening the pain had grown too onerous and he had drugged himself heavily and departed to his room to seek rest. Accordingly a trusted secretary was detailed to take down Baxter's words, copy them neatly and finally despatch them in a letter duly sealed with the South-east region's symbol of anchor and corn-sheaf.

Although he was a man who used speech sparingly, Grand Master Baxter often grew quite expansive in correspondence where, unable to gauge the recipient's immediate reaction, he was inclined to labour and repeat points.

'. . . and so if you will grant me this indulgence in the matter of Father Oakley, I would be very much in your debt. As I have stated it is very much to be desired that I maintain the existing high reputation of the South-eastern region by continuing to recruit senior staff of exceptional talents and wide experience. In this way the present high standard of service to the administrative and governmental echelons in the area will be preserved.

'Furthermore . . . ' He paused. 'Just a moment, Jagger, how much do you think this letter will come to?'

'Just over two pages I would imagine, your Grace,' replied the secretary whose outline was dimly visible in the shadows of the large room.

'Quite enough – more than enough for that impatient crowd in London. Very well, sign it off with the usual stuff and bring it for signing tomorrow morning. I think that will be all for now, Jagger. Goodnight.'

The Grand Master was feeling comfortable and relaxed. A large log fire was warming him nicely on the exterior and a glass of brandy was performing the same task on the inside. Having just dined well, he felt that his material needs were fully satisfied for he was a man of simple tastes in matters not affecting the mind.

His rare trip away from home was not so bad as he had anticipated. A suitably comfortable room had been procured for him at an inn near to the Abbey and away from the Church's rather . . . spartan Whitehall Citadel. Doubtless the innkeeper was fleecing poor distracted Hillaire over money, but the food was both ample and pleasing.

At one point he had been tempted to leave the selection of a new assistant to the relevant Church authorities; however it was *such* an important appointment (to him) that he had forced himself to make a personal effort. Where better to look, in that case, than at a conference packed to the gills with able magicians?

Now it was over and the prospect of home was close, he was glad he had come for he felt he had found just the right person *and* he'd heard some interesting ideas into the bargain. London was awful, however, and the aura of the Archbishop's authority even worse. In fact now he thought upon it, he had allowed his dislike of his spiritual superior to become too apparent and public today. It was a pity that he and the Archbishop did not get on and yet since the same state of affairs prevailed with most of the other Grand Masters it was not of grand import. In practice, if not in theory, the two men were of almost equal power and authority and so neither could unduly harm the other. Still it was a shame to be on bad terms with anyone unnecessarily and he made a mental note to mention the situation to his confessor.

He had spent his brief hard childhood beside the sea and now in his old age he had returned to it. He was never entirely happy away from it and this was part of his general homesickness. Another consideration was that in his home region nothing went on in Church circles (and very little in government circles either) that he did not know about and approve of first, and he missed the feeling of security that this gave. There in his great palace beside the beach he directed the affairs of men, developed his magic to a level entirely unsuspected by others and in broad terms felt safe and happy. His rule in his little kingdom, from the River Test in the West to the Straits of Dover in the East, from Wight in the South to the Thames in the North, was a benevolent one he thought. In recruiting this Oakley fellow he hoped the tradition would be continued; if references were anything to go by all should be well. Everyone from Oakley's Southwark training school through to the Bishops of Llandaff and Reading had spoken of his quiet efficiency. Some baron or other and a couple of decorated Crusaders had testified as to his character. His exceptional ability and brilliant mind were undeniable.

Yes, all in all, the Grand Master thought his guardian angel had smiled upon him in placing Father Oakley at his disposal and he was sure he had made the right decision. Someone endowed with quiet efficiency was just what he needed as the years began to lie heavy on him and his erudite researches became too time-consuming.

His mind thus at rest, Grand Master James Baxter drained his glass, said a quick rosary and took himself off to bed.

CHAPTER 5

In which our hero's sleep is disturbed and he revisits a place from his youth.

Across the river on that cold snowy night, Tobias had taken up residence in a Southwark hotel. He had remembered it from the old days and found it practically unchanged. During the conference he had resided decorously in rooms near the Abbey, provided by the Archbishop; now he need not worry and could follow the dictates of his tastes.

At about eleven-fifteen p.m. when the Grand Master snuffed out his bedside candle, Tobias was fast asleep. More accurately his repose could be described as a drunken slumber for he was slouched in an upholstered chair, fully clothed and still determinedly clutching a half-empty bottle of whisky. Empty bottles of wine lay about him.

Nor was he alone in the rather elegant room for he had spent the evening in the company of a young girl who now sat sulkily in the chair facing his while sipping a glass of wine. She was watching the magician intently.

Linda Partridge was not a regular fixture of the hotel-cum-bordello; she was one of the irregular members of the Bishop of Southwark's legions, a 'street lady' as they were called. Fourteen years old as near as she could reckon, normally she plied and conducted her trade in the streets but on nights such as this it became impossible, so she was particularly pleased to have been picked up by the sorcerer-priest as his partner for the night. It meant a warm room to sleep in, only one customer to please instead of many and, if she was lucky, the chance of breakfast on the morrow. All of which outweighed Linda's fear of magicians. In any case Linda was a brave girl since, in her time, she had to deal with clients more frightening than this quiet, elderly man.

Tobias' selection of this particular girl was in character, for she had almost shoulder-length straight black hair. Another attraction was that at this early stage in her career her face retained elements of childish innocence.

After impressing her by the quality of his hotel and by the meal he'd bought her quite shamelessly in front of all the other guests, later, in his room, Tobias had taken her in several peculiar ways still only vaguely familiar to her and which she'd found distasteful. Then, with surprising speed and quiet determination, he had drunk himself into unconsciousness.

Perhaps because her expectations had initially been raised too high, Linda felt a little upset and disappointed. The sorcerer had hardly spoken a word to her other than to issue orders, had used her in a nasty way which hurt her insides and had now passed out on her. Wizards were much like all other men then, piggish and rather disgusting.

She crouched in the armchair and wondered what to do. How ugly he looked, she thought, his chin was on his chest and his bald pate showed prominently; what hair he had left was arrayed in long and greasy rats-tails. With his powerful eyes closed, his face looked pale and plain and was disfigured by a long scar across his brow. To add to her mounting distaste he began to snore gently. What she had seen of his body had failed to impress either; he was dead-white and running to flab.

All in all she was beginning to feel pleasantly superior and quite bold. Wizards were nothing to fear after all.

It was this self-induced confidence that gave her the idea of taking Tobias' purse from his travelling coat and thus vastly increasing her profits for the night. It would serve him right for being so disgusting; he would never find her and besides her family needed the money.

The deed done, Linda moved quietly towards the door which she knew was not locked and twisted the handle. Or rather she tried to for it would not move at all; she tried again, failed and then pulled on the door with all her might.

At that instant the room was flooded with a flash of light that even Linda knew to be far from natural. There was a noise like a vast drum being sounded in another world far away and Tobias sat up suddenly, his eyes wide open.

He extended his arm and pointed at the girl. A tremendous force picked her up and pinned her, feet off the ground, against the still-closed door. The pressure was such that she could not even make a noise but hung, gaping, as if crucified. In a few seconds she thought her body would burst.

Before then, however, intelligence and wakefulness of a kind returned to Tobias. Recognising his victim, he flicked his finger and then lowered his arm. The girl fell heavily to the floor and lay still, quite breathless. The unnatural light was beginning to fade from the room leaving only the two candles as before.

Tobias staggered up, went over to the girl and stirred her with a foot. She seemed unharmed and was looking at him through fear-widened eyes. His tastes were now such that he gained a pleasurable *frisson* from this.

For no particular reason he went to the window which looked out over the Thames. Swigging from his whisky bottle and looking at the city lights across the river, he suddenly remembered that it was from this very hotel that he had first killed a man . . . a fat American bosun . . . twenty-six years ago. What had he become that he could almost forget that?

Somehow the remembrance had put him in a black mood. Drinking heavily he went to the bed and fell on to it. He saw his black-haired whore get to her knees, still looking at him. From his pillow he regarded her with drunken fatigue.

'I shall deal with you in the morning,' he slurred, 'not gently this time either.' It looked as if he had more to say but at that point a blackout suddenly overtook him.

Linda looked fearfully at the future Assistant Grand Master of Magic in the South-east and resolved never again to provoke the wrath of wizards. Tobias would have a fully compliant and respectful partner the next morning.

CHAPTER 6 – 2011 AD
In which our hero's new life is described and in which he comes to a decision.

Tobias found life entirely agreeable at the Grand Master's lonely palace on the beach at Pevensey Bay. The quiet efficiency discerned in him by successive exploiters of his peculiar talents enabled him to settle in very quickly. After Hillaire's not unexpected death, Grand Master Baxter was impatient to off-load the routine administration of his realm on to Tobias' shoulders. Only then could he return to the vast library where he toiled away, day after day, pursuing his own projects.

Accordingly a very wide range of powers was entrusted to Father Oakley and with very little preparation he found himself responsible for a not unrespectable slice of Christendom. Nor was Baxter's faith in him misplaced, for Tobias had spent his life preparing for just such a task.

Elements of the existing apparatus did not entirely please him and he was allowed to sweep them away. Similarly he found certain members of the Grand Master's staff less than impressive and these he was permitted to replace with men and women of his own selection.

In short, Tobias had the effect of a new broom and he brushed away with a will. Baxter, by now fully confident of his new Assistant's ability, retired thankfully to his research and was rarely seen. Tobias, for his part, found it easy to drop into the system once his reforms were fully established and after a year or so worked only in a supervisory capacity.

Following an initial shaky period when innovation met resistance and a number of enemies were made, the administration of Church thaumaturgy in the South-eastern region was as efficient as it had ever been. The fact did not go entirely unnoticed in certain high circles even though the maintenance of pre-existing high standards was not usually an occasion for praise.

Once upon a time Tobias would have found complete fulfilment in obtaining and holding such a position. He would have constantly compared its importance in terms of power and status with the lowliness of his beginnings. Now he fretted in the free time his efficiency had created for himself.

That is not to say he was not pleased with the operation he ran and the fruition of plans that it represented. Indeed at odd times he would linger pensively before a large map of the area entrusted to him and feel a twinge of pleasure at the scope of his influence. Soon, however, the old vacant reverie would creep upon him and he would emerge from it to find anything up to an hour gone with only the vaguest remembrance of it in his mind.

The truth of the matter was that the South-eastern region was too quiet an area for a man of his type. Upsets or dramas were few and after three years had passed he found he had created a system that functioned so well it rarely really needed him.

As Assistant to a Grand Master he would normally have been fair game for all sorts of political machinations which would at least have provided some distraction. Unfortunately, his burgeoning reputation and whispered history discouraged his fellow magicians from any such moves.

Therefore, for the first time since the talent was discovered in him Tobias lacked any identifiable enemies upon which to externalise his inner conflicts. The closest he came to appreciating this state of affairs was to note a growing tendency for introspection which sometimes left him in his 'nothingness' and other times shaking with a murderous rage. As a conscious remedy he decided to adopt Grand Master Baxter's ways and immerse himself in research.

At the time of making this decision, unusually enough he had no existing project in hand. After studying demonology and self-subjection, his attention had turned to attempts to make himself susceptible to the simpler pleasures: the joys of the table and the bed for instance. When this failed he tried to conjure himself peace, for it now seemed happiness was denied to him. For the first time in his life his hard work, painstaking study and constant application availed him not at all and he had to admit himself defeated by a problem of research. The best result he could show for these several years of work was a kind of self-induced trance deeper than any hitherto taught him which might masquerade as 'peace' but which was really little better than his mindless periods of abstraction.

For once magic had failed him. Alcohol provided only a temporary solace which required steadily increasing doses to achieve the desired effect. Hashish and opium were unobtainable with unjustified effort and the opportunities for sexual expression to suit Tobias' tastes were few and far between at lonely Pevensey Bay.

For a long time he pottered around with several minor research problems which kept him occupied even if they added little to his knowledge. Then after nearly seven years of faithful service to the Grand Master, Tobias had an idea which, if successful, would resolve his nagging doubts one way or another for ever. It had come to the point where certain pressing questions had to be resolved or else mere habit was the only reason for carrying on.

CHAPTER 7

In which our hero's new home and its pleasing environs are fully described.

Grand Master Baxter was a son of the sea and so when, against all expectations, he rose high in the world he invested his new-found wealth in a grand residence in the seaside location of his choice. Such was the traditional right of every Grand Master.

Previous to his arrival, Pevensey Bay had been inhabited by a few impoverished fishermen whose collected dwellings did not merit the name of village. Aside from this intrusion the coast ran from Hastings to sedate Eastbourne without any sign of man's presence.

A little further inland a slightly more cultured community clustered around the ruin of the old Roman shore fort and went by the name of Pevensey village. To say the least it was not an area which figured often in the affairs of Church or government until, that is, Baxter's whim began to take shape on the shoreline.

Looking back, the Grand Master thought the whole thing had been a little overdone: too large for his needs, too fashionable for the region and decidedly too expensive. Still, the extravagance was forgivable for, at the time, he had been rendered slightly light-headed by the scale of his new-found wealth and position. All in all he was happy with the place despite these cavils.

He made his home in the west wing – the house was modelled on the then popular classical Roman style with a central block and two protruding wings – and left the rest of his residence for staff and servants to occupy. From one balcony at the front of his wing he had an uninterrupted view over the sea and could behold both tranquillity and chaos. From the balcony at the rear he could view Pevensey village and the Roman castle, and behold reassuring antiquity.

In the sheltered areas between the two wings he had created an ornate decorative garden, complete with a vastly expensive fountain in which stone sea-serpents cavorted. There, when weather permitted, he would stroll in gentle reflection as a means of relaxation.

It was a pre-eminently civilised dwelling place even if the surrounding country was apt to be a little sombre out of summer. Surprisingly, for a man no longer of very strong opinions, Tobias liked the place from the start. The crumbling Roman fort in the village; the deserted marshes behind the shoreline; the black timber shacks of the fishermen; the grandly incongruous 'palace' of the Grand Master – all appealed to him. He had arrived in February on a day when the sea was stormy and the sky black with rain-clouds. Seeing the huge house outlined against the grey nothingness of the Channel horizon, he was charmed. He was not to know that the scene would be less appealing to him in summer when brassy sunbeams made the area look like one of the sickly watercolours refined young ladies were encouraged to execute. At such times he retreated to the house and had the curtains drawn tight. Fortunately high summer was short in that region and some of the cheerlessness of the nearby scenery that comforted Tobias quickly returned.

He found himself an agreeable suite of rooms in the east wing and was soon very comfortable. Once settled and moderately familiar with the building's geography, he set to work on ensuring his comfort was fully maintained. He quickly ascertained that a number of the senior servants had taken the opportunity of Hillaire's lengthy illness and the consequent lack of supervision to make merry. It seemed clear to Tobias that the amount of fine foods and wines in the storehouse was considerably less than it should be. Suspiciously enough, however, the stock of lesser-quality food and drink put aside for the servants' consumption looked as if it was barely touched.

Even more curiously, the inventory of fixtures and fittings for the east wing had been 'mislaid' and an inspection revealed many wall-niches devoid of their usual ornaments, and rooms significantly sparse in furnishings.

After a purge occupying a full, sulphurous day, order was restored and a somewhat reduced force of servants set to work with renewed vigour and dedication – henceforth the main block and the east wing were as well kept and provided for as the Grand Master's own abode.

The only other occupants of the house were a few journeymen and one qualified magician who performed a few administrative duties and assisted with Baxter's researches. Tobias found them to be competent aides if little else and otherwise rarely spoke to them. In their turn, they went in terror of Father Oakley and avoided him where work did not compel a degree of contact. All of which was rather unfair for he never once did anything to harm or even intimidate them. However, rightly or wrongly, they thought him capable of anything and so avoided him.

In terms of work he was busy. Covering for the Grand Master, he advised ministers of the Crown when they wrote to him with queries and petitions. While Baxter decided on broad policy it was left to Tobias to implement the details of all instructions to the local Deans Temporal. Several days each month were spent exhaustively checking Grand Master Baxter's submissions and returns to His Majesty's Royal and Holy Government. Every point of fact had to be independently confirmed; every opinion expressed had to be reconsidered in the light of current Church policy. The responsibility was such that none but Father Oakley could undertake the task.

By far the greater part of his time was taken up by the myriad petty duties arising from the control of such a large area and so many people. Despite his long service in the magical profession, Tobias had been surprised by the extent and complexity of a Grand Master's responsibilities. Every matter magical was down to him. It was a little daunting to realise just how many men and women, how much money and how many spheres of influence, were at one's disposal.

For instance: Baxter had inherited a number of farms and properties from the previous Grand Master. These had to be administered by Tobias, staffed, watched over and duly milked for money. This and other monies accruing from the post had to be properly accounted for and invested to maximum advantage. Also, aside from the Magicians assigned to him for dispersal to the various Bishops, there was a large number of soldiers and servants to be paid, supervised and utilised.

It can therefore be understood that the correspondence arising was colossal, and the need for vigilance never-ending. And until he had fully created and mastered his reformed system, Tobias was usually glad of his bed at the end of the day.

Remaining with the subject of bed it should be mentioned that, almost as a reflex action, he seduced a number of the girl-servants (deflowering two), but he found the act less and less pleasing. After a year or thereabouts he ceased such activities altogether and felt no loss. Outwardly at least, he effortlessly assumed the chastity expected of him. Inwardly his erotic life continued unabated with increasingly bizarre and disquieting cameos in his mind. Their implementation would have to wait for a time when greater immunity from discovery and subsequent embarrassment was his.

His shadowy libido thus unsatisfied, Tobias turned to other fields for distraction and amusement but found little or none of either. When time hung heavy on his hands and food and drink, books and women, pleased him not at all, then he found himself willing to risk everything for an explanation of his present state.

CHAPTER 8

In which demonology is discussed and our hero is frustrated by conversation.

For as long as demonology had been a part of the magical art, men had been aware that powers higher than the 'common' demons existed. Little was known for certain save that many spirits (for want of a better word) referred to them as if to a higher authority. Many humans, and magicians in particular, had experimented and made attempts to contact these higher forces; but in almost every reliably recorded case such endeavours had ended either in complete failure or disaster. A popular legend always recited to journeymen and usually embellished with all sorts of gruesome details concerned one such attempt by an unspecified early-medieval Pope. The story had it that this gentleman had assembled the entire council of the Holy Thaumaturgic College of the day to summon for him such a 'Demon Lord'. The result was that the twenty-six councillors, the best magicians of the age, were discovered the next day seated at a long table within a pentagram – all with their heads twisted neatly back to front, because of which they were dead.

Although the story was entirely without substance, it served to make the point that assays into the higher realms of demonology were highly dangerous. It was commonplace knowledge that considerable numbers of magicians died every year in summoning quite 'ordinary' demons because of faults in ritual, inadequate preparation or simple lack of power. It took the sort of combined natural ability and years of patient study that Tobias possessed for even minor summonings to be conducted with any degree of confidence. Demon Lords were therefore quite out of the question . . .

However, that is not to say they were entirely left alone as a subject. Drawing on Biblical references, theologians and magicians gratuitously assigned names to these dimly glimpsed Demon Lords and arranged them into the hierarchy of Hell. Books of speculation abounded but the inquisitiveness thereby engendered merely led to a record of disastrous experiments and eventually the Church called a halt to further research.

Of course this did not worry or inhibit Tobias in the least. With his extensive knowledge of the subject he had picked up occasional references which seemed to suggest direct contact could be both possible *and* survivable. In years past he had merely been intrigued and left the matter at that. Now he sought out these few, enigmatic references again and gave them deeper consideration.

If demons were masters of the material world when invited into it, then what was the power and knowledge of the *masters* of demons? he wondered.

His desire for some hint of an absolute explanation had grown desperate but not to the extent that he threw away all caution. Like all good soldiers, suppressing the urge for battle, he would reconnoitre first.

Tobias was quite confident of most summonings now. While questioning demons he was assured enough to be able to relax in an armchair placed in the pentagram. Thus situated, and with a cup of tea on a small table at his side, in the spring of 2011 AD he entertained the supernatural in his locked room. And yet Tobias' vigilance was never lowered; for all his appearance of ease, he kept various warding spells and the phrase of dismissal constantly in his mind. Paradoxically it was at such times, when life had to be lived from moment to moment, that he found the mental peace and freedom which he was seeking. Alas it was only ever a temporary thing, for no life can be constantly lived in such a manner unless it is spent on a battlefield (and thus is short).

All Tobias' tutors and all the manuals advised that no attention should be paid to a demon's appearance or surroundings. Such things were specifically designed to distract and possibly ensnare the summoner. All thought and all concentration must be bent upon the demon's words and upon forcing it to perform one's will. In practice, however, the temptation to marvel at demonic ingenuity was too much for most people and Tobias was no exception; but he had the advantage of experience to excuse such lapses.

Looking into the chalk window he had drawn on the far wall, he could see a smart seafront of the type found in the southern coastal resorts as patronised by Royalty. Evidently it was high summer for sunlight of the kind that Tobias so detested gleamed brightly on the white houses along the road and on the calm blue sea. People in smart summer suits and dresses strolled leisurely in considerable numbers up and down the promenade. Possibly it was a holiday in their world, if world it was. Tobias, quite appalled by the scene, could see no obvious person to talk to, nor judging by their lack of reaction could the holiday-makers see him. Then a woman alone, passing along the street, stopped, looked directly at Tobias through the window and came closer, then spoke in a coarse sullen voice, 'What d'yer want?'

''Ello Threadgold, darlin','' replied Tobias, mimicking a lower-class accent quite accurately.

'She' or Threadgold, as magicians termed 'her', had all the appearance of a blowsy tart. Tobias had seen whole brothels-full of the type in Southwark. The besmirched youthfulness, clumsy make-up and pouting sulkiness were all calculated parts of the attraction. True to the part, Threadgold's dress was cut remarkably low and a frivolous bonnet topped a mop of lanky black hair. Despite the fact that his celibacy was now engrained and his tastes in fantasy roamed elsewhere, Tobias found himself pleasurably, or perhaps dangerously, aroused.

Collecting himself, he said, 'I want information rather than deeds, bound by oath to the black eminence in return for six bodies.'

Threadgold followed the practice of leaning over the window ledge into the room and studied the drawn pentagram very closely. Tobias' eyes were irresistibly drawn to the cleavage thus revealed and he was momentarily distracted.

'OK, I vow,' the demon said as she leant up, obviously satisfied.

'Firstly; your guise is excellent but change it, please.'

'D'y fancy me?'

'Yes, that's the problem. Just how senior are you?'

'Very.'

'I can believe it; ordinarily the flash of a couple of grimy breasts wouldn't affect me in the least. You're exerting some sort of "fascination" aren't you?'

'Yeah.'

'Thought so. Very well – stop it and rearrange yourself.'

'Don't wanna.'

'You're bound to.'

The tart disappeared and in its place was a beautiful boy with the face of an angel.

'No.'

'*Please*, sir . . . ' he said winningly.

'No!'

The boy vanished and was replaced by something totally inhuman, viscous and revolting. The holiday crowds took no notice of it.

'No!'

Finally, after the appearance of a sweet young girl in a party dress and with eyes of sluggish green vomit which Tobias also rejected, they settled for a priest. Admittedly it was an unsavoury priest, all haggard and etched with indulgence and despair but it was recognisably human. He looked vaguely like an unfrocked prelate Tobias had once met and perhaps that was where Threadgold had got the idea. Then, sensing some impatience in Father Oakley, the demon priest forced his ravaged features into an anticipatory expression.

'Thank you – at last,' said Tobias. 'Now, remember you're under vow of truth.'

'Of course,' Threadgold replied, 'unlike humans I'm bound by my oaths . . . '

'Why?' interjected Tobias eagerly.

'I don't know; I just am.'

'Who is your master? Who controls that town?' he nodded towards the promenade.

'*I do* – when it's in existence that is, look . . . '

Threadgold pointed a finger at a passer-by and the woman dropped lifeless to the pavement. The crowds looked alarmed for a little while; a couple caught Tobias' glance in a supplicatory way but they soon gave up. So they *could* see him, after all! Very shortly the pedestrians, hapless prisoners of Threadgold's little world, were picking their way around the corpse with all normality resumed.

'Beyond the town who is your master?'

'I never go there, so the question, my son, does not ever arise.'

'Who created you and when?'

'I am not permitted to answer such questions.'

'*Who* does not permit you?'

'I don't know.'

'To whom do you owe allegiance?'

'You – at the moment.'

'At other times?'

'You have me there. I owe allegiance and obedience to a Lord.'

'Named?'

'The name is not known to humans and would make no sense to you in any case.'

'Nevertheless, I wish to know it.'

'He will kill you and have your soul.'

'Good – name him!'

'If you have power enough he may answer to the name of Lord Burgess – that is a reasonable human rendering of his naming.'

'To whom does Lord Burgess owe allegiance?'

'I do not know, my son.'

'Is he what we would call a Demon Lord?'

'Father, he is *the* Demon Lord.'

'Is he the black eminence?'

'Yes, I suppose so.'

'Does he have ultimate knowledge?'

'I would imagine so.'

'Have you never questioned him on the nature of things?'

'No – such matters just don't occur to my race; we don't think about them. My advice, which you won't take so I'm safe in giving it, is for you to do likewise – it's enough to kill and eat!'

Tobias ignored this.

'Does Lord Burgess answer the call of humans?'

'Occasionally.'

'Can he be bound?'

'Doubtless he could be by some races but I suspect humans are not among them.'

Tobias refused to rise to this bait.

'So you know nothing of the forces that bind you to bargains, nothing of supreme beings, nothing of the universe beyond your demonic Eastbourne, nothing much at all in fact!'

'No to all your questions but, Tobias my son, let's put this into perspective.' Threadgold grinned ingratiatingly but the deep sunken eyes were fish-cold and senseless. 'I *am* a very powerful demon. A fact you seem to forget due to my lack of metaphysical knowledge and interest. Let us keep in mind that released, unbound by such as you, I could ravage and destroy your world all in a single day and night. You seem unaware of it but I am the most senior summoning of your demonological career. The fact that I'm prepared, indeed obliged, to answer your stupid questions is a signal honour to you. There are few humans who could summon and bind me.'

Ignoring this speech, Tobias demanded, 'Do we, collectively as magicians, have the correct names of any Demon Lords?'

Threadgold looked pained and said, somewhat peevishly, 'Tobias, I have already said that as far as I know there is only one Demon Lord and human textbooks do not know his real name.'

'But there have been summonings in the past?'

'Presumably they found his name from other sources – as have you.'

Tobias thought a little while and then, tensing visibly, said, 'Very well, I have finished with you; you may go.'

'Just a moment, Tobias,' replied the priest hurriedly, 'with sufficient safeguards a man of your ability could enter my realm in complete security. I could become the tart again – for you. Powerful magicians such as you have fucked demons before you know – it's an experience worth ten lifetimes, how — '

Tobias threw a cloth containing six consecrated wafers through the window and spoke the phrase of dismissal. Abruptly the window closed and became wall again. Threadgold's last 'How' echoed briefly around the room.

Tobias sipped abstractedly at his tea and hurriedly put it down again because it was cold.

So – demons, even the powerful ones, were more ignorant and incurious of their origin, place and fate than the most brutish of humankind. Power they had sure enough, but of understanding, less than the old ladies who packed Pevensey Church. It remained therefore, thought Tobias in a curious epithet from his Southwark days, to speak to the accordion player rather than his monkey. From this 'Lord Burgess' he would seize back some sort of self-respect and justification for the race he had run and supposedly won.

CHAPTER 9
In which our hero asks some very important questions.

In this quest there was no one and nothing to guide him save his accumulated knowledge and good sense. As far as the magicians' manuals were concerned, contact with Demon Lords was both forbidden and impossible – which covered all eventualities nicely. Therefore, lacking guidance and inspiration, Tobias decided that he had little alternative but to use the pentagram that had held Threadgold (he knew no stronger one) and hope it would similarly hold Threadgold's master.

Laboriously, for he was no seamster, in the evenings he embroidered a smaller model of the pentagram around the hem of a spare gown. This he found was the most difficult and exasperating part of his preparations, as his curses and pricked fingers bore witness.

When this task was at last completed and after a week's fast, he retired to his bedroom. *If I ever leave this room again*, he thought, *it will be with all my unhappiness taken away*. Tobias could hardly remember when he was last actively happy and wondered what it would feel like.

Outside the locked door stood one of the Grand Master's guardsmen, picked by Tobias for his good record and, so far as he could tell, complete lack of curiosity. The man was armed and had been told to admit no one, not even the Grand Master (a tricky instruction this!), whatever might be heard from within. If Tobias had not emerged within twelve hours the guard was to break in himself. Copious rewards had been promised him.

With infinite pains Tobias redrew the pentagram and window then checked and rechecked it. This done, he changed into the embroidered gown. As a last gesture he strapped his sword on, despite feeling somewhat foolish for doing so. The tiny sense of security thus engendered might just make all the difference in so hazardous an enterprise. He had no offering to carry with him this time, for nothing in his possession was of sufficient value to influence a summoning such as this.

Now that there was nothing to do but start, he appreciated just how simple his preparations had been. In truth he was relying solely on his developed powers and his intelligence to carry him through rather than rituals and magical geometry. Perhaps all great magicians came to that stage and finally realised that the essence of magic lay in the mind and anything else was merely auxiliary. Very few, however, Tobias included, ever cared to act upon this and dispense with all ceremony. At this level the penalty for any failure actively discouraged experimentation.

Having lit candles, Tobias stepped into the pentagram and had no excuse for delaying further. He was human enough to take a long look around his room and his few accumulated possessions. If things went wrong this would be his last sight of the world of men.

Then, breathing deeply, he recited the preparation spell and was thus moved one small step sideways from normal consciousness. The force he was summoning was named and worked into the pattern of the pentagram, but still it was necessary to make an act of will and call for oneself.

'Lord Burgess,' Tobias chanted softly. 'I request an audience with you; take my life if you can, I will give it freely.'

Extemporising in this manner, he continued for a long time. In a way that defied words he knew he was succeeding. With every minute that passed he was building up some sort of rapport with something equally indefinable and from beyond the world of ordinary Nature. Each chant added a minuscule amount of awareness to the growing level of contact and he knew that eventually a decisive climax would be reached.

As it happened, just under an hour was sufficient to make the chalked window flash into life. Tobias was very pleased at such swiftness – in earlier years he had been kept waiting longer just to see a mere Bishop. However he had little opportunity to consider, for events moved quickly. All the letterwork and symbolism of his pentagram lit up with a blue light; the whole pattern shifted, dipped and levitated in a way that chalk and paint should not be able to. Simultaneously, the most powerful wind he had ever known ripped into the room from the window. The candles were doused and thrown, candlestick and all, to the far wall. Furniture cartwheeled across the floor and the bed was stripped of blankets. Yet the pentagram held and the wind did not come inside it; Tobias could stand and watch untouched as his room was savaged in the eerie blue light. He had no mind to do so, however; his attention was riveted upon the window, and the line of his pentagram which wavered and shuddered under the storm's force but held firm. For once, there was little enough to see through the window which revealed only an inky blackness.

He did not know it but an icy cold emanated thence as well, and outside the room the slow-witted guard stamped his feet, blew upon his fingers and dimly wondered if he could endure twelve more hours.

Then, after about five minutes as far as Tobias could reckon, the wind suddenly ceased as did the assault on the pentagram. The scene through the window also changed slightly to show points of light in the blackness which was less absolute than before. The gentle sound of the sea came from the darkness. Obviously no one was coming to speak to him, so, as anticipated, he must go and seek them out. Using a spell of transference of his own devising, Tobias raised his arms, palms outstretched, and then suddenly moved them to grip his gown. Instantly the pentagram lost its blue glow and became a mere complex pattern on the floor again. At the same time the pattern embroidered on his gown achieved illumination and, his zone of safety thus successfully shifted, he was ready to move.

Tobias picked his way through the wreckage and walked over to the window. Somewhat cautiously he put his head through it and looked around. Now that his eyes were a little more accustomed to the dark, he could see a stony shoreline. A quite normal-looking moon shone on the sea which, at high tide, lapped gently on a pebbled beach. Of the country beyond the shoreline, he could see nothing for it was in deepest darkness. Far out to sea a few lights were visible, one of them flashing regularly, but Tobias knew they were beyond his reach.

He was beginning to feel a little puzzled when a light sprang into life along the beach. Judging by the way it flickered and danced, it was produced by a bonfire. Since this was less distant and might have relevance to his quest he had little alternative but to investigate it.

Despite the futility of drawing back at this late hour, Tobias hesitated slightly before committing himself entirely and climbing through the window. Only his self-discipline carried him through.

On the other side of the wall and beyond the Earth, Tobias could almost imagine himself on a perfectly normal beach at night. Only the bluish gleam of his gown hem, now slightly dimmed after crossing the divide, served as a material reminder that this was not so. Looking to either side and behind, he could see nothing of interest, but the light of the bonfire ahead served as cause to move on.

This he did, making a seemingly enormous noise on the pebbles where the only other sound was that of the sea. Completely alert, he pressed on for ten minutes or so by his pocket-watch but covered little distance for the rolling pebbles were hard going. Out to sea the lights were still there, arousing a curiosity that could not be satisfied. Inland a single light had come on but it, too, was a very long way off. Then, fully accustomed to the gloom, Tobias noticed a figure standing ahead of him at the edge of the sea. It seemed human in form and to be facing in his direction; more than that he was too distant to tell. The other party did not seem disposed to make a move. Tobias instinctively glanced back at the faint glowing lines of the window hanging in mid-air, but he walked on – keeping to a straight line along the top of the beach which would take him past the figure by the water. As he drew level Tobias could make out a man dressed as if for work in a London accounting house, that is to say in a sombre black suit. Even more surprising was the observation that his face was featureless: lacking eyes, nose, mouth, ears or hair. In fact the head, although human in shape, looked like a perfectly smooth ball of skin. In its hands the figure carried a bloodied axe.

Tobias quickened his step, hoping that this was not part of his quest.

Although eyeless, the figure appeared to watch the priest's

291

gradual progress and its head slowly turned to keep him in 'sight'. Tobias trudged on, for a while leaving the figure behind, but soon he heard pebbly footsteps behind him – the thing was keeping pace.

More than ever disinclined to turn back, he carried on until he was near the bonfire. Close up, he could see the fire was on a massive scale, perhaps twenty feet high and giving out an intense heat. Around it were the bulks of three boats, beached and dilapidated beyond hope of use. They were of the type and size that might be seen fishing off Pevensey Bay, but in the flickering light they looked old and sinister. Realising that this was not an occasion for military-style caution, Tobias walked straight into the middle of the illuminated area. Af first, blinking in the light, he thought himself alone for the footsteps had ceased. But, looking about, he saw a plump middle-aged woman of dowdy appearance who sat with her back to one of the boats.

'Hello,' she said in a voice that belonged more properly to a man of short temper.

'Lord Burgess?' queried Tobias. He had not noticed the glow of his portable pentagram dim a little.

'Yes – you have taken a long time to get here.'

'There were difficulties and you are some way from the portal.'

The woman got up. She might have been pretty once, but no more. When she spoke again her voice had changed from being masculine and abrasive to very feminine and sweet. 'Forgive me, Tobias, but I do not often have – human – visitors.'

'Pray don't mention it; all is well now that I am here safe and sound.'

'Such confidence, Tobias, is a less than endearing characteristic. You are far from safe I can assure you.'

'It was merely a form of speech.'

'Ah –I see; I am unfamiliar with the idioms of your language. Tell me, why is it that I was unable to kill you in your room; that has not generally been the way of things so far.'

'Generally?' said Tobias. 'Who has successfully contacted you before me?'

'I feel disposed to answer.' Lord Burgess replied. 'Two humans only, in your era, but I have made a holocaust of many failures.' The female figure waved a hand towards the fire and Tobias, following the gesture, noticed for the first time that among the planks and sticks were innumerable bones. They looked human.

'What were the two names?' asked Tobias, unintimidated.

'One was Robin Corbishley . . . '

'Of course, I would expect that.'

'Several hundred years ago now – such a charming conversationalist.'

'Who else?'

'Mamarutu, about fifty years ago. You would not know of him, he lives on an island still unknown to your civilisation, around the other side of your world.'

'I see.'

'Of course, you should not deceive yourself that you rank alongside Robin Corbishley and his ilk as one of your world's greatest magicians. You are slightly above average and no more. Only the foolhardy seek to contact me.'

'But I was good enough to make contact *and* protect myself.'

'Pride is another of your faults.'

'This is true.'

Lord Burgess studied Tobias closely, her face lit up crazily by the fire. He found it difficult to imagine this homely woman as a Demon Lord. At length she said, 'I wish you to meet someone well known to you although you have not met.' A raised arm beckoned to something outside the circle of light.

Tobias did not bother to query the paradox since he was sure it would soon be resolved. This was indeed the case for out of the darkness came strolling the faceless axe-man. He, or it, came and stood by Lord Burgess.

'We have met already,' said Tobias.

'Oh – he followed you along the beach did he? Obviously he sensed a kindred spirit and came to greet you.'

'I heard no greeting.'

'Well – that is his way but I'm sure a warm welcome was intended. Allow me to introduce you to Murder.'

'Is that his name?'

'No – that is what he *is*.'

'Can he speak?'

'No.'

'Then how do you know what he is?'

'Do you think I am restricted to communicating through speech alone?'

'I beg your pardon.'

'That's all right. Incidentally, Murder is of both sexes.'

'Naturally.'

'I found "him" on the beach one day and have since kept him as a sort of pet. Of course he spends a lot of time in your world.'

Tobias discovered himself about to launch into a whole range of questions on this interesting topic, but realised he had completely forsaken his purpose there. This was the Demon Lord's deliberate doing – he must be brief and make up for lost time.

'This is all prevarication,' he said. 'I want information which because of my safe presence here you are bound to give me, am I correct?'

'You are.'

'*Truthful* information?'

'That is so.'

Tobias decided to test this assertion. 'What is your name?'

'In human rendering, Lord Burgess.'

'Very well, what I want to know is this: what greater powers surround you; who *binds* you to tell truth to summoners?'

'I do not know.'

'But *you* bind Threadgold to abide by his vows.'

'I do not.'

'But Threadgold said you did.'

This was not *quite* the case. Threadgold had professed ignorance on the matter but Tobias thought it would be interesting to test Burgess' knowledge of his vassal.

'No doubt he genuinely believes that; alas it is not true. As his superior in power and imagination, I am recognised as his Lord and obeyed through fear. But there is no obligation – not from me at any rate.'

'But he said you were the black eminence, the *only* Demon Lord.'

'Nonsense, there are more than you can count and the existence and identity of any "black eminence", as you call it, is unknown to me. Poor little Threadgold. He could destroy your world, but he only *knows* of one Demon Lord; namely me.'

'And you are of equal power with these other Lords?' said Tobias agitatedly.

'By and large, yes.'

'There is no supreme power?'

'Possibly – there *are* constraints on my actions just as there are on yours. I cannot enter your world freely – you cannot jump mountains – it's all the same thing. Where these constraints came from I don't know; they just exist.'

'Birth and death?'

'I cannot remember being born and I've never heard of a Demon Lord dying. Mind you, very occasionally one will entirely disappear; perhaps that is our equivalent.'

'Then perhaps there are beings above you to whom you owe allegiance – other Demon Lords!'

'*Of course* there are, Tobias. However, don't worry your head about them; even to know their names would kill you.'

'But — '

'Neither could they help you for they could only give the same sort of answers you've had from me.'

'Then — '

'That's right, Tobias. We're *all of us* bounded by unknowing – isn't that enough to drive you mad?'

'Blast you,' yelled Tobias. 'You know *nothing*!'

'Is that a crime, Tobias? You are angry with me because in common with other living things I do not know every answer to every question. More to the point, you're angry because I can't justify your life. So what? Does it really matter? Reconcile yourself to the fact that life is pointless and accept the consequences that follow. Be mad and happy!'

'I've been wasting my time – you haven't the wits to justify anything or anybody.' Tobias turned and began to walk away.

'Wait Tobias, wait – I have something more to tell you.'

'Go fuck yourself.'

'Would you like to know what happens to humans after they die?'

Lord Burgess' voice took on a placatory tone. Tobias ignored it and carried on walking, engrossed in his anger and a sense of despair that grew minute by minute.

'I *do* have knowledge of God, Tobias; we are all his slaves willing or not.'

Lord Burgess was shouting now. Tobias heard but knew it for lies because unsolicited information was not bound by the vow and he walked on. Now that their conversation was over he suddenly realised that the glow of his pentagram had dimmed almost to extinction. Burgess had been exerting power against him all through their speech and had been trying to stall and delay. God knows he had almost succeeded. Only Tobias' impatience and disappointment had saved him, or at least given him a few extra moments, and he was under no illusion as to what would happen if the pentagram's life and efficacy should falter and die under Burgess' assault. In this sphere every single atom was a creation of the Demon Lord and would react to a stranger's existence in exactly the way their Lord wished it. Which meant that any such stranger would be snuffed out and left to Burgess' mercy for eternity.

Small wonder, then, that Tobias took to his heels and ran with a speed not seen in him since he had sprinted for the walls of Reading as a young man. From behind him he heard Burgess' voice, now harsh and masculine again: 'Murder – he is yours!'

Tobias had seen many horrific things in his life but the nightmarish chase that followed ranked very high among them. His laboured breath drowned out the sound of the sea, so that all he could hear was the sound of two sets of footsteps – his own and those belonging to a personification of the act he had admired for so long.

Even as he ran, he wondered why he had bothered. Yet run on he did. Tobias knew enough of demons to know that Murder's axe would be but the first part of a death lasting for ever.

So the chase continued; the issue being not so much whether Murder would catch up with Tobias but whether Tobias could reach the safety of his own world before his defences fell to Burgess' sustained attack. He felt almost certain that his own magic would not function in this sphere and he could not spare the time or energy to test it.

It had taken perhaps twenty-five minutes to walk to the bonfire. Going back, because of the various incentives, Tobias made much better time. As he came within clear sight of the window, Murder was running almost side by side with him. The gown pentagram was feeble unto death now and flickered ominously. Each time its light faltered, Murder drew closer and Tobias desperately fended him off with his sword. The gory wounds thus inflicted seemed to cause no worry at all. Ever more bloody, Murder kept pace, ready for the kill.

Tobias was so exhausted that he was beyond rational thought. Otherwise he might have cared to reflect that he was in no small way responsible for his adversary's obvious strength and stamina. Much of his adult life had been spent in carefully making his pursuer as mighty a force as possible. Now his works were turned against him for his own ruin. In later reflection he would spot and appreciate this clear irony.

At last, his mind full of fear and his mouth of bile, he reached the window as the pentagram was on its last breath and Murder was lifting his axe. Most unlike a man in his fifties, Tobias threw himself through the portal and returned to his own world in a very undignified posture. Behind him he had left his sword and one of his shoes. Not noticing his extensive bruising, he crawled the two paces to his old, floor-bound pentagram which instantly sprang into life. In man's world, man's magic was supreme and that little part of Tobias' mind still functioning told him he was safe. He lay on his back panting and feeling sick, waiting for more of himself to come back under control.

From the window came the full measure of Lord Burgess' wrath: the tornado again; tongues of fire and flying pebbles. Within seconds Tobias' bed and curtains were blazing and smouldering pieces of furniture took to the air.

He knew the pentagram was not proof against fire born of this world and so there was an added incentive to recover quickly and say the words of dismissal. He pushed himself on to all fours and croakingly did so. Nothing happened. He was saying them again when his sword came flying through the portal and buried itself deep into the door. Still his efforts met with no success. A third and fourth attempt met with similar failure. Finally, as he was completing his fifth repetition there was a noise like that of the world's greatest cannon and the wall went blank. He was now protected from supernatural threats.

However, Lord Burgess' final efforts had caused untold destruction. The far wall and door were pulverised and within the rubble, just visible, lay the corpse of the sentry. The small fires springing up everywhere were quickly spreading to the corridor outside, for the Demon-storm had already reduced the room, beyond the pentagram, to matchwood.

Still not fully recovered, Tobias was obliged to struggle to his feet and somehow break into a run again if he was not to die in a common or garden fire.

He had some vague idea of raising the alarm but the 'explosion' had been heard as far afield as Pevensey village and nearby Langley. Accordingly, investigations were well underway by the time he staggered, smoke-blackened, out of the nightmare and into the ornamental gardens. The servants were gathered there and Grand Master Baxter, active for once, was organising a bucket chain.

Fortunately the tide was in. After causing an initial shock, Tobias was ignored by all and left to recuperate at his leisure while watching the east wing being consumed.

CHAPTER 10
Postscript. In which our hero is canonised.

Justifiably, perhaps, the Grand Master was rather vexed by the loss of a third of his house and a reasonably full confession had to be made. For a considerable while Tobias' star waned and his ears were daily assaulted with reproaches. However there seemed to be no question of reporting him for forbidden experimentation as he had become so indispensable that his position was not threatened. He worked a little harder, devised new means of raising revenue to finance rebuilding and soon he was rehabilitated in Baxter's eyes. Things went back to normal, vulgar gossip ceased and Tobias continued his life. The only difference was that beforehand Tobias had not exhausted all possibilities and therefore had hope. Now he had none and would act accordingly.

The incident did not *quite* end there. The fisherfolk of the nearby shanties were pious or superstitious people, depending on one's point of view. As chance would have it their boats had just landed and everybody was busy with the catch when the 'big house' was rocked by an unearthly explosion and burst into flames. Some watched engrossed, while others rushed to give assistance.

In the ensuing days there were various garbled reports of the matter from house-servants and the like. The whole affair passed deeply into village consciousness and became the subject first for speculation and, then, embellishment in idle hours.

In time, versions of the story were passed on to new generations and children were told of how Satan himself, Old Nick, had tried to come to earth and work his mischief on their little community. Even when the Grand Master's palace was deserted and largely ruinous, the story still survived of how a priest named Oak had squared up to the devil and hit him a blow that could be heard for miles around. Thus bested, the Prince of Darkness had fled to Hell never to return to the area again so long as brave Oak was remembered. Remembrance eventually turned to reverence and out of priestly earshot the term 'saint' was appended to Tobias' name. Crude little carvings of St Oak adorned the front of each family's boat and hung over each threshold, and thereby kept them from the power of evil. If outsiders ever enquired it was said that they were representations of Christ and no one could gainsay this.

In the less cautious and more secular world which arose many hundreds of years after the time of this story, the legend of St Oak at last reached a wider audience and was accorded a very small footnote in the *Encyclopaedia of Saints*. He was termed: 'Mythical – Local and Specific', which was a niggardly way to repay centuries of providing comfort and a sense of security in an unfriendly world.

Tobias, of course, never knew anything of this. In his younger days he would have been pleased by it; later on he would have been dryly amused. In his old age, which started in his late twenties, he would have lacked sufficient interest to hear out the end of the story. At the same time he would have lacked the will to walk away from the teller. It was a poor pass for a future saint to come to.

CHAPTER 11 – 2023
In which our hero meets Rosemary Archer.

Since it was so fine, Rosemary Archer, housewife of Pevensey village, thought it a good idea to take her child out for a walk in the September sunshine. She had heard that sun and fresh air were good for young bones although her mother-in-law and the other grannies said otherwise.

Taking her five-year-old daughter by the hand, she strolled up the short village street, pausing occasionally to pass the time of day with neighbours. At the end of the village the road curved round the Castle walls and headed off to Langley, but Rosemary carried straight on, passing through the simple arch into the fort.

The Roman wall, still quite high in places, enclosed a huge elliptical area given over to grass. A flock of sheep were grazing there but other than that the villagers did not properly exploit the Castle's interior at all. There were stories of sieges, massacres and evil deeds from the past, and for this reason few people cared to tarry overlong in it at night. The sighting of ghosts and strange lights along the wall were regularly reported. And just as regularly discounted by the priest.

In the daytime, however, it presented a more friendly aspect and people would go there for peace and quiet. Today, since it was a working hour, Rosemary and little Julie had the place to themselves if one discounted the sheep.

In the middle of the Castle was an old cannon, broken down and beyond hope of repair. Tilted at a crazy angle on one remaining wheel, it was a plaything for the local children and a convenient seat for older citizens. Rosemary sought a dry and comfortable place on it and sat down. She had loved this place since she was a child and she liked to repopulate the Castle in imagination. Unlike most of the villagers, she had an enquiring mind and in another age would have responded well to education. However, as a person of churl status her rôle in life was destined to be that of home-maker and child-bearer and for this only a very basic level of knowledge was needed. Yet she was happy because she had a life of the mind to fall back on when Pevensey life occasionally seemed a little dull.

On this bright sunny day Rosemary idly reflected on what the Romans had been like. She realised that in her imaginings they always came out as strangely clad villagers of her own time because this was all the information she had to go on. At times it was very frustrating to be knowingly ignorant and in one such mood she had asked Father Morris, the local priest, to teach her to read. Kind man that he was he had started to do so but – really – there just *wasn't* the time and Samuel had grumbled about his meals being late and mother-in-law had said something about people getting above themselves. In the end she had had to give up the attempt which was a pity because she might otherwise have been able to borrow a book from Father Morris about the Romans.

From Church she had understood that it was the Romans that had crucified Christ. However she knew that this had happened a very long time ago and a very long way away, in another country. She was not like one of these *very* stupid types hereabouts who maintained (when Father Morris wasn't about) that Jesus was crucified in the castle or on Beachy Head and such-like nonsense. No – that had happened in another, hot, country but it was definitely Romans (and Jews of course) who did it. If this was so what on earth were the Romans doing building a castle in Sussex in England? Why had the King of England let the Christ-killing

Romans into the country and let them build a castle? Even the Earl of Sussex needed Royal permission before he could construct a fortified place; she knew that for a fact! It was all *very* confusing.

Suddenly Rosemary realised she had been day-dreaming again and some time had passed. Still – no matter, here, alone, such musings were allowed. At home they attracted criticisms from husband and mother-in-law: 'She's off again', 'another one of her turns', 'wake up girl, there's things to do', and so on.

Rosemary saw that Julie had run off quite a way in pursuit of her favourite pastime – chasing sheep. She watched amused as her daughter's chortles and cries came floating back; so long as she didn't go out of the gate there was nothing to fear in her running off.

Ordinarily Mrs Archer would have been right in supposing this; there were no holes her daughter could fall down, no sharp edges to cut herself on, no animals likely to bite or scratch, in short nothing inimical to life at all. However fate is regularly capable of throwing new factors into even the simplest of considerations. In this particular case that factor was a large black coach drawn by two horses. She glimpsed it briefly through the gate and then heard it stop outside; the noise of male voices and the sound of a door were carried across to her. Drawing on local knowledge this was all the evidence that Rosemary needed to justify prompt action. Raising her skirts, she ran as fast as she could across the green sward in pursuit of her errant child.

Before she could even get halfway, a number of men appeared at the Castle arch and Rosemary had to slow down to as brisk a walk as seemed polite. The men were soldiers bearing the livery of the Grand Master; the villagers knew them well and feared them. They noted Rosemary, the child, the sheep and the otherwise empty Castle, and then relaxed sufficiently to take their hands from their sword pommels. At this sign of implied safety another figure came through the archway and Rosemary's worst apprehensions were confirmed.

At sixty-three years of age, Tobias had failed to grow old either gracefully or impressively. A few trails of hair were all that was left to him and these were greyish-white. Oiled into the strands of a young man's pigtail (fashionable once again), Tobias' last crowning glory looked improper. He had become emaciated through irregular eating and his Grand Master's gown, intrinsically impressive, hung about his frame like a draped flag. But it was first and foremost on his features that Tobias' history was writ: jaw set; mouth in a permanent droop; his brow a mass of worry-lines; his scar an ugly livid line. The magician's eyes burned and wept with a power that could find no release. Even the uncaring Irish mercenaries that he surrounded himself with did not like to meet his glance directly. Hardened as they might be, a residual sensitivity told them that he was a dark and dirty storm always close to breaking.

Whenever his house and gardens tired him, Tobias would call for his coach, cover it with guards and drive off in search of fresh scenery. Usually he avoided the village since he knew his visits upset the inhabitants, but he had expected the Castle to be empty at this time.

Tobias, of course, knew a considerable amount about the Romans. The research of an idle hour had made him reasonably well informed about the castle as well. Armed with this knowledge he could easily distinguish between the Roman masonry of the Saxon Shore Fort and the much smaller medieval structure which occupied one corner of it. He had no idea how valuable and interesting this information, casually picked up, might be to other inquiring but less well provided minds.

He was not quite sure what he would do there; wander round presumably, try and think and hope that time will pass quickly for once. This was what he had in mind when Cormac, his personal bodyguard, had signalled that the way was clear.

Coming through the gateway however he was surprised to see that there were two people already there; a jolly little child running after the sheep and a woman, obviously her mother and a villager, coming towards her.

Tobias meant no harm; he felt a sudden urge to talk to somebody and be pleasant. He would go up to the little girl and ask her name, perhaps give her a silver sixpence as a present. Lord knows he had enough money, why not make someone happy with it? He could ask the woman who she was and find out about her family – that would be interesting. Using his magic he could make a sheep do tricks like 'sit up and beg' to amuse the child; perhaps this afternoon would go easily after all!

But when he began to shuffle forward, the mother gave a scream and ran towards her child with an expression of distress on her face. Tobias was puzzled – what was the matter? – and then angry. The incipient smile disappeared from his face and, knowing the reasons for the woman's actions, he scowled at her bitterly. Just at that moment the little girl turned round to see the newcomers for the first time; she caught his ravaged face which was momentarily animated by hate and instantly burst into fearful tears. A moment later Mrs Archer came thundering to the rescue and snatched the girl up in her arms.

As quickly as it had come Tobias' goodwill passed.

'Cormac', he said, 'bring those two over here.'

Cormac, a large, stocky man with bushy black hair nodded and quickly did what was asked of him.

Brought up close to this ancient ogre Julie Archer screamed and wailed and nestled into her mother's arms as far as was possible. Mrs Archer, realising that she had done wrong, however justified her fears might be, started to say how no disrespect was meant, your Grace, the child was startled your Grace, she's very highly strung, your Grace, and so on. Tobias interrupted curtly.

'I meant no harm, damn you', and he signalled to one of his guards, 'get those two out of here, *quickly*.'

He turned away and did not see a huge gauntleted hand descend on Mrs Archer's shoulder and guide her rapidly away. Gradually the child's cries faded away into the distance and then were lost to the ear.

In a blacker mood than before, the purpose of his walk already defeated, Tobias doggedly shambled around the walls of the fort under the ever-watchful eyes of his guards.

CHAPTER 12
In which an evening at our hero's home is depicted.

At home he found little respite. He ate alone in an inappropriately large dining-room – Stratter, his assistant, being absent that day. Of late, most foods tasted exactly the same to Tobias so the cook's efforts were wasted. Oppressed by the silence, he sloshed some fine red wine into his glass and bore it off to his living room; the silence was still there but at least the scenery was different. First a servant came in and asked if he required anything, and was dismissed; then Clough, Cormac's assistant, entered and asked a similar question.

This was a more important enquiry for it posed a number of questions very relevant to the long hours to come. Did he want a bed-fellow procured for him? Tobias entertained the concept and, disgusted, rejected it. Did he intend to move from this room again before morning and, if not, could the night-security arrangements be put into operation? No, he didn't and yes they could. A number of other minor matters were settled and then Clough withdrew. The door closed and Tobias knew that for the next ten hours or so he would be totally left to his own devices.

This idea always pleased him in principle – nothing and no one to bother him for a while – but after this novelty passed off, he was appalled by the task of trying to endure such a large chunk of time. He slept very badly and then only in the mornings. So there was no point in retiring to his bed early. Alcohol made things easier and in sufficient quantities could even produce a semblance of sleep's blissful oblivion. But then he would be ill for days and sleep even less, so it was a poor remedy.

Even so, Tobias kept large quantities of different drinks in his room, including a bottle of sherry for guests who never came, and sometimes in the long hours of wakefulness he just could not help but drink himself into a stupor.

Reading, the usual relaxation and diversion of the educated, also failed him as a pastime. His walls were lined with thousands of books, mostly Baxter's, and included among them were rare titles which would have been a bibliophile's delight. A true scholar could have been incarcerated in that room for a six-month and not spent an idle or unprofitable moment, but not so Tobias. This particular evening, he rose from his fireside armchair, glass in hand, and moved over to a nearby shelf. Selecting a title, he returned to his seat and began to scan the pages. Within five minutes, he was up again and looking for a new book. This was always the way; while reading one volume his thoughts would wander and think of another title or subject that seemed more interesting. Off he would go in search of this only to repeat the process shortly after. He knew he was doing it but was powerless to stop himself; nothing could hold his attention for long before he rejected it. As such, his inability to read was symbolic of his greater problem which caused him to wander endlessly and aimlessly during the day and lie awake between dusk and dawn.

There were a few books, it was true, that he could read from cover to cover – elegant, sophisticated works of erotica from the secret presses of Paris and, to a lesser extent, London. These, at least, were a success and encouraged his senile lust to rise from limbo and embark on what always promised to be its last adventure. But he found that he required increasingly stronger material until, at last, the Parisian pornographers could not keep up the pace. Beyond this lay the field of Satanism and Black Magic and even Tobias could not afford to be caught with books of *that* nature in his possession.

For a few years after becoming Grand Master, Tobias had indulged his inherent sensuality to a great degree. All, or nearly all, the 'tableaux' that had flitted through his mind in previous years were commissioned and performed. Very soon he'd realised that if he didn't wind down his activities he would be dead of the pox or a prisoner of the Inquisition within a twelve-month. And in truth the curtailment proved to be no great sacrifice. The effort just wasn't worth the game. Henceforth he restricted his bed-partners to one or, at the most, two young girls or boys. The whole thing was unimportant to him and just as incidental as visits to the lavatory. The young people were merely human spittoons and about as highly regarded.

Now he occasionally indulged in a little voyeurism and a few feeble perversions but for the most part was as disinterested as might be expected of a man of his age and time.

In a world where most people counted themselves fortunate to see their fiftieth birthday, Tobias was a venerable old man. Albeit one who was unusually hale and healthy. That is to say, his body still functioned with moderate efficiency and his intellect flourished entirely undiminished. Everything else, however – energy, hope and curiosity – had gone into the grave before him. The thought that he had lived too long often occurred to him but he knew of no other place to go to and so stubbornly, unhappily, remained.

Human pursuits offered nothing to poor Tobias in the twilight of his life. A thousand times daily he would look at his pocket-watch and marvel that so little time had elapsed out of a day already made weary by boredom. When all diversions fail, then tedium becomes the final enemy and will, in its victory, make each sluggish moment an agony. An agony, it should be said, made all the worse by its tolerability.

So, forced at last into inaction, Tobias sat drinking glass after glass of wine while looking out of his window over the audible but invisible sea. From time to time he would hobble round the room or boil a pot of tea over his roaring fire but as the night wore on he got up less often. The reverie he had once sought to escape was now his beloved companion and a blessed release to boot. When it did not come, he would invoke its magical equivalent and thus escape for an hour or so. For a magician to remain long in a magical trance was dangerous, however. Strange things lurked at the edge of reality and it was not entirely unknown for minds resting halfway out of the world to be attacked and suborned. Heedless of this risk, Tobias continued; he thought that a little peace, even if it were that of the grave, was the higher consideration.

When he was too tired to drink any more and could think of absolutely nothing else to do, he retired to his bed. Then after an hour or so of restless twisting and turning, he heard a clock downstairs strike four and shortly afterwards fell asleep. Another day of his sixty-third year on Earth was over.

CHAPTER 13

In which our hero's dotage is described with a note on his unusual assistant.

Grand Master Baxter had died in circumstances of quite impeccable naturalness. Tobias had been the first to discover the body, which was slumped over a desk, head in a vast grimoire. However the rumours this engendered were dispelled by a doctor's inquest which showed that the Grand Master's heart had finally and suddenly given up the unequal struggle allotted to it.

Tobias' promotion soon followed and in this way he, a mere clerk's son, reached the very highest position he could reasonably hope for in the profession of his choice. Unlike Baxter who came from even humbler beginnings, Tobias did not immediately embark on a programme of building and spending. This house in which he had lived for nearly fifteen years by that time was quite satisfactory to him, besides which he could not think of anywhere in the Southeast he would rather go. His only celebratory extravagance was a free-spending week in the winehouses and stews of Southwark where he tested his imagination and his kidneys. But even then he did not entirely forget his rôle in life. An Assistant had to be obtained and, as Baxter had done fifteen years before, Tobias caused a stir by attending the annual Thaumaturgic Conference. Unlike Baxter he gained little from listening to the papers given, for they were uniformly pedestrian that year; but as luck would have it he spotted an entirely suitable magician, a young Welshman, to be his acolyte and disciple.

In this Tobias had been wiser than he knew. While looking for someone who was unobtrusively competent, he found in Father Stratter someone who was not only that but also a shadow version of himself. A battle between inner contradictions raged beneath the young Master of Magic's detached exterior just as it had once done with Tobias.

At first he had seemed no different from the other cardboard characters who flitted through Tobias' life; his unspectacular efficiency seemed to describe him. Then, after about a year, he came to his Master with his first conspiracy theory. On that occasion it concerned a group of suspected Leveller sympathisers in Winchelsea; the evidence seemed reasonable and Tobias allowed him to proceed against them in conjunction with the military authorities. As round-ups went it was conducted moderately and that appeared to be the end of it.

But Father Stratter returned to Tobias with tales of heretical tendencies amongst certain laiety in the Faversham region. The case was sketchy, but he was given the benefit of the doubt and elements of the Holy Office descended upon the unlucky town.

However, when at reasonably regular intervals Grand Master Oakley was asked to believe that every heresy, forbidden grouping and proscribed organisation was flourishing in his area, he took leave to doubt Stratter's testimony. In the course of a long discussion he noted the burning look that came into his Assistant's eyes whenever the persecutions of his making were mentioned. Tobias' curiosity was aroused and, while he thought the matter out, he postponed the suppression of the alleged Pelagian heretics in Lewes that were Stratter's latest obsession. Enquiries were made by discreet people whom Tobias retained for such purposes. Yes – an informant had reported some such unorthodoxy in that town but it only concerned one person; admittedly it was a wealthy and highly respected town burgess but still only one person. Stratter had magnified the merest breath of wrong-headedness into the stench of widely ramified corruption. Doubtless further investigation would reveal that his earlier stories of illegality were equally insubstantial.

Tobias was not particularly worried by this; he had gone beyond being concerned by considerations of Justice or Right. If a few of these stuffy little southern towns were ruffled up and bloodied a bit he, for one, would not protest. So long as the efficiency and general good name of his area was not damaged, he would not intervene.

What did interest him was Stratter's motivation for these little crusades. To use him properly, Tobias needed to know which strings made this particular puppet dance. Detailed questions were asked about Stratter's career and Tobias sought to pry behind the initial glowing references that had prompted him to select the man in the first place. Slowly, but surely, clues began to come in: the testimony of an enemy here, the ugly rumour of a duel there. Tobias wondered if Baxter had trod this path before him and what horrors had been dredged from his own past. The strange thing was that, for the far greater part, the opinions he gathered were warmly approving of his Assistant. He was deemed a good-hearted, kindly and compassionate man. It just seemed that from time to time something bitter within him spiralled up and struck out blindly at the world.

Not unnaturally, Tobias thought unpredictability a dangerous quality and for a while he kept a close watch on his aide. Although the external enquiries ceased, Cormac (not an unintelligent man for all his brutality) was detailed to monitor Stratter's every move and discreetly canvass household opinion on him. With the exception of one senior servant, embittered by mankind beyond hope, everybody had the highest praise for the newcomer. He was described as 'courteous', 'considerate', 'kindly', even 'pious'. It came to Tobias' ears that he performed good works in the village and distributed a secret dole to some of the poorest families. Inevitably, therefore, it was not long before he became a well-loved figure in the area and the object of loyalty and admiration in his Master's house.

This was all in great contrast to the public image of 'that restless spider in the big house', as the Squire of Pevensey called Tobias. But as Grand Master, he was not jealous. And Stratter's work was impeccable; perhaps too good, even, for it left his Master with little to do. Therefore, caring not a fig for the threat to his charges, Tobias

BOOK FOUR

found he had no reason for complaint or disquiet. Presumably, something had filled Stratter with violence, but Tobias did not consider this a matter for his concern.

And so he soon instructed Cormac to leave the young assistant alone and a letter was despatched calling down the wrath of Church and State on the Pelagians of Lewes.

Predictably, new offenders were found to replace them and as time went on a long list of heresies was unearthed. Albigensians, Waldenses, Bulgars, Lollards, Hussites, Arianists, Donatists – and may other footnotes of history – were revived for Stratter's expiations. Tobias only intervened when he thought the credulity of higher authorities risked strain or one bloodbath followed too closely on another. He had a tool who could find the energy to punish the world for his existence where Tobias could not. In this spectacle the Grand Master found the last satisfaction that life had to offer him. Without the bother of having to train him, Tobias had found himself an heir apparent to carry on his own traditions.

To all intents and purposes Tobias' time was already over. He could not remember whether either magic or power had been the love of his life at the beginning. Later on, of course, they had become irretrievably mixed; but now the love was dead. Deprived of this justification his life was an empty shell and just as sterile.

After a fitful sleep he would rise late. While one of his Irish guards stood by, a servant would dress him and then breakfast would be brought into his room. As often as not he would merely toy with the food or send it back untouched. On alternate days there would be a newspaper fetched from the village for him to try and read, otherwise he would shuffle off to his study and pretend to work. No less a personage than the Grand Master of London, England's senior magician, had suggested to him by letter that he should put down his lifetime's experience of the demonological art – a field in which he was 'our foremost expert' – into a book. This would be published by the Church and used as a guide for magicians of all ranks and would 'finally secure a position in posterity' for him.

From such a person, requests were barely distinguishable from commands and Tobias felt obliged to comply with the suggestion. Yet, as in everything else, his heart was not in it. He had seen the ultimate end of demonology and had seen that there was no point to it. Even so, he tried his best and worked hard to collect his memories into a form palatable to the Church. News of the project spread and expectations were high. Yet all that Tobias' executors found were a few sheafs of unconnected, rambling and, in places, enigmatic notes. A rumour spread that the long-awaited exposition on Demons had been destroyed or suppressed by Church authorities because of its scandalous and disturbing content. As rumours go, this was quite entertaining and entered the annals of popular myth but, alas, it was not the truth.

The truth was that Tobias had simply not got the work in him any more. Innumerable times he would sit at his desk, write a few sentences, perhaps pen a diagram, and then his mind would go blank. Thus blocked he would go and drink some wine, stare out over the sea and then force himself to return to his 'book'. By that time his mind had lightly moved on to other fields, other times, and the next thing he wrote would be entirely unconnected with the subject matter preceding it.

No one knew of the countless times he consigned the whole manuscript to the flames and resolved to start again. But whatever he did, it always turned out the same; the book was never written and his hard-won experience was lost.

On most days he would give up the self-deluding struggle around midday and go to the dining room for some lunch. In the afternoons he would confer with Stratter or write up his weekly returns (one task he could complete by force of habit). But otherwise he would wander; he hated it but some restlessness kept him on the move. Round the house he would go, time after time, with his old man's shuffle – having furniture rearranged, finding fault with the servants, trying to catch out Cormac's security arrangements and a host of other pointless, time-killing, activities.

His temper was ever more uncertain now and, aside from his Irishmen and Father Stratter, his household assiduously avoided him. Usually he found himself pacing a long corridor, quite alone and entirely out of the sight and sound of men. Sometimes he grew so bored with this that he even returned to 'work on his book' which meant more wine-drinking and sea-watching. If the sun was not too bright he occasionally varied this routine by venturing along the beach. His coach was kept ready should he wish to depart to more distant places.

Outside of the house his Irish guards accompanied him at all times, partly for reasons of security and partly in answer to his pathetic desire for company. In a world where religion and politics were abrasive callings and where circumstances could change suddenly, his mercenaries were his eyes and ears, sword and shield. He had chosen Irish guards because they were familiar with his culture but not part of it, and he paid them excessively enough to make them loyal and incurious. Cormac, their clan leader, was something of an amateur philosopher and theologian, although he did not allow this to affect his actions, and it was with him, during those interminable afternoon wanderings that Tobias had his last real conversations. Everyone else came for orders or with petitions but cold, hard Cormac was prepared to talk – so long as his salary continued to be paid.

All things pass and at last, around 6.00 p.m., Tobias would have his dinner which he pecked and worried. Then when he could spin this out no more he retired to his private room to endure the sort of evening and night already described.

Barely able to endure his plight, unable when he most needed it, to summon up any remaining will to change it Tobias carried on wearily, hoping for anything that might force change upon him.

In his heart he knew that there was only one thing, now, that would bring release to him. But when every single other hope was dead he continued, against all evidence, to hope that another solution would reveal itself to him. Thus in fighting off resignation this dying ember of hope became one of his major torments. Like a ghost doomed to fruitless quest, Tobias was unable to find peace because, now in his extremity, he lacked the capability to even *look* for that which he sought. Nor would it come to him save in one, unpalatable, form.

He lived on.

CHAPTER 14–2026 AD
In which our hero goes on a day's holiday.

The clock struck ten a.m.; it was a cold wintry morning. Tobias considered staying in bed where he was at least moderately warm. Why not? Give it a try, he thought. So there he lay, staring at the panelled ceiling. After a while a servant appeared carrying breakfast but was dismissed before he even fully got in the room. Silence swiftly returned and he endured an hour or so of thinking of nothing before it became unbearable and he was about his wandering again.

He rang for a servant and ordered outdoor clothes to be set out. With the servant arrived an Irishman and he was told to get the coach ready along with four of his number. Tobias had decided that today would be a holiday from work or, more accurately, from the guilt inspired by an inability to work.

He dressed in a heavy gown, topped this with a sturdy overcoat and ordered a large hip-flask to be filled with brandy. Then, suitably clothed and provided for, he was helped downstairs and into the waiting coach. Cormac and three brooding companions were on top and Maxted, taciturn coachman to successive Grand Masters for thirty years, completed the outing's personnel.

In an effort to spin any recreation out as long as possible, Tobias deliberately did not hurry. They stopped along the coast road and venturing out, Tobias hobbled along the beach a little way. Exhausted by this he stopped and looked out to sea for a long while – it was much the same as seen from his study window he thought – evil and brooding. A bore.

Cormac and his compatriots waited patiently saying hardly a word; they were more than used to this and nothing the old man could do would surprise them any more. After a while he came back and one of them leapt down to help him in. A blanket was draped round his knees, the door secured and at length he tapped the roof with his stick as a signal to move on.

Throughout the remainder of the morning and most of the afternoon the little group trundled around the area. In most of the nearby villages his name and reputation were well known and his passage attracted no welcoming glances. Tobias knew full well that children were being called in, doors shut and curses spoken even as he arrived. It made him hate them all a little bit more but on the whole he didn't care. The ever-vigilant Cormac was on top; he would make a note of the more obvious signs of hostility and these could be brought to Stratter's attention. Tobias considered their enmity unjust; he had done nothing to harm these yokels. Their objections were based on his irregular and withdrawn lifestyle which was none of their petty-minded business. Stratter's attentions would be their just punishment.

In fact he was not entirely incorrect in his assumptions. The farmers and fisherfolk of the surrounding countryside hated his name because of his perverse sexual life and had no way of knowing that the widespread rumour claiming that Black Magic was practised at the big house were baseless.

And so, an unwelcome visitor in the dwellings of man, he moved on with no particular route. From time to time he would spot some natural feature or view that seemed interesting and, stopping the coach, he would be helped out to gaze and pace in silence. In every case however, it was not long before his attention wandered and his old feet were forced to do likewise. By mid-afternoon Tobias thought himself incapable of looking at another natural feature and gave the order to set off home. On the way they stopped at an inn for refreshment; a bottle of wine and some lamb cutlets were brought to him in his coach. He drank and ate but could taste nothing and soon gave up. His guards and coachman, however, ate heartily – as well they might, for it was at his expense. As he sat there he could hear them happily chomping and chewing away and momentarily hated them for their zest. Because of this he hammered on the roof to move on and the merry repast on the coach roof was curtailed.

The light was threatening to fade as they drew near to Pevensey village. Tobias was in no hurry to get home but, even so, was surprised to feel in himself a desire to take a stroll around the castle before calling an end to this 'holiday'. Lacking any reason not to he communicated this wish to Maxted and very shortly the coach pulled up outside the East gate. Cormac jumped down and poked his bushy head through the open window.

'Just the normal stroll, your Grace?'

'More or less. If there's anyone in there, turn them out first.'

Cormac gave a few swift orders in incomprehensible Gaelic. The Irish attendants disappeared into the Castle and returned a few minutes later with a round dozen of disgruntled but acquiescent villagers – mothers and children for the most part but including one obvious courting couple. They looked blackly at the coach and its invisible occupant but moved rapidly off to their respective homes.

Cormac informed Tobias that all was clear and then helped him to dismount. Two Irishmen stayed by the gate and the coach while Cormac and another accompanied the old magician at a polite distance.

Midway along the north-west wall of the Roman fort, just by the edge of a long stretch of fallen masonry, was a small postern gate.

Tobias had seen it during the course of his first visit, pondered briefly on its original purpose and then forgotten it. Today, he would not have noticed it at all if he had not, some thirty yards away, spotted a slim figure emerging slowly from the passage behind the gate. At first he assumed it was another villager and was about to call Cormac. But something made him take a second, closer look and instantly he came to a halt. It was Joan – beyond any mistake. She had not changed at all in the fifty years since their last meeting. Despite this long separation, Tobias had nothing to say to her. He made no move to approach. According to the way of her race Joan maintained an incommunicative silence as well. But if nothing was conveyed by sound, whole volumes were written on their faces. Joan's wrinkled visage beamed with triumph, just as that of Tobias sagged with a defeat whose extent he finally realised. Her yellow eyes challenged him with her malicious victory and for the first time since childhood, he offered no defiance, no resistance. For a long while they expressed their mutual indebtedness in this way until Tobias was interrupted by a polite cough coming from beside him. He turned to look; it was Cormac.

'Your Grace?'

'Yes?'

'Is all well?'

'Do you see her?' Tobias turned to look again. Joan was gone. *'Did* you see her, Cormac?'

'I saw her, your Grace, yes. It was but a female from the village. Is anything the matter? You look pale.'

'Where did she go?'

'Back into the passage – where she came from.'

'Get her – quick!'

Cormac and his companion rushed off to investigate but, of course, there was no sign of Joan.

'Take me home,' said Grand Master Oakley in a weak voice.

'She was lucky,' said one of the Irishmen to Cormac as they trundled homewards. 'The dirty old swine must have taken a powerful fancy to her. I'm glad she got away.'

'Amen to that,' replied Cormac.

CHAPTER 15
In which our hero undertakes a much longer journey.

After this incident Tobias passed into a state of despair which made all past miseries seem affected. He had no doubt at all that this was to be the last evening of his long and eventful life. The knowledge caused neither distress nor rejoicing, but he was filled by a sense of waste. Nothing of this world could touch him now but the past was full of newly discovered pain.

Doctors of an age yet to come would have pronounced him in a state of shock but, as he sat alone at the long dinner table, he was simply seeing his life pass slowly before him in solemn review. He wanted to reach out into this procession to change, alter, correct and transform; but it was far, far too late.

He caused a huge blaze to be built up in the rarely used dining-room fireplace and sat beside it for a long time, drinking brandy which he did not taste. When the procession ended, he was left utterly empty: an old man, useless and finished, duped and destroyed.

After an hour or two Stratter came in, back from some official errand in Hastings. Tobias called him over. As though from a million miles away and another time Tobias wondered what he should do. Kill his assistant? Give him all the knowledge acquired in a lifetime? Cling on to him and plead for another day of life? In the end all the possibilities were equal – equally pointless and unattractive and so he settled for doing nothing.

'Goodbye, Father Stratter,' he said dully.

'I beg your pardon, your Grace?'

'I said "Goodbye".' The Grand Master's tone was decisive and final.

Father Stratter was a magician and therefore capable of accepting abnormal and disturbing events without qualms. He was silent a little while, and then said, 'Have you anything to say – anything to tell me?'

Tobias tried to consider this but swiftly gave up because this was the easiest course of action. No trying or struggling for him any more. He looked up.

'No, I think not; help me up please.'

315

Stratter did so. Tobias turned and looked at the last living creature he would ever see.

'Goodbye,' he said again. Then, pursued by a host of phantoms, he ascended the stairs to bed.

For a while he drank brandy and looked out to sea. The lights on a big ship slowly crossed his view and he watched this sign of life until it was no longer visible. Eventually he got into his large cold bed and soon fell asleep. When he awoke he was unsure of the time but thought it some hours before dawn. He listened to the regular roar of the sea and the miscellaneous noises of his house. As he had done so many times before, he looked up at the decorative panels on his ceiling and waited.

He had been unsure in what form his release would arrive but it came as no surprise to him when, after only ten minutes or so, he felt the terrible blow to his heart. Suffused with pain he gasped and thrashed around in the bed but, at last, his final drop of energy drained, he went peacefully away.

To his surprise, Tobias Oakley woke again – although he was not glad of it. He lay in bed and wondered how it was he knew that he would never sleep any more.

Nor was this the only information vouchsafed him in the brief, dark, interval between life and . . . this. Every cell of his brain, every nerve of his body, was suffused with a harrowing sense of error. He longed for life again that he might reform and amend and so escape this, the very worst of all his agonies. Then, despite the fear of learning more, in some desperate hope of alleviation, he opened his eyes.

Far below, he could see another Tobias Oakley, in another bed, but this version of himself was lying absolutely still. Then the vision blurred and receded, taking in his room, the Palace, Pevensey, England, a blue-green globe, and – eventually – nothingness, a mist-filled void between there and here. Tobias' all-consuming sense of wrong heightened. It was unbearable.

Then, from out of his line of sight, a voice like the end of everything spoke.

'Tobias,' it said, implacable but not unkind, and drawing ever closer. 'Tobias, you were . . . misled.'

Tobias tried to scream but it was the merest mouse-squeak compared to the voice.